"I think you did that on purpose," Austin said, teasing.

"Behave," Leah said, still smiling. Humor danced in her eyes, and her hair danced on her shoulders.

She looked just a little bit tipsy. Her cheeks a little flushed. Or was it just the laughter?

Whatever it was, she looked sexy as hell.

Austin wasn't certain who did it, who closed the small space between them, but their lips met.

The kiss didn't start slow, or hesitant. It went from hot to hotter. Leah's tongue met his and danced. Her hands moved around Austin's neck, pulling his mouth closer, as if wanting it deeper. Deep was good...

Praise for
The Hotter in Texas Novels

Blame It on Texas

"Craig returns to Texas and the hunky boys of the Only in Texas PI agency in this sexy, lighthearted romp centered around a sassy heroine on a mission and the gorgeous hero who falls for her. Complete with genuine characters who have heart, this story will keep you laughing as you turn the pages. A truly fun read!"

—*RT Book Reviews*

"*Blame It on Texas* is contemporary romance at its best, with the right blend of humor, emotion, mystery, and just a hint of sexiness...I can't wait to see what's in store for the detectives in the next book in the series."

—FreshFiction.com

"[Craig] definitely doesn't disappoint here...Both Zoe and Tyler are extremely appealing...[She] writes amusing scenes, believable dialogue, and charming characters...With this second solid book, Ms. Craig solidifies her standing on my must-buy list. In fact, the excerpt for the third book, Austin's story, has definitely titillated my interest."

—*All About Romance* (LikesBooks.com)

"Irresistible…Christie Craig's stories are like an addictive drink. They're refreshing and just what you need to quench your thirst for some steamy and funny romance."

—RomRevToday.com

"Christie Craig is the master of taking a story and rolling out the romance in a way that has every reader begging for more."

—*The Reading Reviewer*

(MaryGramlich.blogspot.com)

Only in Texas

"4 Stars! An entertaining tale with delightful, fully formed characters and an intriguing mystery."

—*RT Book Reviews*

"I lost count of the number of times I laughed out loud… Craig [has a] wonderful ability to write comedic dialogue, appealing characters, tender sentiments, and sexy love scenes…I'm not sure how I missed Ms. Craig's books… Now that I know what is inside the covers, I won't make that mistake again."

—*All About Romance* (LikesBooks.com)

"Fun…[a] caper-filled story…a good madcap-type romance. I look forward to Tyler's and Austin's stories."

—TheRomanceReader.com

"Steamy...Craig seems to have a real knack for writing fun little romantic romps...There is an almost tongue-in-cheek quality to them that just makes them fun to read...I know all I need to do is just sit back and enjoy the ride...Be sure to check out *Only in Texas*."

—TopRomanceNovels.com

"Absolutely a delight to read. Christie Craig has hit a home run with *Only in Texas*. I laughed, teared up, laughed, sighed, laughed, blushed, laughed, and laughed, and finally finished the last page with a bit of sadness because I did not want this book to end. It made for a great weekend of reading pleasure."

—GoodReads.com

"Craig offers up another well-written and nicely plotted story...[She] always delivers enjoyable, light romantic mysteries—add *Only in Texas* to the list."

—BookLoons.com

Texas Hold 'Em

Texas Hold 'Em

CHRISTIE CRAIG

FOREVER

NEW YORK   BOSTON

Copyright © 2014 by Christie Craig
Excerpt from *Only in Texas* © 2012 by Christie Craig

Forever
Hachette Book Group
237 Park Avenue
New York, NY 10017

www.HachetteBookGroup.com

Printed in the United States of America

First Edition: January 2014

10 9 8 7 6 5 4 3 2 1

OPM

Forever is an imprint of Grand Central Publishing.
The Forever name and logo are trademarks of Hachette Book Group, Inc.

The Hachette Speakers Bureau provides a wide range of authors for speaking events. To find out more, go to www.hachettespeakers bureau.com or call (866) 376-6591.

The publisher is not responsible for websites (or their content) that are not owned by the publisher.

ATTENTION CORPORATIONS AND ORGANIZATIONS:
Most HACHETTE BOOK GROUP books are available at quantity discounts with bulk purchase for educational, business, or sales promotional use. For information, please call or write:

Special Markets Department, Hachette Book Group
237 Park Avenue, New York, NY 10017
Telephone: 1-800-222-6747 Fax: 1-800-477-5925

To Jim Houston, a friend, a fan, and a real-life hero who will be missed

Acknowledgments

Thanks to my agent, Kim Lionetti, for giving me her all and making me feel like I'm her favorite client, even when I know she makes all her clients feel that way. Thanks to my editor, Michele Bidelspach, for helping me whip *Texas Hold 'Em* into good shape. Thanks to my hubby for doing laundry, dishes, and cooking while I hide away in my study following my dream of writing books that hopefully make my readers laugh, love, and cope with their everyday stresses. Thanks to my assistants, Shawnna Perigo and Kathleen Adey, who help me cope with my own everyday stresses. Thanks to my friends who are there to laugh with, walk with, worry with, and offer invaluable motivation. A shout-out to Lori Wilde, an awesome writer, whose continued support through the years has been an inspiration. And last, but definitely not least, thanks to you, my fans, who not only read my books, but recommend me to others. I wouldn't be living my dream, I'd be doing laundry, cooking, and dishes, if not for all of you.

Texas Hold 'Em

CHAPTER ONE

AUSTIN BROOK OPENED his front door and stared at his two PI partners standing shoulder to shoulder on the front porch. They looked pissed enough to chew glass. He knew why they were here. He even knew why they were pissed. Still, he decided the best approach would be to take a page from his dating manual and do the same thing he always did when he got in trouble with a woman. Namely, feign ignorance and pretend everything was just fine.

"Hey," he said. "What brings you guys by?"

"What the hell do you think you're doing?" Dallas O'Connor snapped.

Austin grinned. "Well, I was thinking about taking a piss when someone started pounding on my door."

Bud, Dallas's dog, nosed his way between his owner's legs and stared up with the same bulldog face as Austin's partners at the Only in Texas agency.

The fact that Bud was an English bulldog made his look understandable. Not that Austin didn't understand his partners' dire expressions. He knew they were here to derail his plan.

"I thought you guys were in Galveston." And he was hoping to be gone before they got back. Austin raised his foot and with the toe of his boot scratched the dog's neck between the folds of loose canine skin.

"We came back early. Roberto called us." Dallas, a big man carrying a bad attitude, pushed inside, and Tyler, slightly less bulky but equally tall, joined him. Bud, snorting and probably farting, followed at their heels.

Austin shut the door, then regretted it when the strong odor of doggie gas hit him square in the face. Instinctually, all three men waved a hand to clear the air.

Tyler's gaze, his eyes as dark as his black hair, shifted to Austin's suitcases sitting beside the bar. "I thought we decided to let Roberto handle this."

Roberto was the professional informant they had digging up info on the SOB, DeLuna, who'd framed them. And while Austin liked Roberto, or at least liked what little he knew of the man, he was taking too damn long to get the job done.

"No, you two decided that," Austin said, letting the bitterness shine through in his voice. "I distinctly remember telling you that I was tired of handing everything over to Roberto and getting handed back shit. We're paying this guy big bucks and we really don't know crap about him."

"So far his leads have all been on the mark," Dallas insisted.

"True. But it's been six months since he's given us a solid lead on DeLuna." To Austin that meant it was time for one of them to intervene. And since both of his partners now had wives to consider, he figured it was up to him to do it.

Not that he minded. Taking down that no-good lowlife claimed top spot on his bucket list.

"My bet is by now all of DeLuna's men know our faces," Dallas said. "You go through with this, and we'll be buying your casket in a matter of weeks."

Austin sat down on his favorite armchair and stretched

out his cowboy-boot-clad feet. "Just use the one we keep in the entranceway of the office and save yourself some money." The damn casket had been left in the building by the previous owners, who ran a funeral home. Now it was sort of their trademark.

"He's serious," Tyler said, using his calm voice that always reminded Austin of a therapist. Not that he'd gone to one in a hell of a long time. Well, not since he was thirteen and had decided that being a ward of the state didn't mean he had to follow their damn rules.

"You think I'm not serious?" Austin asked. His mind was made up. He didn't mess around with his bucket list.

"What brought this on?" Tyler asked. "Is this about your—?"

"Stop! Quit trying to get in my head." Austin's anger surfaced with a rush. But it was directed more at the stranger who'd shown up at the agency and spilled her dirty laundry right in front of everyone than at his two partners. Still, that didn't mean he had to discuss it. Discussing it meant thinking about it, and he'd spent a whole hell of a lot of energy trying not to do that.

"You want to know what brought this on?" he asked. "It was the year and a half I was fucking locked up in prison. Or have both of you forgotten about that?"

It sure seemed to him they had. Okay, maybe they hadn't forgotten it, exactly, but they'd somehow gotten past it. And while Austin was friggin' happy for them that they'd been able to do that, and he'd danced a jig at both their weddings in the last two months, he couldn't get past it. He wouldn't until DeLuna was behind bars.

Or dead.

Tyler exhaled. "I just think—"

"Then stop thinking!" Austin moaned. The last thing he

wanted was to have anyone rummaging through his mental closet. There were too many damn skeletons, too many nailed-shut trunks of emotional crap, that he didn't want to think about.

"Damn it, Austin," Dallas snapped. "This is shit. We need to stick to our plan."

"What plan?" Austin asked. "We don't seem to have a plan anymore."

Dallas's shoulders tightened. "The plan hasn't changed. We keep picking apart DeLuna's organization until we force him to come out of whatever hole he's taken cover in and face us. Use your brain for once. You know as well as I do that we lose every advantage by going to him instead of having him come to us."

"Look, nothing personal, but you two have other priorities right now," Austin said. "As in wives. And I get it. But what he did still eats away at my gut. I want my pound of flesh."

"Roberto is working it," Dallas said. "If you go in now, you'll probably get him killed. Can you live with that?"

Austin raked a hand over his face. When he opened his eyes, he found himself staring at his partners' concerned faces. Real concern. Damn it to hell, he knew they were here because they cared. And yes, he felt the same way about them. If anything, the bond he had with these two was the closest he'd ever come to having a family, but...

"I don't know what Roberto told you," he said, speaking more calmly, "but I've already worked this out with him. I'm not even going to Fort Worth. I'm checking the other lead that—"

"Which lead?" Dallas asked.

"The sister."

"Half sister," Tyler corrected.

"Whatever," Austin said. "They're Latin, and you"—he pointed to Tyler—"know how important family is in that culture."

"She's half-Latin," Tyler corrected again. "And stop stereotyping."

"It's a good stereotype," Austin said. For someone who grew up without a family, he could have used a little of that stereotype in his life. Of course, when he saw how his partners' families drove them crazy, sometimes he wasn't so sure.

"Roberto watched her for a month and found no connection to DeLuna," Dallas added.

"Yeah," Austin replied, "but I'd bet my left nut she knows what rock he's hiding under."

"You could lose more than your left nut. And even if she knows, why would she tell you?" Dallas asked. "Plus, Roberto tried connecting with her and it didn't work."

Austin smiled. "I'm not Roberto. I'm charming. Women like me. It's a gift."

He was just like his biological father...or so his "mother," aka the woman who'd given birth to him, raised him for a few years, and then abandoned him, had said when she'd shown up last week. The brief conversation they'd shared came back to haunt him, but he pushed it aside. He wasn't going to think about that. Nope. So he shoved the memory back into his mental closet.

Only it kept falling out. She'd come looking for peace of mind and ruined his in the process.

"We know the type of women who find you charming," Tyler said. "Leah Reece is educated, and she's part Latin, which means she's too smart to fall into bed with you."

"Now who's stereotyping?" Austin asked. "Besides, I didn't say I was going to sleep with her. I'm going to charm her. Get her to trust me enough to confide in me. And actually, her being Latin works in my favor." He grinned. "We've discussed this before. I go for blondes. Of all the Victoria's Secret models, there's only one brunette I'd pick before I'd sleep with their whole catalog of blond models."

"How the hell did Victoria's Secret models come into this?" Dallas ranted.

"Anytime you can bring them into the conversation, it's a good thing," Austin added with humor. "Besides, I've already worked out a plan. Roberto rented the apartment next to hers. She's a vet, and I'm thinking about getting a dog. I'll buy one, then pop in to see her and say... 'Hey, aren't we neighbors?' And, *voilà*! Instant connection."

"Right," Tyler said. "Once again, you didn't do your research. Leah Reece isn't a regular vet, she's a specialty vet. Special as in a feline specialist. Feline as in cats." He laughed. "I'd pay to be a fly on the wall. You, an ailurophobe, are going to try to charm a feline specialist. I'll bet she owns at least two or three cats."

People owned three cats? "I'm not scared of cats." But it would be a cold day in hell before he acquired one of those clawed varmints. The scar beneath his right arm started to itch.

"So, the vet angle won't work," Austin said. "I'll find a different way." Somehow he'd win Leah Reece over enough that she'd confide in him about her brother. How hard could it be? She was, according to Roberto, a petite, pretty little thing with a soft spot for animals.

"I still don't like it," Dallas said.

"Me, either," Austin admitted, still thinking about the cats. "But I'm doing it."

Monday morning, Leah Reece was busy doing one of the things she did best.

"I swear, you enjoy this, don't you?" Sara, her vet assistant and good friend, teased as she stroked the anesthetized cat on the table.

"Can't you see the satisfaction in her eyes?" Evelyn, the office manager of Purrfect Pet Veterinarian Clinic, added from the doorway.

Leah grinned but didn't look up until she removed the second testicle from the tiny incision and dropped it into the metal container. It landed with a tiny thud in the pan beside its brother ball. "I was just thinking that I'm good at it, but it doesn't bring me the joy you two are insinuating. Now, if Spooky walked on two legs, thought he was God's gift to women, and spewed out come-on lines instead of purring, then it would do my heart good."

They laughed. Then Evelyn cleared her throat. "It's been two years since the divorce. I think it's time you stop dreaming of castrating them all and remember what a man can do for you."

"You mean like cheating on you with your neighbors and running up your credit cards by having phone sex with strangers?" They laughed again. Sometimes even the truth was funny. Or it could be after two years.

Still in the doorway, Evelyn gave Leah her I'm-serious look. Leah adored Evelyn; she'd been the first employee Leah hired three years ago when she started the practice.

She'd known Evelyn was the right fit when Leah asked her if she had any prior office management experience and the fifty-five-year-old answered, *"Nope, but I managed to keep a household afloat, take in over ten cats, clothe and feed three boys, and get two through college on my husband's car salesman income. If you need someone who can run a tight ship, balance a budget, knows how to get stains out of men's underwear, and doesn't mind picking up hair balls, I'm your woman. Besides, with the economy down, and one boy still in college, I could really use a job."*

Evelyn cleared her throat again, pulling Leah back to the present. "Brandon was an idiot."

And managed to make me feel like one, too. "But he was so good at it." Leah checked Spooky's scrotum one more time.

Sara chuckled. "I think both of us would have helped you castrate Brandon. But Evelyn's right—not all men are scum."

No, Leah thought. Some of them were even worse. Brandon was just the last in a long line of men in her life to disappoint her. First had been her father. Then her half brother. And a few lying-cheating boyfriends along the way. If not for Luis, her younger brother, she'd have given up on the whole male species. But as it was, she would be hard pressed to trust another man. And the only kind she'd let get close were the feline variety that she'd previously neutered.

"Don't you miss it, just a little bit?" Evelyn asked.

"Miss what?" Leah moved Spooky into the cage on a soft mat where he'd wake up. She gave the unconscious feline an ear rub. Hopefully now that he was fixed, she could find him a home. But Lordy, she was such a sucker for a stray.

If only she didn't already have four at home...

"A man's touch," Sara answered for Evelyn, her voice dreamy. "The way the palm of his hand moves over your skin or fits just so in the curve of your waist. The way he looks at you like you're eye candy, making your skin get ultrasensitive. Those sexy bedroom smiles that make you squeeze your thighs together a little tighter. Oh, and that moment when he's naked between the sheets and—"

"Oh, my." Evelyn fanned herself. "I'm calling my Stewart and telling him to come home early." She walked out, her step peppier than when she'd walked in.

"Well?" Sara asked.

"Well, what?" Leah barely got the two words out. Her mind was mush and her body ached for something she didn't think she could ever allow herself to have again. She'd tried it. As wonderful as it all was in the beginning, it cost too damn much. Both emotionally and monetarily. Phone sex didn't come cheap.

"Do you miss it?" Sara asked.

"Nope," Leah lied, and looked down at the removed testicles.

Evelyn appeared in the doorway again. "You have a phone call. He says he's your brother, but it doesn't sound like Luis."

CHAPTER TWO

MONDAY AFTERNOON, AUSTIN waited in his truck for Leah Reece to return to her apartment. His plan was simple. Bump into her, start a conversation, eventually get her to trust him enough to tell him about her long-lost, piece-of-shit brother. If that didn't work, he'd move to plan B.

Problem was, plan B was slightly illegal and could get his ass thrown in jail. He didn't like jail.

He'd concluded that in the first fifteen minutes of his sixteen-month stay.

But it was worth the risk to get to DeLuna—the man who'd put him there.

He frowned. How late did vets work?

According to Roberto's description, the woman was petite, young, and pretty. Which sounded almost as bad as "a good personality." Even if she wasn't some hot babe, she had the young part going for her, so what was she doing working twelve-hour days?

Hell, maybe she left work and went straight to some date. He could be here until midnight. He groaned. Patience had never been his strong point.

A white Honda pulled in a spot across the way. Right

color, wrong car, and parked in the wrong spot. Still, Austin paid attention.

A young, small brunette exited the car. Was it Leah? He should've done a better upfront investigation. Tyler always accused him of not being a Boy Scout and being unprepared, and maybe this one time, his partner had a point.

Roberto had sent some surveillance images when he'd done his own Leah Reece investigation, but, pissed when the report stated Roberto had struck out, Austin deleted them.

He continued to study the Honda's driver. She snatched a baby from the back. Damn! Leah Reece wasn't a mom.

Another car engine roared close by. The brunette with the baby stepped away from her bumper at the same time a red Ford Focus came hauling ass down the parking lot. He slapped one hand on the horn and bolted out of his car. The woman, clutching her baby, jumped back.

"Slow down," he yelled at the fleeing car, but he doubted the driver heard him over the music vibrating the windows. The woman nodded a thank-you. He nodded back and crawled back in his truck.

He'd arrived in the town of Heartbroke yesterday and got settled into the apartment. Not that it required a lot of settling. He'd hired a rental company to furnish the apartment on Friday. All he'd brought with him were a few clothes, his laptop, his phone, some basic tools, and Marilyn.

Some guys named their boats, their vehicles, or their dicks. Austin had named his Glock.

Never leave home without Marilyn. He pulled out his gun from the glove compartment. He'd cleaned the weapon twice yesterday to pass time.

Another car engine roared through the parking lot. He set his gun on the passenger seat. When a silver Toyota passed, he flopped back against the seat.

Call him optimistic, but he'd hoped to connect with Leah yesterday—and to have already scheduled a coffee date or something. But she'd stayed locked up in her place. He knew because his apartment was next to hers and he'd kept an ear to the wall half the time.

She'd watched TV and talked on the phone. Not knowing if perhaps she was chatting with her half brother, Rafael DeLuna, frustrated the hell out of him. Hence plan B.

When he'd woken up at six a.m. and didn't hear anything, he'd run to the parking lot, only to find her white Chevy Cruze gone.

On the way to get plan B supplies, he'd driven by her office. Her car was parked in the back. Why couldn't she have been a regular vet? He really liked his original plan of getting a dog. Partly because he was thinking about getting one. He liked Bud, Dallas's dog. Well, everything but the gas bombs he dropped.

Leaning back, he stared at the roof of his Chevy pickup. Boredom already had him by the neck and threatened to choke him. If at home, he'd be working a case or shooting the shit with Tyler and Dallas. They shot a lot of shit.

At first Austin worried about how the two of them getting married might change things. It hadn't. Oh, they didn't joke so much about getting laid, but he respected that. He'd even found a soft spot for his partners' wives. They, of course, were always threatening to fix him up... "with a good girl."

He told them not to bother. He wanted the bad ones.

Another car's engine sounded, and he bolted up. He was ready to give plan A a shot before risking plan B. He'd brainstormed a few approaches to Leah, but they felt forced, so he decided to wing it.

With women, he could wing it. He might not be the genius like Tyler, or have the diplomatic skills that Dallas had, but Austin Brook had charm. The kind women loved.

Just like your daddy. Tensing to the point his shoulders hurt, he remembered the words of the woman who had the nerve to call herself his mother.

As if fate knew he needed a distraction, a white Chevy Cruze pulled past. *Showtime.* His heart raced as the car turned into the parking spot next to him. The space designated for apartment 212.

He grabbed his phone and pretended to be talking in case she noticed him. She never glanced his way. And he never took his eyes off her. A curtain of thick, dark hair hid her face as she pulled into the spot.

She parked and brushed her hair back. Lots of soft-looking dark hair. He studied her feminine profile, a small nose, best described as perky, and lips that were…pouty. Most women accomplished that sultry, seductive look with the right lipstick.

He could be wrong, but he didn't think she was wearing lipstick.

She pulled her hair on top of her head and shoved something in there to keep it up. With her arms up, he got a glimpse of her upper torso, which included her feminine swell of breasts straining against a pink shirt. He wasn't sure if it was the breasts or the soft cut of her jawline, but it hit. Recognition. She was…familiar. But from where? She turned and glanced toward her backseat, offering him the frontal view of her face.

Shit! His grip on the phone tightened while his other hand locked around the steering wheel. She looked just like the Victoria's Secret model. The one brunette who had him overlooking the blondes. Hell, he'd spent more nights with this woman—in his mind—than he could count.

Was that her? Was she moonlighting as a model? He'd heard some models did that. She exited her car and walked around the passenger side. She wasn't the model.

As Roberto had implied, Leah Reece was petite. The angel he adored from afar who posed in sexy underwear was five feet and eleven inches. He knew 'cause he'd surfed her website—fuel for his fantasies.

He mentally measured Leah as she opened the back passenger door. Maybe five-three. He liked them tall, he reminded himself, when he felt the initial stirring of male interest.

She leaned forward to grab whatever it was in her backseat, presenting him a good view of her backseat—a very nice, rounded ass covered in soft denim. The view had his jeans feeling crowded.

"She's not the model," he muttered to chase away the stirring in his boxers. It didn't work. *She's DeLuna's sister, damn it!*

His crotch listened to the second point.

She raised up with grocery bags hanging from each hand. His gaze stayed fixed on her as she started walking.

That's when he remembered he was supposed to be bumping into her.

She was already in the front of his car. If he didn't do this now, it wouldn't work. He twisted for the door, and bumped the horn with his elbow. When he looked up, Leah Reece had her arms in the air, and raining down on her were the bags' contents.

Oh, hell. This was not a smooth, charm-her-into-trusting-him approach.

Improvise, his gut told him as he reached for the door. Wing it. Hadn't he just admitted being good at that?

The horn blew. Leah's breath hitched in her throat. Her arms shot up and her groceries went up with them, some escaping from the bags, others crashing to the pavement inside the thin white plastic.

"I'm sorry," a deep voice said at the same time her bottle of cheap Cabernet landed with a resounding crack.

Panic still biting her stomach, she took two big backward steps. When her startled gaze spotted the man hurrying toward her, her need to escape vanished. Blond, apologetic blue eyes, clean-cut. *Not Rafael*, a calming internal voice whispered. *Not Cruz. And not someone who looked like one of her half brother's homeys, either.*

She hadn't realized it until now, but the call from her half brother had put her on edge. The alarm tensing her insides faded, replaced with grief—grief for her bottle of Cab.

"Really sorry." He stepped closer. All six-foot-plus of him.

"It's okay." She knelt beside her discarded groceries, embarrassed at how she'd overreacted. She stared at his cowboy-booted feet and not his handsome face. It wasn't this stranger's fault she'd jumped out of her own skin at the sound of a horn. She glanced at the plastic bag holding the wine and saw the red liquid slowly filling the plastic bag. After the day she'd had, she could have used a couple of glasses.

The stranger knelt beside her. His muscled thighs straining against his jeans filled her view. Not wanting to get caught crotch staring, she gazed up at him re-bagging the undamaged goods.

Tongue-tied, she refocused on the plastic bag filling up with wine. Turning her head, she looked to see if the garbage can was still located between the parking spaces. It was.

She reached for the bag with the broken wine, but the good-looking stranger got to it first.

"Let me." Obviously having seen her eyeing the garbage, he picked up the bag and straightened. A piece of broken glass must have poked through the plastic because wine began to squirt out in a steady stream. Bright red Cabernet hit her pink shirt, across her boobs.

She squealed.

"Shit!" He yanked up the bag.

Up, which meant the stream got her in the face. Her eyes started burning. She blinked.

"Damn," he muttered.

She slammed her eyes shut, lost her balance, and plopped back on her butt. She fanned her face, hoping to cool the sting in her eyes. The wine bottle hit the ground again.

She heard him shuffling around. "Here. Take this." Fabric came against her face. "Wipe your eyes?"

She buried her face in the cotton and kept blinking.

"Friggin' hell," he gritted out at the same time the roar of a car's engine and blaring music vibrated the pavement. "That car again!"

Leah felt herself being swooped up. Up into the man's arms at the same time she heard a car zoom closer.

"Slow the hell down! It's a damn parking lot, not a racetrack!" the man bellowed out.

Catching her breath, her body cradled against a warm masculine chest, she pulled the cotton fabric from her face and turned her watery eyes to him. She opened her mouth to speak, but nothing came out. Probably because she didn't have a clue what to say. It wasn't every day she was doused in wine and swooped up by a hot guy whose crotch she'd just stared at.

He scowled. Yet somehow she understood it was targeted toward the driver of the car and not her.

"Are your eyes okay?" Concern tightened the corners of his mouth.

She nodded and tried to blink away the Cab-induced tears. The fruity smell of berry and oak tannins filled her nose, but beneath that she caught the scent of male aftershave.

Spicy.

Earthy.

Nice.

She took another deep breath. Was the wine going to her head? She looked at the bunched-up cotton she used as a towel and realized it was the man's shirt. And that's when she realized all the warmth surrounding her was skin.

Warm naked skin. Yup, the wine had gone to her head.

She cut her eyes to his bare shoulder. Then, aware of the feel of his arms holding her, his muscled chest, she remembered Sara asking, *Don't you miss it?* "It" referring to a man's touch and all the sinfully wonderful sensations that came with it.

Like how warm his solid, slightly bulging muscle in his left arm felt pressed against the side of her breast. Like the tingles his other arm sent pressed to the back of her thighs. Even through her jeans, she felt his corded muscles.

Her heart beat to a tune of romance—well, not romance, she didn't know this man; this wasn't romance. This was pure lust. She drew in a gulp of air to sober her thoughts. Aftershave and wine filled her nose, a combo that reminded her of lusty romantic evenings.

"Uh. Can . . . you put me down?" she managed to say.

"S-sorry." He set her on her feet. "You're so light, I barely noticed I was holding you."

Barely noticed? Just the impression a woman wanted to make.

She glanced at his wine-stained shirt and then down to her wine-stained blouse, which had come unbuttoned and exposed her once white, now Cab-pink, bra. She looked up. His eyes dropped to her chest. She slapped his wine-soaked shirt over her wine-soaked boobs and bra. *Well, he did seem to notice that.*

He swung around as if offering her privacy. "I'm sorry," he repeated.

She buttoned her shirt. After a few awkward seconds, he looked over his shoulder and then turned around.

His blue eyes—baby blue, sky blue—met hers and stayed there for several heartbeats.

"Here." She handed him his shirt. "I...don't know if the wine will come out, but if you wash it now, it might."

"It's not important." He hung the shirt over his shoulder and knelt to collect her scattered groceries. Of course, most of them, like the flattened loaf of bread and the carton of eggs oozing yellow yolks, were toast.

"I should say thank you," she said.

He stood up. "For what? Accidentally blowing my horn and scaring the shit out of you, squirting wine on you and in your eyes, or almost getting you run over?" He laughed.

A really nice laugh. She smiled—especially when she saw what he had in his hands. "How about for saving me from being run over and for...attempting to rescue my tampons." She took the box of smashed feminine protection. His look of embarrassment came and then went when he laughed again.

She moved and tossed the squashed package in the garbage.

When she faced him again, her gaze shifted from his sexy smile to his bare chest. Needing a distraction, she started picking up the other remnants of her purchases to toss in the garbage. She grieved slightly over her flattened, frozen mushroom pizza, oozing out of the box and wearing a tire track down the middle.

Avoiding his gaze, she grabbed the few items that weren't complete roadkill: a can of corn, some soup, and a pack of toilet paper.

He held out a plastic bag.

"Thank you." She took the bag.

Another smile lit up his eyes. "My name's Austin Brook... shire."

He seemed to stumble over his name, telling her he wasn't nearly as confident as she'd originally thought. That made him more likable. She'd had her fill of overconfident, cocky playboys who thought they were God's gift to women. Guys who made you feel complete and loved until you spent a few years married to them. Guys you were trying to start a family with, and then, bam, you realize they were charging phone sex calls on your credit card and having sex with your neighbor. Yup, she'd had enough of that kind.

Then again, she'd had her fill of all men. And she needed to nip this...cute, funny conversation, which entailed thank-yous, apologies, and a mention of tampons, in the bud before he assumed she was interested.

Of course, he hadn't really shown any interest in her. Well, other than sneaking a peek at her boobs; but she couldn't blame him. She'd sneaked a peek at his chest, too. She wasn't counting the crotch stare. He'd put it in her line of vision.

Ahh, but she didn't fool herself. Men like him, even the uncocky ones, with his body and blond hair and blue eyes, could snap their fingers and have any woman they wanted. Women like models, superstars, or high-brow types who wore fancy high heels, worked at their six-figure-income jobs, and drank expensive wine.

Not that she considered herself a bad catch. But she wouldn't trade in her career for anything highbrow. She was good at her job. Even if most of her income derived from removing testicles.

Someday, when her school loans were paid off and her brother's education was taken care of, she'd be able to afford a pair of Christian Louboutin high heels. God knew she could use a few inches. Maybe she'd even find the means to buy something better than a screw-top bottle of Cab.

Realizing his gaze had returned to her chest with interest, she stepped back. It was good-bye time.

She cleared her throat.

He gazed up, looking a tad guilty, and focused on her face. "That's odd," he said.

"Odd?" She glanced down and didn't see anything odd about her boobs. They were perfectly good, wine-doused, small size-C boobs. Well, one was a little bigger than the other, but that was normal. "What's odd?"

He bit back a smile. "Not your..." He almost laughed. "I meant, usually when someone tells you their name, the other person responds by telling you their name. I told you my name. And your name is...?"

She hesitated. "Leah." She sat her salvaged bag of goods at her feet and picked up the last of her run-over groceries. A couple of egg yolks slipped from the bottom of the demolished egg carton. One plopped on her jean-covered thigh, and another made its way down to the toe of her tennis shoe.

Yellow goo ran down her leg and the sides of her right shoe. She realized she was pretty much feeling that way inside. Gooey.

And it was his fault. His smile. His naked chest.

"Just Leah?" he asked.

"Yes." She cringed, realizing how silly she sounded. "No. I mean..." *You won't need to know my name.* "Leah Reece." Ignoring the mess on her jeans and shoe, and the mess that was called her life, she stepped away to toss the items. Moving back to where he stood, she snatched up her bag. "And... I should be... need to get going. I have... calls to make."

"You live in the apartments?" He inched closer.

She nodded, a car eased past and the driver stared at them, and she realized how odd they looked, him shirtless, her covered in wine and eggs.

"Can I help with your groceries?" he asked.

She held up her one bag and tried not to let her gaze go to his bare chest. "I got it. But...thanks."

Offering him her best smile, because that was all she could offer, she walked away.

Don't you miss it? Sara's question echoed in her head again.

Hell, yes, she missed it. But what she didn't miss was the pain that always followed the pleasure.

CHAPTER THREE

NOTE TO SELF, Austin thought thirty minutes later: Improvising and winging it might not always be the best idea from now on.

But, shit! He'd made a mess out of the "chance" meeting. He'd almost given her his real name. And he was paying for that mess now. He glanced around to make sure no one was nearby.

Desperate times led to desperate measures. And this was pretty damn desperate. Not as risky as plan B, but a lot more embarrassing.

Confident no one was watching, he hurried down aisle six with his cart to the smaller boxed items, wishing a pack would just jump off the shelf and into his shopping basket.

Again looking to see if he was alone, he sifted through the bag of run-over items to check for the brand. He found it and then noticed... Who would have ever guessed these things came in sizes? He looked back up.

"Shit," he muttered. This would teach him not to wing it.

It took a good three minutes to find the *slim medium absorbent*. Snatching up the twenty-four pack—just like she'd purchased—he studied the tampons one more time to make sure he had the right kind.

"Crazy what we'll do to get into a woman's pants, isn't it?" A voice came at Austin's right.

Flinching, he dropped the box in his cart and glanced at the man who looked about as uncomfortable as Austin felt. About his age, he stood puzzling over the tampon varieties, too.

"Is she worth it?" the man asked, losing his look of embarrassment, as if talking sex would make this easier.

A denial was on Austin's lips. This wasn't about getting into any woman's pants; it was about getting the woman's asshole of a half brother. But then his mind re-created the vision of her pants, or rather the perfectly round ass inside those pants. Following that vision came one of her dimples. When she smiled, they literally winked at him. Hell, even the Victoria's Secret model didn't have dimples.

But Leah Reece wasn't tall, he reminded himself again. Then he realized the man standing beside him, holding a package of sixty-four name-brand, medium extra-absorbent tampons, was staring at him.

Is she worth it? The man's question repeated in his head.

"Yeah, she's worth it," he muttered, not completely lying because he imagined she would be. Not that he had any intention of getting into Leah Reece's pants. Information. That's what he was after.

"Gotta get the right kind, or she'll send me back," the man moaned. "It's a damn piece of cotton in a tube; how the hell can they be so different?"

Austin looked into the bag one more time, assuring he hadn't messed up, because frankly if he had to shove something up his body, he'd be picky, too. His face reddened just thinking about it.

"Later," he said, not in the mood to discuss tampons with a stranger anymore, and pushed his cart toward the egg aisle.

He was careful to buy all the same items, and only reconsidered when he got to the wine section.

Seriously, how good could a ten-dollar wine be? He stared at the bottle of Napa, California, Cab, one of his favorites that he served when having company and making homemade pizza. Thoughts of pizza had his appetite stirring. Then he looked again at the other items in his cart.

Everything was the store brand and the cheapest on the market. Was Leah Reece cutting corners? The apartment she rented wasn't in the slums, but with not-so-new carpet in the halls, walls that could use a paint job, and speeding demons running through the parking lot, it sure as hell left a lot to be desired. Didn't vets make a decent living?

He considered her age. She might still be paying off school loans. It hit him then what this meant. Her dear ol' brother must not be sharing any of his illegal gains from his drug- and gun-running business. Or maybe Leah didn't want any part of his dirty money.

The sweet smile she'd offered him before walking away flashed in his mind. He liked the thought of her being better than her asshole brother, or he did until he realized what that meant. If she didn't want any part of his money, she might not want any part of her brother. And damn it, if that was the case, she wouldn't know where he was.

Austin stood in the middle of the Cab section gnawing on that thought, when another one hit. Was she the proprietor of her vet clinic? If so, then someone, maybe DeLuna, had helped finance that.

Grabbing his phone from his pocket, he searched for Roberto's number and hit dial.

"Yeah?" Roberto muttered.

"Good or bad time?" Austin asked.

"Give me a second," Roberto answered with all sorts

of construction noises going on in the background. It took thirty seconds before he spoke again. "What's up?"

"You still on the job?"

"Leaving for the day."

"About our subject. Is she hurting for funds?"

"In debt up to her cute ying yang," he said.

So Roberto thought her ying yang was cute? "The clinic she works at, is it hers?"

"And Chase Bank's. A whopping two thousand a month. Add her school loans and her brother's college, and if there's not enough sick kitties that month, she's probably eating rice and beans and beans and rice."

"How do you know this?" Frustration echoed in Austin's voice.

Silence filled the line, and it felt intentional on Roberto's part. Finally he muttered, "I told you guys when you hired me not to question my methods. You three might still worry about abiding by the rules, but me? Not so much."

Austin gripped his phone tighter. "I don't give jack shit how you got it. All I want to know is how accurate it is."

Roberto still paused. "Accurate. Let's just say every time I walked by her mailbox the lock kept falling open."

"And you don't think she's getting any handouts from relatives?" Austin did a few more calculations in his head. "Is she making enough to pay all those bills?"

"You ever taken a pet to a vet?" Roberto asked. "It can run you a fortune. Not that it wouldn't be tight. She doesn't even stop by Starbucks for coffee, and she shops like a senior citizen on Social Security."

Austin looked at the basket of low-cost goods. Roberto hit the mark on that one.

"Like I told you," Roberto said, "I think you're farting in the wind on this one."

Austin ran a hand over his face. "If she's taking care of her younger brother's college, she's into family. My gut says she knows more than we think."

"You've met her, haven't you?"

"Yeah," Austin admitted.

"Cute little thing, isn't she?"

"Not my type," he ground out.

Roberto chuckled. "You tried to pick her up, didn't you? Don't feel bad, she gave me the brush-off, too."

Austin frowned. Half the problem was he *had* picked her up, and there was nothing cold about the experience. She'd been so warm, so easy to hold. The feel of her in his arms was... he couldn't really describe it, but it felt... natural.

She'd even smelled natural, not perfumey, but like... cookies, no... like freshly baked waffle cones in an ice cream parlor.

"I like tall blondes," he added, wishing his libido would remember that.

"Then wait until you get a peek at her vet assistant." Roberto exhaled. "Not that... I mean, she's probably not your type, either. She's got a kid."

Bet she doesn't have dimples. Freaking hell, since when did he give a damn about dimples? He wiped a palm over his face again, as if to wipe away the thought. "I'm not here to pick up women!" he said.

"I wasn't trying to pick her up, either, just attempting to get some info. I'm not interested in chasing tail." Roberto sounded defensive.

His tone felt off. Truth was, something about Roberto had always felt off. At times, he came off as an upstanding citizen. Too upstanding, considering he made money doing dirty undercover work for anyone who'd pay him. He liked putting the bad guys away. Although, he didn't seem to like cops any more than he did the jerks he turned in. Something Austin, Dallas, and Tyler respected.

But Roberto also didn't seem to mind crossing a few lines to get a job done. From what Austin could tell, the lines the man crossed weren't anything Austin wouldn't step over himself. In spite of being slow to get a big payoff on DeLuna, Roberto was good at what he did.

"I'm only interested in finding DeLuna." *Not petite, dimple-faced women with cute ying yangs!* "Her loyalty to her younger sibling is proof that family is important to her."

"Yeah, but the younger one has never been in trouble. I think your girl is squeaky clean and doesn't care to wallow in the mud, if you get my meaning."

"All the more reason for her to want to save her brother," Austin said.

"And I think she knows he's low-life shit and can't be saved."

Low-life shit. It wasn't so much what Roberto said, but how he said it. A tone so much like his and his two partners' when they spoke of DeLuna. Austin recalled how, in the beginning, Tyler had surmised Roberto had his own agenda with DeLuna. They couldn't prove it, but they decided they didn't see a downside if it were true. As long as Roberto's agenda led to the same place theirs did—with DeLuna either behind bars or six feet under—they didn't give a damn.

"What is—" Austin heard the click of the line being disconnected.

Roberto hit the off button the second he heard the footsteps behind him, and spewed out a few lines. "Look, bitch, I've told you. It's over. Pay your own rent." He pretended to hang up.

"Problems?" A deep voice came from behind him.

Roberto recognized the voice. Brad, Roberto's ticket into Cruz's private club. Cruz was the owner of the construction company and Brad's brother-in-law. While the company did fairly well, it was really more of a front. The real money came from the illegal dealings. And the orders came from the Big Boss in charge of all the illegal dealings.

The Big Boss being Rafael DeLuna.

"Just some chick who gave it up a couple of times and now thinks I'm her sugar daddy."

"You seem to have a lot of those kinds of calls." Brad crossed his arms over his meaty chest. And at six-five, there was a lot of meat.

Hell, had Roberto used that line already? He needed to be more careful. "I guess my dick gets me into trouble."

"Let's hope it's just your dick." Brad's tone dropped to a serious range. The man had worked in construction all his life, and his build showed it. He reminded Roberto of one of those television wrestlers, three-hundred-plus pounds of muscle. Almost bald, the burly guy was downright scary looking. But, in reality, he was a wimp. He might do well in construction, but he wasn't nearly bad enough to work for someone like Cruz or DeLuna. Not heartless enough.

"What're you saying?" Roberto forced his tone down to the serious level.

"You know what I'm saying."

"Are you fucking accusing me of being the leak? Are you forgetting I took a knife for your ass? Remind me next time to let you die." Taking the knife had been a stupid mistake. He'd thought he'd step in, take a few punches, and show his loyalty to Brad. Roberto hadn't known the kid had a knife. It had hurt like hell, but the mistake had got him what he wanted. Closer to Brad. Closer to DeLuna's operation. Closer to making that bastard pay.

"I'm not accusing you, but someone will if you keep this crap up."

"What crap? Just because I work for you doesn't mean I can't have a private conversation. Next you'll be saying I can't take a shit alone. You'll want someone to come in there and wipe my ass for me."

"Look," Brad snapped. "If this keeps up, if another delivery goes bad, heads are going to roll. And it might be yours if you don't watch your step."

"Did something else happen?" Roberto saw genuine fear in the big guy's eyes. Of course Roberto knew what'd happened. And with this drug-deal-gone-bad situation, like the last four, he hadn't collected for his services or let Austin and his partners help pull the final strings. DeLuna was bound to start looking at the Only in Texas bunch, and the last thing Roberto wanted was the guilt of someone else's death on his conscience.

His conscience was friggin' full already.

At first, the Only in Texas team was just another way to support his own mission. With them it was a true win/ win. They wanted DeLuna and so did he. But after getting to know the detectives a little, he didn't want to see them go down in the process.

Eventually, when you surrounded yourself with nothing but scum, it was easy to emotionally attach yourself to anyone decent with whom you had regular contact. The Only in Texas PIs were decent. They might have carried a shield at one time, but like him, they now knew how useless the cops could be.

And like him, they had an agenda. Theirs was justice. His wasn't so politically correct. He wanted revenge. It didn't have to be wrapped up pretty. He didn't want it to be pretty. Not for DeLuna.

And if he got a few more creeps off the street while he

was at it, great. He'd need some good karma when he arrived at the pearly gates.

"Fuck, yeah, something else happened." Brad spoke with such emotion that spittle left his mouth. "Someone tipped off the cops in that Austin job."

"No shit?" Roberto asked. "But wasn't that just a small run?" Of course, he knew it was small. He'd borrowed the Only in Texas's method of getting to DeLuna. Keep interfering with his business, and sooner or later the asshole would surface to do something about it.

"Small, yes, but they are adding up. And Cruz and the Boss have lost their patience." Guilt filled the man's eyes and he leaned in. "Johnny . . . you know, the skinny kid, he did the delivery, and because he stopped and made a few calls, they think he tipped off the cops." A frown marred the big man's face. "They sent some guys to post his bail and . . . I'm told they made an example of him as a warning. When the news comes out about his body being found, they're taping it, and I'm supposed to make sure all the guys here see it, as a warning."

"They killed him?" Roberto didn't want to believe it.

Brad nodded. "That's shitty, isn't it?"

"Damn." Roberto's stomach knotted when he remembered meeting Johnny, but then he also recalled the twenty-year-old bragging about taking part in a gang rape of a fifteen-year-old girl. Johnny belonged to part of Roberto's karma plan. His conscience wouldn't have to take a hit on this one. He still felt hit.

Realizing Brad was staring at him, Roberto asked, "So they think he was behind it, huh?"

"Somebody's doing it. And Johnny seemed like the obvious one. At least that's what they said. But, damn it! He was just a kid."

Roberto drew in a sobering breath. "Maybe the cops have just gotten better at sniffing them out?"

"That would be too much of a coincidence. They don't believe in coincidences. And if this shit doesn't stop, some-one here will be the next Johnny. I work with these guys. How am I supposed to just watch them take one of 'em out?"

"We just hope it stops." But it wasn't going to stop and Roberto knew it. The next job-gone-bad deal was tomorrow in San Antonio. He'd dropped that info on an undercover cop and already collected a cool two hundred.

Life was about to get interesting. And not in a good way.

An hour later, Leah ran her spoon around the bowl, watching what Campbell's called stars swirl in the broth. Tiny cubes of chicken and occasional fragments of carrot swam around the bits of pasta.

Skitter, her gray and tan tabby, leaped onto the table and stared at the soup. He raised his paw as if to catch moving parts, but she caught his foot. "This is my dinner. I fed you, remember?"

He looked insulted. Sighing, she fished out a piece of chicken. "You know I shouldn't do that. I jump on my clien-tele for doing that." The cat collected his prize.

Staring back at her uneaten dinner, she gave her spoon another lap around the soup and inhaled the savory scent. She'd already had her taste buds set on pizza and half of the bottle of wine that had perished in the parking lot. Along with part of her sanity.

Pushing her soup and all the parking lot memories to the back burner, she stared at her phone, wishing Luis would call. She'd left three messages. Which was probably why he wasn't calling.

He'd told her that whenever she was upset, her voice was

a dead ringer for their late aunt Nita's your-ass-is-grass tone. Considering their aunt had raised them since Leah was eight and her brother was two, it was no wonder she took after her aunt. And considering how many times her brother's ass had been grass with his aunt, Luis was an expert on the tone. But like Aunt Nita, that tone stemmed from love.

Besides, how could Luis not expect her to be upset? He knew better than to contact Rafael. Every damn time her half brother popped in their life, shit popped up with him. Leah had her quota of shit for a lifetime.

A loud knock sounded at her door, and Leah's heart knocked with it. She recalled Rafael's words when she'd refused to give him Luis's contact information. *Don't piss me off, Sis. Family loyalty has never been big in our kinfolk.*

Old news, she'd thought. She'd discovered that as a kid, when she'd asked her mom how come her daddy didn't live with her all the time like her friends' dads. Mom told her that her daddy had an important job. Mom also told her... *Absence makes the heart grow fonder.*

Even at six, she hadn't believed it. A few years later she learned the truth. Daddy had another family. Obviously, he didn't need absence to make his heart grow fonder for them.

She wasn't sure if Rafael's smart-ass remark had been a threat, but it felt like it. Already, talking to him had cost her a couple bags of groceries, her much needed wine, a blouse, a bra, and a lot of embarrassment.

The knock sounded again. Pressing her hand to the door, she lifted on her tiptoes and spied through the peephole.

"Crap!" She pulled back. Not Rafael. Her racing heart took on a different tune. Austin Brookshire. Why his name had stuck so easily in her memory bank, she didn't know.

Oh, hell, she did know.

She hadn't stopped thinking about him. His smile, the devilish twinkle in his blue eyes, the feel of his naked chest.

Sara! It was Sara's fault for talking about missing a man's touch. But blaming someone wasn't going to answer the door, or fix her problem. Problem being it was getting harder to deny that part of herself that craved a little company. Male company.

"Damn! Damn! Damn," she muttered.

CHAPTER FOUR

AUSTIN HEARD THE expletive and leaned a bit closer.

"Leah? It's me, Austin," he said, even though he'd seen the peephole go dark and knew she'd peered out.

"I'm not home." It was little more than a murmur, but the words still traveled through the cheap-ass apartment door.

"You know I can hear you, right?"

"Shit!" Her voice carried again, and he grinned trying to imagine her expression when flustered. Did her soft brown eyes get a little darker? Did those pouty lips get a little poutier?

"I come bearing gifts," he said, his mind envisioning her mouth.

"I don't want any gifts." Her tone sounded extra-defiant. "I don't like gifts."

"Why wouldn't you like gifts?" He leaned his hip against the door frame, genuinely curious. Every woman he'd dated loved gifts. At the beginning of every relationship, he always brought them gifts.

When she didn't answer, he replied, "They really aren't gifts. They're...replacements. For the groceries I turned into roadkill. Please open the door."

She opened the door, but not enough to be an invitation to come inside. "You didn't have to do that."

"Yes, I did," he said. *How else are you going to trust me enough to tell me what I need to know?* The thought brought tension in his shoulders. Or was the tension from feeling the punch of attraction again?

She'd changed out of her wine-soaked clothes. She wore a light blue T-shirt and a pair of gray sweats. Both fit her very well and showcased a body that was all curves.

"I was careful to get all the same items." He held out the bag in his hand.

She stepped out a few inches, eyeing the bags. Her hair hung loose and locks of it kept shifting over her breasts.

"My frozen mushroom pizza?" Hunger flashed in her eyes. Her tongue dipped out and swiped across her bottom lip.

"Got it." His gaze stayed glued to her mouth when she leaned forward and glanced inside the bag.

She looked up and smiled. "Wow. You must have felt really bad."

"Because I got your mushroom pizza?"

"No"—she pointed inside the bag—"because you bought me tampons." Her dimples deepened in her cheeks. "Never met a man who'd do that."

"There's always a first time. And a last." Damn she was pretty. And in a refreshing way. Not made up, or artificial. Half the women he dated used clothes and makeup as a mask. This petite little feminine package before him wore no mask; there was nothing counterfeit or artificial about her.

She rolled her eyes. "You really didn't have to do this. I didn't blame you."

He didn't blame her, either. The realization hit. He'd thought he'd instantly dislike her. He thought every time he looked at her, he would think of the scumbag who'd framed him and cheated him out of sixteen months of his life.

But, nope. Right now he knew that she couldn't help who her brother was, any more than he could help who his mother was. Or his father for that matter.

But that didn't change anything.

If she knew where DeLuna was, he intended to find out. Just because he didn't hold a grudge against her didn't mean he didn't hold one against her brother.

"The only thing I gave you an upgrade on was the wine." He set the bag on the floor and pulled out the bottle of Cabernet from the other.

Temptation flashed in her eyes.

He couldn't help wondering what else tempted her. "I have a couple of glasses in my apartment."

She jerked her eyes up. The longing and humor vanished.

Glancing at the bag at his feet, she said, "I tell you what. I'll take everything but the wine."

"No. I mean..." He wasn't accustomed to being turned down. "You sharing the wine with me wasn't a condition. I just thought... since we're neighbors..." He motioned to the door to his left.

"You live... *there*?" Her expression looked as if she'd just sniffed sour milk.

"Don't worry, I'm a good neighbor. No loud music, no wild parties." *And as soon as I get the info I need, I'll never bother you again.* His gut tightened. "I'm just new in town and thought..."

"I'm not interested in..." She paused.

"Conversation?" he finished for her. "Because that's all I was asking for."

She bit down on the edge of her bottom lip and studied him. "Gay?"

"What?" he asked, certain he'd misunderstood.

"Are you gay?"

"No! Hell, no. Not even a little bit. I meant...I wasn't looking...I just wanted..."

She leaned closer. "Keep your eye out for the woman who lives in two-oh-six and the one in two hundred. Both blondes, they have guys come and go all the time, so I know they are open to"—she shrugged—"*conversation*."

"You're difficult," he said, not even meaning to state it out loud.

"And you're pushy," she said, pursing her lips into a tight bow.

He frowned. "Because I asked you to share a glass of wine with me?"

"No. Because I refused your offer and you can't accept it."

"I can accept it." He just didn't like it.

"Good. Then enjoy the wine." She nodded at the bottle and reached for the other bag.

"No," he said, getting more agitated, "the wine stays with the pizza." He leaned down and snatched up the other bag before she did, and placed the bottle inside. Then he handed both bags off to her. "Take it."

She did but didn't look happy. "See, you're pushy."

"And you're still difficult," he answered back. But then he spotted the grin flashing in her eyes and couldn't stop himself from laughing. The sound of her laugh followed his and had her dimples winking at him. He got the oddest desire to touch her cheek. Since when had he enjoyed arguing with a woman?

"Okay," she said, her smile still on her lips. "I'll be the bigger person and say thank you."

He quirked another brow at her. "But you still won't share it?"

"Nope." She didn't even hesitate. "But I'm still the bigger person."

Not by a long shot, he almost said, remembering how small she'd felt in his arms. Warm. Soft. Almost fragile. "How tall are you?"

She rolled her eyes. "I meant 'bigger' hypothetically. I'm five-two and a half."

"With or without shoes?" He laughed again. But the laugh was cut short when not one, but two, yellow-eyed creatures appeared at the door. One was black, and one was orange. Their presence had the air he'd just inhaled hitching in his chest. Then the black one hissed.

He forced himself to step, not jump, back. He should have been better at hiding his fear since Tyler occasionally brought his wife's cat to the office. And maybe Austin was better, but his skin still crawled, and the two-inch scar under his arm that he'd carried since he was four started to itch.

"You have two cats?"

"No," she said. "Four. Two are just semi-feral."

"Four," he said. "I thought that was illegal."

She made a cute face. "No. Well, I mean the apartment manager thinks I have two. But that's our secret." She studied him. "You don't like cats?"

His gaze shifted from the devilish-looking creatures to her soft brown eyes. "What's not to like?" It came out sounding sincere, but only because he started thinking about her.

"You have one?" she asked.

"Yes, I mean, no. I just lost one, not too long ago." See, he could wing it.

"Sorry. That's hard. I'm a vet. Purrfect Pets. I specialize in felines." Her empathy-filled eyes widened. "Are you open to adopting? I have one I'm trying to place in a good home."

Oh, shit. "No, I..." Absolutely no more winging it.

"Too soon?" she asked.

"Yeah." He jumped at that answer.

"You know sometimes it can help."

"That's not the case," he said quickly.

She nodded and looked at the wine in the bag and then she met his gaze. Temptation filled her eyes. And just like that, he knew. She was reconsidering. They were going to share the wine.

"Maybe it wouldn't be a bad thing…" A phone rang. She looked back inside, then up at him. The spark of promise in her eyes vanished.

"I should…take this. It's probably my brother. Thanks again."

Austin's gut tightened as she closed the door.

Which brother?

He stood there, even moved in to see if he could hear. The cheap-ass door was just thick enough to prevent eavesdropping from across the room.

Frowning, he swung back to his apartment.

Looked like he was going with plan B.

"Luis?" Leah dropped the groceries on the table and snatched up the phone without checking the number. Her gaze shot back to her front door, and her heart raced at how close she'd come to agreeing to share the wine with her new hot neighbor. Which, no doubt, would have been a colossal mistake.

"Luis?" she repeated.

"Sorry, it's me, Evelyn."

"Oh," Leah said. *Where the hell was Luis? Was something wrong?*

"You okay?" her office manager asked.

"Fine."

"You don't sound fine. It's that half brother of yours, isn't it? He's bad news, right?"

Leah hadn't done a lot of talking about Rafael. As a matter of fact, Evelyn and Sara had sort of been giving her the stink eye, because she out-and-out told them "no questions." She had her reasons, too. Talking about Rafael would lead her to talking about her dad, and some things were best forgotten.

She remembered telling Austin, *I don't want any gifts, I don't like gifts.* She'd seen the gifts her father had brought her mother. Hell, Leah had even gotten a few gifts from him. Something pretty wrapped up in a neat little bow to make up for the fact that they were his dirty little secret.

They weren't even good enough to get his name. Little did he know, Leah would have traded those presents any day of the week for a real father who loved her. And while in his own way he might've loved their mom, he'd proven how little he loved her and Luis when their mom died in a car accident and he disappeared.

"Is this brother causing you trouble?"

"I didn't say that."

"You didn't have to say it. You've been off your game ever since he called this morning. That, and the fact that you've never even mentioned that you have a half brother, tells me he's trouble."

"Yeah, well, he's not worth mentioning."

"Well, if he causes you any problems, let me know. I've got four six-foot-plus strapping men—a hubby and three sons—who'd be happy to teach a guy a lesson."

"I don't think it'll come to that." Her mind ran with Evelyn's six-foot-plus comment and landed right back to her new neighbor. "So you just called to check on me?"

"No, I forgot to tell you that I'm going to be late tomorrow. It's my morning to get my boobs smashed."

"Your morning to get what?" Leah asked.

"Boobs smashed. You know, mammogram. They have you strip down, tape BBs to your nipples, then have you stand there willingly while they put them in a large vise and smoosh the hell out of them."

"Sounds like fun." Leah covered her boobs protectively with her free arm.

"It is. I always ask the technician if I can wear the BBs home to entice my hubby."

Leah chuckled. "You're crazy."

"You need a little crazy in your life," Evelyn said. "How long has it been since you enjoyed yourself?"

Tonight verbally sparring and flirting with Austin Brookshire. "Maybe I'll see about getting a mammogram." But for now, at least she had her pizza and wine. Phone caught between her ear and shoulder, she picked up the bag and went into the kitchen and started putting away the groceries.

"Oh, guess who I ran into today at the grocery store?" Evelyn asked.

"George Clooney?" Leah put the eggs in the fridge.

Evelyn chuckled. "I wish. It was Eric Taylor. He asked how things were going and said again for you to call him if you changed your mind."

Leah closed her eyes. At times she was tempted to call Eric and take him up on his offer. But Purrfect Pets had been her dream, and letting him buy into the business and turn it into a traditional vet office would change things. Eric, who had sold his clinic back in Austin, had moved back home to Heartbroke. He was working part-time with the only other vet in town, and he wasn't too happy and thought they would make good partners. And they probably would. Deep down she knew if things didn't pick up, she might have to accept his offer. But she'd cross that bridge when she was pushed on it. Or would it be too late then?

"What did you tell him?" Leah pulled the box of tampons from the box and smiled in spite of the dire conversation. She still couldn't believe he'd bought them.

"That I'd pass on the message," Evelyn answered.

"And do you have an opinion on the issue?" Leah sat the tampons on the counter. With Evelyn being the office manager, she knew Leah's financial woes.

"It would make your life easier," Evelyn said. "But we're still hanging on."

Her phone beeped. "Hey, I got another call. I should take it. Just come in tomorrow when you're done." She clicked off.

"Luis?" She spoke her brother's name, hoping she was right.

"Is something wrong?" Luis's voice should have calmed her, but instead her anger at him for trying to contact Rafael rose to the surface.

"I've called you like five times," Leah said.

"I know," Luis said. "But I'm out of town and have been with friends all day."

"Out of town?" Leah asked. "Where are you?"

"In San Antonio. Helping a friend move."

"San Antonio? Why didn't you tell me you were going out of town? What about school?"

"Uh, I thought I did tell you. Or maybe I just thought about telling you and realized that you'd get your head up your ass about it, so I decided to spare you the trouble."

She rolled her eyes. "School comes first."

"I know. And I'm sorry for the wisecrack, it's just I wish you'd let up sometimes. I'm not sixteen anymore. If I miss a couple of days this semester to be a good Samaritan, it's not going to hurt my grades."

"A couple?" she asked.

"We're here for a few days. Give me a break. I never skip classes."

"There's a girl involved, isn't there?"

"Could be," Luis said.

She sighed and reminded herself that Luis's grades weren't falling. And just because she had hideous luck with men didn't mean her brother had bad luck with women.

"You should have told me you were leaving." Closing her eyes, she remembered her real beef with her brother. "And what is this about you asking around for Rafael?"

"What? I wasn't...Oh, wait. I ran into that old friend of his on Sixth Street. The one he brought to Christmas that one year, the one you didn't like? I think he went by Cruz? I swear he looked up to something. Made me nervous."

Chills, bad chills, ran up her spine remembering Juan Cruz. She'd been eighteen, and he'd been horny and hadn't wanted to take no for an answer. If her aunt hadn't come home and overheard the fight, Leah wasn't sure what would have happened. And if Juan hadn't run like hell after her aunt noticed her ripped dress, there'd be one less bad guy in the world.

Say what you want about her aunt, stubborn as a pissed-off mule, but she'd been a strong woman, and Leah and Luis had been lucky she took them in.

"Next time you see that jerk, just walk the other way."

Luis paused. "What happened? Did Rafael call you? He give you trouble?"

She heard the concern in Luis's voice. Even though Luis was six years younger, and griped about her playing the big-sister role, Leah wasn't the only one overprotective. Of course, they had to be when all they had was each other.

"Yeah, he called. He said you were trying to get in touch with him."

"I wasn't trying to get in touch with him. I never said that. I ran into the guy. He was acting weird. I joked about him watching out for cops. Told him to tell Rafael hello. I didn't even mean it; I was looking for an exit line and didn't want to seem rude."

"Well, next time you have my permission to be rude to anyone associated with Rafael." *Especially if it's the guy who tried to rape me.*

"What did he say?" Luis asked.

She spotted the wine and opened a drawer to find the wine opener. "He wanted to know how to get in touch with you."

"He didn't call me," Luis said.

"That could be because I didn't give him your number." She pulled out the wine opener, positioned her phone between her shoulder and ear, and peeled off the foil. Pausing, she gave the label another glance. It looked expensive. Just how much of an upgrade had her new neighbor given her? A few dollars? Five? More? She frowned. It was beginning to feel like a gift. She probably should return it to him tomorrow.

"You should have given it to him," Luis said. "You shouldn't have to deal with him."

Leah would rather deal with him than let Rafael anywhere near her baby brother. When Luis was sixteen, Rafael nearly pulled him into a life of crime. Their aunt had just died and they were living on a shoestring. He'd been tempted by the cash he could earn for simply delivering a package.

Thank God she'd discovered what he was up to and put a stop to it before Luis had done the job. Of course, Rafael hadn't been happy when Leah delivered that package back to him and told him in front of his friends that if he tried to get her brother involved in his dirty business again, she'd take the delivery straight to the police.

Of course, her little stunt hadn't gone unpunished.

She pushed the thought from her mind now and focused back on Luis. "I handled it." She gave the wine another glance. She'd buy Austin another bottle of the same stuff and return it to him later. Right now, she really needed a glass.

Luis moaned. "Once again, Sis, I'm not sixteen anymore."

"I know." She screwed the wine opener top into the cork. "You're a whole twenty-one and a little bit smarter. But you will forever be my baby brother, so just get used to it."

"Has anyone ever told you that you're difficult?"

She tugged the cork out. "Yeah, as a matter of fact they have. Just this afternoon."

"And I bet you didn't believe 'em," he said in a smart-ass tone.

"Of course not." She set the wine down and grabbed a glass.

Luis chuckled. "You aren't just difficult, you are a pain in the ass, but I still love you."

"I know." Leah poured the wine. Picking up the glass, she sniffed the Cab. The scent of blackberry and dark chocolate filled her nose. It smelled wonderful. It smelled expensive. "I love you, too," she said. "And from now on, please tell me when you leave town."

"I'll try to remember that," he said. "And you promise me that if Rafael calls again, you'll give him my number and let me handle him."

"Now, why would I make a promise I couldn't keep?" Socks, her black and white cat, jumped up on the counter and rubbed his head against her arm.

"See, you're difficult," he moaned.

"I love you. Call me when you get home." She hung up, set the phone down, gave Socks a stroke behind the ear, and took a sip of the wine. The taste danced on her tongue.

"Heaven," she muttered. So this was what girls with better bank accounts drank? Someday... someday she was gonna be able to afford good wine and wear expensive shoes.

Hell, maybe someday she'd be at an emotional place where she could date again, too. A place where she'd forget about all the men who'd let her down and the power they wielded over her when she loved them.

CHAPTER FIVE

TUESDAY MORNING AT five a.m., Austin rolled out of bed and moved into his kitchen. He poured himself some coffee and then sat at his table, his ears on guard for any noise coming from Leah's apartment.

He heard a low beeping and assumed it was her alarm. That would make sense since his breakfast area wall and her bedroom wall were one and the same. He could swear he heard a moan. Was she not a morning person?

He recalled the wine. Had she drunk it? Too much of it?

A few minutes later he heard light thuds, footsteps moving around. Was she a coffee drinker? Was she going after a cup right now?

Pulling the steaming cup of black coffee to his lips, he thought about her sipping from her own cup. For some reason he tried to remember the last woman he'd shared the simple ritual of sipping coffee together. Had he even had that since...Cara? The one woman he'd almost gone the whole nine yards with, until...a little murder conviction had her running scared. He pushed her memory away because he didn't like thinking about her.

Then he recalled Brenda, the nurse. They'd shared

coffee. They'd dated for about four months last year. A record for him. She'd been…different. Less of a party girl, and more…domesticated. Instead of hitting the bars, they worked out at the gym, rented movies, and had sex. It had been a nice change.

Oddly, he couldn't recall why he'd stopped seeing her.

Oh, yeah. Her ex was moving back into town, and she wanted to give it another go. Perhaps when Austin got back, he'd call and see if it had worked out for them. If not, maybe they could pick up where they'd left off.

But, on second thought, maybe getting a dog was a better idea.

He didn't miss Brenda. He missed the easy company. He missed the comfortable sex. And he missed what they had. Which was almost a real relationship, minus the emotional ties. He hadn't been hurt when she cut things off, not like Cara, nor had Brenda been all that upset to say good-bye. And that's the way he preferred it. No emotional entanglements. Easy in and easy out.

Just like your daddy.

"Get out of my head," he muttered, hearing Candy Adams's words again. The woman had nerve showing up. Even more nerve to call herself his mom.

Why would she even tell him about his father? Austin didn't care. He couldn't recall the man—supposedly he'd impregnated the seventeen-year-old girl, stayed a year, but left because he'd wanted no part of being a dad.

But his mom, yeah, he remembered her. Remembered missing her. He'd been almost three. Just old enough that a few of the memories hung around.

Sometimes he didn't know if he actually remembered it, or if he'd just heard it whispered behind his back by all the social workers over the years.

Dropped off at a new day care by a mother who worked at a strip joint and had a drug problem, and she just got too busy taking her clothes off, or too high on drugs, to come back for him. The boy was so sick over it, he stopped eating. Told everyone he'd only eat his mom's grilled cheeses.

A year later, the system found her. She'd been arrested for selling drugs and hadn't bothered telling anyone she had a son. After her two-year stay in the county jail, the foster program wanted to give her a chance to get her kid back. They hadn't asked the kid what he thought. He'd been more than a little leery of the woman who said she loved him, but left him anyway.

But she got a job, got clean, was taking parenting classes. She actually came to see him once a week. It was those last visits when she won him over. She'd taken him to the park and played ball with him—something his foster parents had never had the time to do. Once she took him out for ice cream and let him order a triple scoop. She didn't even get mad at him when he couldn't eat it all.

But on the next scheduled visit, his mom had been a no-show.

He remembered sitting for hours, waiting on the porch steps for her. His foster mother had forced him to come inside. He'd been certain his mom was just running late. Certain she wouldn't have abandoned him again.

She had.

And it was worse the second time.

Seven years old and he'd stopped counting on people and started counting on himself. And he'd done a damn good job, too. Not that his attitude back then had made him very adoptable, or even easy to foster. He'd quickly gotten dubbed as closed-off, cold, distant. They slapped the title

"troublemaker" on him. How many times had he been told
that he was going to wind up in jail?

And yeah, he'd gotten into some trouble as a teen. Who
hadn't? Nothing serious. Until the murder conviction. But
that had been bogus.

Bogus crap that had robbed him of sixteen months of his
life. And the man responsible was DeLuna, Leah Reece's
half brother. But as much as he resented DeLuna, the thing
that still ate at Austin the most was the pride it had cost him.
He could almost hear the social workers who'd overseen his
case... "Like mother, like son. We knew that boy would
land himself in prison."

He was nothing like his mother. Chances were, he wasn't
like his ol' man, either.

He didn't plan on having kids, but if he did, he'd never
leave, and that child would *never* be sitting on porch steps
waiting for him. He didn't take on much responsibility, but
when he did, he took his responsibilities seriously.

And right now, he felt responsible to make that asshole
pay who'd framed him and his partners. More importantly,
he longed to clear his name.

Yeah, their exoneration had made the news. But until
the courts had someone to lay the guilty verdict on, there
were people who still believed they'd gotten away with
murder.

That was why he had to find out what Leah Reece knew.
That was why he had to find DeLuna. And his gut still told
him the pretty little brunette was the key to the puzzle.

When he'd planned this, he hadn't considered if his
intrusion into her life would cause her any trouble. Now he
thought about it. The idea of tricking her into trusting him
didn't feel right, but it didn't feel wrong enough to stop him
from doing what he had to.

He stared at his handiwork from last night on the kitchen table. His few semesters in computer engineering had taught him a few useful skills. And his few years working as a cop had taught him just how much time he could get for using the skills he'd learned, too.

Risky, yes. Illegal, yes. Necessary, hell yes.

But he'd given plan A a shot and it hadn't worked. Now, with a few wireless webcam transmitters and a few plastic circuit boxes, he had his bugs. Getting them into her apartment and placing them where she couldn't find them, and where he could hear from room to room, was going to be more difficult than building the devices. He glanced around his own apartment, almost the exact layout as hers, and mentally stationed the bugs. Three should allow him to hear any conversation she had throughout her place.

A groan of running water came from the other side of his wall. A shower? His mind created a vision of her shedding her nightgown. He made it something sexy, too. Then his imagination saw her naked beneath a soft spray of water. Pulling his coffee cup to his lips, he put himself in the shower with her. Having never dated a woman that short, he wondered how their naked bodies would meet.

When a few visuals had his blood running south, he shut the image off. He didn't need a hard-on for her getting in his way of getting this job done.

As soon as she left this morning, and the apartment hall cleared, he'd do a little breaking and entering—another thing that could land his ass back in jail—and place the bugs. Hopefully, in a couple of days he'd have the info he needed.

Hopefully her cats would stay out of his way while he did it, too. And if not, he was prepared.

He picked up the new pistol he'd purchased along with

the other plan B supplies. Letting the awkward weight of it fill his hands, he aimed at his refrigerator.

"Hiss at me again and you'll regret it!"

He placed his finger on the trigger, and then what the hell, he pulled it back and watched the supercharged water squirt out of the barrel.

Yup, he was prepared.

Leah let herself into the vet clinic at five forty-five to dish out love and food—after she'd done the same to her own babies at home. Carting a wine headache, every step caused a twinge in her temple. She really should have stopped at two glasses instead of three. Ahh, but it had been so good, she almost didn't regret it.

Almost.

She plopped her purse on the front desk. Spooky meowed from the back room. Apparently, the orange tabby had recovered enough to protest being locked up. Answering his call, she opened the cage, pulled him into her arms, and whispered soft words when he butted his chin against her forehead.

"See, you don't even miss them." She gave him a scratch behind the ears. He let out a pathetic meow, and if her head wasn't slightly throbbing, she'd have chuckled.

"Hey...I think I got you a possible person. He's a tad pushy, but he has great taste in wine. I think you two will get along."

After filling the kitty bowls and checking on her patients, she started a pot of coffee, caught the first drops of it in her cup, and made her way back to the front desk to sink into the chair and baby her headache. The message light flashing on the phone caught her eye. Finding Evelyn's aspirin in a drawer, she downed two with coffee, then proceeded to check the messages.

Six calls.

She hit play. The first one was from a client who rescued feral cats wanting to know if she would offer free neutering for a couple of males. Leah sighed. She was never going to get ahead doing freebies, but she did them anyway.

The second call was a hang up. As was the third and fourth. The fifth…"Shit." Rafael's voice came on the line.

"Still haven't heard from Luis, Sis. Am I going to have to come there myself to get his number? Don't make me do that."

"Shit what?" Sara walked in the front door.

"Nothing," Leah said, and hit delete.

Sara moved in and sat on the edge of the counter. "It's way too early for your brow wrinkle to make an appearance."

Leah forced a smile. "Headache. I had wine last night."

"I told you, take two aspirin before you drink and it prevents headaches. It's like Beano before you eat that nonfat veggie soup, no aftereffects."

"You back on the soup diet?" Leah asked.

"Yeah. Just five more pounds." She pinched her waist, not that there was enough to pinch. Sara looked great. Taller than Leah by at least four inches, and blond, if Sara wore the right clothes and makeup, she looked more Hollywood than Texan. She was classy looking compared to Leah being cute. Sure, Sara had lost a lot of weight, but she'd never been fat.

"Frankly, I don't know why I don't just eat all the ice cream and cookies I want. It's not like anyone appreciates my efforts. The last guy to see me anything close to naked told me to relax and apologized for his hands being cold. And I got his bill a week later."

Leah grinned. "So you dated my ex, too?"

Sara chuckled. "Not phone sex bills, he was my gyne-cologist." She pulled a small envelope from her purse and handed it to Leah. "Brian's birthday invitation. He's going to be two next week. Do you know what that means? It's been two years, eight months, three weeks, and four days since I've had sex. And I can give you down to the hours if you want. Ugg! What's wrong with me?"

Leah opened her mouth to offer some empathy, but Sara held up her hand.

"No, let me rephrase that. What's wrong with us? You're as bad as I am."

"Not quite." Leah smiled. "It's only been two years for me."

Sara shook her head. "Yeah, but you don't even have the excuse that I do."

"I've got plenty of excuses." Leah had covered several of them last night as she drank her third glass of wine and talked herself out of stepping next door to continue the ver-bal rendezvous.

Sara rolled her eyes. "Please, you didn't gain sixty pounds and push a ten-pound kid through your who-who. You didn't get approximately three hours' sleep a night for a year. Nor did you find yourself with a little person who looks at you with so much love that you feel guilty when you want something in your life besides him. I swear, anytime I think about anything outside of being Brian's mommy, I feel like a terrible mother."

Leah rested her hand on top of Sara's. "You're the best mom I've ever known. And single moms date all the time."

Sara sighed. "And kids of single moms end up emotion-ally damaged because of it, too."

"Not if you pick the right guy," Leah offered.

"You're talking about me, remember? If I like a guy, that's a guarantee that he's on meds, illegal or antipsychotics, or has at least three warrants out for his arrest. I fall for mental cases, addicts, or felons." She paused. "And sometimes I get extra points when they are all three in one. Seriously, I've told you about Brian's father."

"And you don't think we can learn from our mistakes?" Leah had asked herself that question last night.

"Do you?" Sara asked.

"I hope so." Leah paused. "Someday."

"You mean someday when we're too old to enjoy sex?" Sara dropped her face in her hands. "God, I'm so..."

"Horny?" Leah downed the last sip of her coffee.

"No." Sara dropped her hands. "Okay, maybe a little. Mostly, I'm lonely. Everywhere I look I see happy couples. Last night I took Brian out for ice cream. There was this couple sharing an ice cream cone, laughing, and whispering. The guy looked at her as if...as if she was his world. With one finger, he brushed a strand of her hair behind her ear and then moved his finger to trace her lips. It was the hottest thing I've ever seen. She said something and he burst out laughing. I sat there watching them and I felt so...empty inside. I want someone to touch me like that. I want someone who laughs at something I say. Someone who melts when they look at me. I want to be that special to someone."

Leah inhaled, feeling as if her friend was echoing her own sentiments. "Then do it." Leah had concluded last night that she wasn't ready to step into the big scary world of dating yet, but that didn't mean Sara wasn't.

"Do what?"

"Start dating. I'll watch Brian for you."

"Date who?"

"I don't know. Go steal ice cream girl's guy," Leah teased. "Wait. What happened to...Mr. Tall-dark-and-handsome, the one who brought in Spooky? You went to lunch with him. You said you had a good time."

"*I* had a nice time. He obviously didn't. He never called back. Besides, I think he was more interested in you. Half our conversation was about you or the clinic."

"Please," Leah said. "He couldn't keep his eyes off you. I almost cracked up the first time he laid eyes on you. He was talking to me and you walked in and bam, he was off somewhere in his head probably making love to you."

"Was it good? Details please." Sara chuckled and pulled up one knee and wrapped her arm around her leg. "He was so good looking, too."

"Call him," Leah said.

"I gave him my number. He didn't give me his."

Leah arched a brow. "But he gave it to me."

"So he was interested in you." Sara almost looked jealous.

"No, he gave it to me when I filled out the form about Spooky." Leah rolled her chair over and pulled out the file. She thumbed through the files. "Here." She yanked it out and slapped it down beside Sara. "No more excuses. Call him."

She shook her head. "I can't."

"Yes, you can," Leah insisted.

Sara frowned. "I told him about Brian. That's probably why he hasn't called."

"Did he act like it bothered him?" Leah asked.

"No, but..."

"Then call him."

Sara dropped her head on her knee. "He's probably a criminal."

"No. He rescued a cat. How many criminals do you know who rescue cats?" Leah knew for a fact that the average law-breaking asshole didn't like felines. Rafael had proven that the day after she'd told him off about not involving Luis in his drug business. He'd sent Cruz to her house to deliver a package. She hadn't opened the door. She'd waited an hour to see what he'd left on her doorstep. And to this day the memory of her beloved cat in that box still horrified her.

Right then Spooky came swaggering in and jumped up onto the counter.

"Look at you. Spry and ball-less." Sara dropped her hand and gave the tomcat a good scratch behind his ear.

"I possibly have him an owner," Leah told her, pushing the ugly memories away.

"Really?" Sara asked.

"Yeah, a new neighbor. He lost a cat not too long ago."

"He? Is 'he' cute?"

Hell, yes. An image of him standing in the parking lot without a shirt filled her mind. The patch of light brown hair spread across his chest like angel wings. She willingly accepted the image to help her chase away the one from her past. "Didn't notice."

"Liar." Sara grinned.

Leah laughed, feeling a bit sinful. "Okay, he's... drool-worthy."

"And?" Sara asked.

"And I think he'd make a good pet owner," Leah said.

"And?"

"And nothing," Leah said.

"Please, what did you just tell me? To start dating."

"That's you. I'm not that horny yet. I haven't salivated over a guy licking an ice cream cone," Leah teased.

Sara picked up Evelyn's smiley face stress ball and threw it at Leah as they laughed. Laughed until the phone rang.

"Purrfect Pet Veterinarian Clinic. Can I help you?" Humor rang in Leah's voice.

"Just the person I wanted to talk to." Rafael's voice raked across her nerve endings, melted her smile, and shot her good mood to hell. And the throb in her temple came on full force.

Leah waved at Sara as she walked away.

"Just a minute," she said. But she didn't say anything else until she closed her office door. "What do you want?"

"The same thing I wanted yesterday. To talk to your damn brother."

"What do you want with Luis?" she asked.

"To ask him some questions."

"About what?" she seethed.

"He ran into a friend of mine in Austin, and he was acting really strange, and then my friend ran into trouble."

"And you think he had something to do with that? He doesn't want anything to do with you or your friends! Leave us alone."

"I need to talk to him!" His tone was dark and dirty.

"He's not home. He's in San Antonio."

There was a pause. "San Antonio? What's he doing in San Antonio?" Accusation rang in his tone.

"Helping a friend move," she answered.

"That better be all he's doing. Give me his fucking number, Leah. I'm tired of playing games."

"Go to hell." She pushed the off button and punched in Luis's number. As expected, he didn't answer. The phone went to voice mail. "Hey . . . call me!"

She hung up and moaned. Then, standing in the middle

of her office, her heart pounding in rhythm with her headache, she got a bad feeling.

What was it that Rafael thought Luis did? Could Luis be lying to her and be up to no good?

No. Luis was a good kid. But he'd fallen prey to Rafael once before. And even if Luis wasn't guilty of anything, if Rafael thought he was doing something, there would be hell to pay.

CHAPTER SIX

FOR LUNCH, ROBERTO hopped on his bike and drove to the diner that was his regular noontime hangout. Brad usually met him for lunch. Roberto didn't completely dislike Brad, he just didn't respect him. Oh, he wasn't all bad, the guy actually loved his wife and kids, but he looked the other way when his brother-in-law, Cruz, did things. Terrible things. And Brad had a tendency to need to talk, to get things off his chest. Since Roberto needed to know things, he pretended to be the man's friend.

However, he hadn't spotted Brad this morning. So today, Roberto might be getting a reprieve from pretending. He stepped into the small hole-in-the-wall café and started to his regular back booth. One step later, he stopped when he spotted the man sitting there. It wasn't the balding, almost forty-year-old big guy at the booth.

Cruz, owner of the construction business, DeLuna's partner, and all around badass, sat in his place.

The man motioned Roberto over.

A bad feeling curled up inside Roberto's gut. Had his cover unraveled? How?

His footsteps faltered. Had someone found out he wasn't

who he said he was? He considered leaving. Then reconsidered. This could just be a test. Besides, if he died getting justice, so be it. That had been his plan in the beginning, hadn't it? Get revenge—even if it was the last thing he did on earth. Funny how lately he'd started thinking more about living than dying. Sometimes that felt wrong.

He plopped in the booth across from Cruz, who now stared at his phone.

"Where's Brad?" Roberto motioned to the waitress to bring him coffee.

Cruz looked up, and his dark gray eyes held a chill of evil. This man had no conscience. Roberto had heard that Cruz kept a count of the people he'd killed. Everyone should be proud of something in their life.

Roberto had met a lot of career criminals in his last two years. Few of them shied away from murder when confronted with the right situation, but none seemed to relish it as Cruz did. He suspected DeLuna was the same. Actually, he knew he was.

Talk was that Cruz and DeLuna were two of a kind, grew up in the same neighborhood, pulling off petty crimes since they were ten years old.

The old adage *Birds of a feather flock together* came to mind. But he thought of a better one—*Just like mass attracts mass, shit attracts shit.* Not that Roberto had the overwhelming need to take Cruz out. It was DeLuna he wanted.

Still, the karma points he could earn from taking out Cruz would secure his stroll through the pearly gates.

Cruz set his phone down. "Brad had business in San Antonio." The man continued to stare. Roberto's brain worked overtime trying to figure out what Cruz wanted. Roberto had seen the man around a lot, but he'd never shown a personal interest in Roberto.

"Brad thinks highly of you," Cruz said.

"But you don't trust Brad." Roberto leaned back into the booth.

"I didn't say that," Cruz said.

The waitress, Rosie, placed a cup in front of Roberto. "You want your regular?" She smiled. Tall and blond, she wasn't hard on the eyes. But she proudly wore a pin with a picture of her husband and kid. And she'd put a number of men in their place who'd tried to order a slice of her instead of pie.

"That'll be fine. Thanks," he said.

Cruz cleared his throat. "You're not going to take my order?"

She frowned. "You said earlier all you wanted was coffee."

"Maybe I changed my mind."

Her mouth pursed as if about to give Cruz a smartass comeback, but then she seemed to think better of it. Smart girl. She recognized trouble when she saw it.

"What would you like?" Her words sounded forced.

"A piece of apple pie." He seemed to purposely stare at her breasts. "And whatever else you might be offering." Sleaze oozed from the man's voice.

Roberto clamped his jaw shut to keep from telling Cruz not to be an asshole. Still frowning, Rosie left without saying a word. Yup, taking Cruz down would be doing the world a favor.

"Okay," Cruz said, still staring after Rosie's ass, "I admit it. I don't trust Brad's opinion. I like Brad. He's married to my sister. But he's about as smart as a dull rock." Cruz picked up his coffee, staring at Roberto over the cup's lip. "You, on the other hand, I haven't decided if I like."

"Because I'm better looking than you? And I know the

difference between a whore and a woman trying to make a living?" He looked at Rosie to make sure Cruz understood what he meant.

Cruz's cold stare grew colder. "You getting some of that?"

"No," Roberto said.

"Then why do you give a shit?"

"I got a soft spot for waitresses. My mama was one." That was the truth.

"A mama's boy?" Cruz smirked.

"Until she died," Roberto answered with pride.

Cruz frowned. "The guys tell me you mostly keep to yourself. Except for Brad."

"I like my own company." Roberto took another sip of coffee, hoping he hadn't blown it. "I didn't think playing nice with others was part of the rules around here."

"Guys also say you don't act like your average Mexican."

"Could be 'cause, like you, I'm not Mexican."

"*De dónde eres?* Where're you from?"

"Born here. My mom was Venezuelan. Like you," he pointed out, hoping to win brownie points. "My dad was a gringo who didn't hang around."

Cruz's shoulders squared off. "How'd you know I was Venezuelan?"

"The accent. Maracaibo, right?"

Cruz didn't seem to like talking about himself. "You spend time on the inside?"

"Nah." Roberto had considered lying about that in the beginning, but decided too many lies could get you in trouble.

"You got a record?"

"Nope."

"Who'd you work for before me?"

"Odd jobs. Mostly in construction."

"You got company names?"

Roberto pitched out a few. The same ones he'd checked into when he filled out the application two years ago. It had taken him that long to get this close to DeLuna. He hoped like hell this wasn't as far as he got.

"Funny, all those guys are either dead or out of business."

"Who did you work for before you got your own company? Bet most of them are the same."

Roberto could see Cruz's mind working, then realizing Roberto was right.

"I hear you earn your pay on the job. That you're good at this. Brad says he goes to you for advice on things." Cruz touched his phone as if waiting for a call.

"This isn't my first rodeo." Not that Roberto thought Cruz cared how anyone performed in his construction business.

Nevertheless, it was true. He'd spent his entire adulthood working construction and was a year away from graduating with a bachelor's in architecture, when his life went to shit.

Cruz stared. "So what convinced a law-abiding mama's boy to come work for me?"

To slit the throat of the guy who runs the illegal side of your operation. "Never said I abided by the law. I just haven't gotten caught breaking any."

"What did you *not* get caught at?"

"Nothing too bad. Sold some weed. Had a thing for nice cars for a while." Unfortunately, both of those were true, too. But they were also before his mom got cancer and he turned his life around to help her get through the last year.

Cruz didn't look convinced. "So you're that good."

"Maybe I'm just lucky," Roberto said.

"Better lucky than good." Cruz leaned back and they sipped their coffees in silence for a few minutes. "You interested in some overtime?"

"Depends," Roberto said.

Cruz's phone rang. He picked up the cell. "Yeah?" His expression soured. "Motherfucker! How does this keep happening? DeLuna's gonna see red. You find out who's behind this or it's gonna be your ass on the line."

Roberto turned his cup in his hands and pretended not to listen.

"Really? He called you?" Cruz said into the phone. "Who?" Pause. "Did she give him the number? Seriously, I'm telling you that kid was up to something in Austin. And his sister is a piece of shit." Cruz closed his eyes and continued to listen.

"Fine." Cruz hung up, lurched up from his chair, and frowned down at Roberto. "Come by the office this afternoon." He stormed out.

Roberto watched him leave, and his chest filled with a sense of success when he put two and two together. The San Antonio deal was supposed to have gone down early. And it must have gone down bad. Or good, as he saw it.

Sooner or later, DeLuna was not only going to see red, he was gonna slither out from whatever hole he'd been hiding in to fix things himself.

Parts of the conversation played in his mind. Who was the kid and sister Cruz referred to? Could it be Leah Reece and her brother?

Couldn't be, or at least it wasn't likely. He believed what he'd told Austin. Leah Reece and her brother had nothing to do with DeLuna.

"Let me guess," Rosie said. "He's not coming back, is he?"

Roberto looked up. "Nope, but leave the pie, I'll pay for it. I'll eat it."

She frowned. "You don't want this one. I had the cook spit on it."

Roberto grimaced. "Remind me to never piss you off."

She set his meat loaf plate in front of him. Her free hand came to rest on her hip. "You know, my mama used to say you could judge a person by the company he keeps. If my mama's right, then I'm wrong about you."

He picked up his fork. "That's just work."

"Construction?" she asked suspiciously.

"Yup." He forked some mashed potatoes.

"Hmm..." She studied him as if questioning her judgment. "Oh, I've been meaning to ask you about that stray cat you rescued from the Dumpster last month. Did it ever find a home?"

"Last I knew, the vet was still caring for it."

"Did they give him the snip-snip?"

Roberto frowned. "Probably." He tightened his thighs at the thought.

She continued to study him. "Do me a favor?"

"What's that?"

"See if you can't take that asshole who just left here in for a neutering." She turned and walked away.

Roberto smiled. Maybe it was Rosie's blond ponytail, the touch of determination in her tone, or maybe it was the question about the cat, but he thought of the blond vet assistant. He'd thought about her on and off a lot this last month, but even more since he'd told Austin about her yesterday. Which he regretted. Of the three Only in Texas detectives, Austin came off as a rounder, and Sara...Roberto hesitated, to remember for sure if that was her name. But yeah, that was it. Sara didn't deserve some rounder working her over.

Sure, he didn't know her well enough to say what she deserved. With the little time he'd spent with her, knowing her wasn't possible. But she was one of those people you met and, oddly, they felt familiar. Not as if you knew them, but in that déjà vu way. Or maybe it was just because the first time he'd seen her she was bottle-feeding a tiny two-week-old kitten and talking to it in that sweet voice; he'd found her so damn refreshing. A nurturer, a damn sexy nurturer.

Then, when Leah Reece didn't respond to his attempts to get info, he'd happily turned to her assistant. Turned to her a little too eagerly perhaps. The next day, he dropped back in with the pretense of checking in on the cat and asked her to lunch. She'd been a breath away from turning him down, but he put on the charm and she fell for it.

Wanna see the true love of my life?

He remembered the look on her face—hesitant but determined—when she asked him that over their one and only lunch. He'd nodded. She'd pulled out her wallet and passed him a picture of a brown-haired, brown-eyed little boy. Her tone, the way she studied Roberto across that café's table, told him it had been a test. Would he recoil at the idea of her having a kid?

Staring right into her blue eyes, he'd had to work hard not to let his true feelings show. Not that he would have recoiled. Just the opposite. That was when he saw more than a pretty face and a source of information.

Having been raised by a single mother, he'd known he was the reason his mom hardly dated. He couldn't help respecting a woman who put her child first.

Respect. The feeling made his lungs feel too big for his chest. He should have been able to handle respect. Then he realized, it wasn't so much respect making him uncomfortable that day. It was respect mixed with his other feelings.

It was the thoughts of how her lips had looked so damn soft that he'd wanted to touch them. Of how he'd wanted to ask her to let her hair down so he could see what it looked like falling around her shoulders. He wanted to know what those blond locks would feel like.

She wasn't the first woman he'd been attracted to lately. But she was the first he'd both respected and lusted for since...since DeLuna screwed up his life. And feeling it now, just felt...wrong. Disloyal.

Rosie placed a piece of apple pie in front of him. He looked up, almost too lost in his thoughts to react.

"You wanted a piece of pie? This one's spit-free."

"Thanks." His cell rang. He half expected it to be Austin again, but his phone readout stated unknown caller.

He almost let it go to voice mail. Then decided against it. "Hello?"

CHAPTER SEVEN

"IT HAPPENED AGAIN," a deep, familiar voice said.

"What happened?" Roberto asked, still trying to register the name of the caller.

"The cops were there. It got ugly. The buyer shot a cop."

Brad. He was probably using a different cell since he'd been sent on the job.

"Who the hell is doing this?" Brad groaned.

I am. "Shit, I don't know. Did you get caught up in it?" Roberto told himself he wouldn't feel guilty. Brad was a grown man who had started making bad decisions way before Roberto came along. The fact that Brad expressed numerous times that he didn't feel as if he had a choice was insignificant. "Brad? Did you get caught up in it?" he repeated.

"No...I wasn't arrested. I was watching from a convenience store. I was supposed to notify Cane, the guy doing the drop, if I saw something. And I called him as soon as I saw the bum hiding behind the Dumpster. He was a cop. Cane no sooner got off the phone with me when they moved in waving guns and badges."

"At least you weren't arrested," Roberto said. But it was only a matter of time.

"Yeah, but you know what this means? Johnny wasn't doing this and they killed him. Fucking killed that kid for nothing. I'm tired of this. And the boss wants me to do a job for him. I told 'im in the beginning I didn't want to do the dirty work. I'm a construction guy."

"Then don't do it," Roberto said, realizing he didn't dislike Brad as much as he should.

"You can't tell the boss no." Brad's voice rose.

"Then tell your brother-in-law you can't do it. Tell Cruz it's for his sister and his nieces."

"He won't give a rat's ass. He doesn't care about my girls. If the boss says do it, he'll say the same thing."

Roberto closed his eyes. "Don't do something you can't live with."

"If I don't do it he'll think I'm behind this. I'll end up like Johnny." The man almost sounded like he was crying.

Roberto massaged his temples with his thumb and middle finger. *He'd tried. Given it an honest shot. Now all bets were off.*

"What does he want you to do?" he asked.

"Fuck!" Brad moaned again. "I'm not cut out for this."

"What does he want you to do? Talk to me."

"It doesn't matter. I gotta do it," Brad said. "Look, you're not in nearly as deep as I am. Do yourself a favor, get on your bike, keep riding, and don't look back." Brad hung up.

"Shit!" Roberto muttered.

You're not in nearly as deep as I am. Brad's words echoed in Roberto's head.

Oh, I'm in deep, Roberto thought. He was in it until it was over. Until DeLuna was six feet under.

Or until Roberto was.

* * *

Austin's phone rang a little after two that afternoon. Pissed that his schedule for plan B had been hijacked, he answered it without checking who it was.

"Hello," he snapped.

"Aren't you in a good mood?" Tyler said. "What's wrong? Her cats hiss at you when you planted the bugs?"

"Real funny!" he muttered. But damn, he wished he could figure out what it was Tyler was afraid of so he could give the guy hell right back.

"Did you get them in?" Dallas's voice came on the line. They were on speakerphone. "We told you to call us after you did."

"So what does that tell you? I haven't done it yet."

"Yeah, like you're really good at reporting in," Dallas came back, letting Austin know he was still pissed at Austin's coming here. "Then just don't do it! The last thing I want to do is make a run up to Heartbroke, Texas, and bail your ass out of jail."

"I'm not getting caught. If the damn painters would leave, I'd have been done." Austin had already spoken with his partners once this morning. Not that he'd filled them in on everything. The whole fiasco of meeting Leah Reece, and then being shot down by her, was something he'd keep to himself.

Hell, he had a reputation to preserve. They thought he was forever getting lucky, and he kind of liked them thinking that. Not that he got turned down a lot, but lately he hadn't put himself out there as much.

"Take that as a sign and just get the hell out," Dallas said.

"No can do," Austin shot back. "How friggin' long does it take three men to paint a one-bedroom apartment?"

No way could Austin risk picking a lock with painters coming and going. "Did you just call to piss me off?"

"No. We actually have good news," Dallas said, his tone taking on a different tune.

"Good news that will confuse the hell out of you," Tyler said.

"What?" Austin stood from his sofa and looked out the peephole to see if the door to the neighboring apartment was still open.

It was.

"Tony dropped by," Dallas said.

Tony, being Dallas's brother who was a homicide detective for the Miller PD. "And you want me to guess what he wanted?" Austin snapped, letting his mood loose again.

"He didn't want anything," Dallas said.

"He brought us a puzzle," Tyler said.

"Would you just tell me?" Austin's hold on the phone tightened.

"There was an incident in San Antonio this morning. A drug bust."

"Tell me DeLuna was arrested and I'll dance naked in the streets," Austin said.

"Only because then you won't have to go face the big mean kitties and possibly have to squirt them with a water gun," Tyler said, laughing.

Damn, he wished he hadn't told his partners about that. He still thought the plan was brilliant. Cats didn't like water. He didn't like cats.

"Hell," Dallas said. "We'd all be dancing naked if that was the case. But it appears to be DeLuna's operation and his men who were arrested. A cop was shot, not by DeLuna's men, by the buyers. But that means San Antonio police are going to be looking into this hard."

"Okay, so why do I feel there's more to this story?" Austin remembered Tyler's remark about there being a puzzle.

"Someone put the San Antonio police onto the drug deal going down," Dallas said. "A paid informant."

"Roberto?" Austin asked. "Did he ask for payment from us? He didn't mention it, and I spoke with him yesterday."

"We haven't heard from Roberto, but that was why Tony came by. He thought we were behind it."

"Let him think what he wants. I don't give a shit." Austin didn't dislike Tony, actually he'd grown to like the guy, but with him still being a cop, sometimes he rubbed Austin the wrong way.

"But there's more," Dallas said. "One San Antonio detective got to looking into who these guys connected with in the past and found out that in the past month there've been five other busts in varying cities with these people. Two of the guys were on bail from another arrest. All of these arrests were handed to them on a platter by an informant."

"The same one?" Austin asked.

"We can't prove it. No one's going to give up their informants." Tyler put in his two cents.

"You think it's Roberto?" Austin asked. "That doesn't make sense. Why would he stop asking us for money?"

"Don't know," Tyler added. "But it's almost too coincidental that someone else is doing this. Getting to DeLuna, one drug deal at a time."

An alarm bell went off in Austin's head. "Tyler, remember when we first hired Roberto, you said it seemed Roberto wanted DeLuna for his own reasons?"

"Yeah, I thought about that," Tyler said. "But we decided it didn't matter."

"And I'm not sure it matters now, either," Dallas said. "If the guy's willing to do the job for free...let him."

"But it's a puzzle," Tyler said. "I don't like puzzles I can't figure out. Unsolved puzzles come back and bite you in the ass."

"Then figure it out." Austin picked up the water gun that was loaded and ready to go as soon as the damn painters left. "Or hell, call Roberto and ask him outright."

"I've thought about it," Dallas said. "But what if he says he was doing it and he's not."

"Weren't you the one who accused me of not trusting him?" Austin asked.

"I do trust him. Or I did until this came out. Hell, what doesn't make sense is, even if he wasn't doing it, if he's really positioned himself in with DeLuna as he says he is, he should at least be reporting things back to us. This isn't making sense."

"You're right," Austin said. "It doesn't make sense. Maybe somebody needs to arrange a little visit with him. We haven't done that in almost a year."

"Maybe," Dallas said.

"But if he's in really deep it could cause trouble," Tyler said.

"Not if we're careful," Austin insisted. But damn his partners were getting to be pansies on doing anything that carried the least bit of risk. Maybe he pushed his luck some, but he had to when working with these two.

"Let me think this through," Dallas responded.

"I want to do a little more investigation on Roberto," Tyler said. "Maybe I can dig something up."

Austin rolled his eyes, aimed his water gun, and squirted the bull's-eye he'd hung across from the breakfast table. "You know, sometimes there is such a thing as thinking something to death."

"And there are such things as idiots, too," Dallas groaned.

Voices and banging noises echoed outside his apartment door. "Hey...I think I hear the painting crew leaving. Let's argue this point later."

Getting into her apartment was a piece of cake. Easier than it should be. Leah Reece needed to replace her lock for one a little more difficult to pick.

Slipping the thin dental-appearing tool in his pocket, he reached for the doorknob and hesitated. He mentally went over the checklist of things he needed: the bugs, his water gun, his gloves—just in case the bugs were found and checked for fingerprints. *Ready to roll.*

Just to be safe, he knocked before walking inside. As expected, silence echoed from the apartment.

He reached for the knob and stopped. His gun—his real gun. Shit! He hadn't brought it. He wouldn't need it, his subconscious insisted. He couldn't actually shoot one of Leah's felines. And to bring it would lead to temptation to do just that.

Oh, hell! He was procrastinating.

The mere idea that not just one, but four felines waited inside terrified the shit out of him. Honestly, he'd thought the time he'd been forced to be in the same room with Lucky, Tyler's wife's cat, had cured him of his only phobia. Obviously not.

He glanced down. His friggin' hands were shaking. Not that he'd ever admit his cowardice to another soul. But who could blame him? Leah had admitted that two of her cats were semi-feral. Meaning semi-wild.

It had been a feral cat that had attacked him. He carried the scars from a whole shitload of stitches under his arm, and the crazed animal had nearly ripped off his ear. If that wasn't bad enough, he'd had to get about a hundred painful rabies shots in his stomach because the cat and her kittens had disappeared.

And what had he done to deserve the attack? Not a damn thing. He'd just wanted to look at them.

Taking one deep breath, he turned the knob and inched inside. He moved in quickly and closed the door. Then, automatically frozen in one spot, he visually searched for varmints.

A gray tabby shot across the room. "Damn!" Austin jerked back, but calmed when the feline disappeared into the bedroom.

The sharp taste of panic on his tongue hadn't faded when he spotted the big orange cat perched on the arm of the sofa. Its gold eyes looked evil as it rocked back and forth as if preparing to lurch at him.

"I wouldn't do that." Austin pulled the gun from the waist of his jeans. "I don't want to use this, but I will." Damn it was good he'd left his real weapon behind or he might have left a trail of dead cats behind.

Almost as if the damn thing could understand English, it settled back on its haunches.

"Good kitty," he said, mimicking Tyler when he talked to Lucky.

Austin was about to relax when something brushed against his leg. "Shit!" He sounded like a scared girl, when he saw the black creature against his shin. He nearly fell over his own feet to escape. It was the same one who'd hissed at him last night at the door, too.

Getting his balance, he aimed the gun at the black feline waiting to see if it planned to attack. It didn't. It just stood there, gold eyes watching him as if debating whether Austin's demise was worth its effort.

"I swear, I'll use this thing. Leave me alone and I'll leave you alone." It had been the peace treaty he and Lucky had made. They'd gotten excellent at ignoring each other.

Rolling his shoulders, he tried to relax. "Place the bugs and get out of here." He whispered his plan. Hearing his own voice in the silent apartment eased his nerves.

He slipped his gloves on. Watching the two felines, he stepped into the kitchen. He kept count of them and their whereabouts. *Two felines in the living room and one hidden in the bedroom.* Which meant one more was hiding somewhere. Probably watching him right now. Shit!

He searched for the fourth cat. When he didn't spot it, he focused on finding a place for the first bug.

"There." In the breakfast nook, he could conceal it in her bookshelf.

He peeled off the back of the sticky tape used for hanging and lodged the bug under the third shelf. Stepping back, he confirmed that the molding on the lip of the shelf hid the little matchbox-size device.

It did.

Remembering he wanted to see if she had a little black book filled with numbers, he stepped into the small kitchen. The bottle of wine he'd bought her sat on the counter.

Half-empty. "So you liked it, huh?"

Looking over his shoulder, confirming no cats were in attack mode, he noticed her surroundings. Her place was neat, not too neat, but cleaner than his own place. Only a coffee mug and the wineglass were in the sink. Remembering what he was looking for, he stuck his pistol into the waist of his jeans and pulled out a drawer.

A little black book sat on top of some papers.

Bingo.

With victory stirring in his chest, he opened it up to the

D's for DeLuna. He stared down at the neat handwriting written across the notebook. *Donaldson, Dixon.* No DeLuna. He checked the R's for Rafael. Not there, either. He went to B for brother. Nope. But one name, Brandon, was circled and a face with horns was doodled beside it.

"What did Brandon do to you?"

Frowning, he placed the book back in the drawer. Carefully, he moved back into the living room. The orange cat sat on the arm of the sofa, looking at him as if to say: *Wait until my master gets home, I'm gonna tell her you were here.*

He pulled out his water gun again, his major fear having subsided, but just to be safe. "I know you can't talk, buddy," he told the feline, and eased to the other side of the sofa and peeled the paper off the second bug. Crouching, one eye on the cat and one on his project, he attached it to the underside of one end table.

While there, his gaze caught on a photograph on the tabletop. A young Leah with a younger male standing at her side. Leah looked around eight, the boy around two or three. She had a protective hand on the young boy's shoulder— appearing to be the picture-perfect big sister. Having never had a real sibling, or at least none he knew of, he wondered if Leah's brother appreciated her. With her paying for his dang college, and penny-pinching on groceries, he hoped the young man valued her sacrifice.

Austin suddenly noted the absence of an older sibling from the picture. How much contact had Leah had with DeLuna? He was only Leah's half sibling, and because of the different names he assumed they shared the same mother. Which usually meant they lived together. Yet he knew what they said about assumptions.

He needed to call Tyler. He'd bet the information guru knew all about Leah Reece, too. Tyler knew everything. A genius, he read about four books a week. He took in more information than he did oxygen. However, asking Tyler for the info would earn Austin another reprimand on his poor investigation skills.

Tyler's reprimands were hard to swallow, too. Mostly because Austin knew he was a damn good investigator. They simply worked differently. He worked best deciphering the situation minute by minute and following his gut. Tyler was a damn Boy Scout. Prepared to the point of boredom, he followed logic. Except when it came to Zoe, his new wife. The genius had gone plumb stupid during their crazy courtship.

Normally, Austin avoided the Boy Scout's reprimands at all cost, but not this time. Austin needed to know everything about Leah Reece, and now. If it cost him enduring another lecture, he'd endure it.

But he was going to make sure it was worth it. Giving the apartment another visual sweep, he started gathering questions about Leah. Did she ever live with Rafael growing up? How did Rafael end up so bad and Leah so... different? Why was she antisocial? Questions started popping in his mind from every direction. Why didn't she insist her younger brother get a school loan? Why didn't she like gifts? Who was the Brandon dude, and what had he done to deserve a devil doodle by his name? Was Brandon the reason she'd refused to share the wine with him?

He realized most of his inquiries were personal and not investigation related—and Tyler would be the first to point that out. Frowning, Austin picked up the picture and stared at the younger Leah. Discontent filled her eyes. From an unhappy childhood? Or did she not like being photographed?

"Bet my sob story is worse than yours," he muttered. Then

he remembered the number of domestic violence cases he'd worked on the force. Violence in a home usually spilled over to the kids. There were parents who treated their own flesh and blood worse than the foster parents had treated him.

As bad as he'd had it, he'd never gone hungry or been beaten. Not physically. Knowing nobody really ever gave a shit—no one cared if he made good grades, if he got the spot on the football team, or did his homework—might not have been the best way to grow up. But some kids living with their parents got rawer deals than him.

Thoughts of the past led back to the recent past and his unwanted visitor. Candy Adams's words floated through his head. *I thought we could just get to know each other.*

Did she really think she could just waltz back into his life?

Get to know each other, my ass! She probably realized she was getting old and wanted him to take care of her. Hell, she could wait on him on the front porch steps somewhere and see if he showed up.

Passing a palm over his face, he pushed his mother and the uncomfortable feelings from his mind and focused on Leah Reece.

Still holding the photograph, he stared harder at the sad girl in the image. "What's your story?" Personal or not, investigation related or not, he wanted to know it.

Setting the frame down, he started to stand up, but a flash of fur caught his eye. That damn orange cat now sat on the other arm of the sofa, less than eight inches from his face. Those claws could take out an eye in seconds.

Tamping down the temptation to blast the animal with water, he slowly rose. "Look, I know another cat your color. He's a little uglier than you, not that it's his fault, having been caught in a burning building. But the point is that we made a deal? You stay out of my way, and I'll stay out of yours. Got it?"

The animal meowed almost as if he understood.

Forcing himself to relax, Austin shifted his gaze around the room. Feminine touches were splashed here and there. Throw pillows in matching colors, fancy drink coasters, and that dried flower crap in crystal bowls that made the room smell like...like cinnamon and apples.

With one more bug left to hide, he started toward the bedroom. In the hall, she had a set of louvered doors, only half closed. His apartment didn't have these.

He opened the doors and stared at the stacked washer and dryer and open space that held a litter box. Returning the doors to their half-open position, he paused in the doorway and stared at the bed.

His steps faltered on the threshold. He remembered the one cat that had earlier scampered into the room. And he still hadn't seen the fourth cat. Was it in there hiding? How wild was it?

He peered inside. Not a feral kitty in site, but the bed ruffle stirred as if recently moved.

"Shit," he muttered, but determined not to let his fear best him, he inched inside. His next intake of shallow air filled his scenes. It smelled different in here. His mind stopped thinking about cats and started thinking about Leah. The scent was...vanilla. A soft, warm, musky perfume that reminded him of waffle cones. He remembered catching a hint of that smell when he'd picked her up in the parking lot.

Austin's gaze moved to a white, fluffy-looking blanket resting on top of the unmade bed. On the corner of the bed rested a silky-looking rose-colored nightshirt.

He moved farther in and stared at the piece of soft-looking fabric. His hand, without permission, reached out and touched it—slid his glove-covered fingers over what looked like a low-cut neckline. An image of her wearing it filled his head.

Realizing his behavior bordered on perverted, he pulled his hand back. Moving to the head of the bed, he got on his knees and stuck the bug at the bottom of the bed frame. Then he heard it. A loud half moan, half cry. Still on his knees, he glanced back.

The gray cat stood between him and the door. It arched its back in an unnatural way, its neck extended, its tongue hanging out as weird noises spewed from its mouth. Austin bolted to his feet. Was this an attack warning, or was the animal convulsing and about to die?

Before Austin could decide which it was, the animal bolted forward. Austin lurched back and hit the side of the bed.

As if the sound was an alarm, the other two cats came running through the door. Holy hell. Three of them—all looking at him as if they were hungry and he was a salmon.

Grabbing his water gun, prepared to shoot, he watched as the gray cat suddenly went from howling to hacking. A projectile spew of fluid came from the animal's mouth, and then the most disgusting three-inch tubular thing shot out behind the water and landed right beside Austin's shoe.

"Gross." He'd heard of hair balls, but never believed they were that big, or that... disgusting. Why would anyone own one of these creatures?

Staring at the hairy glob of goo, his stomach turned. And wouldn't you know, that was when the fourth cat, another gray one, came shooting from under the bed, hitting Austin's ankles. Austin shot forward. The black cat, positioned a few feet in front of him, hissed.

"Friggin' hell!" He leaped onto the bed. The back of his head hit the ceiling fan blade, and he took several steps back on the mattress.

His heart pounding in his chest, he pointed the gun—daring one of them to try anything. Then with his other hand he rubbed the back of his head. The cats didn't move. All four sat glaring at him. This was absolutely his worst nightmare.

He shifted his eyes from one to the other. And that's when he noted the hair ball was no longer on the floor. He looked down. The disgusting ball of hair clung to the side of his shoe. But even worse were the footprints he'd made on the pristine white comforter. Footprints Leah was bound to notice.

"Shit! Shit! Shit!"

In spite of the cats, he jumped down. They scattered. Two out the door, one under the bed, and the orange one landed on top of the dresser. He pointed his gun at Big Orange. "Don't mess with me."

He looked back at his friggin' footprints on the comforter and then at his watch. He didn't have time to take it to be cleaned.

Her clinic closed at five. Which meant, in less than two hours, if she didn't stay late, she could be strolling home.

His heart thumped with indecision. If she thought someone had been here, she'd call the police. If she called the police, they might find the bugs.

He was screwed.

"Damn it!" He took a deep breath. He could do this. He had an hour and a half. Tucking the water gun back in his waistband, he paced out into the hall. Maybe she had some spot cleaner and he could manage to get the footprints off the damn thing and make it look like the cats threw up on it instead. Or maybe…His mind stopped working. The creak and clink of Leah's door opening echoed in the silent apartment.

Oh, damn! Had she left work early?

Okay, he wasn't just screwed. He was screwed, glued, and tattooed.

CHAPTER EIGHT

BREATH HELD, HE eased into the washer and dryer closet and closed the louvered doors enough that he couldn't be seen. This wasn't by any means the answer to his dilemma, but a temporary reprieve. Because the way his luck was running, the first thing she'd do was start a load of laundry. Or decide to change the litter box. And from the smell of things, it needed it.

He heard footsteps in the living room. Damn, this was bad.

He leaned forward to peek through the slats in the door. The only thing he saw was Big Orange slinking toward the louvered doors.

The door creaked and a paw poked inside the opening of the door. Austin's breath caught again. He watched in horror as the animal used his paws to open the door a few inches and slink inside.

Big yellow eyes looked up at him, then the animal brushed between Austin's legs and went inside the litter box. He cringed when the sounds of litter being tossed around filled the small space. Would she hear it? Come check on her shitting cat?

The sounds stopped, but what came next was worse. Much worse.

Damn, he was going to have to apologize to Bud, Dallas's dog, for saying his farts were unbeatable. This was much worse. His gag reflexes start to quiver.

Putting his hand over his mouth and nose, he wondered how long he could hold his breath. A sudden hiss echoed from the living room, and two cats came hauling ass into the hall and darted into the bedroom. So focused on not breathing the aroma of cat shit, it took a second to realize that wasn't right. Leah's cats wouldn't run from her. Tilting his head, he concentrated on the sound of the footsteps. Heavy footsteps. That wasn't Leah. Who the hell was there?

Through the slats, he spotted a man in the living room. A supersized man with a gun. He reached for Marilyn—and pulled out the water pistol. Okay, he wasn't just screwed, glued, and tattooed.

He was fucked.

Sara Clare gave the injured kitten a couple of swipes behind his ear. "You'll be all better in a few days," she cooed.

Leah, her boss and friend, popped her head into the room. "Hey, Evelyn's here and there are no appointments for another hour. I'm gonna run to the grocery store. Do you need anything?"

"A guy who's mentally sound, no criminal past, preferably with a job, and doesn't mind two-year-old boys," Sara teased. "Oh, and make him a complete hottie."

Leah hugged the door frame and grinned. "Did you call him?"

Sara rolled her eyes. "Not yet."

"Why not?"

"'Cause it's awkward." Sara closed the kitten's cage but

reached between the wires to offer the feline one last touch. She was a firm believer in the power of touch. Something she'd been missing lately, if you didn't count it coming from her son.

"Hey." Leah drew Sara's attention. Her boss nipped at her bottom lip as if thinking. "Why don't you call and tell him we have an owner for Spooky. Tell him it's our policy to make sure he didn't change his mind and want the cat before we adopted him out."

Sara arched a brow. "That's not a bad idea. I mean, I wouldn't be calling to ask him out or anything."

"Do it!" Leah disappeared, her footsteps echoing on the tile floor. Then the footsteps came tapping back. She plopped a file down on the examining table. Spooky's file with a certain tall, dark, and handsome's telephone number in it.

"No excuses. When I get back from the store, I want to hear how it went." Leah started out, then turned back. "You sure you don't want anything? I'm gonna be in the wine department."

"Wine?" Sara asked. "I thought you overindulged last night."

"Just three glasses. I'm a cheap drunk. Besides, this bottle isn't for me. It's for my neighbor." She pushed away from the door frame.

"Wait just a minute, Miss Reece." Sara crossed her arms. "Which neighbor? The drool-worthy guy you're after?"

Leah frowned. "I'm not after him. I'm replacing the wine. It was his bottle I drank most of last night."

"What?" Sara gaped. "You two shared a bottle of wine? What else are you *not* telling me?"

"We didn't share it." Leah backed up, clearly inching away from telling the truth.

"Why do I think there's a story here?" Sara asked.

"No story," Leah said, but Sara smelled a lie. Leah continued, "I'm just wanting to soften him up so he'll take Spooky." She turned, took one step out, and then swung around. "Oh, I told Evelyn—but in case you pick up the phone—if Luis calls tell him to call my cell. ASAP!"

"Is everything okay?" Every time the phone rang today, Leah had popped out to the front desk asking if it was Luis.

"Fine," Leah said again, and took off. And that smelled like another lie. She and Leah had become good friends since Sara started working here a year and a half ago. And while they shared a lot of things with each other—Leah's disastrous marriage to Brandon, and her disastrous relationship with Brian's dad—Sara always got the feeling that Leah had secrets.

"Be sure you make that call," Leah called back.

Sara rolled her eyes but picked up the file. The idea of calling under the ruse of securing a home for Spooky wasn't a bad idea. Or was it? She pulled her cell from her scrub uniform pocket.

Damn it to hell and back! Austin needed a weapon, something other than a friggin' water gun. He also needed clean air. He'd take Bud's farts over this smell, hands down.

The nearing footsteps brought Austin's gaze up. Through the slats, he watched the gun-toting man walk past the opening in the hall as he made his way into the living room. Rummaging noises filled the apartment. Was he just the average burglar? Austin's mind flashed with the image he'd gotten of the man. Big. Really big. A little older—wearing khaki pants and a dress shirt. He didn't look like your average burglar.

So who the hell was he? Could he be connected to DeLuna?

The cat poked its head out of the box and looked up. Then it went back and started shoveling litter around. The noise seemed loud. The footsteps started moving his way.

Desperate, he grabbed a toilet plunger from a shelf. Beggars couldn't be choosy.

Austin's heart thumped against his chest bone as those steps neared. The cat hopped out of the box and slipped through the crack of the door.

"Damn cat!" the intruder moaned. "You almost got your ass shot."

The man inched closer to the louvered doors, reaching for the knob. Austin bolted out, remembering his football-playing days. His shoulder rammed the man right in his gut. Austin's water gun hit the floor. A gush of air left the man's throat at the same time the bozo hit the wall. The intruder's gun fell from his hand and skittered across the floor. As the man slid down the wall, out of breath, Austin tossed down the toilet plunger and went after his assailant's weapon.

Face it, gun trumped toilet plunger.

When Austin turned around, the bozo was no longer trying to catch his breath. He was going for the toilet plunger.

"I wouldn't do that." Austin pointed the man's gun at him.

He didn't blink. He snatched up the plunger and swung. Hard. The bottom of the plunger might have been rubber, but it was hard rubber. And it didn't feel good hitting the side of Austin's face.

"Shit!" He ducked the second plunger pass and put his hand on the trigger. "I swear I'll kill you with your own gun."

"Go ahead!" the man growled. The plunger smacked Austin square in the face.

Austin stumbled back. Pain throbbed against his lips and he tasted blood. Pissed, he lowered the gun toward the man's legs so the shot wouldn't be fatal and pulled the trigger.

Nothing happened. The damn thing wasn't loaded. Turned out plunger trumped gun after all.

The second Austin took to even consider shooting and not killing the bastard cost him another blow to the face, not even the plunger this time, but a fist. He ducked the direct blow, but the fist got him in the corner of his eye.

Falling against the louvered doors, he heard several of the paneled slats cracking. The man bolted out the hall. Austin dove after him and tackled him to the ground. They rolled on the floor, hitting end tables and bringing a lamp down on top of them.

Austin threw a couple of good punches, one to the man's gut and one to his face. It might have taken a lesser man down, but not this hulk. Nevertheless, the asshole had to be hurting, because even through the gloves, Austin felt the man's teeth cut into his knuckles. The man's shoulders collapsed back on the floor. Austin thought his assailant had passed out.

He went to get to his feet, but the big bastard must have been playing possum. Austin barely saw the lamp coming at his head. And it didn't miss. A thud sounded and caused a ringing in his ears. Momentarily stunned, he fell back against the end table. The blow hadn't been that hard, but his vision swirled. He rose to his feet again but kept one hand on the wall to avoid falling. When his world stopped spinning, he saw the man hauling ass out the apartment door.

Austin shot after him. The man was gone. Austin made a complete circle. Had the bozo entered one of the other apartments? A light click filled the hall. He spotted the door to the stairs slipping closed.

He went after him. The man's labored breathing echoed below, followed by the sound of a slamming door. When Austin made it down and outside the apartment, he saw a black Ford truck racing down the street. He recognized the monster of a guy driving the truck but caught only the first two letters of the license plate.

Wiping the blood that ran down his cheek from his temple, he grunted a much-felt string of four-letter words.

"Are you okay?" A hot blonde wearing a skimpy sports bra and tight stretchy pants ran up to him.

On a normal day he might've considered letting her play doctor, but there was nothing normal about this day.

"I'm fine." He turned back to the building. Adrenaline coursed through his body, so instead of waiting for the elevator, he shot up the stairs.

Rushing back into Leah's apartment, he slammed the door. He looked around, praying her cats hadn't escaped. Although, after seeing the hair ball incident and smelling the cat shit, it'd be doing her a favor to lose one or two.

He let out a frustrated moan. What the hell happened? He spotted the gun on the floor. The unloaded gun. What kind of criminal carried an unloaded gun? What kind of idiot left without his gun?

Maybe the same kind of PI who brought a damn water gun with him instead of a real one.

He stared at the weapon. What were the chances of its being registered? Low. But the man hadn't been wearing gloves. He might be lucky and get a print.

Wiping another stream of blood, he noticed the mess in Leah's apartment. His phone tucked inside his pocket vibrated. He ignored it and walked into the hall. The louvered doors hung off the hinges.

The lamp lay broken on the floor. He glanced inside the

bedroom, frowning at the bed with his footprints—which were the least of his problems now.

His phone vibrated again. Knowing it was probably Dallas, he yanked it out of his pocket.

"You get the bugs planted?" Dallas asked.

"They're planted." *But probably not for long.* "Gotta go." He hung up. Dallas would be pissed, but Austin didn't have time to explain. He had to come up with a plan. And fast.

CHAPTER NINE

LEAH SET THE wine in her floorboard for fear the bottle would break before she got it to its rightful owner. Why did he have to buy such an expensive bottle? She knew it tasted expensive. Or at least better than stuff she'd had lately, but forty-two dollars? Maybe she'd get an extra neutering in this week to pay for it.

She'd slipped behind the wheel when her cell rang.

It was her office. Had Luis called? "Hey," she answered.

"Hey," Evelyn said. "You got a strange call."

"Luis?"

"No," Evelyn said.

Rafael? Leah dropped her head on the steering wheel and fought back a moan. "What kind of strange call?" If Rafael didn't stop calling, she was going to have to tell Evelyn and Sara everything. She'd probably have to explain that she'd lied about her dad being killed shortly after Luis was born.

Not that it was completely a lie. The man was dead, only it didn't happen until she was eighteen. Not that she'd cried or anything. When she'd seen his picture in the obituaries, she'd been emotionally baffled—unsure what she should feel. Especially after she read the two little paragraphs naming all the loved ones he'd left behind.

It's official. Leah had come running into her aunt's house that night. *Luis and I don't even exist.*

"It was your neighbor," Evelyn said, drawing Leah away from the past.

"Who?" Surely he wouldn't be calling her. Had she even told him where she worked?

"An Austin Brookshire."

She must have told him. "What did he want?"

"He said…" Evelyn paused. "He said someone broke into your apartment."

"Crap," she eked out.

"That's what he said."

"Damn you, Rafael," she muttered under her breath.

"What?"

"Nothing." She remembered finding Snowball those years ago, and instant panic filled her chest. "Are my cats okay?"

"He didn't mention the cats."

"Did he leave a number?" Leah's heart raced.

"Yup."

Leah dug in her purse for a pen. She pulled one out along with a small pad. Holding phone to ear with her shoulder, she said, "Give it to me."

Leah jotted down the number. "Thanks. Bye."

She dialed, praying and hoping with everything she had that her cats were okay. Unfortunately, she knew what Rafael was capable of.

Austin had removed the bugs. He didn't see any other option. He'd also hidden the assailant's gun in his apartment, and as soon as he was done with Leah, he'd call Dallas about having it checked.

Now, while waiting for Leah to call him back, or to show up—he didn't know which she'd do—he pressed two fingers to his swollen eye and went into her bathroom mirror to check out the damage. He looked like shit.

He'd gotten in a couple of good licks on the attacker and could only hope the bozo looked worse than he did.

His cell rang. He didn't recognize the number. Leah?

"Hello?"

"Austin?" She said his name. She had one of those lyrical voices.

"Leah?"

"Yeah. What happened?"

He'd worked on his story. "I saw your door open, I knocked and called your name, and this guy, I'm guessing he was there to rob your place, came at me. I tried to stop him, but he got away."

"My cats?" Her voice sounded strained. "Are they okay?"

He looked at the bedroom door, which he'd shut when he noticed all four of them were in there. "They're fine."

"What did the guy look like?" she asked.

"I didn't get a good look at him." He spouted out a lie. "It happened so fast."

"Was he Hispanic?" she asked.

No, but were you expecting him to be? Did she think her half brother had done this? While the guy hadn't been DeLuna, he could still be behind it. But why?

"He could have been. I'm not sure."

"How big was he?" she asked. "Smaller than you? Thin?"

Austin weighed her words. Smaller, thinner, and His-panic. A perfect description of DeLuna.

"Bigger than me," he said, thinking about having to explain how he got a black eye. "I didn't call the police, I thought you..."

"No," she said quickly.

He'd been prepared to try to talk her out of calling the

police. *Nothing was taken. No harm done. The cops probably wouldn't even come out.* His black eye was going to be the only thing hard to make light of.

"Did he take anything?" she asked.

"I don't think so."

"Then there's no reason to call the cops."

"I guess not." He was getting what he wanted, but it was too easy.

"Did he break in my door?" she asked.

"No. He must have picked the lock." *Or I forgot to lock it after I picked it.* "You should get a new lock. The locks on these apartment doors are a joke."

"Yeah." She paused. "Is the place ransacked?"

He walked out of the bathroom, stepped over the broken lamp, and headed into the kitchen, where the bozo had emptied out the drawers. If the guy hadn't been robbing the place, what had he been looking for? "A little."

"Okay, I'm going to see if they can do without me the rest of the afternoon at the clinic and I'll head that way."

"You sure you don't want to call the police?" If she was, he could replace the bugs.

"Positive."

"Okay." His suspicions grew. "I'll see you when you get here."

"Yeah," she said. "Thanks."

"No thanks needed." He continued to look at the contents spilled out of the kitchen drawer. The line had gone silent when he realized something was missing. Squatting down, he rummaged through the items. Her little black book wasn't there. And it had been in the drawer.

Why would someone want that?

The same reason he'd looked at it. To find someone, but who? Was someone else looking for DeLuna?

*   *   *

Roberto was finishing up for the day when his cell rang. Hoping it was Brad, he snatched his phone from his jeans. He'd tried to call him back but hadn't gotten an answer. The fact that he cared about the big bruiser wasn't good. Caring about anyone associated with DeLuna could be detrimental to his cause. Caring about anyone could be detrimental. When you cared about someone and they were yanked out of your life, it just hurt too damn much.

"Hello?" he answered.

No one said a word. "Hello?" he repeated.

The click of the call being disconnected sounded ominous. Was Brad in trouble? Roberto cut his phone off and then checked the number.

It wasn't the same number as before. Had Brad ditched one cell and gotten another? He hit redial and listened to the phone ring. And ring. It went to voice mail.

"I'm sorry, the person at this number is not available. At the beep leave a message."

He hung up.

"Hey, Rivera," someone called out.

It was Patrick, another of Cruz's main guys.

"Yeah?"

"Cruz called to make sure you dropped by the office when you leave."

"Got it," Roberto said. But he didn't get it. And he liked it even less. Something bad was about to happen. He felt it in his bones.

"I just got off the phone with Nance," Austin said. "He's agreed to drive up here and bring the gun back. I was hoping you could get Tony or Rick to run a check for us."

"What gun?" Dallas's voice bellowed from the phone.

"The guy had a gun." As soon as Austin had spoken to Leah, he replaced the bugs and called Nance, the nineteen-year-old college kid who worked at Dallas's wife's art gallery and who did odd jobs for them. Then he'd called Dallas and Tyler to fill them in.

"You didn't say anything about a gun," Dallas snapped. "Were shots fired?"

"It was unloaded." Austin glanced at his watch. Leah could be walking through the door any minute.

"What kind of criminal carries an unloaded gun?" Dallas asked.

"A stupid one." Austin answered. *And a big one.* He touched the knot on his head.

"Wait a minute." Tyler spoke up, letting Austin know they were on speaker again. "Do you think this guy's connected to DeLuna?"

"I don't know," Austin said. "That's what I'm hoping to find out. I'm hoping we've got some prints. But my gut says he's involved."

"Why?" Tyler asked.

"Because I'm pretty sure he took one thing." And Leah's not wanting to call the police was suspicious as hell. For some reason he hadn't told them about that.

"What?"

"Her little black address book."

"That doesn't make sense," Tyler said.

"I know," Austin said.

Tyler spoke up. "I started snooping around Roberto's past. I might have stumbled onto something."

"What?" Austin asked.

"I don't want to say until I make sure I'm right."

"Just spill it," Austin said.

"Not until I know for sure," Tyler said.

"He won't tell me, either," Dallas said.

Austin heard the ding of the elevator opening. "Gotta go. But Tyler, I want to pick your brain about Leah Reece tonight."

"What?" Tyler asked. "You didn't do your research before you left."

"Don't make me kiss your ass. Because then I'll want to kick your ass." Austin clenched his fist and realized his eye wasn't the only thing swollen. Footsteps echoed outside the front door. "Later."

CHAPTER TEN

LEAH STOPPED AT Austin's door and considered knocking, then decided to check on her cats first. Besides, she needed a few minutes to confirm she was doing the right thing by not calling the cops. Oh, she knew the right thing, as in the good-citizen thing, would be to report it. But she'd tried that when Snowball had been killed. And what had the cops done?

Not a damn thing.

They'd patted her on her shoulder and told her they needed proof. She'd asked them how seeing the scumbag leave the box wasn't proof, but they'd informed her that investigating a dead cat wasn't what the city's taxpayers intended them to do with their money. As if their sitting at the donut shop down the street, stuffing their faces with jelly-filled donuts, was better. She knew they were jelly-filled because the big guy wore the drippings on his shirt.

In their defense, if she'd told them why the cat had been killed—in retaliation for her storming into her half brother's drug house, slamming a bag of weed on the table, and putting him in his place in front of his boys—they might have gotten involved. Involved by way of arresting Luis, or her, for that matter.

Decision made. *Not* calling the police was the right thing to do—at least for now. While she hated admitting it, her reasons were only partly due to wanting to confirm Luis wasn't somehow involved. God help him, and her, if he'd let Rafael pull him into some illegal shenanigans. But her main reason for not calling the cops was Rafael's threat. Even years later, it stayed with her. *Talk to the police again, Sister, and the body you'll be finding on your front step will be your little brother.* She still didn't know how he'd found out she called the police when she'd found Snowball. Did he have cops working for him, or was he watching her place? Either way, it was a risk she didn't want to take.

But what did this all mean? Was Luis associating with DeLuna and Cruz again? She loved her little brother with all her heart, but if he was up to that again, she was going to kick his ass all the way to tomorrow. She hadn't sacrificed all she had for him to go do something enormously stupid. But wasn't Luis smarter than that now?

Oh, hell, she didn't know. And she wouldn't because Luis wasn't calling her back.

Moaning, she checked her phone again to see if he'd returned one of the fifteen calls. Nope.

Okay, that did it. Even if he wasn't doing something with Rafael, she was kicking Luis's ass for not returning her calls.

She went to unlock her door but discovered it wasn't even all the way shut. Her emotions went from fury to fear in a nanosecond. Butterflies flapped around her stomach. She reached into her purse for her small can of mace. If Rafael or one of his men had come back...

She hesitated and looked back at the neighbor's door, but determined not to let some thug make her afraid to walk into her own apartment, she pushed open her door.

Silence filled the apartment. Telling herself she was

overdramatizing this, she stepped inside. Looking around, she walked straight to the broken lamp on the floor. She squatted down to pick it up when footsteps came from her kitchen. She sprang up. Her mace and her heart fell at the same time.

A scream rose in her throat, but she managed to stop it when she recognized her neighbor.

"Sorry, I was picking up a few things for you," Austin said.

She put her hand on her chest. "I didn't know you were still here."

"Sorry. I thought I told you I was here." He shrugged. "And considering what happened, I assumed you'd want someone here when you came home."

She had wanted that. Or would have if she'd thought it was an option. She wasn't used to someone worrying about her.

Right then her thoughts took a total U-turn when she noticed his face. "Oh, my God. Did he do that?"

"He?" he asked, his one good eye tightening a bit. "Do you know who did this?"

"I mean 'he' as in the person who broke in."

Austin nodded. "Yeah, he did this, but I got in a few punches, too," he said as if the question dinged his male ego.

"I'm sorry. I asked about my cats and I never considered that you'd been hurt. I...Maybe we should call the police. Or get you to the hospital." The thought of calling the police gripped her gut, but could she allow someone else to be hurt? She moved in and looked at his bruised face.

"Not for this." He pointed to his eye. "Please, when I play basketball, I walk away looking worse than this."

"I don't know." She noticed his hand was swollen. She caught it. "Does it hurt to move?"

"No." He wiggled his fingers.

Still holding his hand, she frowned at the puffiness and purple color already circling his entire eye. "That looks painful." Their gazes met and held. "Seriously, I'm so sorry."

He frowned. "You know you have a habit of apologizing too much."

She recalled her aunt telling her the same thing. *Everything isn't your fault, Leah. Sometimes the wind just blows shit your way and it ain't nobody's fault. So stop taking the weight of the world on your shoulders, girl.*

This was different. This wasn't her blaming herself for her mom's death or their father's abandoning them. "You got this trying to protect me... well, my... apartment."

"True, but I'm fine." He slowly pulled his hand away. Then he raked the injured fingers through his blond hair.

She tossed her purse on the small breakfast table. "Sit down and let me get some ice." She pulled out a chair. "Sit down." When he didn't move, she snapped, "Sit."

"You're being pushy again," he muttered, reminding her of their conversation last night.

"Only because you took on my role of being difficult," she answered.

"So you admit you're difficult?" His left eye crinkled with a smile.

This was no time to restart the flirting. Pointing to the chair, she didn't move until he dropped into it. Hurrying into the kitchen, she stepped over the mess on the floor. "Tell me what happened?" She glanced over her shoulder.

"I told you." He lifted his gaze from the clutter she'd just stepped over. "I saw the door open and thought it was strange. So I stuck my head in and called your name. A guy came running out of the hall. We fought."

Pulling out a bag of frozen peas and a bag of corn from

the freezer, she suddenly noticed the absence of her furry
pets. Her heart clutched. "My cats? Where are they?"

"In the bedroom," he said. "I closed the door to keep
them contained."

She exhaled the growing sense of panic and hurried back
to stand in front of him.

Only the sight of his painful-looking eye allowed her
to ignore her need to see that her cats were all unharmed.
Then she spotted a dark red stream of blood oozing down
his temple.

"You're bleeding." She dropped the frozen veggies in his
lap and grabbed her phone out of her purse. "I gotta call the
police."

In no hurry to see Cruz, Roberto had gone to his apartment and taken a shower. Now about a block from the office,
he pulled over at a park entrance and tried to think. The
sound of innocent laughter bounced around the trees. His
gaze involuntarily went to a mother chasing her little boy
around the playground.

Closing his eyes, he tried to calm the swell of doom
growing inside him. He wanted to chat with Brad before he
saw Cruz. If the shit was about to hit the fan, he needed to
know exactly what kind of shit was coming.

But Brad wasn't answering. Not his regular phone or the
number he'd called him on after lunch. What happened? Had
Brad got himself caught up in something and was behind
bars? Or worse, dead?

Had Cruz had his own brother-in-law killed? Roberto
wouldn't be surprised.

Pulling up his recent calls, he studied the number of the
hang-up he'd gotten earlier.

He still didn't recognize it.

It could've been a wrong number. A butt call. Somebody trying to sell him funeral plots. Hell, if so, he ought to get back with them; he might be needing one.

He hit redial. It rang.

"Hello?" a feminine voice hesitantly answered.

Who the hell was this? Had to be a wrong number.

"Hello?" she repeated.

"Yes..." He thought he recognized the voice. "Uh, someone from this number called me earlier."

"Yeah, that was me. It's about Spooky."

Spooky? "About who?"

"Oh, I'm sorry, you don't know his name."

"Know whose name?" Was this some kind of prank call?

"The cat you brought in."

"Sara?" He said her name. He hadn't given her his number. Then he remembered the first time he'd gone in, he'd filled out paperwork hoping Leah Reece might call him.

"Yeah, but I'm calling about the cat. Not...anything else."

"Okay," he said, not sure what else to say.

A long pause hung in the air and he felt the need to fill it.

"What's up with the cat?" he asked, feeling guilty for not giving her...closure. For not calling her back after their lunch date and just tossing out some stupid excuse why he wasn't interested in seeing her again. Right then he knew the reason he hadn't, because he had been interested.

That felt so wrong.

"We think we've found a home for him, and before we place animals that were brought in by someone, we check to make sure they haven't...changed their minds."

"Yeah," he said.

"Yeah, you want the cat?"

"No, I meant, yeah I get why you called. But I can't take the cat. I work construction and I'm sometimes out of town."

"Okay," she said. "That's all I wanted. Thanks for—"

"Sara?" He interrupted her hasty good-bye.

"Yes?"

"That's why..."

"Why what?" she asked.

"Why I didn't call you," he said. "I had a job come up and I had to go."

"Right," she said, and he realized his lie sounded as false as hers in the beginning. "Well, have a good...life." The last word came out snippy.

"How's Brian?" he blurted out before he could stop himself.

His question drew silence.

"Sara?"

"You...remembered my son's name." Had that made her nervous?

"Yeah." Actually it surprised him that he remembered, but hearing her voice brought a lot of their conversation back. Brought back the way her eyes had lit up with love when she'd talked about her son. "You talked about him a lot at lunch that day."

"That's because he's important to me," she snapped.

"Whoa, I didn't mean that in a bad way. I was just... making conversation."

"That's the reason you didn't call me again, isn't it?" she asked. "Well, let me tell you—"

"No. I thought it was great that you cared so much for your son."

"But he's extra baggage that you don't want to deal with, right?"

"I already said that wasn't it." Her accusation stung.

"Oh, right. You suddenly had to go out of town and couldn't find the time to call." She sighed. "Hey...forget I even said anything. It doesn't matter. Sorry I bothered you. We'll place Spooky in a good home. Bye!"

She hung up, "Damn it!" Without thinking, he hit redial.

"What?" she answered.

"It *does* matter," he spit out. "It had nothing to do with you. It's—"

"Oh, it's me, not you, right? Is that the best you can do? Really? You called me back to give me *that* line?"

"I called you back because I didn't want you to think you'd done anything wrong."

"You don't have to tell me that. I know I didn't do anything wrong."

"The fact that you love your kid had nothing to do with why I didn't call you back."

"Then what did? Or is it some classified secret?" she asked.

CHAPTER ELEVEN

AUSTIN FELT THE blood trickle down his brow. "Don't call the cops on my behalf." He caught Leah's hand before she grabbed the phone. The two bags of frozen veggies landed in his lap. Since she'd already touched him, touching her shouldn't have felt like a big deal. It felt big. Like one of the first touches between two people who'd really like to get to know each other better—better in an intimate way. Holding her hand made him want to hold more. To get closer... remove clothes.

Realizing where his brain had gone, he pushed that thought back. Thinking about her like that would get him in trouble and sabotage his plan. Sure, he'd planned on charming her, but as he'd told Tyler and Dallas, he didn't plan on sleeping with her. Yet he hadn't expected to be attracted to her. Suddenly, aware he was still touching her, he pulled his hand away.

"But you're hurt," she said. "We have to call the police. When we go to the hospital they'll make you report it."

"Hospital? No. Look, if you want to call the police because some creep broke in, then call them. Just don't do it because of me." He held his breath for her answer. If she called the police now and they found the bugs, he was screwed.

Well, not totally screwed. The cops would think the guy who broke in had planted the bugs, but it would mean all efforts today were in vain. Not to mention he'd gotten the crap beaten out of him for nothing.

"Didn't you hear me? You have blood running down your forehead." She snatched a tissue from the bar between her kitchen and dining room and patted his brow.

"This is nothing." He said it with conviction because he'd checked. "It's a scratch. Head wounds just bleed a lot."

"Let me see it." She slipped between his legs to stand. Close. So close that her soft breasts were inches from his face. So close his hand itched to reach out and fit his palm around the sweet-looking curve of her waist. But damn, what he wouldn't give to lean into her just an inch more. To bury his face in all that soft-looking cleavage that smelled like soft woman and waffle cones.

"He could have killed you." She gently parted his hair with her fingers.

"He didn't. As a matter of fact this happened when we were scuffling around on the floor, and the lamp fell off the end table and hit me." It was a lie, but now that Austin thought about it, that bozo could have swung twice as hard as he did. It was as if he hadn't wanted to hurt him.

"Lean forward." She put a hand on each side of his face and tilted his head. His forehead practically rested on the swell of breasts. She wore a fitted white T-shirt with a scooped neckline. Not too scooped. Not as scooped as he would have liked, but for sure low enough to make it interesting. And with the current position of his head, it was really interesting.

He took in the sweet-looking mounds of flesh covered

by a beige lacy bra—lace that was basically transparent. He could make out her nipples—a soft rose color.

Feeling perverted, he closed his eyes. Then opened them. Okay, so he was perverted.

Or maybe he was just a man.

Her fingers moved over his scalp. Her touch came so damn soft that the tension he'd been holding melted away.

"It's not bad." Her voice came out feminine. "But you should see a doctor. You could have a concussion."

"I don't have a concussion." Still mesmerized by the view, he wondered where else her sweet touch would work magic.

"How do you know?" Her fingers stirred in his hair as if to get a better look.

He lifted his face. "Because I didn't pass out. And my eyes are dilating properly. See." He closed his eyes and then opened them.

"You could still have a concussion," she argued.

Her small hands caressed the sides of his head. "Feel this." He moved her right hand a little to the right to one of his permanent dents. "This was a concussion. Now this over here." He moved her to the left. "That was just a few stiches."

She frowned, her fingers now gently threading through his hair, feeling for imperfections. Her touch was both relaxing and sensual. His shoulders gave up another bit of tension. Some of which he felt as if he'd been carrying for weeks.

"What's this?" She touched another lump.

"That I was born with." He grinned, glad she wasn't looking at the scar behind his ear. "Thank God baldness doesn't run in my family." Or did it? Hell, he didn't know what ran in his family.

She made a cute face. He wanted to pull her into his lap

and taste that smile, to dip his tongue in those dimples. To put his lips around her dusty-rose nipples. His heart raced. "Besides, you're a vet," he said. "You can take care of me."

"That's right. I'm a vet. And you're not an animal."

You wanna bet? She wouldn't say that if she knew what all he'd like to do to her right now. Tear her shirt off her, toss that lace bra across the room, rip those uniform pants off, get his fingers in her panties, and taste . . .

"I'll be fine." He tried to stop his thoughts from going south. Who was he kidding? Things had already gone south. Even with two packs of frozen vegetables in his lap, his jeans felt tight. He didn't need a hard-on for her muddling things up. They were muddled enough.

"I'm not so sure." Their eyes met and held. Damn it if she didn't look like a woman who wanted, no, needed, to be kissed.

And she wasn't alone in the wanting and needing department.

"It's a simple question. Why didn't you call me back?" Sara repeated.

Roberto's grip on the phone tightened, as he mentally searched for an answer he could give her. One that made sense. One that didn't have any element of truth to it.

"It's complicated." He pinched the bridge of his nose.

"What kind of complicated?" she asked. When he didn't answer she continued, "Married complicated?"

"No," he said. *Not anymore.*

"Criminal past complicated? Have you been arrested, robbed a bank, killed anyone?"

"No." *But the killing part could change.*

"Drug complicated? And by that I mean either illegal or prescription, like Prozac, Xanax, or antipsychotic drugs."

"No," he bit out, realizing how stupid this was. He should just hang up, but he didn't want to.

"Gay complicated?" she asked cautiously.

"Please," he mumbled.

"Then why don't you just tell me. Is it… 'just not into you' complicated? Seriously, that would have been better than what I got. Which was nothing. I thought we had something. A spark, a connection. Guess I was wrong."

"You weren't wrong. It's just…" The pause hung on. What could he tell her?

She let out a big puff of air. "Like I said, it's not important."

It felt important. It felt wrong. Both wrong not to explain, and wrong to have played her like he did. Yet he didn't get why. It wasn't as if he'd slept with her. He hadn't even touched her. All he'd done was buy her lunch to get a few answers. Okay, he'd gone in under false pretenses, as if he was interested in her. But then again those hadn't been false.

"Look, I'm in the middle of something, okay?"

"Well, that explains everything," she said, sarcasm so thick in her voice he was amazed it didn't clog the line.

His gaze shot back to the park. The mother waited at the bottom of a slide, encouraging the boy to slide down. "Do it," the woman called out. "Just do it."

It was as if she was talking to him. Roberto swallowed. "I lost my wife and boy."

Sara took in a sharp breath. "Shit!" she muttered. "Now, I feel like a total bitch. I—"

"You didn't know." His line beeped. "Look, I'm getting another call." He raked a palm over his face. "Can I call you back later?"

She hesitated. "Yeah. But you don't have to. I get it. I mean, I understand if you don't."

He understood if he didn't, too. That made sense. What didn't make sense was how much he wanted to talk with her again. He hung up and took the other call.

"Are you coming?" the male voice snapped.

Roberto recognized Cruz's voice.

"Yeah," he said. "Be there in five." He hung up. Looking back at the woman and child playing in the park, he gave himself a second to enjoy the view. There was something about it: innocence, beauty, love. Like a piece of living art. He'd had that. And Rafael DeLuna had taken it from him.

He glanced at the mother again. She was young, dark hair, dark eyes, and attractive. Like his Anna had been. He searched himself to see if he'd feel that longing, that almost instant connected feeling he'd felt with Sara. It wasn't there.

What was it about Sara? Physically, she was the complete opposite of his wife. How in the world had a woman he barely knew crawled under his skin?

Oh, he understood the attraction. She was beautiful. Yet he'd been in the presence of a lot of beautiful women since he lost Anna. This . . . it was something else.

But it wasn't important. Because after he did what he needed to do, he'd either be in jail or dead.

He pulled up Brad's number and hit dial one more time to see if he would answer. He didn't. Roberto slipped his cell into his pocket, got on his bike, and went to do what he had to do. Because the closer he got to Cruz, the closer he would get to DeLuna.

"I'm not going to the hospital," Austin said.

Kiss her.

Don't kiss her.

His willpower kept switching on and off so fast, he was surprised he didn't blow a mental breaker switch.

Kissing her would be so easy. Slip his hand around her waist and pull her an inch closer. Her lips looked sweet, moist, ready. He was ready. His gut said she wouldn't refuse him. Said she'd lean into him, let him taste her lips, and who knows where it would lead.

As if she'd read his mind, and knew her own willpower, she dropped her hands from his head and took a step back. "What do you do?" When he didn't answer, she continued, "You have a scar here, too." She pointed to his brow but didn't touch him; that's when he knew he was right. She'd felt it, the lure, the temptation. "What do you do that gets you beat up so much?"

He had to clear his head to answer. The truth was he'd gotten a few on the job working for the force, the few others while doing time in prison. He couldn't tell her either of those.

"I'm a day trader." He told her the lie he'd already planned out. Which was only a partial lie. "And a financial advisor." Dallas, Tyler, and now their wives came to him to help make their investments. It was something he was good at besides being a cop. Hell, he'd earned more money day trading than working as a PI.

"What brought you to Heartbroke?"

He had this one worked out, too. Another lie, but if it took that to get what he needed, it was justified. "I have a client here. He's making some big investments and wanted me close for a few months."

"So you're just here temporarily?" she asked.

Until I learn the info I need. "If I like it, who knows." He didn't want that to keep her from chumming up with him.

She frowned. "That doesn't explain getting hit in the head four or five times."

So she'd figured that out. He had to think quick. "While starting the business, I worked as a bouncer for a club.

Things got crazy." That was true, too. He'd worked a security gig for a club.

"Good thing you got out of it. A couple more licks and you could have hid your own Easter eggs."

He laughed. "Good one. Tyler would...like that one." *Shit!* Why was he talking about Tyler?

"Tyler?" she asked.

"A friend. He's always quoting things."

"I don't know if it's original, but my aunt said it. She was brilliant and a hoot at the same time."

Her tone told him her aunt was important to her. He wanted to ask, but wasn't sure how. Then the opportunity seemed to fade.

She bit down on her bottom lip and looked at his mouth. Was she still thinking about being kissed? He sure as hell was.

"Okay, so no police. No hospital." She picked up the two bags of frozen vegetables.

That was still too easy. She didn't want to call the cops. Why?

"But you stay here for a couple of hours so I can keep an eye on you. If you slipped into a coma or died, I'd feel guilty. At least a little bit." She smiled.

If he'd known it was this easy to get her to spend some time with him, he'd have had someone hit him over the head the first day.

She pressed one of the frozen bags of vegetables to the side of his face. "Hold this to your eye and this on your swollen hand." She set the second bag on the top of his hand that rested on his leg.

"Be careful," he said. "You're almost being nice."

Through one eye, he watched her do that cute eye-roll thing again. She grinned. Her dimples winked. She stepped back and kicked a pen that was on the floor, reminding him of what he should be concentrating on rather than her dimples.

"You know, I told you the guy didn't take anything, but he did have something. A small black book—an address or phone book."

Color washed out of her face. She looked at the stuff on the kitchen floor, knelt, and rummaged through the items.

Looking for her black book, no doubt.

"Was it yours?" he asked.

"I don't know." That sounded like a lie.

"Why would someone take it?" he asked.

"I don't know." She looked up, and he recognized the emotion filling her big doe-like brown eyes. Fear.

Of what?

He dropped the cold pack of peas from his face. "Is something wrong?" He hoped it would be this easy, that she'd just explain things. Maybe even throw in the whereabouts of her low-life brother. He could thank her and leave before things got complicated. Hell, if it was DeLuna causing her fear, he'd solve her problems right along with his.

"I need...to check on the cats and...and get some supplies to clean that cut."

She snagged her phone from the table.

And make a phone call to someone, he thought.

She backed up and looked at him. "Hold the peas to your eye."

He did, then with one eye he watched her walk away— the soft sway of her hips hypnotic. Who the hell was she calling?

He heard her open and close her bedroom door.

She was definitely hiding something. But what?

He inhaled a deep breath and mentally thanked Tyler for

reminding him to put a receiver program on his laptop and have it set to record.

Which meant, just as soon as he got back to his place, he'd know what had put the panic and fear on Leah Reece's pretty face.

Leah passed out quick scratches behind every cat's ear, then let out Bob, her orange tabby, who looked like he needed the litter box. Then, emotionally reeling, she called Luis.

It went to voice mail. Tears filled her eyes. "Luis? Where are you? Are you still in San Antonio? Call me. Now!"

Brushing her first tear from her cheek, she caught her breath and tried to catch her emotions. Crying wasn't going to solve a damn thing. She'd learned that early on. At eight years old, she'd cried nonstop for a week when her mom had been killed in the car crash. Aunt Nita had tried to soothe her by telling her that sometimes God just needed to take people up to heaven to be with Him. That hadn't helped.

Leah had cried harder and told her aunt that God was selfish and unfair. If He needed someone, why hadn't He taken some kid's mom who had a dad? It had been a few months since her father had even dropped by. Not that Leah had missed him. But her mother had. Leah had known because she'd heard her mother crying at night.

Pushing the past to the far corner of her heart where it wouldn't hurt so much, Leah inhaled a shaky breath. Then she dropped on the bed and hugged Socks, who gave her chin a concerned bump with his forehead.

"I'm okay, as long as you guys are okay," she said to her cats.

As long as Luis is okay. His address and telephone

number were in that black book. Was that why the intruder had taken it? It had to be Rafael or one of his friends, didn't it?

What she didn't understand was why Rafael was intent on finding Luis. The idea that Luis might have gotten pulled into something with their half brother hit a few more nerves. "Please," she murmured. *You can't end up like him.*

Her gaze fell on her white blanket and she saw...footprints. Crap. Why the hell would the intruder be on her bed? She recalled Austin's description of the man. It hadn't sounded like Rafael. It hadn't sounded like Cruz, either, but she could see him getting some kind of perverted pleasure from getting in her bed.

Feeling violated, she hugged her arms around herself.

Her phone, still clutched in her hand, rang, and she answered it before the first ring finished. "Luis?" She breathed out her brother's name.

"Sorry, it's me, Sara."

"Is everything okay at the office?" Leah asked.

"Here, yes. Evelyn told me your place was broken into. Is everything okay? Did they steal much?"

"No," she said. "My neighbor...Everything's fine. Has Luis called?"

"I don't think so, but let me ask Evelyn," she offered.

"No." Sara came back. "Evelyn says no one's called since your neighbor. Is everything okay, Leah? Is something going on with your brother? Is that connected to your place being broken into?"

"It's...complicated," Leah said.

"Wow, that's the second time someone's used that line with me in the last hour. I hope you're not gonna make me feel like a bitch, too."

"Why would I...I'm not following you."

"I did what you suggested and called that guy. The guy who brought in Spooky."

"And?" Leah asked, pushing her own issues aside.

"His wife and kid died," Sara said.

"What? When? He was married?" Leah asked.

"No, not when he was here. But when I called him, he apologized for not calling me back after our lunch, and I got bitchy about it and asked for a reason. He told me he was still dealing with their deaths."

"Do you think he's telling the truth?" Leah asked.

"It didn't sound like a lie." She paused. "I don't really know him, but I feel like I do. You know that weird feeling . . . as if it's synchronicity or something. I felt that with him."

"You mean horny?" Leah asked in a teasing voice.

Sara chuckled. "That, too."

Leah suddenly remembered her bleeding guest in the other room. "So that's it. You're not going to see him anymore?"

"I don't think so. I think me having a kid reminds him too much of his own kid and wife. Then again, he said he'd call me back. But I don't think he will."

"I'm sorry," Leah said. "But he's not the only guy out there."

"I know," Sara said. "There's a ton of fishes in the sea. Just none of them seem to be for me."

"And you're a poet—"

"And didn't know it," Sara finished.

Leah smiled, letting go of her woes. She glanced at the door. "I should go. Austin's still here."

"Austin?" she asked.

"The neighbor," Leah said.

"How is Mr. Drool-worthy?" Sara asked.

"He's bleeding. He caught the guy here and they fought."

"Wow, that's kind of hot. He's a hero."

Leah didn't believe in heroes. "It's not hot," she said. "I'm not the horny one, remember?" But it was hot. For a minute there, she could swear he'd been going to kiss her, and for a minute there, she would have let him.

"Liar," Sara said.

"Okay, I'm horny, but not as much as you." She chuckled. "I'd better go."

They hung up, and Leah was about to walk out of the room when she saw something else, something half sticking out of the bed skirt. What was that?

CHAPTER TWELVE

ROBERTO SPOTTED TWO of Cruz's goons in the office reception room.

"You Roberto?" the crooked-nose man asked.

"Yup."

He motioned for Roberto to go on back.

The office door stood ajar; Cruz spoke on the phone.

"It's him, I'm telling you. That Johnny kid, he went to the same high school as him. I don't know," Cruz said. "But give me five minutes with him, and I'll find out. I'll take care of her, too." The man almost smiled; started twirling a pencil in his hands. "Why not? Do you want her taught a lesson, or not?" Pause. "Fine. I'll wait. But you know we'll end up doing this anyway."

Roberto hung back, feigning disinterest. Something had happened, but what? He hoped it didn't involve Brad.

Cruz looked up and motioned him inside. Roberto moved in and sat in the chair opposite the desk.

"Yeah," Cruz said. "I will." He hung up and let out a frustrated breath.

"Problems?" Roberto asked.

"Nothing I can't handle," he said. "What the hell took you so long?"

"Needed a shower," he lied.

"I sent word for you to come straight here."

"I didn't know it was urgent." He leaned back in the chair.

"Is this how you operate? If so, pack your shit and leave. I need people who know how to follow orders."

"Like I said, I didn't know it was urgent."

Cruz met his gaze. "Whenever I tell you to do something, assume it's urgent."

Go fuck yourself. "Easy enough." Roberto's gut gripped. If there was one thing he wasn't good at, it was kissing ass. "So what's the overtime job involve?"

Cruz hesitated as if debating. He leaned back in his desk chair. It squealed in protest. "We need you to make a delivery."

"What kind?" he asked.

"Does it matter?"

"It does." He leaned forward. "I've heard the last few deliveries have gone bad."

"Who told you that?"

"The guys talk."

Cruz frowned. "We've had an issue lately. That's why I want you to do this. Didn't you tell me at lunch that you're lucky?"

"Yeah."

"Do you want the overtime or not?"

"If overtime pays well, I do."

"You'll be compensated." Cruz nodded. "You'll be going with Luke. You know him?"

"Big guy with the crooked nose out front," he said.

"Yeah." He paused. "The drop's Thursday. You got your own piece?"

"I do," Roberto said.

"Bring it with you and show up here at midnight on Wednesday."

"I thought it was Thursday."

"It's not around here."

"Where is it?"

"You'll find out Wednesday. Or is there a reason you need to know now?" The man might as well have asked if he was planning on contacting the police.

"No reason, just curious."

Cruz leaned forward. "Curiosity can kill the cat."

"I'm not a cat." Roberto knew he'd screwed up the moment the words left his lips.

"Yeah, but you can die just as easily. I know. I've killed more than my share. Both cats and men. If you work for me, you do what I say and don't fucking ask questions. Got that?"

Roberto nodded.

"And if you're late, that'll piss me off. And you never want to do that."

"Got it." Roberto got the feeling they were done. Or at least he hoped so; he'd kissed all the ass he could for one day. He stood to leave.

"Hey," Cruz said.

Roberto turned around.

"Have you spoken with Brad?"

Roberto nodded. "Yesterday after work."

"Nothing today?"

"No," Roberto lied, remembering Brad's panicked call this morning. "Is something wrong?"

"I hope not. If you hear from him, tell him if he knows what's good for him, he'll call me."

Roberto walked out more worried than ever about what

Brad had gotten himself into. And worried what he'd just gotten himself into.

Austin moved closer to the bedroom, hoping to hear the conversation going on inside. But when Big Orange came strolling out, he shot back to his chair and plopped in it. When the cat kept coming he muttered.

"Stay back." Holy shit, how was he going to get through the next few hours without completely making an ass out of himself? Especially if the other three cats came in. Hell, she'd know he'd lied about owning a cat. His heart pounded. This was bad. He envisioned Tyler laughing his ass off at the situation. Not that he would tell Tyler.

The cat moved closer. The thing was huge, too. Bigger than Lucky. Austin had to get out of here, but how?

His gaze shot to the hall, praying another varmint didn't come stalking in. None were. He refocused on Big Orange. He'd stopped inching forward but stared at him like prey. Austin stared back.

Then, remembering that ignoring Lucky had encouraged the cat to do the same, he looked away but kept the animal in his peripheral vision.

Obviously, Big Orange hadn't gotten the "ignoring memo," because he darted across the room and leaped up on the table, which put him less than six claw-range inches away.

Austin jumped out of the seat. Aware that Leah could walk out at any minute, he went and sat on the sofa. Realistically, he knew being afraid of something a tenth of his body weight was ridiculous. However, as Tyler had so enjoyably pointed out, phobias weren't logical.

Tyler had also suggested a few books that might help Austin deal with his phobia. Tyler knew a book for every problem known to mankind—and had read them. But

Austin knew how to deal with this. Stay the hell away from cats. And since he and Lucky, who only came to the office once in a while, had come to the ignoring understanding, he hadn't worried about it.

The cat jumped off the table and strolled toward him. Austin waved his arms. The cat hopped up on the chair Austin had vacated.

Leah walked back into the living room. "Look what I . . ." She stared at the cat in the chair where Austin had been seated a minute earlier.

Austin cleared his throat.

She swerved and studied him. "You okay?"

"Yeah, I just remembered I have some e-mails to send. That's all."

"You look tense. You don't have a headache, do you?"

He relaxed his posture. "No. Just the e-mails."

She didn't look convinced. After a second, she said, "Look what I found."

His gut knotted. Had she found the bugs?

She held up a water gun. His water gun.

He'd forgotten all about that.

"I found it almost under the bed." She sounded puzzled. "It had to belong to the guy who broke in here. But why would someone have a water gun?"

Because cats don't like water. "Wouldn't have a clue," Austin lied. And when Big Orange leaped up on the arm of the sofa and actually brushed against his arm, he popped up. "I'm going to run and take care of those e-mails."

"Not until I clean your wound. Sit down."

His gaze met hers. She looked damned determined to play doctor, and if the cat wasn't there, and Austin wasn't here under false pretenses, wild horses wouldn't have been able to drag him away.

He considered coming clean, telling her the truth. But damn it, he couldn't. He couldn't until he knew for certain what her relationship was with DeLuna. For all he knew, she could be protecting her brother. She could know exactly where he was.

Austin's gaze shifted to Big Orange again, but thinking of DeLuna upped his courage.

"Fine." He plopped down on the sofa. She dropped the water gun on the end table. Big Orange bounced off the arm of the sofa, landing on the cushion. It took everything Austin had not to grab the dang gun and shoot the beast.

"Let me get the alcohol and gauze from the bathroom." She walked into the hall.

The cat inched toward him. Austin bolted up.

He hadn't completely gotten his footing when Leah popped back out of the hall doorway. "He messed up my laundry doors, too."

I couldn't help that. Sorry. "I saw that." Austin, standing by the sofa, tried not to look awkward or worse yet, terrified.

She studied him. "You sure you're okay?"

He had to get out of there. Now.

Roberto straddled his bike and was about to pull out of the office parking lot when his cell rang. Brad? He looked at the number. Familiar, but who? His mind went to Sara, but it wasn't her number.

It was Brad's home phone. The man had only called him a couple of times from that number.

He picked it up. "Where have you been?"

"Roberto?" A female voice came across the line.

"Yes?" Had he been wrong about the number?

"This is Sandy, Brad's wife."

Okay, not wrong about the number. But why was Sandy

calling him? His mind raced. He'd met the woman once when she'd picked Brad up from work. But Roberto had seen her picture every time he went into Brad's office. Brad kept the photo of her and his two girls front and center on his desk, unlike some men who had a picture pushed back on a bookshelf. Brad's picture was placed for optimum viewing.

"I'm worried," the woman continued. "Brad hasn't come home. He's not answering his phone. And Kelly, our daughter, had her dance recital. Brad wouldn't have missed it. He loves the girls and..." Her voice shook. "I know he's friends with you. He spoke highly of you. I thought maybe you might know where he is. If he's okay?"

Roberto closed his eyes. "I...I haven't spoken with him, Sandy." It was a lie, but how could he tell her that her brother and DeLuna had sent Brad off to do something he didn't want to do? He didn't even know if Brad was alive.

"Have you asked your brother?"

"Cruz says he hasn't heard from him. I think he's hiding something. I'm worried. I thought about calling the police, but my brother would be furious. He's up to no good. Now I'm worried it's somehow caught up with my husband. I regret the day I suggested he go to work for him."

A sick feeling hit Roberto's gut. "I'll run up to Jimmy's Ice House where the guys hang out after work. See if I can find out anything."

"Thank you. Brad said you were...different from the others."

Yeah, but what your husband didn't know was that I was just using him to get to DeLuna. Guilt knotted Roberto's shoulders. Not guilt for going after DeLuna—that asshole deserved it—but guilt for...for how easily he used others for his own means these days.

He pinched the top of his nose. "If I find out anything I'll call you."

Before he slipped the phone back into his pocket, he tried again to call Brad. It rang. No answer.

Hanging up, he started his bike and drove to Jimmy's Ice House.

"The cut doesn't need to be cleaned," Austin said, ready to bolt.

"Yes, it does. Don't you dare leave!" Concern tightened Leah's expression, and she went for supplies. Left him alone with the feline.

Austin glared at the cat. Sitting on the opposite end of the sofa, it raised its paw at him, as if toying with him.

"Stop it," Austin whispered. He could swear that cat knew he was terrified and was determined to out him to Leah.

When she came back a minute later, he and the cat had traded places again. "Are you two playing musical chairs?"

Austin smiled. "I think he's toying with me," he said, hoping that came out sounding humorous and not like a person scared shitless.

"Yeah, sometimes he likes to hide and jump out at you. He gets a kick out of scaring you."

"Thanks for the warning." He eyed the feline.

"Oh, it's cute."

"I bet." How could that be cute?

She sat on the coffee table and positioned her supplies beside her. "Lean toward me."

The soft request had his nerves subsiding. He came forward but kept his head turned so he could keep an eye on the cat.

Her hands moved in his hair like before, and if he wasn't so tense about Big Orange, he would have enjoyed it again.

"This might sting," she said.

She was right. It stung like the devil, but it was the cat leaping into his lap that had him cursing.

"Shit," he muttered, fighting the urge to bolt. He'd personally witnessed what cat claws could do to a human ear; he didn't want to imagine what they could do to . . .

"Sorry," she said, thinking it was the alcohol, and she leaned in and blew on his scalp. The stinging stopped, but he didn't dare breathe. Not with the animal in his lap and its sharp claws right above some important, tender male parts. The cat rearranged itself in Austin's lap, faced Leah, and raised its paw, claws extended, to Leah.

"I'll love you later," she cooed.

Love? She was a friggin' vet. Didn't she know the damage a cat could do?

When the cat repeated the motion, she waved the feline off his lap. The animal strolled into the hall. But he shot Austin one parting "go-to-hell" look.

When Austin saw the long yellow tail disappear, his heart, which had crawled up his throat, slipped back into his chest. He glanced up and was immediately caught up in her warm brown eyes—eyes that still held the hint of her earlier fear. God, he hoped his own fear wasn't as apparent. Then again, he'd spent years hiding his emotions. His motto: never let them know they are hurting you.

"I can't believe you got this because of me." She frowned. "It's going to be all sorts of bruised tomorrow. I'm sorry." Sincerity rang in her voice.

"You're apologizing again," he muttered.

"Sorry." She clamped her mouth shut; a smile appeared in the corners of her eyes. "Bad habit."

He supposed she could have worse ones. He smiled back.
And this close all he could think about was waffle cones and
kissing her. Sitting back, before he could claim her mouth,
he picked up the picture of her and her brother.

"Your brother?"

"Yeah." She reached in her pocket and pulled out her
phone, as if checking for missed calls. "He was supposed to
call me."

Was that who she'd called? Was her younger brother connected to the missing phone book?

"How hard would it be to make one little call?" She
stared at her phone.

"Is there a problem?"

"No. I mean...he's out of town." She glanced away as
if to hide something. "I just worry. Being the bigger sister."

Did she also worry about her big brother? "You two
close?"

A nostalgic smile appeared on those sweet lips. "Yeah.
He's in college and busy with girls and such. We see each other
twice a month. He's a good kid." Emotion sounded in her voice.
Again he wondered if her younger brother knew how lucky he
was. Austin hadn't had anyone to care about him.

He glanced back at the picture; the sadness in her young
eyes seemed even more apparent. "How old were you here?"

"Eight."

"Is he your only sibling?" He worked to keep his voice
casual and met her gaze, hoping beyond hope that she'd
be honest. Hell, he could find out what he needed to know
tonight and get out of here before...before things got any
more problematic.

She hesitated. "Yeah." The one word sounded heavy. As
if it cost her to lie.

He focused on the image to hide his disappointment.

Why hadn't she told him the truth? He started to judge her, then stopped. Did she lie for the same reason he lied when asked about his past? Because it was nobody's damn business but his own?

He should be able to respect that. He did respect that. But he needed to know about DeLuna. And that meant he couldn't let up.

"You don't look happy," he said. Her brow pinched as if she didn't understand. "In this picture."

She stared at the image and he stared at her. She didn't answer, as if deciding what to tell and what to keep to herself.

"I wasn't," she answered in a whisper, as if she spoke the words to herself.

The silence in the apartment grew loud.

"Why?" He leaned in closer.

She blinked, and the way she inhaled led him to believe she was trying to push thoughts away. Something he'd been doing a lot himself this last week since his unwanted visitor.

"Who knows, maybe I was forced to eat my broccoli that day. I hated broccoli, and my aunt thought it was a magical food." She went inside her head for another second, but he doubted her memories had anything to do with broccoli.

She looked at him. "Would you like something to drink?"

"I think it's more," he said, unsure why he couldn't let it go. It wasn't even just about DeLuna anymore. It was about her. She was a...puzzle. For the first time, he understood Tyler's obsessive need to solve something.

He wanted to understand her. Oh, hell, he wanted to save her—not even knowing why she needed saving. He also wanted to get her naked, but he seldom got everything he wanted.

She pretended she didn't hear him. "I still have half a bottle of the wine left. And I have your replacement in the car."

He ignored her question the way she'd ignored his comment. "Your parents get a divorce?" He waited to see her expression. He'd know if she lied again.

She started to the kitchen, stopped halfway, and faced him again.

"No," she answered. It didn't come with any of the heaviness of an untruth. "Would you like that glass of wine?"

He looked back at the photograph, then up at her. "It's more than broccoli." Damn, he should let it go, but he couldn't.

"And you're an expert at reading kids' faces in old photographs, huh?"

He squared his shoulders. "Not an expert. But…I didn't like broccoli, either. This…" He sat the picture back on the end table. "This look isn't about eating your vegetables."

"Maybe you just didn't hate broccoli as much as I did?"

"Oh, I pretty much hated it." He knew they weren't talking about vegetables anymore.

"What happened?" she asked.

Her question had discomfort swelling in his chest. Damn it, why had he pushed? Maybe because he hadn't figured she'd push back.

She stood there, as if now she had her own puzzle to solve. Then she repeated it. "What happened to you?"

"Nothing." He feigned innocence, banking on his years of never showing his cards.

She arched one brow. "When you're really good at recognizing something, most of the time it's because you've experienced it, or something close to it. Your parents get a divorce?"

Yup, he should have friggin' kept his damn mouth shut. "Wine sounds good."

She laughed, and he joined her. It was like an emotional release. As well as an unspoken compromise that neither had to spill their guts. The laughter wound down and they were left simply looking at each other, knowing they both had secrets.

The difference was, his secret wasn't just about his past, but about the reason he was here. He wasn't going to stop trying to uncover her secrets. Not if they involved the man who framed him for murder and sent him to prison for a year and a half.

"I'll get the glasses." She moved into the kitchen.

Big Orange came strolling back into the room. Only he wasn't alone this time—he'd brought reinforcements. Two other cats bracketed him, all three moving with purpose, slow and determined, as if on the hunt. And they seemed to have a certain prey in mind.

He was it.

The black one, the one who'd hissed, hung to the orange cat's right, and the gray one, who'd hacked up that disgusting hair ball, lurked at Big Orange's left.

"Looks like my pack's hungry," Leah said, looking at the cats as she came back.

See, he knew he was right.

"That's Skitter, Bob, and Socks." She introduced them proudly. "Henry, the really shy one, doesn't come out much around strangers."

"Quite a pack." He nodded, unsure what she expected him to do or say. "Why don't you bring the glasses to my place?" Austin shot up. "I have to send those e-mails."

She opened her mouth to argue. He didn't give her a chance. "See ya in a couple minutes."

"I'm not . . ."

"I thought you wanted to watch me for a while—to make sure I didn't have a concussion?"

She frowned. He walked toward the door, past his own version of hell—a line of three felines, all watching his every step. Heart thumping, he didn't breathe until he shut her door.

CHAPTER THIRTEEN

AUSTIN RUSHED TO his laptop and tapped a few keys to make sure he'd caught Leah's earlier phone conversation in her bedroom.

As he waited for the VLC—VideoLan—program to boot up, he glanced around the room to make sure nothing might give him away. At home, had he been waiting for some female company, he'd be looking for misplaced dirty socks and attempting to do a fast change of the sheets. He hadn't been here long enough to leave out dirty clothes, and the bed wasn't part of this equation. Tonight wasn't about getting and giving mutual sexual satisfaction. But damn if the idea didn't appeal to him. The vision of her nipples playing peek-a-boo behind her lace bra filled his head.

Damn it! Tonight was about getting information. Nevertheless, the anticipation low in his belly didn't share his plan.

His eyes hit on the plastic baggie holding the gun on the coffee table. "Shit." That would for sure have her asking questions. He looked at his watch. Nance, the makeshift delivery guy who would be transporting the gun back to his partners, should be here any minute. He found a plastic grocery bag and hid the gun inside. Knotting the top of the bag, he set it on the bar between the kitchen and living room. Easy reach if Nance showed up while she was there.

And if that happened, he'd improvise to explain who he was and what he was passing off. Suddenly remembering how well improvising had gone for him yesterday, he formed a plan... Nance, an associate of the guy he was working for, had left his wallet in Austin's truck. Feasible. Believable.

He walked back to his computer and checked the screen. He'd set each bug at a different frequency, given them names, and had set his backup disk with a voice-activated program to save all the segments with sound. He already had several files in the program—most of which were from her living room. Then he saw a file saved as "bedroom, 17:24."

Not wanting to turn the volume up in case she walked in, he looked around for the Best Buy bag, which held a set of headphones. Spotting the bag in the kitchen, he got up and saw the phone book opened to a local Italian place. He'd been planning on ordering pizza for him and Nance.

Not anymore. Hopefully, he would be having dinner with Leah. And if he ordered it now, she couldn't say no.

Snatching the phone, he dialed the number as he shot into the kitchen to collect the headphones. He ordered a large pizza, and remembering her frozen mushroom pizza, he made it just mushroom. It wouldn't be as good as his home-made pizza with pepperoni and all the fixings, but he'd take what he could get.

While he called out his credit card number, he used a knife to open the earphone package. He'd just gotten them out when his doorbell rang.

Crap. He wasn't going to get to hear her conversation before she arrived. Resigned, he set the headphones down, changed his computer screen, and went to answer the knock.

Leah or Nance? He didn't bother to check the peephole. He opened the door.

Turned out it wasn't either one. He heard Leah's door open.

Oh, shit, this wasn't good.

Since Sara's son had skipped his regular afternoon nap, he went down early. She stood by his bed and stared at his perfect little face, perfect little hands and toes. Awake, he was a handful. Asleep, he was an angel. Her angel. And moments like this, she accepted that whatever she had to sacrifice to keep him happy and safe was a small price to pay. If that meant she went to bed lonely, so be it.

Single moms date all the time. She remembered Leah's words. Sara wasn't stupid, she knew they did.

She also knew she shouldn't feel guilty for wanting to be a part of that crowd. But wanting it and figuring out how to fit it into her life was different. Sure, she could find a sitter once a week and go out and get laid. And yes, Leah was right. She was horny. But she didn't just want sex. She wanted…more. She wanted the fantasy. She wanted what the couple had in the ice cream shop. She wanted to be somebody's everything. Wanted that wonderful gooey-feeling connection two people shared.

She recalled the strange phone call she'd had with Roberto. *You weren't wrong. The connection was there.*

Had he been lying about that? No, she didn't think so, which made it even worse. Her heart clutched thinking how it must have hurt him to lose a child. His wife, too. But a child; that seemed too much to overcome.

Moving into her bedroom, she fell back on her bed. Little Bit, her gray cat, came to collect some TLC. When the sound of the cat's automatic feeder went off, the feline dove off the mattress, proving the animal chose food over TLC.

Wanting to chase away the blues, Sara reached for the romance novel—a loaner book from her mom, who was an avid reader—on her bedside table. According to her mom, a widow for nine years, if they couldn't have the real thing, they could at least have the fantasy. Not that her mom hadn't moved past just dreaming about it. In the last six months, she had started dating again.

Turning on her reading lamp, Sara found where she'd left off and got submersed in another world. And just when that fantasy got hot—the heroine's bra getting unclasped—Sara's phone rang.

She checked the bedside clock. Her mom. She called each and every night to say good night to Brian. Setting the book down, she picked up her phone. "Sorry, he's already in bed. And so are the characters in the book. They're about to do the deed. Bad timing."

"Brian's already down?" her mom said. "I missed him?"

"Sorry, I called you. He missed his afternoon nap and he practically fell asleep in the bathtub. I had to carry him to bed."

"Poor fellow," her mom said.

"Hey, I'd kill for someone to pull me out of the bathtub and carry me to bed."

Her mom's sigh filled the line. "Just keep reading. It's a great book. Have you gotten to the hot tub scene?" Her mom giggled.

"No," Sara said. "The heroine just burned dinner, and she and the hero are getting naked for the first time."

A click came on the line. "Oh, I think that's Harry," her mom said. "He's taking me to San Antonio to a hotel with a hot tub. I'll call you back in one minute."

Frowning, Sara dropped the phone in her lap. Wasn't it in some rule book that a mother shouldn't be getting luckier than her daughter? And in a hot tub? The images flashing in her mind weren't pretty. Harry was…well, hairy. Sara didn't mind a little body hair, it was masculine, but this man had locks of gray hair trying to crawl out of his shirt.

Oh, goodness, she wasn't sure she could enjoy the book's hot tub scene now. But after a second, she picked up the book again.

It took one line to pull her back in. *The bra strap slipped off her left shoulder.*

Moaning from yet another interruption, she snagged her ringing phone. "The panties are coming off. Can I call you back after the deed is done?"

"Say what?" Two words, spoken in that deep tone— that's all it took for Sara to recognize his voice. Two words for her to feel like a complete and utter idiot.

Oh, sure, he'd said he would call her back, but she hadn't believed it.

"I thought you were my mom." She realized that didn't sound much better than the first statement. "We were discussing a book and…she was calling me right back. Then you called and…"

He laughed. A masculine sexy laugh. A little rusty, as if he hadn't used it in a while, but the kind of laugh that made a woman want to soak it up.

Or maybe she was just caught up in the scene. The line beeped.

"That's my mom. I should…"

"Call me when the scene's over." He chuckled again.

Her face grew warm. She hung up. She didn't say bye. Frankly, she'd already said too much.

Embarrassed beyond embarrassed, she debated not answering her mom's call, but knowing her mom she'd just call back.

"So what scene are you on?" her mom asked.

"The first love scene." Her face was still hot, but she was happy her mom didn't want to discuss her upcoming hot tub weekend. She loved her mom and appreciated her no-topic's-off-limit approach, but when it came to her mom's sex life, the less Sara knew, the better. "Can we talk tomorrow?"

"You okay?" Leave it to her mom to pick up on her emotional cues.

"Fine. We'll chat tomorrow." She dropped the phone and buried her face in her pillow. While she could cry from the embarrassment, she started laughing instead. Wait until she told Leah this one. Or maybe she wouldn't tell Leah. Oh, yeah, she would. They told each other most everything.

Call me back when... the scene's over. His words floated through her head.

Not happening. He'd explained why he didn't want to get involved with her. She could respect that. And the only reason he'd called her back in the first place was because... because their call earlier had been interrupted. Basically, there was nothing more to say.

Which was a shame. His laugh played in her mind. Yup, a shame. Especially if he was telling the truth about not having a criminal past, or being on any meds. He might have been one of the first good guys she was attracted to.

Austin stared at the blonde in his doorway, holding a plate of cookies in front of her oversized breasts. It was the same blonde he'd seen earlier today when he'd been bleeding. Leah's apartment door opened.

"Hi," the blonde said. Austin's gaze flipped from Leah's door to the blonde. "I'm Tina, your neighbor." She shot him a sexy smile. "That eye looks bad." She paused. "I saw you earlier..."

Leah, a bottle of wine in her hands, gazed at Blondie and frowned.

Oh, hell.

The elevator, a few feet down from his apartment, dinged. Nance walked out.

Leah put it in reverse, moving back into her apartment.

"No!" He looked at the blonde. "Excuse me." He slipped the rest of the way out his door and caught Leah. "Please. Come on in."

She frowned. "Why don't—"

"No. Come inside." Gently, he moved her past the frowning blonde and her cookies, and ushered her inside his apartment. He swung back to the door, purposely centering the threshold so Leah couldn't slip out, and the cookie carrier couldn't slip in.

He remembered Nance. The dark-skinned nineteen-year-old kid stood in front of the elevator, smiling, as if reading the scene all wrong.

Austin held up a finger to Nance asking for a second, then glanced back at the blonde. His gaze zeroing in on her exposed cleavage before he could stop himself. She might have been holding a plate of cookies that looked like Thin Mints, but she was no Girl Scout.

"What were you saying?" he asked her.

"I…" She looked at Nance and then back at him. "I wanted to welcome you to the apartment."

"Thank you for the welcome and for the cookies." He took the plate, offered one polite good-bye nod, then stepped inside and shut the door.

"One second," he told Leah, who stood staring with a frown. "I gotta give this…the kid…the one out there. He left his wallet in my car." He dropped the plate of cookies on the bar and grabbed the bagged gun. Smiling, trying not to react to the apparent chaos, he shot back into the hall and shut the door behind him.

His neighbor was halfway down the hall. Nance hadn't moved, except to turn his head to watch the blonde as she sashayed off.

"Hey," he said to Nance.

The kid's head jerked back. Laughter lit up his brown eyes. "Two women. Did one of them give you that shiner?"

"No." He tried to come up with a short explanation. Then quit trying. "Here." He handed him the bag. "Get it to Dallas ASAP to give to his brother and see if we get a name on who owned it. Tell Dallas to call me as soon as he gets something." He looked back over his shoulder. "And thanks. I owe you."

Nance looked puzzled. "I thought you were buying me dinner."

"Yeah. I need a rain check."

The kid smiled. "Ah, hell, I'd do the same if I had a woman in my apartment. But I have to tell you, the one you sent packing got my vote. She looked more ready to...you know."

Austin frowned. "This isn't...I'm just..." Why ruin the boy's fantasy. "Bye." He turned for the door.

He grabbed the knob, then hesitated. He recalled Leah's expression when he walked out. Several years back, he'd actually screwed up and invited two different women over. One left pissed off, and the other stayed only long enough to dump the chili he'd made for her in his lap.

Tonight might not go well.

Cautiously walking into his apartment, he spotted Leah sitting on his sofa smiling and talking on her cell. Who was she talking to? She glanced up. His shoulders relaxed when she didn't frown or start throwing the fake apples in the wire basket on the coffee table at him.

"Yes. I know. But just to be safe." She nipped on her bottom lip while she listened to the person on the other end of the line.

Austin studied her. She'd changed clothes. She wore a pink long-sleeve tee and jeans. Not skintight jeans like the ones the neighbor had poured herself into, but fitting enough to show off her shape. He remembered Nance saying he'd have preferred the blonde. The kid had no taste.

"I know," she continued. "I love you. I will."

Who did Leah Reece love?

"Later." She ended the call. "My brother." She looked relaxed for the first time since she came home. "He finally called me."

Austin nodded, assuming it was her younger brother she spoke about. But he could be wrong. "Yeah, you were worried about him...being out of town, right?"

She nodded.

When she didn't elaborate, he asked, "So everything's okay?"

"Yeah." Her gaze shifted to the bar, or rather to the plate of cookies, then back to him. "So you took my earlier advice, huh?"

"What advice?"

"To go meet the neighbor."

He shook his head. "No. I didn't...This was the first time...We saw each other earlier, but we barely spoke."

"She brought you cookies." Leah reached for one of the apples from the bowl.

She didn't throw it at him though; she just turned it in her hand and then replaced it. He looked at the plate of cookies. "I think they're store bought."

"Just the cookies?" she asked, and grinned.

He laughed. "Probably those, too."

She put a finger over her lips to hide the widening smile and then spoke behind the digit. "That was bad of me. I'll bet she's a nice girl."

"Probably." He couldn't help wondering exactly what it was about Leah's conversation with her brother that put her in a good mood.

"Are you ready for some wine?" He nodded to the bottle on his coffee table. And if they needed more, he had another bottle. "The pizza should be here shortly." He stepped toward the kitchen to grab the glasses.

"Pizza?" she asked. "I'm sorry, I didn't…"

He looked back. See, he'd known she'd fight him on this. "I already ordered it."

She stood and tucked her phone in her pocket, her expression no longer playful. "I really think your head is fine now. I should—"

He stepped closer to her. "Don't run out on me." When she still looked about to refuse, he threw down his last card. "It's the least you can do after I…" *broke into your place and got caught by a real intruder,* "…got this." He pointed at his eye.

She hesitated; he continued. "Doesn't getting a black eye earn a guy a couple hours of your company?"

She still didn't answer, so he went for the kill. "I ordered mushroom, regular crust. I know you like mushroom because that's what you got at the store."

CHAPTER FOURTEEN

AUSTIN WASN'T SURE if it was the black-eye comment or the mushroom pizza, but from her expression he knew she'd relented. And damn if he didn't like that look. He could imagine her wearing that look and nothing else.

"Just this once." She crossed her arms, and the posture accentuated her breasts. He remembered the view he'd gotten when she checked his head wound earlier. Something twitched in his jeans.

They weren't the D cups Blondie had, and even though Leah's smaller breasts were mostly concealed, they were more appealing. And...real. Everything about Leah Reece came off as real. And until this moment, he hadn't realized how damn attractive "real" was.

Then again, he needed to remember why he was here. "I'll get the glasses."

She grabbed the wine and moved to the kitchen table.

He brought the glasses and set them on the table, then pulled the cork out of the bottle. "Sit down."

She lowered herself into a dining table chair and glanced at his computer. "You get your e-mails sent?"

"Done." He poured her a glass, handed it to her, and dropped into the chair on the other side of the table.

He accidentally nudged the table and the cork rolled off, but he was too busy watching how she caressed the glass of wine to pick it up.

"Do you always work from home?" She ran her finger down the side of the glass as if needing something to do with her hands.

"Unless a client needs me to come to their office." He sipped from his glass, wanting to get the taste of the lie from his tongue. He watched her twirl her wine, spinning the red fluid in her glass, and then she put her nose to the lip and inhaled like a wine connoisseur.

"This is nice," she said. "Don't let me forget to get your bottle out of my car."

"My bottle?" he asked.

"Yeah, I'm replacing the one you gave me."

"Why? I broke yours. That's why I gave you this one."

"Yeah, but you upgraded, so it wasn't a fair trade." She took her first taste, and her dreamy expression said she really liked it. She inhaled again. "This is the good stuff. The bottle that broke—that *I* dropped, by the way—was a hair better than Boone's Farm."

He enjoyed the look of pleasure on her face as she sipped again from her glass. "And you don't like gifts," he said, remembering, thinking again of puzzles.

She paused as if trying to recall imparting that piece of information. "Right."

"And why is that?" He leaned back in his chair, just enjoying looking at her.

He saw the shutters go down in her eyes. He'd trespassed on private property—parts of her past she wouldn't share. She lifted one shoulder as if to make her lie sound more casual. "I guess I don't like being beholden to anyone."

Yeah, but why? Who hurt you? He wanted to push, but knew better.

She looked around at his place. "So you moved every-thing up here and you're only going to be here for a couple of months?"

"No. This isn't my stuff. I had a service furnish everything."

"Everything?" she asked.

He nodded.

"That explains it." She looked at her wine and took another sip.

"Explains what?" he asked.

She held up the glass. "Why the wine you drink is more expensive per glass than the glasses you serve it in." She shifted her gaze around the apartment.

He looked at his glass. He hadn't considered them to be cheap. But, on second thought, they were clunkier than those he had at home—which hadn't been cheap.

"So you're an expert on glassware?"

She chuckled. "I'm an expert on cheap. I have the same glasses, bought at the Dollar Store."

He was trying to figure out how to ask about her reasons for being so cheap, when she spoke up again. "But it's not just the glasses, it's the whole place. It doesn't look like you."

He looked around. "What doesn't look like me?"

She made that cute face of hers that had her dimples winking. "The striped sofa. The burgundy chair. The fake apples. The pictures of pears on the wall."

He hadn't even noticed what hung on the wall. "So you're anti-fruit?" He grinned.

She smiled back. "No, but..."

"But what?" he asked, having to force himself not to stare at the sheen of moisture left by the wine on her bottom lip.

"It doesn't suit you." She ran her finger over the stem of her glass. What the hell was it about her that seemed...erotic? Innocently erotic. But damn if he wasn't getting turned on just watching her touch a cheap wineglass. "I'll bet you don't have pictures of pears on your walls at your real place."

He laughed. "So what do you think my real place looks like?"

She tilted her head to the side, reminding him of a curious puppy. "Leather and lots of wood," she said. "If you have anything on the wall, it's...masculine. You had cowboy boots on yesterday, so I'm thinking you go with the rustic type of art."

He was stunned at how right on she was about his place. He actually had an old piece of barn wood with an antique pair of horseshoes hanging above his leather sofa. Not that he'd come up with the idea, but one of Tyler's cousins was an interior decorator and she'd helped him fix up his place to match his style. He hadn't thought he had a style, but he'd liked her work.

He raised his cheap glass. "You're good." It was a bit frightening that she read him so well.

She shrugged. "Or maybe you're just easy to read."

"Maybe." He took another sip and hoped that wasn't the case. "So now it's my turn to surmise why you enjoy good wine, seem to know how to judge it, but drink the cheap stuff, out of cheap glasses, even when I've heard vets do well for themselves."

She did another sniff of her wine. "That's easy. A couple of years ago, I took a class on wine. As for me being frugal? School loans, owning my own business, and...helping my brother with his college, it...oh, and phone sex, it isn't cheap."

He had just taken a sip of wine and it went down the wrong pipe. He coughed.

She laughed. "Sorry, I should have kept that one to myself."

But from the twinkle in her brown eyes, she'd liked surprising him. He liked her liking it, too.

He coughed again. "So you're into...phone sex?"

She rolled her expressive eyes. "No! Not me, my ex. When he left, he didn't quite get the fifty/fifty split rule. He thought that meant he took everything we had, and I got to keep the bills." She took another sip of her wine.

"He sounds like a real champion." He wondered if this was the guy with the devil doodled by his name in her phone book. He also found it odd that she didn't seem to mind talking about some things, but others were unapproachable. Then again, wasn't he like that?

In most cases, he could even joke about the whole framed-for-murder situation, he even made some jokes about losing Cara, but mention his childhood and you'd get shit.

"So no exes in your past?"

"Nope."

"No close calls?"

The doorbell rang. "That should be our pizza."

"Or your secret admirer," she said.

"My who?" He stood up.

She arched a brow. "The neighbor with the store-bought cookies."

He laughed again and it felt good, too. He glanced back. A tiny little thing, a perfect body, the face of a model, a witty personality, and every inch of her...real. This was the most fun he'd had with a woman with his clothes on in a long time. And damn if he wouldn't like to see how much fun they could have with them off.

He brought the pizza to the table, hoping the food would up his willpower. They continued to chat about local restaurants, different types of mushrooms, and even her cats. She really loved her cats. And when she brought up him losing his cat, his manufactured lie, he quickly changed the subject to his homemade pizza.

"You really make your own crust," she said.

"I swear it." And right then he planned to make her one, but he didn't say it because he sensed she'd rebel. He hadn't forgotten her comment, *just this once,* when she'd relented to have dinner with him.

Somehow, someway, he'd change her mind.

He opened the other bottle of wine and refilled their glasses.

He'd eaten five slices of pizza to her two. He pushed the box toward her to have the last one.

"No," she said. "I love pizza, but I limit it to two slices. Especially since we didn't even have anything healthy to counter the bad calories."

"I could make a run to the store and buy some broccoli," he teased, remembering their conversation about broccoli. Then he remembered what the conversation had really been about. Secrets.

Her smile came on timid, as if she was remembering their conversation as well. She picked up her nearly empty glass and took a small sip. "So your parents didn't get a divorce?"

Her question shocked him, but also told him she was as curious about him as he was about her. He enjoyed knowing it. Still, his first instinct was to shut the questioning down, but something told him that if he wanted answers, he should be able to give a few. And why not? In a few days, a week at the most, they wouldn't see each other again.

"No divorce." He took the last swig of his wine. Liquid courage. "I was raised in foster care."

"I'm sorry." Pity filled her eyes.

He hated pity. "You're apologizing again," he said, uncomfortable in his own skin.

"Were your parents killed?" she asked.

He wanted to lie and say yes.

"I'm sorry, you don't have to—"

"My dad ran off after I was born. My mom made a living taking her clothes off, and she had a liking for drugs. When I was three, she dropped me off at day care and forgot she had a son." Damn, he hadn't meant to tell her all that.

Her brown eyes widened. "That's awful."

"Nah, it worked out all right." He set his glass down. "And you?"

From the look in her eyes, he knew she understood exactly what he meant. This was tit for tat? "Or are you sticking to the broccoli story?"

She blinked. The look in those brown eyes told him she'd mentally tossed in the towel. "That picture was taken a week after my mom was killed in a car accident."

His chest swelled. "Foster care?"

"No. My aunt, my mom's older sister, took us in. Having kids wasn't in her... plans, but after she got used to the idea, she made a damn good parent. We were lucky."

He turned the cheap wineglass in his hand and figured he had to go for it. "What about your dad?"

"Dead." The way she said it told him that wasn't the whole story. He glanced briefly at his computer and wondered if it would be more forthcoming with information. What was she hiding? Who had she been afraid of, and who had she called when she'd run out on him and went to her bedroom?

"And?" he asked.

She looked down at her glass. "He..." She stood up, grabbed his glass, and carried them to the kitchen counter to refill them.

"He what?" He wasn't willing to let her off the hook that easy. The silence reigned as she poured the wine. As she stepped closer, she lost her footing. He saw the damn cork he'd dropped earlier shoot out from under her shoe. Before he could even attempt to catch her, she managed to right herself, but not gracefully. Her arms went up and then down, and the contents of the two glasses of wine shot forward. Right at him.

Right in his face.

The cool red splash hit. The alcohol stung his pupils and he automatically squeezed his eyes shut.

"Oh, damn," he heard her say. Then she giggled.

He knew why, too. He remembered doing this same thing to her in the parking lot.

"Let me get you some paper towels," she said.

In seconds, he felt her press a handful of paper towels to his face. He felt her closeness. "I think you did that on purpose," he said, teasing, and beneath the smell of wine, he inhaled her scent of waffle cones again.

"No, I swear." She giggled. "Let me wet some towels and that will help." She moved away. He managed to open his eyes, but barely.

She moved in and pressed the moist towels to his face, covering his eyes. "I think I gave you my shirt." He lowered the towels. His gaze lowered to her breasts. She stood, her legs apart, straddling his knees.

"Behave." Humor danced in her eyes, and her hair danced on her shoulders.

She looked just a little bit tipsy. Her cheeks a little flushed. Or was it the laughter?

Whatever it was, she looked sexy as hell. Maybe she wasn't the only one a little tipsy.

He dropped the paper towels and caught her by the waist. His palms fit perfectly into that sweet curvy spot of her body. He pulled her closer and settled her on his lap.

She didn't resist. If anything, those last few inches were her own doing. Her weight, so light, came against his thighs. But when her soft ass pressed against all the right places, he went hard. He lowered his head, and through watering eyes, he stared at her mouth.

He wasn't certain who did it—who closed the small space between them, but their lips met. She tasted like . . . wine.

Like pizza.

And sweet woman.

All the things he loved.

The kiss didn't start slow, or hesitant. It went from hot to hotter. Her tongue met his and danced. Her hands moved around his neck, pulling his mouth closer, as if wanting it deeper. Deep was good. He'd kill to be deep inside her body right now.

He shifted his palms up from her waist, and his thumbs brushed against the soft sides of her breasts. Nothing blatantly forward. Just a slight brush. But damn if he didn't want more.

She moaned, and her pelvis shifted ever so slightly against the hardness pressing against his jeans. Blood shot to a certain body part, and he became harder still.

He slipped his hand up under her T-shirt to her bare back. He memorized the feel of her skin, silky soft, and instinctively he went for her bra clasp. One tiny twist and it fell open. The slightest weight of her breasts landed against his chest. His right palm found its way back to her front, to the soft supple flesh. He held her breast in his hand and brushed his thumb over her nipple. Her pelvis shifted against him again, only harder, a sure sign that she was with him. He imagined her already wet, and he ached to feel that dampness. Yearned to slip inside it.

Lowering his hand to the button of her jeans, it took

nothing to free it. He tucked his hand inside to touch the silk of her underwear. She did another slight rocking motion against him. His hand slipped deeper, to the moist place between her thighs.

She moaned. And did another rock motion against him.

All he could think about was getting her clothes off and getting inside her. She slipped her hand inside his shirt. That sweet touch, her soft palm against his chest, sent all sorts of warning bells ringing.

This wasn't supposed to happen.

He was here for information, not...

He hesitated. She bolted off his lap.

She was breathing hard. He wasn't breathing. He couldn't. Everything hurt.

They stared at each other. Her nipples pebbled against the soft pink cotton of her blouse.

And her lips, still wet from his tongue, and his hand, still wet from her desire, gave him all sorts of fantasies. He throbbed with the memory. He wanted her back in his lap, now, minus the jeans and panties. He wanted her naked on his lap. He wanted to take her in the chair.

She shook her head and took another step back. "This... this can't..." She turned to leave.

"Wait." He jumped up. His crotch throbbed. He got between her and the door. "I'm sorry."

He heard the shakiness of her breath. Or was that him now trying to get air?

He raked a hand through his hair and flinched when he hit his wound. "It's too soon, too fast. I...I'm sorry."

Her wide eyes filled with a wild look of passion. He knew he probably had the same in his eyes.

"I told you that you should go to the neighbor," she said. "I can't—"

He exhaled. "I...don't want the neighbor." *I want you.* Those three words echoed inside him like a mantra. He wanted her. This was so not what he had planned to happen.

She shook her head. "No. This isn't—"

"I said I'm sorry. I meant it. I won't—"

"Won't what?" She rolled her eyes and then shook her head. "Now who's apologizing? And what are you apologizing for? I'm the one who kissed you."

"Okay." He held up a hand as if to calm her down. To calm them both. "That's...that's good to know," he said. "I wasn't sure who'd done what. But...I'm sure it's still my fault."

"How?" she asked.

"I don't know." He met her gaze again. Her lips looked swollen. Her hair a little disheveled. Damn, she was beautiful. "For being irresistible." He shot her a smile, hoping humor might help.

A laugh bolted out of her. He laughed with her. It was cathartic. It was good.

"This is why you can't walk out of here and be...mad."

"Why?" she asked, the humor lessening from her eyes.

"We make each other laugh. What just happened probably shouldn't have happened...but this..." He waved a hand between them. "This is good."

There wasn't even the tiniest thread of untruth to his words. Letting her walk away knowing she wouldn't want to see him again felt so damn wrong, and not because he needed information so he could bring down her low-life half brother. Not because he needed to bury himself deep inside her so badly his teeth hurt. It wasn't about sex.

He needed... As fucked up as it sounded—and yeah, he accepted he was a little drunk—he needed her smile. Her laughter. The way his hands fit around her waist. The way she felt on top of . . . Okay, maybe it was a little about sex, but not all about it.

"No," Leah said. "I can't. I'm not open to . . ." She put a hand to her head. "How many glasses of wine did I have?" She started for the door. "I'm leaving."

He wanted to stop her so bad it hurt.

His door shut with a click that echoed inside him. She hadn't slammed it. It hadn't been loud, just a sad sound.

His chest gripped with something that felt like loss. Like the seven or eight times different foster parents walked out, leaving him behind with a social worker.

CHAPTER FIFTEEN

LEAH CHANGED HER footprinted sheets, dropped in her bed, grabbed a pillow, and moaned into it. Bob jumped up on the bed and put his paw on her arm. She looked at the cat. "I did a bad thing. A really, really bad thing."

She closed her eyes, and her mind played images of just how bad. "I practically gave the guy a lap dance. Rubbed against him like a feline in heat. I'm so screwed up! So very, very screwed up!"

She blamed the three and a half glasses of wine she had consumed. She blamed her hormones. She blamed the fact that she'd gone soft when he confided in her about his screwed-up childhood. But damn, she was always a sucker for a stray. And that's the way his story made him sound. A stray, someone who'd been abandoned by the person who should have loved him.

And she thought she'd had it tough. Oh, it had been hard, but she couldn't imagine how it would feel if her mom had left her willingly. Dropped her off and just didn't come back for her, instead of dying.

Okay, having a reason for her stupid behavior didn't change a thing. Didn't change the fact that she wanted him.

Wanted to kiss him again. Wanted to feel his hardness slide between her legs.

She wanted to laugh. To listen to him talk. Just his voice turned her on. She wanted to learn all the little details about his life. Did he really make his own pizza? Did he really have leather furniture at his real place? Did he really turn down a hot blonde just to have wine with her?

A knot rose in her throat. She wanted to tell him things. Things she hadn't told anyone. About her mom basically being her dad's whore. About how she'd seen her dad at her mom's funeral, standing in the back behind some trees. About how when his eyes met hers, for one second, she thought he loved her, too, that he was there to take her and Luis with him. But then he left, and she'd never heard from him again.

But she hadn't told anyone about that. Never wanted to tell anyone. Not even her aunt. It was too private. It hurt too much. Maybe that was why she could relate to how it must have felt for his mom to walk away from him. Her father had abandoned her, too.

She closed her eyes. Knowing his childhood was as crazy as hers somehow made her feel connected to him.

But it didn't really mean anything. She'd thought she had a connection with her father. She'd thought she had a connection with Brandon. Wrong on both accounts. She had to remember that.

Austin stood there staring at the door, fighting the urge to go after her. He didn't. He couldn't. It wasn't right, wasn't logical.

But he didn't follow logic. He wasn't a Boy Scout, like Tyler. He followed his gut. But he wasn't a scumbag. And having sex with her when...when he was there under false pretenses would fall in the scumbag category.

He'd come here for a reason. To get information. Nothing more.

He spotted his headphones on the kitchen counter. He plugged them in, brought up the program, and sat down to listen to the phone conversation she'd had earlier when she'd left him in her living room.

"Luis? Where the hell are you? Are you still in San Antonio? Call me now!"

So she'd only left a message and hadn't actually spoken to anyone. The sound of her voice replayed in his head. She'd sounded desperate. Scared. He remembered the look of sheer panic on her face when he'd pointed out the address book was missing. How was the book connected to her younger brother? And did it have anything to do with her older brother?

"Shit!" he muttered, now even more confused.

He was about to jump over to listen to the live tape, when he noticed there was another "bedroom" file, a few minutes after the first one.

The second sounded like a call from her work. *"It's complicated,"* Leah said.

From the conversation, Austin got the feeling Leah wasn't confiding in her work associate. Which really seemed odd the longer they talked because they were obviously friends. The conversation changed to them talking about a guy her friend was dating. Then Leah even mentioned Austin, and it appeared as if she'd mentioned him earlier to this person.

He listened for any info that might be important. But he heard her say, *"Okay, I'm horny, but not as much as you."*

He moaned. That wasn't important, but the tightening low in his belly started picking up again.

When the conversation was over, he clicked it off. Yet another file started uploading, a recent one. Had she gotten a call? He clicked it open. Her voice came through the earphones.

"I did a bad thing. A really, really bad thing."

Who was she talking to? Had she called someone and bypassed the "hello" part of the conversation? He heard a slight meow. Was she talking to her cats?

"I practically gave the guy a lap dance. Rubbed against him like a feline in heat. I'm so screwed up! So very, very screwed up!"

The memory of how unscrewed up and good it felt ran through his mind. Then shot straight down to his crotch. The file ended.

Oh, hell! He took off his earphones and went to take a shower. A cold one.

Roberto sat at his kitchen table, worried and waiting. Worried about Brad. His trip to the ice house hadn't revealed a thing. No one had heard from him.

He was worried that Brad's wife was going to call again and expect Roberto to have news. Roberto wanted to assure her it was okay, but he didn't think it was. He had learned enough about the man to know he really loved his wife and kids. And he wouldn't just disappear without a damn good reason. And right now, Roberto was worried that the reason was that Brad was dead.

Roberto was also worried about what tomorrow night and the Thursday drop would bring. Would he be joining Brad as a missing person?

A missing person no one would miss.

After Anna and Bobby Jr. died, he'd walked away from the friends they'd had. He'd been consumed with fury toward Rafael DeLuna, and even the police who'd refused to believe that what happened that night hadn't been an accident.

He looked at his phone. Waiting for the damn thing to ring and offer him a much-needed distraction.

Call me when the scene's over.

She hadn't. He picked up the glass of water he'd used to down the fast-food hamburger he'd called dinner.

He should forget about the call. Let it go. But hell! He didn't want to let it go. He needed a distraction from all the crap going on. She was the only distraction he could think of besides the bottle of whiskey waiting in the kitchen. And he didn't want that kind of diversion.

He dialed her number.

It rang four times. He was about to hang up when her timid "Hello" answered.

"Must be a long scene." He ran his finger over the scarred wood of the table in his cheap-ass apartment. The table should be thrown away. The thought hit that on the inside he was just as scarred.

There was a pause. "I . . . it's a romance novel."

"I figured that," he said. "My wife . . . read them." His chest gripped. His first impulse was to hang up. Talking to a woman, a woman who intrigued him, about Anna had to be wrong, didn't it?

Silence filled the line. He pulled the phone away from his ear and had his finger on the end call button.

"What were their names?" Her voice finally came and had a quality that he liked. Smooth and yet bubbly at the same time.

He pulled the phone back to his ear. "Anna and Bobby Jr."

"How did they die?"

Some low-life scum killed them. Swallowing, he told her what most people believed, but what he knew to be a lie. "A car wreck."

"Damn," she said. And that one word came filled with emotion.

"Yeah, damn," he said.

"I want to say I'm sorry, but I hated hearing that. Most people don't mean it. They just say it."

He took a deep breath, the focus shifting away from his own pain. "Who did you lose?"

"My father."

"How old were you?" he asked.

"Seventeen. He was this big, barrel-chested man. Bigger than life. And even though I was mostly grown up, I was still his little girl. He was so good at giving advice. Love advice."

"That's rare," Roberto said. "Most dads just want to kill anyone who touches their little girls."

"Yeah, but he wanted me to have what he had with my mom." She chuckled. "He said love made you glow." She paused as if missing him now. "Anyway, I know how it feels to lose someone you love. But I can't even imagine how hard it would be to lose a child."

"Yeah." One word was all he could say. After a second, he asked, "What happened to him?"

"Heart attack," she answered. "It was the middle of the night. Mom says he sat straight up in bed, grabbed her hand, told her he loved her, and then slumped over." Silence filled the line. "You know for a year, every time I heard her tell that story, I was jealous. Jealous that I didn't hear him tell me that one more time. Grief can make you so crazy."

"Yeah," he said.

"How long has it been?"

"A little over two years." He reached for his glass of water and turned it in his hand.

"You know, I also hated it when people told me it would get easier." She swallowed. "Then when it did get easier, I got angry. I felt like I was betraying his memory."

"Sounds about right," he said. Just talking to Sara made him feel like a cheater. Cheating on his dead wife.

"But that sort of goes away, too. It did for me."

"That's good to know." He stretched out his legs.

"We sound pathetic. We should change the subject to something upbeat."

"To what?" he asked.

"I don't know."

After a pause, he asked something he'd wondered about. "What happened to Brian's dad?"

"I said upbeat." She chuckled.

"Sorry," he said. "Forget I—"

"No, it's fine." She hesitated. "He was in the banking business. We were engaged. On our way to happily ever after."

"So what happened?"

"I accidentally got pregnant. And he accidentally turned into the world's biggest asshole. Or not really turned into one. He always was one. He just showed his true colors then."

"What did he do?" Roberto already hated the guy. How could he willingly walk away from the things that Roberto had been robbed of.

"I told him I was pregnant; he suggested an abortion. I refused, so he packed his stuff up and disappeared."

"And you haven't heard from him since?" he asked.

"I wish. About a month after Brian was born, he called me."

"Wanting to get back together?"

"No. He'd been arrested and wanted me to bail him out of jail. See, I wasn't joking when I said he was an asshole."

He chuckled. "Arrested for what?"

"For holding up a bank. Supposedly, that's what he'd meant by the banking business. I felt like an idiot. I lived with a bank robber and didn't even know it."

"If you bailed him out, you were an idiot. If not—"

"Oh, hell no. I said I felt like an idiot, I didn't say I was one." She sighed. "What really got to me, though, was that he never asked about Brian. As far as I can tell, he doesn't even know if he had a son or a daughter."

"He doesn't deserve to know."

"I agree."

The line grew quiet. He wanted her to keep talking. He wanted something to focus on besides his own miserable crap. "So what do you do when you're not taking care of your kid and kittens? Besides reading romance novels?" He chuckled.

"There's nothing wrong with romance novels," she said.

"I didn't say—"

"Have you ever read one?"

"No."

"Then don't judge them," she answered. "As a matter of fact, you should read them. All men should read them."

"Really?" He smiled, and it felt like a first in a while.

"Really," she said.

Silence reigned again. "So what else do you do, Sara?"

She paused as if to shift mental gears. "Well, I'm into music. Singing that is."

"Like performing?" he asked.

"Yup, I do my share of performing."

"Where?" He wondered if he could ever manage to go hear her. "What kind of music?" He hoped it wasn't opera or anything. He wasn't sure he could even pretend to like that crap.

"I dabble in different kinds. I'm known mostly for the ABC song, and 'Little Bunny Foo Foo.' Oh, and outside of music, I'm an expert in all things SpongeBob."

He laughed.

"What about you?" she asked. "What do you do besides work construction?"

Besides endlessly hunting down the killer of my wife and son? Which means, as of Thursday, I'll also be delivering drugs...And now trying to find my boss, who I'm pretty sure is dead.

His grip on the phone tightened. It occurred to him how stupid he'd been to call her. He had nothing to offer. He'd just selfishly wanted to reach out and touch something... normal. Something not tainted by the ugliness he'd surrounded himself with for the last two years.

"Not a whole lot," he finally said.

"Do you read?" she asked as if she somehow sensed he'd withdrawn.

"I used to," he said.

"What did you read?" she asked.

He let himself get pulled back in. "Not romance." He listened to her laugh. Soft, sweet. "Some mystery, intrigue. You know, Patterson."

"How did you end up in construction?" she asked.

"I was always good at building things. I was going to school for architecture," he said, remembering when his life had been so different. It hit then, a revelation. He no longer just missed Anna and Bobby, he missed his old life. He missed who he'd been.

"You didn't finish school?" she asked.

"No," he said.

"Do you ever want to try to finish? I do."

"You want to finish school to be an architect?" he asked, knowing that wasn't what she meant, but curious to learn more about her and not really wanting to talk about himself.

"No." She laughed. "I was a year away from graduating to be a vet when Brian was born."

"Why don't you go back?"

"I want to. But it's hard. I'm already away from Brian forty hours a week to work. The thought of having to be away from him even more, it feels impossible. Mom's offered to let me move in with her and just work part-time and go to school part-time. But that's if I could even get back in. And moving in with Mom feels wrong."

"She wouldn't have offered if she didn't mean it," he said.

"I know, but she's got her own life and she already watches Brian two days a week. Plus, I see how much time Leah, my boss, puts into having her own office. It's a lot of overhead, a lot of work. I'm not sure I want to give all that right now. Maybe when Brian's older. And besides, I get to do most everything I wanted to do. Taking care of animals. Except the surgery, I kind of liked doing that in school. I actually got to take a bullet out of a dog once. I even considered specializing in it."

"Did you have a lot of pets growing up?" He leaned his head back and enjoyed the cadence of her voice. He wondered if she'd ever really tried to sing. Her voice had that quality to it.

"Oh, yeah. Dogs, cats, hamsters. I even had an iguana once. A male." She chuckled. "But I cross-dressed it. I used to tie a pink bow around its neck because I was afraid people would think I was a tomboy having a big lizard."

"I can't see you as a tomboy," he said.

"I wasn't. I was Nurse Sara. Took care of all the injured animals in my neighborhood. I was eight when I told everyone I wanted to be a vet."

She paused, and he worried where her mind had gone.

"Why did you call me back?" she asked.

"I don't know," he lied, knowing he'd called her just to feel a part of something decent, something not sleazy.

"It's not that I mind, or that we can't just talk, but—"

"Then let's do that. Let's just talk."

"I think I've done most of the talking," she said.

"All women do," he said. "Haven't you ever noticed how many more words a woman says a day compared to men? So, don't stop."

"I don't know what to say."

"Tell me why I should read a romance novel?"

CHAPTER SIXTEEN

THE NEXT DAY, Roberto pulled into the diner for lunch. He wasn't sure why he'd even come here. His appetite had seemed to go the way of his sanity. Had he really stayed up talking to Sara until two in the morning? Time had flown, and when he looked at the clock and saw it was two a.m., he thought the damn thing had gone haywire.

It hadn't. He'd been the one to go haywire. Crazy to have called her in the first place. Before he'd hung up, he'd heard it in her voice. The question. *What now?* She hadn't verbalized the question, but he knew she wanted to.

He'd almost answered it, too: *What now? Nothing happens now.*

As much as he wished it wasn't so, he owed it to Anna and Bobby, Jr. to get the piece of shit who took their lives. There was no going back.

He got off his bike. The store in the strip center right behind the diner caught his eye. Funny how he hadn't noticed the store until now. He started toward the diner, then thought *what the hell*. Turning around, he walked to the store.

Ten minutes later, he sat at his regular table with his

bagged purchases at his side. Rosie delivered his coffee. "Fried chicken's on special," she said.

"Sounds good," he said. "Thanks."

She hung there. "You gonna be by yourself today?"

He remembered how Cruz had treated her yesterday. "I think so."

"Well, if you get company, not that big, bald guy—he's a nice guy—but that one from yesterday, I'm getting Bea to take over the table. That guy gives me the creeps."

"I don't blame you," he said. "Sorry about that." When she left, Roberto's mind went to Brad, and he wished he had a clue as to what was happening with the guy.

But focusing on what he didn't know wasn't going to get him anywhere. He reached down into the bag and pulled out one of the books. He folded the cover completely back so no one could see what he was reading, and then he dove right in.

Two chapters later, he heard Rosie clear her throat. "You wanna eat, or read?"

"Sorry." He dropped the book in the booth's seat. As she placed the plate on the table, she glanced down at the book.

She smiled. "I read that book."

He almost blushed. "It was recommended by a . . . friend." The last word caught in his throat. Was Sara a friend?

"Your friend has good taste." She lowered her voice. "Wait until you read the hot tub scene."

Now he did blush. He slipped it back in the bag with his Patterson novel.

He'd barely picked at his food when Rosie came strolling back over. She had an odd expression on her face and the restaurant's portable phone in her hand.

"It's for you." She offered him the phone.

"Me?"

"It's the bald guy. Said he had to talk to you."

Leah forked a piece of chicken from atop her salad and looked up at Evelyn and Sara across her desk. Jamie, the young intern from college who came in once a week, was watching the desk. And since they didn't have appointments for the next hour, Evelyn decided they'd have lunch together.

Normally, Leah would've been thrilled, but for the second day in a row she had a wine headache. Of course, the wine wasn't the only culprit. She regularly got headaches when consumed with worry. And she had plenty to worry over. What did Rafael want with Luis? Had it really been one of Rafael's buddies who'd broken into her place and stolen her address book—which had Luis's address in it? And although Luis had promised to stay with a friend for a few days, had he just been placating her?

Not that worry and wine were the only reasons her right temple throbbed. Regret always had her reaching for the Advil. Only this time her regret was bigger than the three Advil she'd popped. How could she not regret losing her inhibitions and climbing into Austin Brookshire's lap and behaving like some stripper looking for a tip?

"Okay, do you two wanna come clean?" Evelyn crossed her arms.

"Come clean?" Sara asked, sounding guilty.

Leah realized Sara *had* been quiet. "Is something wrong?"

"Of course it's wrong," Evelyn said. "And don't act like it's all on Sara just because she's been checking her phone every fifteen minutes. Because there's the whole thing with your apartment getting robbed and you not calling the police. And you've only asked about a hundred times if Luis called. And if you don't stop frowning, I swear that crease between your brows is going to become permanent. So spit it out, both of ya. What's going on?"

Roberto waited for Rosie to walk away before he put the phone to his ear. "What the hell is going on?"

"It's bad," Brad said. "You need to get your ass out of there. Quick. Walk away before it's too late."

Roberto shook his head. "What's bad? Too late for what? Why are you calling on the restaurant's phone?"

"I had to make sure you weren't with anyone. 'Cause if you were, you'd have to lie about who it was, and I don't think you're that good at lying."

You'd be amazed at how good I am at it. "Where are you? Cruz is looking for you. Your wife called me looking for you. I didn't know if you'd been arrested or dead."

"Neither. Not yet. But that could change anytime."

"Have you gotten with Cruz?"

"Forget that asshole, worry about yourself." Brad moaned. Roberto heard so much in that desperate sound—the sound of a not-so-bad guy put in a very bad position.

"Look, if you tell me what's going on I might be able to help."

"That's why I'm calling you. I need you to get a message to my wife. Tell her…tell her I'm okay and that…just tell her I'm okay."

"That's not what I meant by help." Roberto's gut clenched. "Tell me what's happening."

"I'm not pulling you into this," Brad said.

"Brad—"

"Talk to Sandy for me, please."

Roberto closed his eyes. "I'm sure she'd rather talk to you."

"I can't call her. She...If she figures out what I'm doing—"

"What are you doing?" Roberto asked.

"Just call her, okay?" Brad insisted.

Had Brad killed someone? Had DeLuna made him do his dirty work? "Look if you did anything, you did it under duress."

"Hell, yeah, it's under duress, but what the fuck difference does that make? I'm screwed no matter which way you look at it. And I'm probably going to end up losing the only thing that matters to me. My family. But I'll lose them before...I gotta go."

"Brad..." The line went silent.

"Shit!" he muttered. What the hell had Brad done?

"Fine," Sara said. "I'll go first. I made an idiot out of myself on the phone with the guy."

"What guy?" Evelyn asked.

"The guy who brought in Spooky."

"Ohh." Evelyn wiggled her brows. "He's worth making an idiot out of yourself over. But I didn't think you'd heard from him again."

"I hadn't. Leah convinced me to call him."

"Good for you," Evelyn said to Leah, then turned back to Sara. "So what happened?"

Sara told them about how his wife and child had died in a car crash and then went into answering his call thinking it was her mom. "I think I said, 'The panties are just about off, can I call you when the deed's done.'"

In spite of her headache, Leah, along with Evelyn, laughed so hard she had tears in their eyes. Then Sara went into how she was supposed to call him back, and hadn't. Then he'd called her back and they'd stayed on the phone talking like teenagers until two in the morning.

"And?" Evelyn said.

"And what?" Sara asked.

"When are you gonna make your own losing-your-panties story?"

"He's working in Dallas," she said, but something about her tone sounded off. And Leah wasn't the only one picking up on it.

Evelyn frowned. "What does that have to do with the price of bread? It's like a three-hour drive. What? He doesn't think you're worth coming up here on his day off? When I first met Stewart he lived in Florida, and let me tell ya, he didn't let a few thousand miles get in the way of some good lovin'. He drove down sometimes two times a week. And I made sure it was worth it."

"Stewart hadn't lost a wife and kid," Sara said, but didn't sound convincing. There was something else going on; Leah heard it in her voice.

"Yeah, you said that was two years ago," Evelyn said. "I think—"

"Evelyn?" Jamie called from the front, sounding panicked.

"I swear," Evelyn said. "That girl couldn't make a decision on her own if there were neon signs pointing the way. Bless her heart." Evelyn sighed. "Gimme one second." She popped up.

Leah looked at Sara. "What's got you spooked about Spooky's hero?"

Sara frowned. "It's partly what Evelyn said and part... Oh, hell, I'm attracted to him. And while there's this part of me that wants to believe everything he says—that he's not on drugs and he doesn't have warrants out for his arrest—I always fall for bad boys. He's like this expert at avoiding questions about himself. But I'm falling. Falling hard. He's all I can think about. I forgot to pack Brian's lunch today. I had to go back to the house. I don't know if I can do this. Whatever the hell 'this' is."

"Leah!" Evelyn called, panic now ringing in Evelyn's voice. "I think you'd better come out here. Now!"

CHAPTER SEVENTEEN

LEAH TOOK OFF with Sara beside her. Evelyn stood by the front door, a box in her hands. A shoe box. And it looked like blood dripping from one corner.

Leah's heart stopped. She flashed back in time when another shoe box had been delivered. Her chest swelled, and she had to force herself to move closer.

As she got a foot from Evelyn, she saw the note taped on top of the box. "Don't piss me off."

She swallowed bile down her throat and took the box from Evelyn's hands. Leah wasn't sure who was shaking the hardest, her or Evelyn. Knowing she had to look, prepared to see one of her cat's mutilated bodies, she opened it.

No body. But internal organs. Oh, God!

She dropped the box and reached for her phone. Barely able to think, much less push the right buttons, she hit the recent calls link. She didn't breathe until she found the one she needed.

Turning away from the other three people staring at her, she put the phone to her ear and waited for Austin Brookshire to answer.

*   *   *

"If you remember, at first I couldn't find shit on him," Tyler said.

Austin sat at his kitchen table, his phone to his ear, his mind rewinding to last night. Rewinding to what happened. To why it shouldn't have happened. To why he wanted it to happen again.

"I was worried he was illegal," Tyler continued.

"Yeah, I remember." Austin had to focus on the conversation. He wanted to mull over what he'd learned about Leah from Tyler. DeLuna was her half brother on her father's side. The father had been married to someone else. Leah's mom had been his longtime mistress.

It appeared that after her mother died, her father completely dropped out of the picture. In his obituary, the only kids listed were those from the man's marriage. The man hadn't died when Leah was young the way she'd led him to believe. She'd have been around eighteen.

And since they lived in the same small town, Austin couldn't help wondering if Leah had seen the obituary.

"Then it finally hit me," Tyler continued. "Surnames. It's common for Latinos to have two last names. But since he didn't have his father's last name, I found both his mother's surnames. And bingo. Roberto Rivera had nothing on him. But Roberto Marcos, aka Roberto Rivera Marcos, has some history. He was married. Had a kid. Both killed in a car accident."

"That sucks," Austin said, meaning it.

"Yeah, but there was one article that claimed the husband and the wife's brother didn't believe it was an accident. The brother, a Freddie Gomez, said that his sister and nephew were murdered because she'd witnessed a murder that took place near her house. So I looked up all murders in the area about that time. And you'll never guess whose name popped up as a person of interest in one of them."

"DeLuna." So DeLuna killed Roberto's wife and kid. Fuck, was there no end to what this guy would do?

"Yup. I knew Roberto had a personal agenda."

"What does Dallas say about this?" Austin asked.

"He said we need to put our heads together. Decide if we should call him on this, or not. Part of me says it doesn't change anything, but it feels..."

Austin's phone beeped with an incoming call. He looked to see the number. His breath caught. Leah. "Gotta go," he said.

He took a deep breath, clueless to how this call would go. Even though she'd admitted to initiating their kiss, he was prepared to apologize again. She hadn't been the one to unhook her bra and unsnap her jeans. He'd spent all day regretting his actions. Or trying to regret them.

"Hey," he said. "I'm glad you called."

"Are my cats okay?" She sounded breathless.

"What?"

"My cats? Has anyone broken into my apartment today?" He shook his head "no," and then said, "I don't think so?"

"Can you check? Please. Please check on my cats."

"Sure." Then he remembered she wasn't supposed to know he could get into her apartment. Was this a test? Was she onto him? "I don't have a key."

"Break it down. I don't care."

It wasn't a test. Panic rang in her voice. But for her cats? "What's going on, Leah?"

"Just check on my cats, please." Her voice stuttered.

The fear in her voice reminded him of when she'd left a message with her brother. "I'll call you right back," Austin said. "And calm down, I don't think anyone has broken in."

Dropping his phone in his pocket, he grabbed his gun from the top cabinet and his lock picks from under the kitchen sink. He hurried out into the hall and turned the knob to her apartment door to see if it was open. It wasn't.

He went to work. Was done in seconds. He dropped the picks in his pocket. Remembering her fear, he pulled his weapon and quietly opened the door.

Two cats came hauling ass at him. The orange and black ones.

Shit, he'd come to calm her fears and hadn't considered his own. The cats stopped less than a foot from him and stared as if he was an intruder and they were the guards. He cautiously stepped around them until he could see in the kitchen. It took a second to take his eyes off the two felines. He didn't trust them. Finally, he glanced up. Kitchen empty.

As he crept past the two creatures again, he listened to see if he heard anything anywhere else in the apartment. Nothing. He stuck his head into the bathroom. It smelled wonderful—soft, sweet, with hints of waffle cone. He went into the bedroom. The other two cats were on the bed, but at the sight of him they both scrambled up and darted under the bed.

Seeing them move so fast had his heart moving with them. He backed out of the room. Before walking completely into the living room, he located the other two creatures on the sofa. Job done, he hurried out the door.

The moment he stood in the hall, he grabbed his phone.

She answered before the phone rang. "Are they okay?"

"Yes. I didn't get really close, but they seemed fine. What's going on, Leah?"

"You saw all four of them?"

"Yes."

He heard her exhale. "Thank you."

"Tell me what's up?"

"Someone just played a mean trick, that's all."

"This is no trick!" Austin heard a female say in the background.

"What kind of trick?" He got a bad feeling.

"I'll explain later," she said. "No, don't call the police," Leah said, but she wasn't talking to him.

"Why would you call the police?" he asked, but too late. She'd hung up.

He stormed into his apartment, snatched his keys, and lit out.

Less than five minutes later, his speed ticket-worthy if he'd been spotted, he walked into Purrfect Pets. Leah stood behind the counter. She frowned.

His heart did a crazy leap in his chest at the sight of her. And damn if his first thought wasn't of kissing those sweet frowning lips. He spotted the desperate look in her eyes and decided instead of kissing her, he wanted to pull her against him, to let her lean on him.

Leah Reece needed someone to lean on. And as crazy, as utterly ridiculous, as it was, he wanted to be that person.

"You didn't have to come here."

"I know," he said. "I wanted to." The way he'd wanted to kiss her last night. The way he'd wanted to rid her of her clothes. His mind churned, and he realized he hadn't considered if coming here was right or wrong. He'd done it on impulse. Suddenly, noticing Leah wasn't standing alone, he nodded at the three women beside her.

Her posse of women, he thought. And they all looked willing to let Leah lean on them. But somehow he got the feeling she didn't regularly lean on anyone. One of the posse was a blonde, tall and attractive. One was an older, dark-haired woman, and the other was a redhead who barely looked legal, but dressed like she was.

Leah spoke up. "Austin, who is…just my neighbor, this is Sara, Evelyn, and Jamie." She waved her hand to each one as she spoke their names.

Just her neighbor? He pushed the thought aside to deal with later. More important matters warranted his attention. "What happened?"

"Nothing happened," Leah said.

"This happened!" The older woman pointed to a box on the counter. She shot him a quick look, pleading him to talk some sense into Leah. "Where I come from, when people send you bloody packages, it's not 'nothing.'"

Leah shook her head. "I panicked. After I calmed down, I realized the organs are either chicken or turkey. Someone probably bought them at the grocery store."

"I don't care if they belonged to Big Foot or where they bought them," Evelyn snapped. "They were put in a shoe box, had a threatening note on top, and were dropped off at our doorstep."

Austin stepped closer. "Where's the threatening note?"

Everyone looked at Leah.

"She has it," said Sara, the blonde, speaking for the first time.

Leah pulled the sticky note from her pocket and slapped it on the counter. "It's not really a threat."

Austin read the four words. *Don't piss me off.*

"Well, it's not a love letter," he told her.

"My words exactly," said Evelyn. "I like this guy. Where have you been hiding him?"

"He's just my neighbor," Leah repeated, and damn if it didn't hurt more the second time. Did she let any neighbor unhook her bra and jeans and…

"What's not to like? Except the black eye." The redhead shot him a look of interest.

One he wasn't even the slightest bit flattered by. She was way too young, and...*and didn't have dimples.* He pushed that thought aside.

"It was a stupid prank," Leah said.

"Sorry, but I agree with Evelyn. This is more than a prank." His mind started forming questions and he spouted them out. "When did it arrive? Did anyone see who dropped it off? Has anything similar to this ever happened before?"

"You sound like a cop," Redhead said. "I like cops. Is that how you got the black eye?"

"I'm not a cop," he said, but she was right, he was acting like one. He needed to watch himself. Then again, someone needed to figure out exactly what was happening before someone ended up hurt. Someone being Leah. "But we should all be thinking like one."

"I think we should be calling one," Evelyn said.

Austin looked from Evelyn to Leah. "She might have a point."

"Call them for what? To interrupt their donut time and have them tell me that they don't have time to be looking into dead cats? Been there, done that, got the T-shirt, and I'm not doing it again."

She stormed off into a back room, but not before he spotted the emotion in her eyes.

Evelyn looked at him and sighed. "I don't know what's going on. She's never been so unreasonable."

Austin heard Evelyn, but his mind was still digesting what Leah had said. "So this has happened before?" he asked the three women remaining.

"No," Evelyn said.

The blonde spoke up. "But Leah just said...or basically just said it has." Her gaze turned to Austin. "It's never happened here."

"No one ever told me getting bloody packages was involved in my internship," said the redhead.

"What's Leah hiding from us?" Evelyn glared toward the back where Leah had disappeared.

As eager as he was to find Leah, he guessed his best bet at getting information was from these three.

"When did this arrive?" he asked.

"Twenty minutes ago," Evelyn said. "Which means it's not too late to call the police."

He didn't want to tell her to do it. Something about Leah's tone earlier sent a warning straight to his gut. "Did someone deliver it? Who found it?" His gut said it was a big, bald guy. The two incidents had to be connected.

Jamie, the redhead, spoke up. "I saw the man who left it. He looked Hispanic, early thirties maybe; he tapped on the window and set the box down in front of the door. I thought it was kittens. Then I saw the blood."

Hispanic? "Was he tall, short, dark-skinned?" The thought that it might have been DeLuna had Austin's mind spinning.

She hesitated as to think. "Sort of tall, not as tall or as built as you." She smiled. "Not very dark-skinned. Just olive. Dark hair, but more brown than black." She lifted one shoulder as if proud of her description.

And damn if that description didn't match DeLuna to a T. Not that it didn't also describe half the Hispanics out there. "You didn't recognize him, then?"

"No," she said.

Have you met Leah's piece of shit half brother? What he wouldn't give for a picture of DeLuna right now. "Would you recognize this man if you saw him again, or saw a picture?"

"Maybe."

Could he show her DeLuna's picture without Leah finding

out? He started formulating a plan. "You know, I have a friend who's a detective. Can you give me your number? He might want to talk to you."

"Of course you can have my number." She shot him a sultry look. He saw Evelyn rolling her eyes.

"So do you think this detective will take care of everything?" Sara asked.

"I don't know. I'm not even sure if he'll look into it. Leah may need to make an official report."

"And it appears that we have about a snowball's chance in hell of that happening," Evelyn said. "I really don't understand what's gotten into that girl. She's been in a frenzy these last few days. Worried about her brother and then her place is broken into." She looked at Austin. "Maybe you could talk some sense into her?"

"I don't know," he said. "We aren't really—"

"Don't lie to me. You were the first person she called. And there was enough heat in the look you two gave each other to deep-fry a chicken."

"I thought he was just her neighbor." The redhead sounded upset.

"And it wasn't too long ago you thought Santa was real, child." Evelyn looked at Austin and pointed to the back. "She's in her office, first left and last door on the right. See if you can make her see reason."

Austin got to her office door. It stood ajar. She was on the phone. Pausing, he stopped to listen.

CHAPTER EIGHTEEN

"WHY THE HELL would Rafael send you a dead chicken?" Luis asked Leah.

"It wasn't a whole chicken." *Which made it worse.* Leah closed her eyes. Why had he done it? To scare her. To remind her that he or his dear friend Cruz had killed her cat. But more important was why this had all started. What did Rafael want with Luis?

"What have you done, Luis?" She gripped the phone.

"I haven't done shit," Luis answered.

"You saw Cruz. Why did you see him?"

"I told you I accidentally ran into him," Luis barked. "Jeezus, Sis, get off your high horse, would ya?"

"I'm not on my high horse."

"The hell you're not. What if I was accusing you of something you didn't do? How would you feel?"

"There has to be a reason this is happening, and it has to do with you seeing Cruz."

"I admit your house getting broken into and you getting dead chickens is weird, especially after Rafael called you. But I swear I'm telling the truth. I saw the guy on the street and spent less than three minutes talking. But what I don't understand is why you hate that guy so much."

"Because he nearly raped me! Because—" Damn, she wanted to pull those words back into her mouth.

"He did what?" Luis's tone turned dead serious.

Leah dropped her chin on her chest. She'd never told Luis. Why should she? He'd been too young and…she'd wanted to shelter him from…from more ugliness. He hardly even remembered their mom. And when he got old enough to ask about their father, she'd told him he'd died right after he was born. Sure, when Rafael showed up in all his glory, a few months after she'd seen her dad's obituary, Luis learned Leah had lied to him.

He'd been eleven and pissed that she'd robbed him of a chance to meet his dad. Leah hadn't held back then. It was the only time Leah remembered really losing her temper with her brother. *He didn't want us, Luis. Why would you want him?*

Absence makes the heart grow fonder. Her mother's words vibrated through her head. It had been seven years since her mother's death, and her father hadn't bothered to come to see them. Absence didn't make the heart grow fonder; people chose to be absent when they didn't care.

"When did Cruz do this?" Luis asked, dragging her from the past.

Leah took a deep breath. "A long time ago. Forget about it."

"Like you've forgotten."

Actually, his killing Snowball had been his most unforgettable crime. She hadn't told Luis that, either. He'd loved that cat.

"Luis, I'm worried about you. If you're into something illegal, you have to stop."

"Illegal? Give me some goddamn credit. Once. Just once

I almost did something, but I didn't even do it. And right now the only illegal thing I want to do is beat the shit out of Cruz. I friggin' can't believe you didn't tell me this."

"Luis, what happened isn't important. I'm worried about you now. Promise me you won't go to your place for a while?"

"I can't crash at Cassandra's place much longer. She's gonna think I'm mooching off of her."

"If it's a problem, I'll send you a couple hundred dollars and you can get one of those weekly hotels."

"No, I can stay here," he muttered.

She paused and her brother's earlier words repeated in her head. "So it's a girl you're staying with? You didn't tell me it was a girl."

"I didn't tell you? Oh, crap, how could I not tell you? Oh, I know, it's because I take after my damn sister, who freaking doesn't tell me shit! Like about some asshole raping you."

"I said he tried to rape me. He didn't do it. And you were too young. And I'm telling you everything now," she said.

"I swear to God, Leah, if I see Cruz again I'm knocking his teeth down his throat." Even though he was angry, she heard the brotherly love in his voice.

"Look, I appreciate you wanting to defend me. But that happened years ago, so leave it alone." There was a pause. Deciding to change the subject she asked, "Are you coming up Sunday?" He usually came up every other weekend. It wasn't enough for her, but it seemed plenty of family time for him.

"I don't know, if I don't have too much make-up work," he said.

I told you that you shouldn't have skipped classes. She bit her tongue to keep from reprimanding him. "Are you going to bring your girlfriend...Cassandra?"

"The last time I introduced you to a girlfriend, you asked her if she was on the pill."

"Well, the question seemed appropriate since you were barely eighteen and I walked in and found you two screwing on my sofa." Leah snatched her stress ball from her desk and squeezed.

"You weren't supposed to be home until a day later. Besides, I thought you should have been happy we didn't use your bed."

"Seriously?" she asked. "The bed had sheets and I could have changed those. I couldn't sit on that sofa for a month."

He moaned, reminding her of the disgruntled teenager he'd been not so long ago. "Look, I need to run. I'll call later about this weekend. And for God's sake, be careful. If you see hide or hair of Cruz or Rafael, call the police. Then call me. I swear to God, Sis, I won't let either of them lay a hand on you. I'll kill 'em."

"You're not going to kill anyone!" she said. "But I love you for wanting to protect me."

They hung up, and she must have heard or felt something. She turned and saw the door slightly ajar.

Austin Brookshire stood there. Frowning.

Friggin' great. How much of her conversation had he been privy to?

Austin took a deep breath, hoping to come off calm, but calm was the last thing he felt. Someone had tried to rape her and she thought this was the same person breaking into her apartment and sending her bloody packages, and she wasn't calling the police?

She wasn't doing shit but waiting for him to strike again? And she hadn't even told him.

He stepped inside the office and closed the door. The

click of the door shutting seemed too loud. She stood from her chair and again he noticed how small she looked. Vulnerable. Fragile, almost. And damn if he didn't want to volunteer to take care of her.

"Didn't anyone ever teach you that eavesdropping is rude?" she said with bravado. But the courage in her voice was all bluff. Odd how he could read her so well.

He stepped closer. "I didn't exactly have the proper upbringing, remember?"

The words no longer slid off his tongue when he realized this was the first time he could remember making light of his past. And for some reason that seemed important.

"Well, someone should have enlightened you." She wasn't backing off.

He shifted his gaze. The office was small. Feminine and filled with cat paraphernalia. Her scent of waffle cones hung in the air. He inched forward another step. With her standing less than a foot from him, he could see the fear in her eyes.

"What's going on, Leah?"

She had to tilt her chin to look him in the eyes.

She opened her mouth, and he saw in her expression that she was going to lie to him.

"The truth," he insisted.

She closed her mouth almost as if reconsidering. "It's complicated."

Slowly, he reached out and put his hands on her shoulders and pulled her against him.

He felt her give, and she rested her forehead on the center of his chest. She needed someone to lean on, and damn was he glad he'd come here.

He dropped his chin down and buried his face into her soft brown hair and wrapped his arms around her back. Inhaling her scent, he held her for several seconds. Then he inched back and with one hand gently raised her chin to look at him.

"Let me help uncomplicate it," he said. "I'm good at that."

As if realizing how close they stood, she pulled back. Her eyes had a watery sheen to them.

"Are you sure?" she asked. "Because I've only known you a few days and"—she waved a hand between them—"this feels complicated."

Damn if he didn't agree with her. This, whatever this was, felt complicated. But now wasn't the time to consider that. "Who's Cruz?"

"This is something I have to deal with."

"Why?"

Her shoulders slumped. "He's someone I knew a long time ago. And he's not a nice person. My brother ran into him, and since then everything's gone crazy."

"Ran into him where? San Antonio, isn't that where you said he was?"

She shook her head as if his questions were unimportant, but the more information Austin could get the better he'd be.

"No. He ran into him in Austin, where he lives."

"But he's in San Antonio?" For some reason that seemed to be important, as if it mattered, but he couldn't put his finger on the reason.

Leah brushed a strand of her hair back. "He's back now."

She was telling the truth, but only part of it. "Is Cruz this asshole's last name?"

She frowned. "It's not important."

That pushed his button and his gut clenched. "He tried to rape you and you say it's not important."

"That was years ago."

"But it was yesterday that your apartment was broken

into, and less than an hour ago someone sent you a pack of chicken guts. And it doesn't sound like this is the first time you've gotten a less than desirable delivery, either."

A knock sounded at the door. Leah took a step back, then called out, "Come in."

Evelyn poked her head in. "Our appointments are showing up."

Leah nodded. "Just put them in rooms, I'll be right out."

Evelyn hesitated. "Are we calling the police?"

"No." Leah said. "No one was hurt. And I don't want to scare off business."

Evelyn frowned at him. "And I thought you had enough charm to make her see reason."

"She's not so easy to charm," he said.

Leah huffed and walked out.

Evelyn walked in and leaned closer. "Can I trust you to look after her?"

He nodded.

She let go of another sigh. "Do you not find it suspicious that she doesn't want to call the police? First with her place and then this?"

Yeah, I do. "Some people don't trust them," he said. But there was usually a reason. And he needed to figure out why.

He checked to see if Leah was out of earshot. "Where's the package?"

She quirked an eyebrow. "It's up front behind the counter. Why?"

"Can I...take it with me? And the note, if it's still up there."

She studied him. "You know, Jamie's right. You act like a cop."

"Not a cop," he said. "But I know a few."

She tightened her brows, still looking slightly suspicious.

"Well, I was going to make giblet gravy with it," she teased, "but sure, take it."

"Evelyn!" Jamie screamed out.

"What the hell is it this time?" the older woman snapped, and they both took off toward the front.

Jamie stood behind the counter, a disgusted look on her face and pointing downward. He and Evelyn moved closer.

"Stop him," Austin snapped, when he spotted the big orange and white cat, even bigger than Leah's Big Orange. The cat had his face buried in the shoe box on the floor, eating the evidence.

"That's just gross!" Jamie said.

Roberto went back to work, but he kept thinking about Brad. What was the guy up to? Then Roberto thought about his promise to Brad: to call Sandy. Roberto really didn't want to do that, but he was going to...just as soon as he decided what to tell her. She was going to be pissed. The message from Brad would bring on more questions than answers. And he didn't have answers.

When he wasn't worrying about that, he was thinking about Sara and that damn romance novel. It had pulled him in about as quickly as Sara had. The author had used suspense, some humor, and lots of steamy parts to keep the reader turning pages. And while he'd been turning pages, he wasn't dwelling on his own problems.

Not that reading was as good as talking to Sara. But it was less complicated. When he finished a book, it was finished. Every time he spoke with Sara, he felt as if he owed her something. A promise of them getting together, or an excuse of why he couldn't.

He didn't need to be in debt to anyone. He sure as hell didn't need anyone counting on him.

After about an hour of taping Sheetrock, he decided to take the rest of the day off. Considering he had to meet Cruz at midnight, he could claim he needed time to get his shit ready.

He packed up and started out. One of Cruz's overseers saw him walk out. "Where you think you're going?"

"I'm taking the afternoon off. I'm doing some overtime work for Cruz tonight."

"Whatcha doing for him?" the guy asked.

"Whatever Cruz needs me to do." He walked off.

He climbed on his bike, but instead of heading back to his apartment, he headed toward Brad's home. He might as well get this over with.

Holding the box carefully in one spot, so as not to disturb any prints, he placed it on the floorboard. Once he crawled back behind the wheel, he dialed Tyler.

"I got something else I want checked out for prints. Can you send Nance back this way?"

"Another gun?" Tyler asked.

"No. A shoe box with chicken parts, or it had chicken parts in it."

Silence crawled into the line, and he realized how crazy that sounded.

Tyler spoke up. "Why is it that I'm not nearly as shocked as I should be? I swear, you are always getting yourself into more shit."

"What shit?" Dallas's voice echoed in the background.

"Let me put you on speaker; Dallas just walked in and he has to hear this one from you. Oh, by the way, who was it that really gave you the black eye, the blonde or Leah Reece?" Tyler laughed. "Sounds like things are really getting interesting there."

So Nance was running his mouth. "Look, I'm not joking. This is serious," Austin bit out. The line clicked and he knew he was on speaker.

"What do you have this time?" Dallas asked.

"Leah was delivered a bloody shoe box with chicken parts in it and a threatening note. But a cat ate the parts." He shuddered remembering, too.

"Voodoo?" Dallas asked.

"No, just a threat. She thinks it's from a guy who almost raped her a while back. All the name I could get from her was Cruz. I don't know if that's a nickname or a last name. Oh, and she thinks it has something to do with her brother meeting up with this guy."

"So she knows you're looking for her brother?" Dallas questioned.

"Not DeLuna, her younger brother." Austin started his truck, giving Leah's vet office one last look. "And do me a favor, Tyler, do a good check into Luis Reece. I want to know everything."

"Will do," Tyler said.

"Austin," Dallas said, and then paused. "Just so I'm clear. Do you think this . . . the break-in and now this bloody package has anything to do with DeLuna?"

"I was about to ask the same question," Tyler replied.

Austin realized the problem his partners were having. His interest in Leah had gone beyond his need to get DeLuna. And it was a real problem his conscience said, but his conscience could just go to hell. Keeping Leah safe was his main concern.

"It could be," Austin said. "Someone at Leah's office saw the guy dropping off the shoe box. Latin, not quite six feet, dark hair, medium build, light olive skin. You know who that sounds like?"

"Me and about fifty percent of the Latin population," Tyler said. "That's not enough to—"

"Fine, it's a long shot. But we could send someone up here and show her a photo lineup."

Dallas spoke up. "I'll look into it."

But his tone said he thought Austin was getting carried away.

"Just do it!" But damn, his feelings for Leah were nothing more than him being a man and her being a woman. A decent woman who stirred up his protect-and-serve gene that had landed him as a cop.

So what if he wasn't a hundred percent about DeLuna being involved.

Wanting to help someone didn't mean anything. Maybe it was just about him being a decent human being and not wanting something bad to happen to someone who didn't deserve it. Wasn't that part of what Dallas had set out to do in the first place with opening the detective agency? To help people?

"Look, Austin," Dallas stated. "I just—"

"I shouldn't have to explain myself. I want Nance to come pick this up and have it checked. And don't just send it to Tony. Send it to Logan at Lab, Inc. I heard he's doing some initial fingerprinting for a couple of the detectives in Houston. If he gets a print, then send it to Tony and beg him to run it. But I don't want it to get lost in their backlogged cases."

"Logan charges an arm and a leg to check for prints. Blood is his specialty," Dallas said.

"Damn it, have I questioned how you guys want to run a case? If it's a friggin' problem, I'll pay for it myself. Just do it."

His outburst warranted him nothing but silence from his two partners. And he knew the reason for it, too. This wasn't like him. He was a damn good detective, and part of the reason he was good was because he always kept his perspective, never let things get under his skin. It was a job. The only case that got under his skin was finding DeLuna. Part of him felt as if he was holding his breath waiting to prove to the doubters that he hadn't followed in his parents' footsteps.

Realizing he was having a mental conversation with himself while his two partners waited, he said, "Have Nance call me and let me know exactly when he'll arrive. I've got some things I have to do."

"Okay," Dallas said. "And, Austin, don't get in too deep."

Tyler broke in, "If you don't know exactly what Dallas means by that, he's saying don't sleep with her."

"I'm not sleeping with her!"

"Tell me you haven't even thought about sleeping with her and I'll feel a hell of a lot better," Tyler said.

"Tell Nance to call me." Austin hung up. Then remembering something he wanted to pick up for Leah, he turned his truck toward Main Street.

Leah with her I-don't-like-gifts attitude was probably going to get pissed, but she'd just have to get over it.

CHAPTER NINETEEN

Even with the hum of his bike beneath him, Roberto felt his phone vibrate. He suspected it was Austin again. He'd left a message wanting to know if there was a Cruz in DeLuna's operation. Roberto needed to call him back, but he had a bad feeling. A feeling like Austin or one of the other guys would try to step in. He was getting close and didn't want their impatience ruining anything.

He pulled his bike in front of Brad's house—a nice home in a decent neighborhood, but nothing too showy. And considering Brad's salary, he could have afforded better. But Roberto remembered Brad saying they were putting money away to pay for his girls' college funds.

Cutting off his motor, he sat there for a second. He'd been here once, but had waited in the car while Brad ran in to get the phone he'd left behind. *Come in and meet my girls,* Brad had offered. He hadn't. He hadn't wanted to. Hell, he'd turned down at least a dozen dinner invitations from the man, too.

From the beginning, Roberto had worked to keep their budding friendship from going anywhere. Worked at keeping Brad at a distance. Apparently, all his efforts were in vain, because like it or not, he actually cared what happened to the big guy. He shouldn't, but he did.

He got off his bike and walked up to the door. Knocking, he hoped she wasn't home. He could say he tried and have a clean conscience. His hope fell flat when footsteps sounded from behind the door.

The door opened. Seeing Sandy punched him in the gut. She looked emotionally spent. Tears glistened in her eyes.

"You got news?" She swung open the door.

He followed her inside, but when she motioned to the sofa, he shook his head. "I need to run. Brad called and—"

"He called you? He's okay?" She pressed her hand over her mouth and her eyes grew wetter. "Where is he? Why hasn't he called me?"

Roberto opened his mouth to explain and didn't have a clue what to say. Finally, he went with the truth. "Look, Sandy, I don't know what's going on. All I know is he called and he asked me to tell you that he was okay."

She inhaled a shaky breath. "Did my brother send you here? Is this all a lie?"

"No. I swear."

"But you work for him?"

"I do, but... your brother doesn't know I'm here, or that Brad called me. And if you don't mind, I'd like to keep it that way."

She nodded. "I just don't understand. Why... what's going on that he can't tell me?"

He shrugged. "I don't know." He wondered what all Sandy knew about her brother's illegal operations. She had some knowledge because she'd told him she knew Cruz would be furious if she called the cops. But did she know he killed people, that his operation turned innocent young girls like her daughters into addicts?

"Is it another woman?" she asked.

Roberto shook his head. "I'd be stunned if that was it. He's all about you and the kids." And that was probably why Roberto liked Brad, too. He was decent.

She shook her head as if she believed that. "He's alive. I guess I should take comfort in that."

"Yes." He paused. "I should go," he said.

She walked him to the door. As he drove his bike away, he hoped Brad stayed alive. And while Roberto couldn't be certain, he had a feeling that after tonight, after getting his hands dirty in Cruz's little operation, he'd learn something about the missing boss.

He just hoped he didn't end up missing right alongside Brad.

That afternoon, Leah parked in her spot and eyed Austin's truck. She remembered how good it had been to lean on him today. To have someone to hold her for just a few seconds in a melt-down moment. Calling him had been a huge mistake, one she wouldn't have made if she hadn't gotten the damn package. Sure, calling him had been the easiest way to make sure her cats were okay. But if she hadn't panicked, she'd have realized the organs in the box weren't feline. She should have calmly left the office, driven home, and checked on her cats herself.

What was wrong with her? She wasn't accustomed to relying on anyone. Since her divorce, she'd decided that making it solo was her best course of action. And she hadn't been tempted to stray from it.

Until now.

Until Austin.

He tempted her. Tempted her in every way possible, too. She wanted to flirt with him, to laugh with him. To let down her guard and just have fun. Even worse, she wanted to confide in him. She wanted him to confide in her. This afternoon, she kept thinking about what he'd said about his mom.

God that must have hurt. Who was she kidding, she knew exactly how that felt.

Oh, Lordy, but she wanted to lean on him. It felt so good that few seconds she'd allowed herself to fall against him and let him hold her. As if the weight of her problems was being supported by someone other than herself.

But that wasn't all she wanted. Hell, she'd admit it. She wanted to have sex with him—sweaty, lusty, in-the-dark, get-naked sex.

Closing her eyes, she bounced her head on the headrest. Maybe it was time she pulled out the ol' battery-operated boyfriend from her underwear drawer. How long had it been since she'd taken a bubble bath, lit a candle, and treated herself?

A long time.

But for a good reason.

Solo sex was like eating fat-free, sugar-free chocolate. It might cut the craving for five minutes, but it was never truly satisfying.

Letting go of a deep sigh, she realized how crazy this was. She had big problems and instead of trying to figure out one of those, she was thinking about sex.

What the hell was wrong with her?

Austin, crouched down in front of Leah's door, was still screwing in the new doorknob when he heard the elevator ding. He glanced back. Nance had come and gone, but it was about time for Leah.

She stepped out into the hall, a bottle of wine in her hands, and came to an abrupt stop when she saw him.

She looked tired. And stressed.

Unhappy.

He wished he understood exactly what was going on so he could help her.

"What are you doing?" she asked.

"Replacing your doorknob." He stood and slipped the screwdriver into his back pocket. His shirt fell open. It had gotten warm and he'd unbuttoned it.

Her gaze lowered to his bare chest with a sweet female type of interest. Not the hot come-and-get-me looks some women used to get a man's attention, but he saw enough interest to feel a sense of pride.

She shook her head and seemed to struggle to move her gaze up. "Why are you replacing—"

"I messed it up when I was getting in earlier. So I decided to replace it." When her gaze lowered to his chest again and she frowned, he started buttoning his shirt.

"When you what?" She watched the shirt close up.

"Remember, you told me to break it in? To check on your cats? I tried to pick the lock, but I messed it up." A complete lie, but it sounded good.

"Oh. I forgot that." She closed her eyes.

"It's practically done, replacing it, that is. I need to secure a few things on the inside and you'll be in working order." And a hell of a lot safer. He couldn't even break in anymore—if he didn't have his own key, that is.

He glanced at the wine. "Did you buy us some more wine? Someone recommended a Chinese place down the street and they deliver. I thought I could—"

"I don't eat Chinese. And the wine...It's not...for us. I mean, it's yours. It's the one I bought to replace the one you gave me." She held it out.

He didn't take it. Instead, he tucked his thumbs into his

pockets. "Didn't I help you drink that bottle? I say we share this one."

"And I say I've had two headaches in the last two days, and I need a break."

"No problem. Just one glass, and we don't have to do Chinese. But why don't you like Chinese? Everyone likes Chinese."

"Not everyone. It's greasy, it's salty, and it doesn't have cheese in it."

"Okay, how about Italian, and I'll limit you to one glass of wine?" A meow sounded behind the door. Austin's gut tightened. He'd spent the last hour inside her apartment, removing the old doorknob and putting in the new one while keeping an eye out for the felines. Twice, he literally ran from the apartment. Only his pride and concern for Leah's safety had driven him to finish the job.

"I don't think so." She pulled the wine back to her side. "Sounds like I'm wanted inside."

He opened the door and let her in first, then he followed. Big Orange was on the arm of the sofa. Blacky, the one who liked to hiss, was a foot away from the door, but was too busy brushing up against Leah's leg to care about Austin. Thankfully, the gray hair ball–hacker and the super-skittish gray cat hadn't come out at all today. And that was fine with him.

She scooped up the black cat and held it against her breasts. His heart raced. Didn't she know what those claws could do to the tender skin of a breast?

"Did you miss me?" Leah cooed.

At the sound of her voice, the two other cats came rushing out of the room.

Oh, shit!

He turned and stared at the door. The scars under his arm and behind his ear itched like the devil.

"Hey, babies," she said, and he heard movement, and then the sigh of someone sitting on the sofa sounded in the room.

Glancing over his shoulder, he spotted her with four cats practically in her lap.

She met his gaze. "They demand attention after I've been gone all day."

"I can see that." He tried to smile, but damn it, part of him wanted to rush over there and protect her from the evil little gremlins. The other part wanted to run for his own life.

"Of course, they smell the other cats on me and are probably jealous."

"Probably," he said. He was feeling perturbed himself at the warm welcome they got considering he hadn't even gotten a smile. Especially considering he'd put his life in danger to replace the locks with cats around.

"Did you see Spooky while you were at the office?" she asked.

"Spooky?"

"The big beautiful orange tabby."

"Yeah, I spotted him." He almost mentioned the evidence the feline had eaten, but decided Leah didn't need to be reminded about that.

"He's a sweet cat."

"Yeah, I got that," he lied.

Watching them paw at her, he recalled Zoe, Tyler's wife's, words, *Have you ever seen Lucky try to bite or hurt any of us? Your fear is totally unfounded. Whatever happened to you when you were young has screwed up your judgment. If you spent a few minutes every day petting him…*

Like he'd have done that. And damn it, he knew his fear seemed unfounded to others. But it wasn't to him. He'd been attacked by a cat. Had umpteen stitches thanks to that damn feline. Cats could hurt you. Just because no one else seemed to know it, or believed it could happen, it didn't change the facts.

His gaze fell on Leah, looking perfectly content, looking...real and beautiful.

Tell me you haven't even thought about sleeping with her and I'll feel a hell of a lot better. Tyler's words played across his mind like a warning.

He should finish securing the locks and be on his way.

"What?" she asked, as if questioning his stare.

"You like grilled cheese?"

"Huh?"

"I make a killer grilled cheese. To be fair, it's sort of grilled bacon and cheese on sourdough bread. But it's good. Really good. And while it wouldn't seem like it, it goes great with a good Cab." When she frowned, he said, "One glass. Come on. You've had a hard day."

He saw her spot the bag from the hardware store, and she stood up. "How much did this cost me?"

"I told you, I broke yours, so I'm replacing it."

"I don't think so. And besides, I didn't have those bolt locks."

"But you need them," he said.

She frowned. "Is the receipt in the bag?" She took a step, and he went into action. He dove for the bag as she rushed forward.

He got to it first. Once he had it in his hands, he rolled over and then sat up. Waving the bag at her as if tempting her to come and get it. She was on her knees and she frowned at him.

"Give it to me." She held out her hand.

"I broke it, I replace it. That's the rules. Besides, I found it on clearance."

She knee-walked closer and reached for the bag. He

caught her hand. "You are one difficult woman." Albeit a predictable one. He'd already planned for this.

"You are one pushy man," she said. Both on her living room floor, they were close, but not nearly as close as he would have liked.

He smiled and she returned the favor. Her eyes twinkled. Her dimples winked. Damn, it was fun being with her, but the humor twinkling in her eyes faded too quickly.

"Why are you doing this?" she asked.

"Why am I doing what?"

"All of this. You're too nice. I don't trust nice people," she said.

He laughed. "I thought I was pushy?"

"You're pushy nice," she answered. "So answer my question. Why are you doing this?"

"Because you seem like a nice person and because I want to help you." And it was the truth.

"I don't need help, Austin. I can take care of myself. I know I called you today and I shouldn't have, I..." She stopped talking. "Give me the receipt."

Still holding her hand in his, he ran his thumb over her wrist. Her gaze met his. Her tongue came out and swept across her bottom lip. She leaned in. Her sweet mouth came closer as if to kiss him. And damn if he was going to stop it.

But before her lips touched his, she snagged the bag from him and bolted up.

"That was dirty," he said. "You tricked me."

She grinned, a little victory in her step. Then she plopped down and pulled out the receipt.

She stared at it and then looked at him. "That's all it cost? The doorknob and the extra locks?"

"Yeah, it's all there. I told you they were on clearance."

In truth, the piece of junk knob and lock she'd bought with that receipt were hidden under the seat in the truck.

"I can handle this," she said. "I thought it was going to be five times this."

"Fine." He frowned at her. "Be difficult." He got to his feet and went back to the lock to finish tightening the last screws.

He felt her staring at him.

"So you're a handyman on top of being a one-time bouncer, and you cook, and you're a stock investor/financial planner?" she asked.

"I'm multitalented," he said.

"I bet you change your own oil in your truck, too?"

"I do," he said. "Although, I don't do plumbing. I can't even unstop a toilet." He suddenly remembered the cats and swerved around to see where they were. One was on the chair stationed beside the sofa, one sat on the coffee table, and the two others sat in dining room chairs. All staring at him.

His gaze found Leah again. She picked up the water gun that he'd brought here yesterday to protect himself from the cats and turned it in her hand as if needing something to do. "Where did you learn to do all this . . . stuff? Did you have a foster dad who taught you?"

He started tightening the screws again. Even having told her about his childhood, his first instinct was to back away from the conversation. "No. I pretty much taught myself." He pulled at the bolt to see if it was solid. It was.

"What was it like?" she asked. "Being in foster care? Was it . . . terrible?"

"I imagine it's not much worse than losing your mom."

"It hurts worse when . . . people just walk away." There was so much emotion in her voice that he knew she wasn't just talking about him.

He looked back, expecting to see the emotion in her expression, but it still punched him in the gut.

She kept turning the gun in her hand. "I know because my father didn't die until I was eighteen. He came to my mom's funeral, then…then he left and I never saw him again. And that hurt, it hurt more than losing my mom." She paused. "And it shouldn't have. Because I didn't love him and I knew he didn't love me and Luis. But it still hurt."

"I'm sorry." He stood, then walked to where she sat and eased down beside her.

She shook her head. "I'm sorry for you. I can't imagine what it would have been like if Luis and I hadn't had my aunt."

He brushed a long strand of hair from her cheek. "You would have survived. We're survivors."

"Yeah." She nodded. "We are, aren't we?"

He inhaled and he knew it wasn't smart, but he leaned in for a kiss. Just a kiss. He wouldn't sleep with her, but how bad was a kiss?

CHAPTER TWENTY

AUSTIN'S LIPS ALMOST touched hers, when she shot him. Right in the face with the water gun. Then she laughed and bolted up.

"Real funny." He wiped the water from his face.

"Okay, here's the deal," she said. "I'll try your bacon grilled cheese sandwich, and I'll have one"—she held up her index finger—"*one* glass of wine. But no . . . no hanky-panky."

"Hanky-panky?" He smiled. "Is that another of your aunt's sayings?"

She nodded. "She was quite colorful with her language and had this witty sense of humor that could have sent the pope into a fit of giggles."

"Then you take after her," he said.

Leah smiled. "I'll take that as a compliment."

"It was meant as one." He wiped his face again of the remaining water droplets and stood up. "Okay, I'll go to my place and start slaving over a hot stove to cook you dinner."

"You do that. I've got to feed my pack, change the litter box, and freshen up. I'll be over with the wine in about forty-five minutes."

"Sounds like a plan." He stared at her and the moment just felt so right. "I like you, Leah Reece."

She bit down on her lip and aimed the water gun at him, looking playful, looking happy, and looking so damn adorable it almost hurt to watch her.

"Behave." She tilted up the pistol and blew on the barrel.

"That's not hanky-panky. It's just the truth." He walked to the door. She followed him. When he walked out, he turned around to look at her standing in the doorway.

"Oh, here. Your new key for the door." He'd kept one for himself. He pulled it out of his pocket and dropped it in her hand, and as his fingers brushed her palm he was zapped by the sweetness of that brief touch.

"See you." But he didn't step back. He wanted to kiss her so badly his chest hurt.

She nodded. "Go."

He turned, opened his apartment door, and had one foot inside when he felt the spray of water hit the back of his head.

Laughing, he turned to give her a little playful hell, but her door slammed shut. He heard her laughter from the other side. And damn if it wasn't a beautiful sound.

He stood there a few seconds, his chest swelling with something he hadn't felt in a long time. Happiness. Just plain ol' happiness. As if things in life were better than they'd been in . . . in forever.

She—Leah Reece—made him happy.

But one question hit and hit hard. Why the hell did she have to be DeLuna's sister?

Austin took a quick shower and was frying the bacon when his cell rang. He flipped the strip of meat and went to grab the phone. His gut feared it was Leah canceling. She'd let down her guard more than ever before, and he worried she'd realize it and try to rein herself back in.

He didn't want the reined-in Leah, he wanted the real one.

He checked the number and smiled when he saw it was Tyler.

"Yeah," he answered.

"I ran a search on anything and everything about Luis Reece. There's nothing. The kid's clean. Hell, I even had a professor friend who works at the college he attends look into him, and he's a good student."

"Okay. Did Nance deliver the package?"

"He dropped it straight off at Logan's lab."

"Good." Austin moved back into the kitchen to watch the bacon. "Have you heard from Roberto?"

"No, and I left a message this afternoon. Dallas wants me to come out and ask him about the Austin and San Antonio deals getting busted. See if he'll come clean."

"Shit! That's it." Austin set his fork down.

"What's it?"

"Luis Reece. He lives in Austin and he just took a trip to San Antonio. And I'm pretty damn sure he was there when the deal went down."

Tyler paused. "You think the kid is involved with the drug deals?"

"Yeah." And that's what Leah thought. He knew it.

"I don't know," Tyler said. "The kid reads clean."

"Or maybe he just hasn't been caught yet." The realization of how Leah would feel if her brother got caught up in something illegal had him hoping he was wrong. But wasn't it too much of a coincidence?

"So you're thinking that the break-in to her apartment and the bloody shoe box are also related to DeLuna?"

"It would seem that way." He listened to bacon sizzle and

pop. "Oh, hell, I don't know. I'm just trying to put the pieces together."

"Well, keep trying; generally they fall together sooner or later."

"Yeah." He paused. "See if you can find out if there's anyone who has ever worked for DeLuna named Cruz. It could be a last name or a nickname. I don't know."

"And this is the guy you think tried to rape Leah Reece?"

"Yeah." Austin frowned, realizing he liked it better when he felt Leah's issues weren't DeLuna related.

"What's your gut say? Do you think she knows where DeLuna is?"

"I don't think so. But...she's secretive." Austin recalled her confession about her father. He also recalled that he hadn't pressed her to get more information. If he'd prodded her, she might have told him about DeLuna.

Why the hell hadn't he tried? The answer rolled over him. Because he'd wanted to console her, not interrogate her. But now to get her back to talking about that could be difficult.

"Shit!" he muttered, realizing he'd screwed up.

"Shit what?" Tyler asked.

"Just shit," Austin said.

"Well, if you're in a bad mood now, I'm about to make it a lot worse."

"What?" he snapped.

"Don't be mad at Ellen. It wasn't her fault."

"What wasn't her fault?" Austin couldn't think of one thing Ellen could have done to make him mad. He liked their receptionist. And if he had a problem with her, he'd probably have to go through Rick, her new husband, who worshipped the floor the woman walked on.

"Your...Ms. Adams—"

"Candy Adams?" His stomach knotted. Damn. He wasn't

used to that name coming up in conversations. He worked too hard all his friggin' life to forget it.

"Yeah, she's been dropping by the office every day looking for you."

"Call the friggin' police. I told her to get lost."

"Look, she hasn't done anything wrong. Just asked for you. She's been polite and seems harmless. But this afternoon, she dropped by again. Ellen came back to ask me what to do. When she went back out there to nicely ask her to leave, Ms. Adams was sitting at Ellen's computer. Ellen had the address book open on her computer because she was going to call you and let you know that Logan at Lab, Inc. and...Look, there's a good chance she got your phone number and address."

"Oh, that's just fucking great!" Austin bellowed.

"Ellen feels terrible."

"Fuck," he gritted out again.

Leah grabbed the wine and stood at her unopened door with all the new, fancy clearance-priced locks that her sexy neighbor had put on. It was crazy. She must be losing it. Here she was going to his apartment for dinner, feeling plumb giddy about it, and yet, yet...she had so many problems that she had no right to be giddy about anything.

Something was going on with Rafael and Luis. Even if Luis was telling the truth and nothing had gone down, Rafael was up to no good. And his no good was bad.

She went back to the sofa, dropped the wine on the coffee table, and reached for the phone in her pocket to call Austin and beg off. She had her finger on the call button and... paused.

Was there anything she could do tonight besides worry? She could call Luis and beg him to come clean...again. But their last conversation convinced her he wasn't lying. That made the situation feel even worse. How could she fix something that was nothing more than a fabrication in Rafael's mind?

She sighed. Calling Luis wouldn't do any good. He'd promised to stay with his girlfriend and not go home. Sunday when he came to visit, they'd have a long talk and maybe figure out what was really happening. But tonight...?

Staying home, fretting, wouldn't solve anything. She might as well go eat a grilled sandwich, drink one glass of wine, and let herself forget she had so many problems. Not that she could forget to the point that she might...do something she would regret.

Okay, she was going to dinner, going to enjoy dinner, but she had rules. No kissing. No more spilling her guts to him. No more...She recalled the electrical feeling she'd gotten when he'd passed her the key. No more touching. And absolutely no sex.

She snagged the bottle of wine, started out, then swung back. Smiling, she grabbed the water gun. She might need it.

Austin paused before answering the knock. He pushed a palm over his face hoping to wipe the scowl from his expression.

He opened the door. "Come in. The sandwiches are almost done."

She glanced at his face, and he worried he hadn't chased away his scowl. She walked past him, and he got a sniff of waffle cones again.

"It smells good."

"So do you," he said, not thinking.

She quirked an eyebrow at him as if to remind him of the no hanky-panky rule. Little did she know, she didn't have to remind him. He'd already given himself a good swift kick in the ass.

"I brought the wine." She held up the bottle.

"Great." He took the wine and saw the water gun in her other hand. And just like that, he remembered he hadn't put away his Glock. *Shit!* That could cause questions.

As he walked past the dining room table, adjacent to the kitchen, he saw the gun on the table.

He looked back at her following him. "Can you turn the sandwiches? While I open this?"

"You bet." The kitchen, nothing more than a nook, hardly held two people.

"Spatula's there." He pointed to the counter.

She grabbed the spatula and set her water gun down on the counter. "These look good."

"They are." He snagged the wine opener and then went to the table to open it, hoping to snag the gun and hide it.

With his back to her and praying she wasn't looking, he reached for the gun.

"I hope you're licensed to carry that."
Busted.

"Of course I am. Sorry. I meant to put it away earlier." He walked in the bedroom and put it in a drawer. He got a glimpse of himself in the dresser mirror, frowning. Inhaling, he went in to face the music.

He went straight to the wine and waited to see if this was going to cause a wrinkle. He didn't need any more wrinkles tonight.

"Why do you have a gun?" she asked. "Do you consider your job dangerous?"

"No," he lied. "But when traveling, I feel a little safer." He removed the cork and stepped into the kitchen to grab the glasses.

"I guess I should be fortunate you didn't have it on you when you found the guy robbing my place."

He pulled the glasses down. "If I'd had it, I'd been able to detain him and he'd be in jail." Moving to stand beside her, he said, "For a girl who doesn't like guns, you sure do like to use one." He tried to make his tone sound teasing, but he wasn't sure he'd pulled it off.

She looked down at the sandwiches, still cooking. "I think these are done."

"Perfect." And she was. She'd changed clothes. She wore a pair of light-colored jeans and a gray long-sleeve T-shirt with hearts printed on it. Her hair was the only thing he would change. She wore it up in a ponytail. He liked it loose.

"Do you want some water?" he asked.

"Sounds good. Where are your glasses?"

He motioned to the top cabinet. While she filled the glasses with ice and water, he set the table.

They didn't talk, and it felt awkward. Was she still thinking about the gun? He walked back into the kitchen, brought the skillet to the table, and put their sandwiches on the plates.

She set the glasses on the table and dropped into a chair. Then she met his eyes and neither of them said anything.

Finally, she spoke. "Is something wrong?"

"No. Why?"

She looked at him. "You're frowning."

"No, it's..." He didn't want to lie. "Sorry, I just got off the phone right before you came in." He remembered the chips and guacamole. Popping up, he grabbed the chips from the pantry, then snagged the prebought guacamole from the fridge.

"Bad news?" She reached for her wine as he opened the chips and pulled the top off the dip.

There wasn't a reason in the world for him to tell her the truth, but since he'd already told more than he normally told anyone, he decided what the hell. He dropped back in his chair.

"Yeah. The woman who...who dares to call herself my mom is trying to nettle her way into my life. She wants us to talk."

"Wow. That would be...tough. I guess. But it could be good."

"Not good." He held out the bag of chips. She took three and put them on her plate. He dropped a handful on his.

She picked up one chip. "What does she want to talk about?"

"Don't know, don't care," he said.

He cut his sandwich in half, and even with his anger popping off like fireworks in his chest, he realized this might be the opening he needed to move the conversation back to her dad.

"If your dad hadn't died, and he came to...talk, would you let him back into your life? Forgive him?" He handed her the knife to cut her own sandwich.

She cut her grilled cheese. What she didn't do was answer. She picked up half the sandwich, and cheese oozed out of the two slices of grilled bread.

"Man, this looks good." She took a bite and he watched her savor it. She closed her eyes and flicked her tongue out to catch a loose string of cheese.

"You like?" He smiled for real for the first time since she showed up.

She moaned. "Like? No. This is love. True love." She talked around the melted cheddar, crisp bacon, and good sour dough bread lightly toasted and cooked in real butter. "I think I just died and went to heaven. Of course, I think I just gained an inch around my hips, too."

He glanced under the table and then came back up. "Your hips look fine."

She rolled her eyes. "How many pieces of cheese did you put in here?"

"Only three." He reached over and caught a piece of cheese that hung on her chin.

"Sorry." She grabbed a napkin. "You can't take me anywhere."

Yeah he could, he thought. And first place he'd like to take her was back to heaven, but in a completely different way. A completely sexual way. And he could think of a dozen different things he'd like to do to match the expression the sandwich had netted.

She looked at him, looking at her. And she pointed at his plate. "You'd better start eating. If I finish first, I can't promise you I won't steal yours."

"And just when I put my gun away." He ate a couple of bites and watched as she continued with her meal.

"Guacamole?" He nudged it to her after he'd used a chip and put two heaping scoops on his plate.

"No, thank you." She picked up her other half a sandwich. "I think my fat intake has hit the ceiling already. For the next two weeks."

"Don't tell me you're one of those women who worries about every bite you eat?"

She made a cute face. "I'm short and that means I have to eat like a short person, but I think I got a tall person's appetite. Not that I don't eat bad stuff all the time. I'll just have to do my aerobics video twice tonight."

"You're not short."

She cut him a get-real look.

"Well, I mean you are ... short, but you're proportionate."

"Now there's a compliment I won't forget." Smiling, she put her sandwich back on her plate.

He pointed a chip at her. "What I meant was ... you look great."

She grabbed a chip off her plate and dipped it in the

guacamole. She bit the end of the chip and sighed. "Oh, my. I might have to do the video twice and get on my elliptical."

He grinned. "If you want, I can take the rest of that sandwich off your hands."

She frowned. "Over my dead body."

"Fine, but save room for ice cream. Pecan cheesecake. And I picked up some of that Chocolate Shell."

"Kill me now," she said.

The conversation moved around for the next twenty minutes. He helped himself to ice cream and talked her into a very small bowl. Which she ate slowly. He hadn't missed the fact that she never answered the question about her dad. But he knew better than to pry.

At the first break in the conversation, he leaned back, pushed his empty plate and ice cream bowl aside, and said, "Tell me about your brother." He didn't even feel like a lout asking, because he wasn't just digging for information, he was genuinely concerned.

She smiled, and affection flashed in her eyes as she did a lap around her bowl with her spoon. "Well, he's a royal pain in the butt sometimes, but…he's a good kid." She popped the spoon in her mouth and licked it clean.

"Do you want more?" he asked, watching her eat. Getting hot watching her work the spoon.

"No." She dropped the utensil in her bowl.

He recalled her telling him that her aunt had died. "He's a lot younger than you, right?"

"Six years."

He picked up his wineglass, then stood up and snagged the bottle from the counter. "I'd offer you more, but I promised that—"

"No. This is all I need." She put her hand over her glass, which still held some wine.

He settled back into his seat and topped off his glass. "What's he taking in school?"

"It was a toss-up between law or hotel management. I wanted law, he wanted hotel management. But since I know how important it is to do something you love, I gave in."

"So you really love taking care of cats?" he asked, hoping he didn't sound cynical.

"Yes." She sighed, and he could tell she meant it. "Neutering is the most fun," she teased.

"Ouch!" He grinned. "So, Luis...that's your brother's name, right?" And when she nodded, he continued, "So how old was Luis when your aunt died?"

"He was fifteen and I was twenty-one."

"Did you take over custody?"

"Of course," she said. Wasn't that what family was supposed to do? Take care of each other?

He sipped his wine and studied her. She was easy to look at. "That must have been tough becoming a parent of a teen. And you were in school, too. Did he give you hell?"

"Depends on what you mean by hell. Did I find him drinking beer when he was underage a couple of times? Yeah. Did I find his stash of *Playboy* magazines? Yeah. Did I have to push him to do better in school? Yeah. But he's smart, supersmart. And sometimes he'd make a B on a report card, not because he didn't ace the test, but because he wouldn't do his homework. But really, other than one time being led astray by some not-so-good people and almost following the wrong path—which, thank God, he didn't do—he's been good."

Austin turned his wineglass in his hand. "Not to bring up a bad subject, but this afternoon when I overheard—"

"Eavesdropped," she corrected, and shot him a look of discontent.

"Okay, when I eavesdropped. It sounded like you were worried he'd gotten himself into trouble again."

She nodded. "Yeah, well, he assured me that wasn't the case."

He paused, unable to come up with a way to bring up the subject, so he just blurted it out. "Do you want to tell me more about this Cruz guy?"

She looked up at him disapprovingly beneath her long lashes. "No. Why end a perfectly good dinner with that?" She pulled out her phone. "Oh, my, it's almost nine. I should help do these dishes and then head back."

"You turn into a pumpkin at nine?"

"Yeah, and you don't want to see it. I get the same look on my face as when I'm neutering."

He grinned.

She started gathering dishes.

"You don't have to do this," he said.

"Please. It's the least I can do." She walked into the kitchen, opened the dishwasher, and started loading them up. He enjoyed the view as she bent over, too.

He moved in beside her and started putting the chips and guacamole away. Stepping by the sink to stand beside her, he decided to give it one more try. "I know a few good detectives. I bet they could run some checks on this Cruz guy and—"

"No," she said. "I'm handling it."

"How?" he asked.

She glanced back at the table. "Are you done with your wineglass?"

Her ponytail shifted over her shoulders. This close he caught another whiff of waffle cones. He reached up and caught a strand between his fingers and brought it to his nose.

She cut her eyes up to him again. "Are you smelling my hair?"

He chuckled. "I'm trying to figure out if that's what smells like . . . like waffle cones."

"Waffle cones?" She pulled her hair from his hand.

"Yeah, like toasted cookie with extra vanilla."

"That would be my shampoo."

"I like it." He leaned in closer.

She reached back and brought the water gun around. "Remember the rules."

"I never was much of a rule follower." He bumped his shoulder with hers.

"You're going to be a wet non-rule-follower."

"You wouldn't do that again, would you?" He loved the humor dancing in her eyes.

She shot him, right in the chest. He grabbed the squirter attached to the back of the sink. She turned to run, but the spray got her between her shoulders. She squealed, turned, and shot him again. He gave her another squirt right in her face this time.

"Okay, I give up. You've got a bigger gun." She held up her arms, emphasizing her breasts, and damn if he didn't want to pull her into him. "Drop your nozzle," she said.

"Drop your gun," he countered.

She squirted him and turned to run. But the tile was wet and she lost her footing. He grabbed her, but she fell and he lost his balance. They went down together on the wet tile. Both of them laughing. She landed on top of him. And holy hell, she felt good there.

CHAPTER TWENTY-ONE

THEIR EYES MET. The humor sobered. "We're being silly." She started to get up.

He caught her. Not enough force to stop her, but enough to let her know he didn't want her to leave. "No. We're having fun. And I haven't had this much fun in . . . in a long time."

She put her hands on his chest to push up, but she hesitated. "I have to go."

"One kiss," he said without thinking.

"I already kissed you once." She didn't push away.

He raised his head, his lips a breath away from hers. "Then one more," he whispered. His lips met hers. Soft, supple, and so sweet. She was the one who deepened the kiss. She was the one who moved up a few inches, so the position was more comfortable. He rested his back on the hard cold tile.

Her hips fit against his. And when her body did that light shift upward, he went hard in zero flat.

She pulled her lips from his, lifted her head, and glanced at him. Her wide eyes looked dazed and her lips well kissed. "That's two."

"We could go for three." He held his breath.

She leaned down and this kiss was different. No holding back. It was her in pure abandonment. On her part. And on his.

Her hand, soft and hesitant, slipped inside his T-shirt and moved up over his abdomen.

Up, when he ached for it to go down. He reached down, unhooked the top of his jeans, and lowered his zipper to ease the pressure.

Then his hands moved up and under her shirt, all the way up, and slipped the soft cotton over her head. She held her arms up to make the removal easy.

Now sitting up, straddling his pelvis and his hard-on, she reached back and unhooked her bra. His breath caught as the straps slipped down and breasts were bare, and beautiful.

Reaching up, he traced her dusty rose–colored nipples. "You're so beautiful."

Then sitting up, he rested her on the floor and settled on top of her. With his weight on his elbows, he kissed her lips and then moved down to her breasts.

Gently, he suckled her nipple and slipped his hands down and unsnapped her jeans. The zipper eased down as he slid his hand inside.

He found her wet and soft. His chest clutched with want.

His dick throbbed.

His phone rang.

Their eyes met.

"Shit!" he said. What the hell were they doing?

She took a deep breath and her eyes widened, and he knew she was thinking the same thing.

She pressed a palm on his shoulder. "I shouldn't have… I should…go."

He rolled off her. His phone continued to ring.

She leaped up, snagged her shirt, and slipped it over her head. Then she took a bolt to the door.

"Leah?" He shot up and caught up with her right before she walked out. "Don't...leave mad." He raked a hand through his hair, and he smelled her scent on his hand. His dick hardened to new levels.

She turned around. "I'm not. I just can't. I can't do that... this."

"Why?" He knew his reasons why he shouldn't, but he didn't understand hers.

"I'm...I'm not ready."

He fought the need to straighten things in his crotch. "Your ex hurt you that bad?"

"Yeah." She nodded. "Him and a few others before him."

"Cruz?" he asked, and instantly wanted to catch that asshole and make him hurt.

"No, well, maybe. But...I really have to go."

He watched her step out, but then she turned back. The look of passion in her eyes had faded. She paused as if she wanted to say something, but was hesitant.

"What?" he asked.

Her big brown eyes blinked. "The question you asked me, the one I didn't answer. The one about my dad and if I would have wanted him back in my life." She paused. "Before he died, I used to dream about him showing up, wanting that very thing. I'm not sure I could have really forgiven him, but it would have been nice to know he tried. But he didn't. He didn't try. At least your mom is trying. You may not be able to forgive her, but one day you might not be able to forgive yourself for not listening. So my advice, not that you asked for it, is to just listen to her."

Roberto finished the book at ten that night. Reclining on the sofa, he looked at his phone. He wanted to call Sara. Wanted to tell her he'd read the book and agreed with her. Men should read romance novels.

It validated men's drive for sex, but left him with the realization that the true satisfaction came with emotion and sex. Men needed the emotion women brought to the table, or to the bed...or in this case, the hot tub. Sure, there were some touchy-feely scenes that certainly resonated more with the feminine point of view, but the fun was seeing how the male characters responded to those scenes. And damn if in the end, even the emotionally packed scenes were, well...enjoyable. It made him realize what was important. Not the job, not the material things. It was the people in your life.

And it made him think about sex. It wasn't written like porn, it was like a Hallmark card, but with sex. It was wholesome but still sexy. He hadn't felt his dick twitch so much in a long time. As if the damn thing was coming back to life and making demands.

He closed his eyes and imagined Sara reading those scenes. Did she respond to them the way he did? Then he wondered why Anna hadn't ever encouraged him to read romance novels. She'd read them all the time.

Because you were too busy trying to get through school and make a living at the same time. What he wouldn't give to go back and change things. To have spent more time with his family and less time trying to make a dollar and get through school. Sure, it had been for their future, but with the future robbed from him, the price felt too high.

Regrets. Funny how much you could regret doing the right thing.

He could still remember Anna running home crying. *I saw...I saw something crazy.* She'd been shaking so hard, he'd been afraid she would drop Bobby. *I was putting gas in and a car pulled up and then one guy got out of the car. He had a gun. I dropped the gas nozzle and got in the car. I had to get Bobby away. But I looked back and I saw like a flash.*

I think he shot someone. And the bad thing is, I knew him, I went to school with him. His name is Rafael DeLuna. He was always getting in trouble then.

"Wait! You actually saw this guy shoot someone?"

She'd started crying. Roberto had done the right thing. He'd held her for a long time and then called their neighbor to watch Bobby so he could drive Anna to the police station. She told them what she'd seen, about how she'd left the parking lot because she'd been so scared.

They stayed at that precinct for several hours. They'd even shown her pictures of several guys and she'd picked DeLuna out. Supposedly, he already had a record for some stuff.

A couple days later, the cops dropped by and told them that they'd brought DeLuna in for questioning, but he'd had a solid alibi. He'd been at a girlfriend's house. They wanted Anna to look at some more photos. She argued that she knew what she'd seen. She'd been certain.

Less than a week later, Anna and Bobby were gone. They said she'd driven across the train tracks right in front of a train. He knew better. Anna was the safest driver he knew. Hell, her cousin had been hit by a train and lost his leg when she was young. Trains scared his wife. She never crossed a railroad track without stopping and checking several times. Even Freddie, Anna's brother, didn't believe it.

She wouldn't have crossed a train track with a train coming.

On top of that, Anna had no reason to be on that road.

The cops wouldn't listen to him. It made sense that if she recognized DeLuna, he must have recognized her. And when the cops told DeLuna they had a witness, he must have remembered seeing Anna and gone after her.

Roberto told that to the cops, but they insisted he had

no proof. No evidence. And DeLuna had an alibi. So there was no arrest. He walked away clean, and Roberto had lost everything.

Regrets. He'd done the right thing making her go to the police. Doing the right thing had gotten his wife and his son killed.

Right then he realized why seeing Sandy, Brad's wife, had hurt so much. She had that look about her, like someone who had already lost someone they loved. Leaning his head to the side, he glanced at the clock on the wall. He had less than two hours before he had to meet Cruz and Luke, the crooked-nose goon. Two hours with nothing to do. Two hours to convince himself that if things went badly and this was the end, it was okay. He'd be with Anna and his son.

So why didn't it feel okay?

His gaze went to the clock. Was Sara asleep? Had she expected him to call her tonight? Was she disappointed when he didn't? He reached for the phone.

"No." He dropped his arm over his eyes. Calling her was wrong. He'd managed to hang up last night without making promises. He didn't think she'd let him get by with that this time. She'd figure it out, if she hadn't already. She'd know that something was going on in his life. He considered being honest.

What the hell was he going to say to her? *Hey, if I live through catching and killing the bastard that killed my wife and son, I'd like to maybe come out and see ya*?

Yeah, that would go over like a fart in church.

All of a sudden his phone rang. Shit. Was it her? He shot up, his chest expanding with a kind of sweet excitement. He snatched the phone and checked the number. All the excitement deflated.

Tyler. He'd phoned earlier, too. Roberto almost took the

call, but decided against it. Odds were Tyler had gotten wind of the other drug deals gone bad and wanted to confront Roberto about it.

Roberto was in no mood to be confronted. He let the phone go to voice mail, then set it back on the coffee table.

Not one minute passed when his phone rang again. Probably Tyler again. The man had a little case of OCD. To confirm it, he grabbed the phone.

Not Tyler. His breath caught. Sara.

When he didn't pick up, Sara hung up. She didn't leave a message. She even tossed the phone on the other side of the bed.

Why had she called him? She should move on. He'd told her it wasn't happening. Why couldn't she just accept it?

Seriously, how much time did she have to offer a relationship? She'd stopped playing Bunko with her neighbors, hadn't met with her old high school friend in two months. The only thing fun she did was get together with Leah occasionally, like once a month, and share a bottle of wine and some commiseration. And see her mom.

Nope. She was done. Finished thinking about Roberto. Especially when . . . her gut told her that there was something she didn't know.

She fluffed her pillow and was about to cut the light off, when her phone rang.

"Not answering it," she said, and gripped two handfuls of comforter in her fists. Nope, not answering. Then she jackknifed up and desperately searched for the phone that had sunk in the covers.

"Talk me out of this," Leah said as soon as Sara picked up. She'd left Austin's apartment, come home, and put on her exercise video. She'd probably worked off the sandwich. She'd tried to work off the want, the need, the achy feeling deep in her belly, but it hadn't worked. Never, ever had she wanted someone so badly. She wasn't pretending it was love. But it had to be a really hard case of like, and lust.

"Talk you out of what? If it involves the neighbor, Mr. Oh-so-hot Brookshire, I'm probably going to talk you into it."

"It's not him—well, it's his fault, but it's not him."

"Am I supposed to understand that?"

"No," Leah said. "I think I was wrong."

"Wrong about what?" Sara asked.

Her gaze went to her bedroom wall, the one that separated hers and Austin's apartment. "Wrong about you being hornier than me." She laughed, a nervous laugh. "I'm thinking of doing something that I know I'll regret."

"What's that?" Sara asked.

"I pulled out the battery-operated boyfriend. I'm seriously thinking about letting this big guy have his way with me."

Sara's laugh came from the line, but Leah suddenly heard a noise from behind her wall, as if a chair had hit it. She remembered Austin always leaning his chair back on two legs. Had he fallen? Or had he slipped on the wet tiles... again?

The desire to run over and check on him bit hard. Nope.

"Wow, you are desperate," Sara said. "I had to twist your arm to buy one. Not that there's anything wrong with owning or using one. It's not nearly as good as the real thing, but it cures the itch."

Leah hit a switch, and the purple tubular thing started pulsating.

"Is that what I think it is?" Sara asked.

"Yeah. Why did I pick out a purple one? Do you remember?"

"You said purple was a party color." Sara paused. "Are

you drunk? I remember we were a little tipsy when we bought our boyfriends."

Leah laughed. "What I can't believe is that Evelyn was the one who took us there. But...no, I'm not drunk. Just desperate."

"Her taking us there wasn't what shocked me, it was when she started pointing out all the stuff there she'd already bought."

Leah giggled.

"Do you think Evelyn's exaggerating about...about her sex life?" Sara asked.

"No," Leah said. "I think she's just one of the lucky-in-love people."

"You sound tipsy," Sara said.

"I had one glass. I'm breathless because I did sixty minutes of aerobics. I'm not going to be able to sit down to pee tomorrow."

"I've done that before." Sara got quiet. "Okay, so explain to me why you can't just play musical beds with Mr. Blond and Sexy."

"He is sexy, isn't he?" Leah flopped back on her mattress.

"So what's stopping you? You're willing. And I know he's willing. You should have seen how he looked at you today, all concerned like."

"I'm not ready. I think my body's ready, but my heart... not ready. I think I'd go straight to rebound city. I'd probably fall for him. Do all sorts of sexual favors for him." She laughed. "Who am I kidding? I'm already falling for him."

"It's been two years. I say it's time to bite the bullet," Sara said.

"I'm slow to recover," Leah said.

"Or maybe our hearts won't ever be ready. Maybe we should listen to our bodies." Sara paused. "If we desire it, do it. To hell with the outcome."

"You mean start acting like men?" Leah giggled.

"Yeah, pretty much." Sara sighed. "Is it a full moon or something? I mean, we both seem to be in this same crazy romantic chaos."

"I don't know." Leah looked at her alarm clock. "Damn, I just looked at the time. You were probably in bed."

"I was, but not asleep."

"Did he call you again?" Leah asked, remembering Sara telling her about the conversation she'd had the night before with Spooky's rescuer.

"No, I broke down and called him."

"And?" Leah asked.

"He didn't answer. What does that tell you? I'll bet if you called Austin, he'd answer."

"I don't know," Leah said, but she remembered feeling the hard evidence pressing against her thighs, and she suspected he would answer. "Maybe the guy will call you tomorrow."

"If I'm smart I won't answer it. Something's amiss with him. I'm getting a bad vibe."

"Ugg," Leah said. She suddenly realized she wasn't getting any bad vibes about Austin. She felt this crazy connection, a bond. Normally, a guy got within two feet of her, and she was second-guessing everything he said and trying to figure out his angle.

"I don't know why we want them," Sara said. "Well, besides giving us babies. And great sex." She moaned. "Do you think I can raise Brian to be a decent man? I wish my father was here to help."

"You're a great mother. You have all sorts of powers."

Leah's thoughts went to Austin. Her heart ached remembering the pain she saw in his eyes when he talked about his mom.

"I hope so. I don't want to think about him growing up and treating a woman bad."

"He won't," Leah said. "There are decent guys out there. Few and far between, but...they do exist." Her brother was good. And she really thought Austin was decent. So why couldn't she take a chance on him?

The thought came back like an echo. *Because he's not the problem.* It wasn't that she didn't trust him. She didn't trust love. How sad was that?

"Do you want me to bring you Starbucks in the morning?" Sara asked.

"Starbucks? Don't tempt me."

"It's my treat."

"No, I'll stick with office coffee. When I add enough cream and sugar it's not that bad."

They talked a bit longer, then Leah said, "It's late, I'd better let you go back to bed."

"Why? Do you have a hot date with Mr. Purple?" Sara teased.

"I don't think so. He's not doing it for me."

"You're prejudiced?" Sara teased.

"Against what? Purple dildos?" They laughed and finally hung up. She stared at the bedroom wall and wondered if Austin was still at the kitchen table.

As crazy as it was, she liked knowing he was on the other side of that wall. Liked thinking he might be thinking about her. Maybe even a little sexually flustered like she was.

Something wasn't right. There wasn't a light on in the office. Roberto pulled his bike in the lot and pulled his phone out to check the time. Three minutes until midnight.

Had Cruz screwed up? The wrong night? The wrong time? Or was this a setup?

The sound of the motor seemed too loud for the cold night air. He cut his engine off. His Glock tucked into his waist holder gave him a little comfort. He sat straddling his bike, looking around for shadows that didn't belong. Not that a lot of shadows were around. Glancing up at the telephone pole, he could barely see the light fixture at the top. Had someone purposely shot it out?

A stirring of cool wind brushed past, but he felt warm inside his leather jacket.

Should he try to go inside? Or was someone waiting to grab him? But why? Had his cover been blown?

The night's silence split with the sound of an engine. Headlights sliced into the dark road. The sedan, one of three company cars, rolled forward. As if someone had turned up the volume, the sound of its wheels hitting pavement sounded too loud. Chills ran up his spine when the vehicle turned into the office parking lot.

It slowed down as if the driver was looking for something. For what? Him? The sedan headed toward him. The crunch of the rough pavement as the car slowly came forward sounded like an omen. A bad omen.

Reaching into the warm leather jacket, he wrapped his palm around his gun. He might go down, but not without a fight.

CHAPTER TWENTY-TWO

ROBERTO HELD THE gun as the buzz of electric windows, accompanied by the sound of an engine, filled the night air.

"Hey, Rivera. You ready?" Luke's bulky voice rose above the car's engine.

Roberto's heart pounded, the sound of blood rushing filled his ears. He needed to relax, stop thinking people were out to kill him. Then he wondered if Johnny, the kid who met his maker at DeLuna's hand, had worried about that. Maybe worrying would keep him alive.

"Where's Cruz?" he called back, but he didn't put his gun away.

"He had to do some stuff out of town. I got our orders and the merchandise. Park the bike in the back. I left the gate open. We got to get our asses in gear. It's a seven-hour drive. And we need to be there a few hours early to make sure the cops aren't crawling all over the place."

Seven hours? Where the hell were they going?

Figuring he'd get the lowdown later, Roberto started his bike and parked it around back. When he left, he shut the gate and locked it. If he lived, he'd like to have his bike back.

Luke stood waiting outside his sedan, a lit cigarette in his hand.

He hated riding with a smoker. Maybe the goon only smoked out of his car. As Roberto neared, he got that bad feeling again. Not really like Luke was going to try to do him in, just that whatever was about to happen was going to change things. As if the shit was a lot closer to hitting the fan.

With a barely-slept headache, Leah hurried out of her apartment at six. She glanced at Austin's door and imagined him still in bed. Did he sleep in pj's or was he an in-the-buff kind of guy? Probably in-the-buff. An image filled her head—him in bed, the sheet hanging low on his waist, a sexy come-hither smile on his lips.

"Stop it!" She gave herself a mental kick in the butt.

Fixating on Austin only made things worse. Wanting to burn off her nervous, naked energy, she took the stairs instead of the elevator. Bad idea. She'd gone five steps when her thigh muscles screamed at her for doing too many lunges.

She grabbed the stair rail to turn around. It took one step for her thighs to scream louder. Up was worse than down. Taking a deep breath, she pulled up her big girl panties and continued down without moaning...too loudly.

Strolling at a no-pain pace across the parking lot, a gust of winter-scented wind blew past. Almost to her car, she saw something on her hood. The sun hung low, so it took her a few steps before she could identify the item.

A cup...a Starbucks cup? Had Sara...? She saw the gun. Her water gun.

Or the water gun some low-life criminal had left at her place.

Seeing the thing shouldn't make her smile, but it did. The

smile brought on the memory of her and Austin acting like a couple of kids. Or rather, acting like a couple of hormone-crazed teenagers. She recalled with clarity the feel of his hand inside her panties, the feel of his mouth on her breasts. It was so wrong. She still didn't stop smiling.

We're having fun. His words played in her head. Could fun be wrong?

A note was lodged beneath the gun. She picked up the coffee. Palming the still-warm cup, she searched for him. He must have just left it.

The parking lot appeared empty. She grabbed the note.

Good morning. Wanted to say I'm sorry. Won't let it happen again. I swear. I won't kiss you. Won't let you kiss me. But, please, let's not stop having fun.

Austin

P.S. The coffee isn't a gift. It's a bribe.

"Damn!" Emotion thickened her throat. Why did he have to be so sweet?

Dropping the gun in her purse, she clicked her car door open and slowly got in. Obviously, the same muscles used to go upstairs were used to climb into a car.

Finally settled, the scented steam seeping from the cup filled the car. She pried off the top and stared at the caramel-colored liquid. She took a sip, the warm, sweet taste dancing on her tongue.

How did he know I took my coffee with cream and sugar?

She sat in her car savoring the coffee and lingering happiness. *Why can't I just let it happen?*

What was the worst thing that could happen? They'd

break up? She'd feel like shit for a while? Wouldn't whatever they had, for whatever time they had it, be worth it?

Maybe Sara was right. Leah'd never stop being afraid. Maybe she had to dive right into the deep end to move past the fear. And if there was a deep end where relationships were considered, Austin was it. Sweet. Sexy.

But maybe. Just maybe.

Austin hid behind a van. Hiding seemed immature, but he wasn't sure she wanted to see him. Or maybe he was still reeling from the conversation he'd eavesdropped on last night.

A conversation about purple dildos and sexual favors. He'd hardly slept a wink. And yet he felt strangely energized—as if he'd downed a six-pack of Red Bull.

Half the night he'd spent thinking of her with her purple toy and considering all the different sexual favors she'd provide... and those he'd feel obliged to offer in return. He'd had to take two showers.

He hadn't done that twice in one night in forever. Not by himself. She had him acting like a teenager.

When her car left the parking lot, he came out of hiding. The sun was only pushing away the darkness. Had she really been smiling when she read his note? For certain she'd sipped the coffee. A good sign.

He was all into good signs.

He headed back to his apartment, pleased with himself. A little too pleased.

Managing to convince her not to push him away for letting things get carried away was one thing. Figuring out how to stop from repeating the same mistake was another.

He was *not* going to sleep with her.

Not until he came clean.

That's what he'd done with the other half of his night...
tried to figure out how to salvage the chemistry they had, and
still do what he had to do. There had to be a way of getting
past this so they could explore this thing between them.

Not that he saw the thing as serious. It would be a long-
distance thing, but a hell of a lot of fun. Long weekends, cooking for each other, laughing, and making love. Running around
his apartment naked, squirting each other with water guns.

Hell, they were already having fun. How good would it
be when they added sex to the equation? The only negative
thing was her cats. But he could continue to lease the apartment and they could hang out there.

He ran a finger behind his ear. He'd probably have to be
around them some. Hell, maybe he'd take Tyler's advice and
buy a book about overcoming phobias. If there was one good
reason to overcome... what was it Tyler called it? Ailurophobia. Well, Leah Reece was that reason.

She'd be worth it. He'd even attend one of those confession meetings and stand up and say, *My Name is Austin
Brook and I'm an ailurophobic.*

Yup, he wanted to explore this... thing they had.

And his best plan was to come clean. And fast. If she'd
tell him the truth, then he could spill his own truth. *Yeah, by
the way, that's the reason I'm here.* Or maybe... *I've been
waiting for you to tell me this so I could tell you...*

He wasn't fooling himself. The odds of her forgiving him
were up there with winning the Texas lottery. He wasn't a
gambler by nature, but he occasionally bought a ticket.
More importantly, he liked winning. Especially if the prize
intrigued him. Leah Reece intrigued him.

Intrigued him more than any other woman. She was... real.

He wanted real.

He walked into the apartment building and went for the

stairs instead of the elevator. He pondered his odds of winning this—of winning her. If it was DeLuna behind Leah's problems, she might be more out to forgive him for wanting the man stopped.

If she wasn't so anti-gift, he'd buy her something. Something more than a cup of coffee. Some diamond stud earrings maybe, or a...

He stopped in front of his door. Did she wear any jewelry? He couldn't recall her wearing any. Not that she needed help being noticed, she had that smile and killer dimples. And that small perfectly proportioned body.

Walking into his apartment, he stood in the middle of the living room trying to figure out if he wanted to make coffee or grab a couple hours of sleep.

He'd already tried to call Roberto. The man wasn't answering. Austin passed a hand over his face. Had something happened to Roberto? Or was this just Roberto behaving like Roberto? The man seldom answered his phone.

Remind you of anyone? Dallas had tossed out when Austin complained earlier. He didn't care about that. His thoughts returned to Leah. Should he call her? Would she call him?

Aware he still stood in the middle of his apartment just thinking, he turned to the sofa. Obviously, the lack of sleep had him dazed, but he didn't feel dazed or tired. He felt buzzed, a little anxious, but good.

He felt hopeful. Hopeful he could pull this thing off with Leah.

Nevertheless, he needed sleep. If he was going to see her tonight—and he planned on it—he needed his wits. He took off to his bedroom, walked out of his shoes, and started stripping down. The shirt and jeans landed on the dresser, his boxers came off next but didn't quite make the dresser. They cascaded down to the carpet—which he ignored. He crawled beneath the cool sheets and when he reclined, he landed on his earphones.

Unable to sleep last night, he brought his computer in here and replayed her conversation with her friend. Then listened to the live tape in Leah's bedroom. Once, he could swear he'd heard her roll over, even snore. Would he find out what it was like to sleep with her?

Realizing he might have missed a conversation, he snatched his computer from the nightstand. There were six saved files this morning.

He snapped on his headphones and hit play. *"My goodness, aren't you a lover this morning."*

He played all six of Leah whispering sweet nothings to her cats.

Just for grins, he played them again.

Listening to her soft voice, he fell asleep.

Roberto sat in the parked sedan, watching the sun climbing the Louisiana horizon. Supposedly, DeLuna had grown tired of playing with Texas cops and decided to see if the coon-ass cops were more fun. Or less out to get him.

If Roberto had known he was coming to New Orleans he might have called Freddie, Anna's brother. Freddie was the only other person who'd believed Anna's accident hadn't been an accident. Then again, he wouldn't have called him. Seeing Freddie would remind him of all he'd lost.

Roberto pushed his mind away from the past that he couldn't do shit about and focused on things he could do shit about. He'd pulled information from Luke about Brad.

Unfortunately, the information told him nada. Luke said DeLuna had sent Brad on a job and he'd dropped off the face of the earth.

And if Brad wasn't dead, Cruz was supposed to take him

off somewhere and teach him a lesson. Not kill him, but rough him up enough that he'd learn a lesson.

Shifting his gaze, Roberto looked at the convenience store where Luke was finishing off his cigarette before going to take a leak. The man had the bladder of a puppy. Of course, every time he stopped, he got another cup of coffee.

And when he drank coffee, he smoked. The smell had permeated into the car. Which meant Roberto was infused with the smell. He sniffed the warm leather material of his jacket that until today had smelled of wind and sun.

Maybe he was hard on smokers, but watching his mom die of lung cancer when she was fifty, and he nineteen, had left an impression on him. He wanted to hand Luke his gun and say, "Make it easy on yourself."

Luke, standing by the door, stomped out his Marlboro and reached for his fly. Shit, the guy'd probably have his dick out before he got to the bathroom.

Finally alone, Roberto checked his phone to see who was responsible for his phone's vibrating.

He hit missed calls. Austin, Tyler, Austin, junk call, Tyler. Roberto had no plans to call them back, not now. The next time he called he hoped to give them Rafael DeLuna's funeral announcement.

Frowning, he went through the calls one more time— hoping Sara's name would appear. Not that he'd call her back. He hadn't answered her call last night. He still liked believing she was thinking about him.

His phone vibrated again. His breath caught when he saw the number.

Checking to make sure Luke was still inside pissing, he answered the call.

"You aren't at the diner," Brad said. "Did you take my advice and leave?"

"'Fraid not." Roberto sighed. "Look, Sandy's freaking out. Call her."

"Not yet," Brad said. "Did you see my girls, too?"

"No, just Sandy."

He sighed and paused. "So where are you?"

About five miles from becoming a drug runner. "With Luke. I'm helping with a drop."

"Goddamn it. Please tell me you're not in Louisiana."

Roberto's shoulders tightened. "Why? What's happening?"

"There's gonna be cops all over that place. Get out. Get out before you get killed or locked up."

"How do you know this?"

"It doesn't fucking matter. Just trust me."

The phone went silent.

"Shit!"

Roberto's mind raced. He could just walk away. Get out of the car and disappear while Luke had his dick in his hands. That would be walking away from DeLuna and his need to vindicate his wife and son. He could go in and either get shot or arrested. Maybe both. Or pray Brad was talking out of his ass. How the hell would Brad know this unless . . . ?

Was Brad now trying to sabotage DeLuna's operation? He had to be if . . . DeLuna had more people going after him than a dog had fleas. Staring at the phone, Roberto knew he had to make a decision and fast. That's when he realized Luke had left the keys in the car.

CHAPTER TWENTY-THREE

"WHAT THE HELL are you doing?" Luke asked when he stepped up to the car.

"I'm driving," Roberto said. "You drove the whole way here."

"It's my car, asshole. Get out."

"No can do. The reason Cruz wanted me here was to make sure the drop sight was cop-free. I want to drive around before the deal goes down."

"Then tell me where to go," Luke snapped.

"If I'm giving directions, I'm not focusing."

The big goon's crooked nose reddened with obvious blood pressure. Roberto didn't care. Behind the wheel, he had more control. He'd rather take on Luke than the Louisiana police. Although, Luke would probably be willing to kill him a lot quicker. Risky? Yes. But he wasn't walking away from his chance at DeLuna.

"Get in." When the man didn't budge, Roberto added, "I swear if this goes down wrong, I'm gonna tell Cruz and the Boss that you stopped me from doing my job. If you think what Cruz plans on doing to Brad's bad, imagine what he'll do to you."

Luke fisted his fat hands as if wanting to yank Roberto

through the window. Then the goon huffed and moved around to the other side of the car.

One problem solved. Now all he had to do was figure out if the cops were really at the drop site. And if they were, he had to convince Luke to call off the drop. While the deal wouldn't go down, they wouldn't be handing over more of DeLuna's powder product to the cops. Of course, Roberto would need proof that the deal had been compromised.

No easy task, considering he had less than an hour. But if successful, this might work in his favor. Cruz would trust him. The closer he got to Cruz, the closer he got to DeLuna. The sooner he could walk away from this seedy life. Maybe he could start over again. Give life another try.

An image of Sara filled his head. He pushed it away. "How's this supposed to go down?" he asked as Luke dropped into the car.

When the man didn't answer, Roberto hit the steering wheel with his palm. "Talk, or I call Cruz and tell him you're not working with me."

"We sit out front of the coffee shop a block off Bourbon Street," he said. "One of us wears a red baseball hat. I got it in the trunk. They find us, show us the dough, and we show the powder. We switch off."

Not if the cops were watching. "Have you met these guys before?" Roberto asked.

"No."

"You sure?"

"Positive."

Roberto gripped the steering wheel as an idea formed. He needed help. And he knew the perfect person.

"You're a good boy." Leah set Spooky on the examining table.

No threatening phone calls. No wine headache, and a shot of caffeine. Even with the poor night of sleep, and after glancing at her office's shrinking bank account, it felt like a good day. She was being optimistic, both about her decision to talk with Eric Taylor, the new vet in town, and about her half brother. But she hoped Rafael had realized he was wrong about Luis's involvement and had moved on.

"You used it, didn't you?"

Leah glanced up at Sara. "Used what?"

"Your purple friend."

"No." Leah chuckled.

Sara pointed a finger at Leah. "You sure? Because you're smiling, and that's not been the norm lately."

Yeah, Leah had hit a rough patch. But things were looking up. "Positive."

"What are you doing?" Sara moved in.

"Giving this guy his shots. Tonight, I'm delivering him to his new owner." She'd thought about it driving here. He bought her coffee; she'd bring him a cat. Seemed like a fair trade.

"He agreed to take him?"

"Not yet, but I'll persuade him."

"How?" Sara wiggled her eyebrows.

"I'll get creative," Leah teased. She gave Spooky a scratch behind the ear and reached for the needle.

Sara moved in and held the docile cat. "You're going to start seeing him, aren't you?"

The question had played on her mind all morning, but hearing it aloud caused an emotional knee jerk. "Maybe." She dropped the syringe in a metal pan. "I might regret it."

"Or you might not." Sara bumped her shoulder. "Go for it."

Leah inhaled. "It happened so fast. Five days ago, if you'd

told me I was planning to let some guy into my life, I'd have asked what you were smoking."

"Love at first sight," Sara said.

Leah shook her head. "It doesn't exist. Lust at first sight, maybe."

"But according to the experts, that's a good start. Studies show that within three minutes a person recognizes a possible mate." She tapped her nose. "Have you smelled his armpits?"

Leah laughed. "No."

"You should. If his pits smell good, he might be your man." When Leah continued to giggle, Sara said, "I'm serious. Google it. You'll see. Good armpit smell means, come on, baby. Bad armpit smell...back away from the merchandise."

Leah gasped. "Okay, what have you been smoking?"

Sara scratched Spooky behind his ear. "I'm not making this up. I sniffed Spooky's rescuer's arm pit."

Leah rolled her eyes. "You did not."

"That's why I agreed to have lunch with him."

"What did you do? Raise his arm, bury your nose in his pit, and say, 'Okay, lunch is on'?"

Sara laughed. "No. It was an accident. I was putting some old files up in one of the high cabinets and he came up behind me to help. I didn't know he was there and I swung around, and that's where my nose went. One sniff and I could have stayed there all day."

Longing filled Sara's voice.

"He hasn't called you back yet?" Leah asked.

"No, and I don't think he will." She shook her head as if to shift her thoughts. "So now I need to find me another armpit to sniff." Humor laced Sara's voice, but disappointment still shadowed her eyes.

Leah remembered Austin giving her his shirt that day in

the parking lot. She'd believed the wine had made her drunk. Could it have been his smell instead?

"Why did you tell me this?" Leah frowned. "Now, tonight all I'm going to think about is sniffing his armpits."

"Whose armpit?" Evelyn appeared at the door. "The neighbor's?"

"You two are incorrigible," Leah said.

"We try." Humor left Evelyn's eyes. "Eric Taylor's on the phone. He said you called him about lunch today."

Leah's chest ached. She'd wanted to tell both Evelyn and Sara first.

"You're gonna sell half the business to him?" Sara asked.

"I'm talking to him."

"I don't think it would be a terrible thing," Evelyn said.

"Me, either." Sara glanced at Leah. "But I kind of like our all girls' club."

"Me, too," Leah said. "I just want to hear his ideas."

"I think he wants more." Sara made a funny face.

"If he says all the right things, then—"

"I'm not talking business. I'm talking about *your* business." Sara waved her hand in front of her boobs. "He just got a divorce."

"Please. He's not interested in me."

"I don't know," Evelyn said. "I saw him checking you out. Actually, I saw him checking you both out. Not in a disgusting way, just a second-glance kind of way. The way a man will move his eyes past you and then come back for another eyeful. Then their eyes twinkle a bit." Evelyn sighed. "I love that look."

"Me, too," Sara said.

Leah sighed. "You two are such a bad influence." Yet Leah couldn't deny loving that same twinkle when she'd seen it in Austin's eyes.

*　　*　　*

Roberto knocked and stood back on the porch steps. He held the red hat and an empty briefcase in his hands, praying this was the right thing. If this went wrong, Roberto wouldn't be able to live with himself... or die with himself. Even in the afterlife, Anna would kick his ass for getting her baby brother in trouble.

The door opened. "Friggin' hell!" Freddie hugged him. "We thought you were dead."

"You thought wrong." Roberto looked back to make sure Luke hadn't followed. He'd parked a block up and walked. He'd only told Luke that he had a plan and would be back in five minutes.

He was down to three minutes now.

"Come in." Freddie, looking half asleep, stepped back. Was the kid still tending bar? "Where the hell have you been?"

Roberto didn't have time for chitchat. His phone in his pocket vibrated. He knew who it was, too. He'd barely gotten away from the car when Luke called Cruz.

"Look," Roberto said, "I don't have time to explain. But I need you to do something. And I'm not going to lie to you. You might have the cops up your ass, but they can't get you on anything. You won't be doing anything illegal."

Freddie studied him and then smiled. "This is about Anna, isn't it? You're still chasing that son of a bitch."

"Where the hell did you go?" Luke waited outside the car. "Cruz's livid."

"He'll be more livid if we end up losing his merchandise to the cops."

Roberto's phone vibrated again. He pulled it out and got into the passenger side of the sedan. He checked the number to make sure he was right about the caller.

He was.

"What the fuck are you doing?" Cruz asked.

"You sent me here to do a job." Roberto gripped the phone. "I'm doing it."

"If you were doing the job, you'd be casing the diner right now!"

"That's where we're going!" He waved at Luke to start the car.

"What the hell are you up to, Rivera?"

"I told you I was lucky. Well, I lied. I'm more than lucky. I'm a damn psychic. And right now I sense trouble. I've gotten this far following my instincts, and that's what I'm doing now. Making sure we either walk away with your money or with the Boss's powder. Or would you prefer we get arrested and lose everything?"

"If you screw this up, I'm personally going to slit your throat. And I'll enjoy it, too." Cruz's tone told Roberto he meant it.

"And what if I'm right?" By damn, Roberto hoped Brad wasn't shitting him.

The phone wouldn't stop ringing. Austin buried his head in the pillow. Leah? He jackknifed out of the bed, snatched his jeans from the floor, and searched his pockets for his phone.

"Hello," he said, afraid to take the time to check the number.

"What took you so long?" Tyler asked. Frowning, Austin eyed the clock. How long had he slept?

Only two hours.

"What do you want?" he asked.

"I got news. But why don't you call me back when you can be nice."

"Sorry," Austin bit out. It wasn't Tyler's fault Austin had stayed up all night fantasizing about a petite brunette with dimples. "What you got?"

"Tony called. He ran the serial number on the gun."

"And?"

Tyler always needed prodding to get to the point. "It's registered to a Brad Hulk."

Hulk. The name fit the guy who'd broke into Leah's place.

"The man has no priors. But he works construction...in Dallas."

"With Roberto?" Austin ran a hand through his hair.

"Not sure. His company leases out equipment and labor to construction companies. There may be a connection."

"But it's obvious that Hulk isn't just some two-bit burglar," Austin said.

"Right, but we don't have proof that this is tied to DeLuna yet."

Austin growled. "Did Roberto ever confirm that the construction company he works with has direct ties to DeLuna?"

"All he'd said was a few guys who worked there had ties."

"And knowing what we know now, do you believe Roberto?" Austin asked.

"I think that guy has more secrets than a hooker in D.C."

"Did you ask him about Brad Hulk?"

"Roberto's gone MIA. I've called him a dozen times."

"Me, too," Austin said. His mind chewed on the info and spat out questions. "Do you have descriptions on Hulk and Cruz?"

"Do I ever let you down?" Tyler asked.

"Just tell me!"

"Hulk is white, and matches his name."

"Let me guess. Big, but bald, right?"

"You got it."

"It still doesn't make sense. If Hulk's a badass working for DeLuna, he'd know not to use his own piece, and especially an unloaded one."

"That's part of the puzzle," Tyler said.

"You get a description of Cruz?" Austin asked.

"Six feet, medium build, dark hair, and light olive skin. He could be the man you said one of the employees spotted dropping off the bloody package."

"Shit." It looked as if all Leah's problems were tied to DeLuna. "So is Dallas sending someone here to show the vet intern a photo lineup?"

"Yeah, Rick's doing it."

Rick was Ellen—their receptionist's—husband and Dallas's brother's partner. Austin trusted Rick. "When?"

"Not sure. You think she'd talk to Rick?"

Austin remembered the redhead practically hitting on him. "Yeah."

"Dallas also sent Perry, the new guy he hired to keep an eye on Luis Reece. But the kid hasn't been home in days."

"You should've asked me," Austin said. "He's staying at his girlfriend's place."

"You have a name?"

"No," Austin said.

"By the way," Tyler said. "Have you gotten any unwanted phone calls?"

Austin's grip on the phone tightened. He hadn't thought about Candy Adams since last night, and he kind of liked it that way.

"No." He pushed that from his mind and thought about DeLuna. If he was directly involved with Leah's issues, his odds of Leah forgiving him for lying would increase. He liked that.

Then he realized it also upped the odds of Leah getting

hurt. And the assholes knew exactly where she was, too. What if the guy delivering the package was Cruz and he returned to her office?

Austin considered telling Leah everything, but like Tyler had said, they didn't have proof. He might not have enough evidence to convince Leah, but it was enough for him.

"Gotta go. Call me when you have anything!" Hanging up, he dressed, then lit out the door, praying some murdering, raping son of a bitch hadn't already gotten to her.

CHAPTER TWENTY-FOUR

"YOU BETTER HOPE you're right, or you're gonna die." Luke glared at Roberto from across the table. Luckily, across the street from the coffee shop was a donut shop with a glass storefront. A perfect view.

"Let's not discuss this now." For all Roberto knew, the guys sitting two tables down were cops.

Luke eyed his watch and frowned. Freddie should have been here already. Had he backed out?

Hell, it was probably best. It was risky.

Realizing he was tapping his fingers on the table, he stopped and turned the page of the magazine he pretended to read.

Minutes ticked by—one, two, three.

Two rough-looking guys carrying a backpack sat at one of the tables. Roberto did a visual of the street, guessing who carried a badge. The crew working on a storefront a few doors down looked suspicious. As did the couple sitting and chatting on the street bench.

Luke looked at his watch again. "You're a dead man."

As Austin drove, he pulled out his phone and debated calling Leah. Then he remembered Evelyn would probably answer. Sensing the woman liked him, he hit dial. He could always count on his charm.

It rang. And rang. His panic rose.

"Purrfect Pets, can you hold?" someone finally answered.

"Sure," Austin said, relieved.

"Can I help ya?" The feminine voice had a deep Texan twang.

"Hi, Evelyn. It's Austin. Leah's...neighbor."

"Yes. How are you this fine, sunny October morning?"

"Great. Just wanted to make sure y'all's day is going smoothly."

"No dead chickens delivered yet."

"Good." He smiled.

"Did you wanna speak to Leah?"

Want to? Yes, but... "Just tell her I called."

"You bet," she said. He was about to hang up when she said, "Austin?"

"Yeah?"

"You seem like a nice guy. But, just so you know, Leah's one of the sweetest gals I know, and if anyone hurt her..."

So much for his charm. "You'd come after them."

"Don't be silly. I'd send one of my six-foot, two-hundred-pound-plus sons after their ass."

"I understand." As Austin passed the vet office, he looked around for a place to park to keep surveillance. Then he realized his red truck would stick out like a sore thumb. If spotted spying, he'd be busted. He tried to convince himself he didn't need to be here. But images of the couple DeLuna framed Austin and his PI partners for murdering flashed in his mind's eye.

He needed to be here.

Roberto's dead-man status changed three minutes later. Freddie, wearing a red hat and carrying a briefcase, strolled

into the café. Shortly later, he walked outside with a coffee
and sat at the one of the umbrellaed tables.

Setting the briefcase on the table, he appeared to be just
someone passing the morning.

The two shady-looking individuals with the backpack
joined Freddie at his table. Roberto prayed Freddie would
follow the plan. Stall. Don't say anything. Look puzzled at
the guys' presence, but not so much that they left.

A second later, the men working on the storefront
stormed over with weapons pointing.

One of the guys with the backpack pulled out a gun.
Roberto gasped. Coffee shop patrons started scattering.

"Damn," Luke muttered. "Guess you aren't gonna die
today. And I was looking forward to it."

Roberto didn't even glance at the goon. He was too busy
fearing the worst for Freddie. Then, as if the kid with the
gun had second thoughts, he set the gun down. He and his
buddy, knowing the routine, got on their knees and lay facedown out on the ground.

The cops still weren't happy. They kept yelling at Freddie, and he kept yelling back. Another cop jammed a gun in
Freddie's back and forced him to the ground.

Freddie kept arguing, but he didn't fight them. Smart kid.
One officer cuffed and frisked his brother-in-law. Even from
this distance the shock showed on the officer's face when he
didn't find a piece.

The cop pulled out Freddie's wallet, no doubt confirming
his identification.

The cops separated Freddie from the two guys. One cop
opened the backpack belonging to the two thugs. Then with
a smirk on his face, he opened Freddie's briefcase and pulled
out some papers.

A couple of officers stomped off—no doubt searching

for another suspect wearing a red hat. Then the cop who'd cuffed Freddie released him.

Roberto had to work not to smile. He shifted his focus to the goon sitting beside him. Cruz and DeLuna might not be happy the deal didn't go down, but they would be thrilled to know their powder hadn't been confiscated. "You ready to leave this Popsicle stand?"

Roberto felt a tad cocky. Hell, if luck hung on, he might even get out of this alive. He might live long enough to start feeling human again.

Austin had made a decision. If his red truck would stand out, he needed a new vehicle. He'd rented an old silver Cavalier with slightly tinted windows. The car hadn't actually been a rental but had belonged to one of the employees at the place. He made up a tale of how he was seeing some girl and they'd dated years back and he'd driven a Cavalier with tinted windows.

It was just crazy enough that they believed him. The guy wanted to sell it to him, but Austin persuaded him to rent it. The man agreed to let him leave the truck there and pick it up whenever he brought back the car. Of course, the guy should've been accommodating. He charged twice what a regular car would've cost. Not that Austin complained. He'd have paid double that amount.

Parking the Cavalier across the two-lane street, he faced Leah's office. If anyone fitting the description of Cruz or the big bozo showed up, he'd be on them like stink on cat shit.

He shivered remembering being locked in that closet with the cat box and feline.

The vet's office had a glass storefront. He held on to the steering wheel hoping to catch a glimpse of Leah. No luck.

He wondered what she was like with other people. Did

she smile, and wink her dimples at other people as much as she did him? Or was she more serious? Did she have water gun battles with other people?

He hoped not. He liked thinking that was just with him.

Time passed with mind-numbing slowness. Stationary surveillance was as interesting as watching a leaky faucet drip. Add in his lack of sleep, and it was understandable why he was grumpy. Or it could be he hadn't eaten.

He glanced down the street for a fast-food joint, but then a white Porsche pulled into the vet's parking lot. Some rich-looking guy, light brown hair and wearing Dockers, got out of the car. Fancy attire for a vet visit. Austin waited for him to reach in his backseat for a cat carrier. He didn't. He did reach in for his sport jacket.

Maybe he was picking up a cat. But Austin's gut said that wasn't it. Not that this guy looked like anyone who would be associated with DeLuna.

The man stood by his car, reached into his pocket, and drew out what looked like breath mints and popped one in his mouth. After pulling at his belt and finger-combing his hair, he walked inside. A man on the prowl. Prowl for who? Sara?

Austin grabbed his phone. Should he call Leah? He glanced back up. The vet office's door swung open. Leah came out. He was so hungry to see her that he didn't immediately realize she was with the damn Docker-wearing, mint-chewing, Porsche-driving man.

And chapping Austin's ass was that the man had his arm around her, his hand way too casually resting in the sweet curve of her waist. And it stayed there as he walked Leah to the passenger side of the Porsche.

What the hell? Leah wasn't open to...conversation. Or was she only closed to conversation with Austin?

No. She'd kissed him. They'd had a water fight. Almost . . . She'd accepted his coffee.

Realizing his thoughts were ridiculous and suddenly uncomfortable, he let the seat back, then forward. He shifted his legs. He felt cramped.

As the man got inside the Porsche with Leah, one word flashed in Austin's mind: *Mine.*

Who the hell was this weasel?

With the sound of the wheels on the freeway, Roberto slowly woke up. Having barely slept in days, he went out hard. Pushing a palm over his face, he remembered a dream. He'd been running toward Anna, almost gotten to her, and then when he got there, it wasn't Anna anymore, but Sara. He exhaled, trying to shake the remnants of guilt brought on by the dream.

Sitting up, he blinked the sun from his eyes. How long had he slept? Fighting his mental cobwebs, he realized something wasn't right. They weren't on I-49. He saw an I-10 sign.

He looked at Luke. "You lost?"

"Cruz called. He needs us in Austin."

"Needs us for what?" Roberto straightened in his seat. He didn't like last-minute changes.

"He said to head that way."

"Does he remember we got a package in the trunk?"

"He doesn't forget much," Luke said.

Shit. What was Roberto up against now?

When the Porsche purred to life and drove off, Austin followed.

He stayed a couple of cars behind the Porsche. His hands curled around the steering wheel as he drove, and he fought the uncomfortable feeling consuming him. Fought it because it felt too damn much like an emotion he didn't do. Jealousy. He hadn't done it since his fiancée, Cara, dumped his ass over the murder charge and started dating a pilot who flew celebrities around.

He'd spent about a month of his time in prison imagining her having sex in tiny airline bathrooms. Then, one day, it hit him. It hadn't been the first time he'd been abandoned. If someone didn't want him, why should he want them? He knew how to deal with this.

Stop caring. And that's what he'd done. He'd stopped caring about Cara just like he'd stopped caring about his mom and all those foster parents who'd turned him back over to the state. He was starting to care about Leah, and that was dangerous. Then again, with DeLuna after her, she was the one in danger.

He continued to follow the car. When the Porsche turned into a parking lot, Austin parked on the street.

When he looked back, he realized where the man was taking Leah. Lunch.

She got out of the car, and the man met her at the car door. He placed his hand on her lower back, and she darted forward as if to avoid his touch. Austin smiled.

Then he noticed the name of the restaurant. Not only did Leah not want the man's hands on her, Mr. Dockers didn't know her very well. Leah Reece didn't like Chinese food.

Austin still wanted to know who the hell this guy was. He could have Tyler call in the license plate to his Highway Patrol cousin.

But there was another way.

Since he didn't believe this guy was connected to DeLuna, it felt safe to leave her for a few minutes.

He drove back to a What-a-Burger restaurant and ordered

two cheeseburger meals. Ten minutes later, one bag in tow, he walked into Purrfect Pets.

Evelyn, manning the front desk, looked up. He shot her his best smile, and in spite of her earlier warning about him not hurting Leah, she smiled back. See, he did have charm.

"Well, look what the dogs dug up," she said.

Maybe not a heck of a lot of charm, but then he saw the humor in her eyes. "I thought I'd bring Leah lunch."

Evelyn hesitated. "She's out."

"Out?" He leaned in. "Is someone trying to steal her before I convince her I'm better than sliced bread?"

Evelyn smiled. "I don't think he's a threat to you."

He feigned surprise. "So it's a man she's out with?"

"It's business. For Leah. For him, I think he'd take both."

Yeah, I noticed that. "Thanks for the warning." He wanted to pry more: What kind of business? How long had the hound dog been hanging around? But not wanting to push his luck, he dropped it. "Then I bought lunch for nothing. Have you eaten?" It couldn't hurt to get on her good side.

"I have, but Leah might come back hungry." She leaned in. "Mr. Taylor took her to Oriental Gardens. Leah worked at a Chinese restaurant as a teen. She won't touch the stuff."

He tried to imagine a younger Leah working at a Chinese restaurant. The big orange cat, the one who'd eaten the evidence, leaped up on the counter beside him. It took effort not to jump back.

"Leah's right. Spooky likes you. He doesn't normally take to strangers."

Austin forced a smile. *What did he normally do to strangers?* "That's because I'm a nice guy."

Right then, the damn feline pressed its paw against Austin's ear. The same ear a different cat had nearly taken off.

Austin's breath caught. The razor-sharp claws rested on

his earlobe. *Friggin' hell!* He wanted to coldcock the cat. "Good kitty." Fear rushing through his veins, Austin nudged the paw away, then bolted toward the door.

"Good-bye," Evelyn said as if his quick departure was odd.

He nodded. "Make . . . sure Leah gets the hamburger."

"Did you agree to his offer?" Evelyn asked.

Leah leaned against the counter. "I told him I'd think about it."

"Think about him or his business offer?" Sara stepped up.

"His business offer." But Leah could no longer deny that Eric might have a thing for her. That, or he was an extra touchy-feely guy. Considering he was rich, handsome, and they had tons in common, she'd waited to feel a flutter of interest. Especially after her need for male companionship had reared its ugly head this last week.

Nevertheless, for Eric, she'd felt . . . nothing, nada.

"That's best," Evelyn said. "Because your boyfriend brought you something. I think he was jealous."

"Austin came by?" Leah smiled before she could stop herself.

Evelyn looked at Sara. "Did you notice she didn't argue when I called him her boyfriend? I think romance is in the air."

"I noticed." Sara smiled at Evelyn. "She's gonna smell his armpits tonight and see if it's real love."

"Did you see that article, too?" Evelyn asked.

Leah rolled her eyes. "Where do you two find articles on sniffing armpits?" She held up her hand. "Forget I asked." She walked away.

"Wait." Evelyn held up an orange and white What-a-Burger bag. "He brought you lunch. It's still warm."

Leah frowned. "He shouldn't have done that."

"You want me to dump it?" She shook the bag.

Leah shot back and snatched the bag. "I'm starving. Even their fried chicken tasted like soy sauce." She'd been so hungry she'd almost eaten her fortune cookie until she read the saying tucked inside: *Absence makes the heart grow fonder.* What a load of crap.

She started to the back, hamburger bag in hand, and pulled out her phone and dialed Luis. It went straight to voice mail.

She left a message. "Hey. You planning to come Sunday? If you'd like, I could drive to Austin. I think I could use a long drive." *To clear my head, because I think I'm losing it.* "Call me please. And charge your phone."

Ten minutes after following the Porsche back to the vet clinic, Austin got her call.

He barely said hello. "You shouldn't have done that," she insisted.

"Done what?"

"Lunch."

"It really set me back."

"That's not the point."

"Did you eat it?" Had she really returned from her date hungry?

"That's not the point, either," she said.

"Then what is?" he asked. When she didn't answer, he said, "I think you're taking this 'no gift' thing a little far."

She paused. "It would help if you'd let me give you something."

His mind created all sorts of ideas. "Hey, I don't have *any* problems with gifts." As those images got erotic, he reminded himself of the no-touching rule.

"Great." She sounded happy. Had she sounded like that with the Porsche driver? "See you tonight then."

"Okay." Smiling, in spite of knowing how hard this evening was going to be, he added, "What's for dinner? Chinese? Or did you get enough of that at lunch?"

She paused. "Evelyn told..." She let out a huff. "I don't like Chinese food."

"I know that, but your friend didn't." He ran a hand over his face. "You ate your hamburger, didn't you?"

Silence hung there, until she said, "Yes, I ate it. Thank you."

"You should practice that." He imagined her sitting at her desk. Then he heard a meow, probably that damn office cat. He ran a finger behind his ear.

"Practice what?"

"Saying thank you when people give you something. It sounded a little unappreciative."

"It did not. I meant it. The burger was good. I was hungry. And it had cheese on it."

He laughed, but it ended when a dark sedan pulled up in the vet parking lot. "How did the business lunch go?"

"What all did Evelyn tell you?"

Not nearly enough. The car pulled up in front of the doorway and idled there.

"Did she give you my bra size, too?" Her tone rang with humor and frustration.

He laughed but didn't look away from the car. *Were they dropping someone off?* He noticed the car had dark-tinted windows. He recalled wanting tinted windows himself to hide behind. Was someone in the car hiding? "No bra size information." His attention stayed on the car. "But I've got that one figured out." Had she forgotten he'd gotten to see them?

"You're good at that, huh?" she asked.

"Most guys are." *What was the damn sedan doing?* "All Evelyn said was that you were at a business lunch at a Chinese restaurant."

"Well, that's all there was to say." In the background he heard Evelyn tell Leah she had clients. "Gotta go."

"See ya tonight. We'll figure out dinner then." Leaning forward, he tried to make out the license plate. He couldn't.

Was someone looking at the hours of operation they posted on the doors? Or were they looking for Leah? The car backed up and then drove to the back of the parking lot and stopped as if casing the place, or looking to see what cars were back there. Like Leah's car. Finally, it pulled away.

Suspicious, he followed. He'd at least get the license plate.

CHAPTER TWENTY-FIVE

AUSTIN FOLLOWED LEAH home. He'd gotten the suspicious sedan's license plate and called Tyler with instructions to get the number run ASAP.

When Leah pulled into the parking lot, he pulled past the apartment building and parked up the street. He waited several minutes before calling.

"You home?" He ran a finger behind his ear, which still itched.

"Just pulling up. I saw your truck wasn't here."

"My meeting with my client ran long. I'm getting home in ten minutes. Why don't you give me time to shower and come over? We'll discuss dinner."

"We don't have to do dinner," she said.

"We both have to eat."

"But…"

"I promised no more kisses. Just fun, okay?" He held his breath.

"That was pretty fun last night."

He laughed. "I thought so, too. But tonight we'll take it down a notch."

She sighed. "Fine. I got your gift. I hope you like it."

"I will." Whatever Leah gave him, he'd like. He didn't care if it was a pair of polka-dotted underwear.

"See you," she said sweetly.

"Are you in your apartment?" he asked.

"No, I told you I just pulled up."

"Then talk to me until you get inside," he said.

"Why?"

"Because your place was broken into and you got a bloody package delivered to you."

"You worry too much."

"You don't worry near enough."

"Fine." He heard her shuffling. "I have to get your gift out."

"Is it heavy?"

"A little," she answered. They talked a few minutes. "Are you in your apartment yet?"

"Leaving the elevator."

"I could swear I heard your cats." He scratched his ear.

"Maybe you're hearing things. All those hits on the head." She chuckled. Her keys jingled in the background. "Okay, I'm in my apartment."

"Good." Cat noises filled the line—a lot of cat noises. Thank God she agreed to come to his place. His ear hadn't stopped itching since that varmint put its claw on him.

Thirty minutes later, shaved, showered, and scared shitless he wouldn't be able to keep his hands off Leah, he answered her knock.

"Come in." He stepped back.

She stood in the doorway, looking nervous and sexy as hell. Her hair hung loose. She had some gloss on her lips. She wore a pair of fitted jeans and a button-down pink shirt. The first two buttons were undone. His fingers itched to release the rest of them.

"Ready for your gift?" she asked.

"Sure," he said.

She reached to the side and brought a cat carrier into his apartment. He took three steps back. A meow echoed and an orange paw poked out of the carrier.

He blinked. She nipped at her bottom lip. "I know it's a surprise and—"

"No." One word managed to leave his lips.

"He needs a home." She shut the door, set the cage down, then released the door of the cage. "I'd keep him myself if—"

"No." The cat poked his head out. It was the friggin' cat from the office.

"This isn't fair, Leah. I can't—"

"I know," she said. "That's why I decided not to give him to you, but just ask you to foster him for a while." She scooped the feline out of the cage and stepped closer. He stepped back. "Three days," she pleaded. "If you aren't in love with him by Monday, I'll take him back to work with me."

"I can't," he said. "I don't have food, a box, or..." *Or the courage...*

"It's all in the car. And if you keep him, all the supplies come with him."

"You're asking too—"

"Three days." Her soft brown eyes widened with hope.

He shook his head. "Can't do it. You'll be upset when I say no." He backed to the sofa and dropped down.

"I won't be upset. I know how hard it is to lose a cat. After what happened to Snowball, it was years before I got another cat."

He remembered his lie about his cat dying. She moved in, cat in her arms, and sat beside him. The cat hissed and then shot off and darted back in his cage.

"See, he doesn't like me."

"He's just scared," Leah said. "He's been moved from one home to another."

Austin could relate to being afraid. He was so afraid he considered coming clean, telling her he'd lied about his cat, about being here, about DeLuna, but she might be mad. And if she pushed him away, how would he be able to protect her?

"Leah, I have meetings and—"

"As long as you give him a few hours of affection, keep his box clean, and feed and water him, he's fine. Of course, when you fall in love with him, you'll do more."

The cat peered at him from the carrier. "He doesn't like me."

"He does. He's just shy around strangers. But Evelyn said he was all over you today."

And I ran like a scared girl.

"Please? Just three days."

Three days sleeping in the same apartment with a cat?

"He was brought in by this guy who rescued him from living in a Dumpster. Someone abandoned him. He was starving and scared, but so hungry for love that it broke my heart. He followed me around the vet office but wouldn't let me touch him for days. I really want to keep him myself, but I can't take in more."

He frowned.

She smiled. "Say yes and you'll be my hero."

Her hero? Damn, he wanted to be her hero. "Will I lose the title when I give him back to you in three days?"

"No." She tilted her head to the side, her expression so damn cute. "He's neutered, too."

The cat, hunched down in the opening of its carrier, did look scared. And no wonder. "He trusted you and you cut his nuts off."

She leaned against him—practically buried her cheek in his shoulder. Her gentle weight was sweet. And tempting. For a woman who'd run out in a huff after they made out last night, she was getting cozy. He liked cozy.

Had she had second thoughts? If so, he'd be in trouble. Saying no would be hell.

"Say yes," she pleaded.

Leah wasn't sure who was more hesitant about this whole deal. Spooky or Austin. But her gut said it would work out. Spooky would win Austin over. And Austin would win Spooky over. That was a no-brainer, because both of them had won her over.

After setting up the litter box, and getting food and water out, she tried to call Luis. His phone went straight to voice mail. Again.

"Something wrong?" Austin asked.

"Luis isn't picking up his phone. Like always."

They sat at the kitchen table. Spooky hadn't come out of the carrier yet. Though he sat at the opened door and watched them. Austin, pushing his chair back on two legs, watched him back. "You could probably pick him up," she suggested.

"No," he said. "He needs to make the first move."

"Sometimes they need reassurance." She stood up.

"No!" He caught her hand. "We'll work this out between us. Or we won't."

She sat down.

Austin poured them wine. "How about going out for Italian? Chicken Marsala or Shrimp Alfredo?"

"No." She was overdrawn in her weekly calories allotment and overdrawn on her weekly budget due to doorknob repair and wine. Not to mention she might have to put out a couple of hundred for Luis if he needed a hotel. She had an emergency fund, and this qualified as an emergency, but being broke stunk. Right then she decided to take Eric Taylor up on his offer. Her penny-pinching days needed to end.

"If you want Italian, go," Leah said.

"It's my treat."

She frowned. "You already bought me coffee and lunch."

"Fine. What are we going to eat?" He crossed his arms.

"I'm thinking scrambled eggs and a piece of dry toast."

"Ugg."

They compromised on omelets. She offered to go back to her place and cook, but he insisted they stay here and do it together.

She insisted on supplying the eggs and cheese.

He called her difficult. She called him pushy. She won.

A few minutes later, she beat the eggs while he cooked the bacon. They worked together in the tiny kitchen, brushing up against each other every few seconds. Those seconds felt good. Too good. And a couple of times, she did it on purpose.

While they worked he told her about teaching himself to cook after a bout of the flu and getting caught up in cooking shows.

"You watched cooking shows?" She chuckled.

He shrugged. "The cook was sexy."

In spite of his promise of no kissing, she noticed him studying her mouth and knew he thought about last night. Not that she hadn't thought about it. She had.

A lot.

Repeat performance, she wanted to say, and fought the urge to go grab her water gun and restart the fun and games.

But embarrassingly enough, she mostly thought about getting close enough to smell his armpits. When she leaned into him on the sofa, she'd hoped he'd put his arm around her—which would've made it easy to bury her nose in the right spot.

He hadn't put his arm around her. If anything he'd pulled away.

When he'd been setting up the kitty box, she'd tried to close in, but he'd scooted away.

It sounded crazy, even gross, but before the night ended, she was going to sniff his pits. And tomorrow, she was giving Sara and Evelyn hell for putting this nonsense notion in her head.

"We'll need some butter," he said. When he opened the refrigerator, she saw her opportunity. She ducked under his arm, and popped up. But since she didn't have a nose in the back of her head, she needed to turn around. She hesitated, instantly aware of his warmth behind her. All she had to do was turn around and plop her nose where it didn't belong.

She did it. He flinched but didn't step back.

"You need something from the fridge?"

She tilted her head up and their eyes met. His arm remained stretched out, holding the fridge open. Her gaze shifted down. His armpit was inches from her nose. She inhaled, but only frying bacon filled her senses. She leaned a bit closer.

"What are you doing?" he asked.

She listened to the hum of the ice maker as it joined in with the sizzling coming from the stove. She cut her eyes up. "I...was...going to suggest you use margarine instead."

"I only have butter." His gaze lowered to her mouth.

She ran her tongue over her lips. "I have margarine at my place."

"Butter's better," he whispered.

She eased closer, her chin practically resting on his chest, and inhaled again. *Still nothing.*

"You're making this hard for me," he said.

"Because I want margarine?"

"Hard to keep my promise not to kiss you."

She smiled. "I'm sorry." But she wasn't. Her gaze flickered to his arm again. "Do you wear cologne?"

"Sometimes. Why?"

She leaned in and sniffed his chest then turned her face and...bingo. Drawing in a deep breath, she forgot about everything but his wonderful addictive scent. Sara was right. The armpit test worked.

"Didn't I put deodorant on?" he asked.

She looked up, her face heated. "You're...fine." *So fine.*

He laughed, probably at the embarrassment on her face. "You're adorable."

She inched up on her tiptoes. Her mouth brushed his, but he slid his fingers between their mouths.

"I'm not supposed to let you kiss me, either, remember?"

"I didn't bring my water gun," she said, feeling breathless.

"I noticed that." His voice sounded like velvet.

"What if I released you from that promise?" She moistened her lips again.

He almost looked panicked. "No."

"Why?"

"Because..." He hesitated. "You've had wine."

"Barely a glass."

"But you haven't eaten, so it could've gone to your head."

Was he really telling her no? Talk about an ego bruiser. "You don't want to kiss me?" Confusion and embarrassment filled her chest.

"I want that and more. But last night you lit out of here

after we'd taken a few clothes off, just like you did the night before." He poked his hands in his pockets like a kid who'd just been told he couldn't touch. Then he pulled one out. "I'd like for this"—he waved a hand between them—"to not fall apart before it starts. So I think we should take it slow."

"Odd," she said.

"What's odd?" His voice sounded tight.

"I didn't know guys ever went for slow."

He frowned. "This is my first time. It doesn't feel natural." He tucked his hands back into his pockets. He exhaled. "I'd love to take those clothes off of you and make love to every inch of you, but—"

"Stop." She took a step back and bumped into the refrigerator shelves. She welcomed the cool air, because she felt hot all over.

"I was only talking about a kiss, I didn't mean…" It was a lie. She'd already admitted to playing with fire. She wanted his hand between her legs again, his mouth on her breasts. She wanted all their clothes off. The sizzle and pop from the frying pan filled the tiny kitchen, the cold air came at her back, but all she felt was the heat in his eyes. He wanted her.

"We couldn't stop at a kiss," he said.

Self-conscious, she said, "I could have." *Maybe.*

"No, I'd be that good at convincing you not to stop." His smile came with confidence and more heat. So sexy, her breath caught.

"You're that good, huh?" The humor offered escape from the embarrassment, but the sweet tightness between her legs grew tighter. The idea of him making love to every inch of her made her dizzy.

"Really good."

She fought the temptation to kiss him again. To seduce him into forgetting slow. "Your bacon's gonna burn."

"It's not the only thing burning." He released a deep frustrated sound, then turned back to the stove.

She smiled. It was good to know she wasn't alone in the wanting department.

CHAPTER TWENTY-SIX

"DON'T GO SILENT on me." Austin flipped the bacon and listened to her whip the eggs within an inch of their lives. His jeans still felt tight. He wanted to throw caution to the wind.

"What do you want me to say?" she asked.

Tell me about your half brother so I can come clean and we can take this where we both want it to go. "Where did you grow up?"

"Here," she said.

He moved the sizzling bacon to a cutting board. "Who was the first guy to break your heart?"

She stopped beating the eggs. "My dad."

The weight of her words hit him right in his chest. But this was where he needed to go. "What was he like?"

She looked up. "I don't like talking about him." She brought the eggs over. "Who was the first girl to break your heart?"

When he didn't answer, she said. "Your mom?"

He pulled another frying pan from the cabinet. "I suppose." Stepping over to pull out the butter, he glanced at her. "Butter, okay?"

"This once," she said. "I'll bet I've gained a pound this week."

His gaze whispered down her. "It looks good on you."

She rolled her eyes.

"You want to make some toast?"

"Sure."

He put some butter in the pan to melt. Not liking the silence, he offered up a mood changer. "The second person to break my heart was Peggy Darlene Delmar."

She glanced back, curious. "What happened?"

"She took me behind the swings, asked me to be her boyfriend, and told me she'd kiss me the next day. I met her on the playground to claim my kiss and got punched in the nose instead. She said I should've brought her flowers."

A smile lit up Leah's eyes. "So you've always had problems with girls, huh?"

"In my defense, I brought her a flower the next day, but she'd already fallen in love with someone else. He got punched in the nose a week later." Austin opened the bag of cheddar cheese.

Leah laughed, and damn if he didn't love hearing it.

"Well, my first real kiss was..."

"Define *real* kiss?" he asked.

She grinned. "I was twelve so it had to come with tongue."

"That's the only kind, isn't it?" He remembered her tongue against his and felt the stirring below his belt again. "Go on."

"It was at a football game; we were under the bleachers. I was so nervous, I got the hiccups." She dropped bread into the toaster. "The kiss had barely begun when someone dropped their chili fries from the bleachers and I got christened."

He laughed. They shared funny stories through dinner. He remembered she'd been married and his curiosity finally got the best of him. "What happened to your marriage?"

"You mean besides him screwing my neighbor and running up my credit card with phone sex charges?"

"He really did that?"

"'Fraid so."

"He was an idiot."

She made a cute face again. He wondered if the idiot ever realized what he'd lost. "We should introduce him to Peggy."

They laughed. "How long were you married?"

"Three years. I was a fool. Even before we married, I started uncovering his lies. Stupid stuff, like he'd never mountain-climbed in Colorado or backpacked in France. I convinced myself he was just trying to impress me. Now I know, a guy who'll lie to you, he's capable of anything." Her phone rang. She grabbed it.

She looked at the screen and frowned. He frowned, too, but for a whole other reason. What was the chance of her overlooking his lies?

"Just a junk call." She sat her phone down. "I'm killing Luis for not calling me back."

Roberto pounded on Luke's hotel door located beside the cheap-ass room he'd been hanging in the last four hours.

"What?" Luke yelled from behind the door. Roberto heard moaning like some porn movie.

"I'm going out. Call me if you need me."

The door opened. "Cruz said for us to wait here."

"I'm hungry." He turned to leave.

"You've gotta be patient if you work for the Boss."

Roberto turned around. "Is the Boss here?"

"Yeah. He's the one that calls the shots on this stuff."

"Will I meet him?" Two years Roberto had dreamed of this. He'd killed him a hundred times in his mind.

"He usually takes us out afterward. To celebrate. Sometimes he gets us girls."

Roberto had no interest in whores. "Celebration for what? What are we doing here?"

"Taking care of some mess."

"What kind of mess?" Roberto asked.

"The kind that needs to be six feet under."

Roberto's gut spewed acid. Trafficking cocaine was bad enough. Murder, or even covering up a murder, was another matter. If that's what it took to get to DeLuna, could he do it? But wasn't he here to get justice for that very thing? Wouldn't this make him the worst kind of hypocrite?

Luke's phone rang. He glanced at the number and his sagging cheeks inched up in a smile. "You aren't going anywhere."

"Shit!" Austin muttered, still sitting at the kitchen table after Leah left. He wore his headphones and listened to her talk sweetly to her felines. He wasn't even sure what his frustration was targeted toward—the lowering odds of Leah and him ever becoming something real, or the damn cat eyeing him from the carrier. Oh, hell, it was both.

When she'd mentioned a gift, he'd thought she might've picked up another water gun or another bottle of wine. But no, she'd brought him a damn cat.

He didn't want a cat, not even for three days. He wanted Leah Reece. He wanted her completely naked, willing, and eager. With a water gun.

He recalled her words. *Say yes. And you'll be my hero.*

He wanted to be her hero. Fat chance now, and all thanks to some asshole ex-husband who'd lied to her.

Yeah, Austin was lying, too, but this was different.

Tossing the headphones on the table, he glanced back at

the cat. The dang feline hadn't moved. He stared at Austin as if...terrified.

He's a little scared right now. He recalled Leah saying, *He keeps getting moved from one home to another.*

"I'm not going to hurt you. You stay away from me, and I'll stay away from you."

The cat blinked its big oval eyes. And for some damn reason, Austin suddenly related to the animal. He knew all about being dropped off at strange places, temporary places. From one foster home to the next.

Realizing the animal hadn't eaten or drunk, Austin got up. He cautiously walked around the carrier and collected the food and water bowls from the bathroom. Easing in, he set the bowls down, then nudged them closer with his foot.

"Now, eat and drink. You die on me, Leah will hate me. Not that she won't anyway." Backing away, he sat down on the sofa. "Eat."

The cat didn't move. They had a staring competition for almost an hour. Austin finally lay down on the sofa thinking the cat might eat if he ignored him. Not that he let himself relax. He liked his body parts too much to let down his guard.

Luke drove into an abandoned warehouse parking lot. "You sure this is the right place?" Roberto asked, but his gut said it was. It looked like a place murder happened. Pitch-dark, nobody around. But damn, he didn't want to be here. His fingers itched to pull his gun. But it was too soon.

"Don should be arriving shortly."

"I thought the Boss was supposed to be here."

"Change of plans."

Did that mean someone was already dead? It might be too late. But if the person was alive, Roberto knew what he had to do. He couldn't stand by and let someone be murdered, even if it cost him his whole plan.

He got out of the car, and the October night felt cold. Pulling his leather jacket closed, he looked up at the stars staring back at him. Hell, it was as good of a night to die as any. Oh, he wouldn't go down easy—he hadn't stopped wanting to kill DeLuna—but he wasn't going to let anyone else die, either. Not if he could stop it.

A pair of headlights sliced through the dark parking lot. "It's Don," Luke said.

The sedan, exactly like the one Luke drove, parked. Don, bigger than Luke, crawled out.

"Open the door, kid." Don tossed a heavy key ring to Roberto.

Roberto, who hadn't been called a kid in over ten years, caught the keys. In the back of his mind, he wondered how many bullets it would take to stop Don. He wondered if he could stop this and still get to DeLuna.

"It's the key with the green tip." Don turned to Luke. "Help me get this piece of shit from the trunk."

"Is he dead?" Luke asked.

Roberto's breath caught as he listened.

"Not yet. But close."

"Did he cop to it?" Luke obviously knew more about what was going on than he'd let on.

"Swears he's innocent. Cruz's bringing in his sister and gonna use her to make the kid talk."

Innocent. Was this kid being blamed for being the snitch? Was it Roberto's fault the kid got in this mess? Roberto recalled Cruz saying something about a brother and sister on the phone that day in his office. Clenching his fist, Roberto considered his next move. He hadn't made up his mind, when the sound of squealing tires sounded behind him. He turned.

A white Saturn hauled ass straight for them. Before Roberto could get to his gun, a string of gunfire exploded. Luke fell facedown on the cold parking lot gravel. Don dropped to his knees, then collapsed.

The last thing Roberto saw before a bullet claimed him was the shooter's face.

Austin roused up, unsure what had stirred him awake. He wasn't even sure where he was. He opened his eyes and found himself staring at a cat plopped on his chest. "Friggin' hell!" He jackknifed up off the sofa. The cat bolted into the air and landed on the dining room floor, then shot back into the carrier.

Heart pounding so hard it hurt, he struggled to breathe. It took another second to realize his phone was ringing—his phone sitting on the dining room table. Which meant walking past the damn carrier.

Manning up, he forced himself to move. He snagged the phone. "Hello," he growled.

"Austin?" An unfamiliar female spoke.

"Yeah?" He squinted at the clock. Just ten. He couldn't have slept more than thirty minutes.

"I wanted to talk to you in person, but you haven't been home."

"Who is this?"

"Your mother."

"I don't have a mother." He hung up and bolted across the room into his bedroom and slammed the door.

Leah's words floated through his head. *You may not be able to forgive her, but one day you might not be able to forgive yourself for not listening.*

Leah was wrong. Candy Adams didn't deserve the courtesy of him listening.

*   *   *

Roberto watched the white Saturn spin off. Had Brad known it was him? What if he came back… "Damn!" He pulled out his gun. His leg didn't hurt; it felt icy numb. He forced himself to get up. Blood seeped through the hole in his jeans—not too much blood. The bullet hadn't hit an artery.

He limped over to Luke, and the cold numbness in his leg became hot pain. He knelt and put his hand on the guy's neck. Not a flutter of a pulse. He managed to get to Don, but he didn't check for a pulse. He'd taken a hit to the head. Ugly.

Remembering the kid in the trunk, Roberto looked around for Don's car keys. He found them clutched in the man's hands. Limping to the back of the car, he pointed his gun, just in case whoever was in there decided to come out swinging. He clicked open the trunk.

No one came out swinging, or otherwise. The trunk light barely reached the body.

"Hey?" Roberto squeezed his stinging thigh. "You alive, kid?"

Only silence answered. Roberto stepped closer.

Austin had just fallen back to sleep when his phone rang again. Sitting up, he grabbed the cell off the nightstand and checked the number.

Not Candy. Holly Macon. A flight attendant he saw on and off. He looked at his alarm clock. Why was she calling at midnight? Who was he kidding? He knew why she was calling.

"Hello?"

"You tucked into bed all warm and naked?" Holly asked.

"Yup." He rubbed his eyes, and that's when he saw the cat curled up on the foot of the bed. "Shit!" He folded his legs up. How had the cat gotten in here? He recalled going to pee once.

"What is it?" she asked.

"Nothing." Austin kept his eyes on the feline. "What's up?"

"I was hoping *you* were. Pun intended. I've got a layover. I'm standing at your door not wearing very much, but you're not answering it."

"I'm not home."

"Could you come home? I'll be better than whoever's bed you're leaving."

"I'm out of town. Sorry," he said, but realized he wasn't. He wasn't in the mood to…An image of Leah filled his mind.

"Shit."

"You keep saying that," she said.

"Sorry, you'll have to go to a hotel."

"A shame. I fly in next week, too. How about a rain check?"

He opened his mouth to say yes, but that wasn't what came out. "I don't know when I'll be back."

She seemed to know what he really meant. "Your loss. I'm a good fuck."

"Yeah, you are." He gave her that much.

"You meet someone?" she asked.

"Not like you think." It wasn't like he was in love. He just…needed something more real than what he'd experienced lately. And Leah was as real as it gets. Not that he was going to get that chance now. But he didn't think he'd be in the mood to see Holly next week, either.

She offered an awkward good-bye, and he took it.

He leaned against the headrest and stared at the cat, who had curled back up. The animal stood up, did a front-to-back stretch, and moved closer. Austin held out his hand. "No! Get. Go!"

The cat kept coming. Scared to make a sudden move, Austin froze. The cat stepped up on his thighs, moved up a couple of inches, right above boys and friend.

Austin didn't even breathe. "Hey, buddy, I wasn't the one who neutered you."

The cat did a circle, then curled up as if he'd found his new sleeping spot.

"I don't think so." Austin tried to wave him away. The cat looked at Austin, then put his paw over his eyes.

Austin chuckled. "Don't pretend you can't see me. Come on, move." He went to push the cat away. But instead he gently touched the cat's fur. It was softer than he imagined. The cat moved his paw from his eyes and dipped his head under Austin's palm as if pleading for him to touch him. Shocked by his own bravery, Austin did just that. He petted the damn thing. Then the most amazing thing happened. The animal made a soft rattling sound. A purr. The cat was purring.

"Hey there, Spooky. You're not so spooky after all."

Roberto came up with a plan. It had flaws, but he had to do something. The kid was in bad shape. He hadn't spoken and was in and out of consciousness. And he wasn't breathing right.

"Don't you dare die on me." Roberto put the kid in the backseat of Luke's car and then got behind the wheel.

Blood oozed out his own wound. The kid wasn't the only one who needed medical attention, but he was the only one getting it now. He felt the kid's wallet in his pocket, which he'd snagged in hopes of figuring out who he was, but first he needed to get away from the crime scene. He drove toward downtown, sure a hospital would be around there. Hearing the kid's shallow breathing, he drove faster.

Ten minutes later, he pulled up into the emergency

entrance driveway. He flipped opened the kid's wallet to see his name. Luis Reece.

"Fuck!" This was Leah Reece's brother. That meant Cruz had gone after her. The kid moaned. Roberto didn't know what to do first, get the kid to the hospital or call Austin.

The kid gasped again. The kid came first.

Roberto reached for his bag with the few clothes he'd brought with him. Removing his bloody, and now holey, jeans, he traded them for a different pair. Lifting his leg hurt like hell. He'd bleed though this pair in no time, but maybe anyone seeing him would think it was Luis's blood and not his. He figured the hospital probably had a surveillance camera, so he snagged Luke's Dodgers hat from the seat and put it on.

He got out, spotted a wheelchair at the glass doors, and grabbed it. When he set the kid in the chair, he slumped over, unconscious again. Keeping his head down, Roberto wheeled him into the emergency room.

Three people sat in the waiting room. The nurse behind the glass window stood up. He'd done all he could. If he stayed, they'd ask questions. He ran out, which wasn't all that fast considering he had a bullet in his leg. But he got in the car. As he sped off, two security guard types ran behind him.

He drove five miles, looking for cops in every direction. Only when he got on the freeway heading toward Heartbroke did he remember to call Austin.

He pulled out his phone. His dead phone. Fuck! He'd left his charger at the hotel.

Tossing it in the seat, he saw the kid's wallet. He'd meant to leave it with the kid. Then again, maybe it was best they didn't know his identity. Maybe DeLuna would be less likely to find him.

*   *   *

At five forty-five the next morning, Austin followed Leah to work, staying a few cars behind. He parked his car across the street and watched the lights come on in the vet office. His phone rang. He hoped it was Tyler with the license plate info. If that came back connected to DeLuna, he was going to come clean with Leah and insist she leave work and go somewhere safe.

Pulling his phone out, he saw the number. "About damn time!" he said in lieu of hello.

"Chew my ass out later," Roberto said. "We've got bigger problems."

CHAPTER TWENTY-SEVEN

"WHAT PROBLEMS?" AUSTIN asked.

"Where's Leah Reece?"

"At her clinic, why?"

"Then you'd better get there and fast. Cruz has orders to take her."

"I'm parked across the street." Austin's gaze didn't stray from the building.

"They got to her brother."

"Shit. Is he dead?"

"I hope not. I dropped him off at the hospital. But he didn't look good."

"Damn." Austin started the car and drove to the stoplight at the parking lot exit. "Why? Was the kid dealing drugs for them?"

"I think DeLuna suspected he was the snitch."

"He got blamed for what we were doing?"

"Looks like it." A black sedan pulled into Purrfect Pet's parking lot and drove to the back. "Fuck. He's here."

Austin punched on the gas through the red light and dropped his phone. He barely dodged being T-boned.

They were not getting Leah.

* * *

"Who's there? Cruz?" Roberto asked. The line went silent. "Shit!" He lit out of the twenty-four-hour Walmart parking lot where he'd purchased a car phone charger. Even speeding, he was thirty minutes from Heartbroke. Austin was on his own.

Roberto shifted and used his left foot to push the gas. His leg throbbed like a friggin' toothache. It had stopped bleeding, but he knew he had to get help. And he could think of only one person to turn to.

His phone rang and he reached for it to see the number. Frowning, he snatched up the phone. "You shot me, you asshole!"

"I shot you?" Brad asked. "That was you? What were you doing with them? They killed that boy. I tried to stop 'em, but I was too late. I'm ... I'm the one who gave DeLuna his address. I might as well have killed him myself."

"They didn't kill him. He was still alive in the trunk, but *you* damn near killed *me*."

"If you were helping them, you deserved it. I can't watch them do this anymore. It's got to stop. My own brother-in-law was blackmailing me. He threatened to hurt my girls—his own damn nieces—if I didn't do what DeLuna wanted. But this stops now."

Roberto gritted his teeth. "I was trying to stop it, too, but next goddamn time, look who you're shooting at!"

"Luke and Don?" Brad asked.

"They're dead."

Brad made a noise of pure regret. "I had to do it. I had to stop it. Luke told me he killed Johnny. And Don beat that boy. I thought he killed him."

"I know," Roberto said.

"The boy is really alive?"

"Yes. I took him to the hospital."

"They're going after the sister, too," Brad said.

"I know. Don mentioned it." Roberto remembered why he was really doing this. "Where's DeLuna, Brad?"

"He was with Cruz."

"In Heartbroke? Are they going after the sister themselves?"

"Don't know. I lost them when I followed Don." Brad got quiet. "It was you, wasn't it? You were the snitch. You were doing it the whole time."

Could Roberto trust Brad?

"Shit," Brad said. "They're here."

"Who? Where are you?" Roberto asked, but for the second time the line went silent.

Austin sped the silver Cavalier to the back of the parking lot where the black sedan had disappeared. When he made the corner, his headlights splashed on the sedan—motor still running. The driver's door opened, then slammed shut. Austin rolled down his window and pointed the gun out.

"Stop right there!" he yelled.

They didn't stop. The engine roared; the car whipped around the parking lot and raced right at him.

Austin felt the impact all the way in his backbone. The air bag exploded. The car skidded a good five or six feet back. Blinking the white air bag powder from his eyes, he pointed his gun at the car. When the car started revving its engines again, he fired. The bullet went through the windshield; the car swerved and fishtailed.

A gun appeared out the sedan's window. The pings and thud sounds of the Cavalier taking bullets shot adrenaline through Austin's veins. But better the Cavalier take them than him. Except for the fact that it was a rental car. Fuck, he'd just bought himself a Cavalier!

Austin got another well-placed shot off. Another pair of headlights sprayed across the parking lot. He expected it to be cops, but a white Saturn came to a tire-squealing stop right next to him. A gun appeared out that window.

Shit! Two against one.

Flashes appeared in the Saturn's window. Austin ducked. More popping sounds rang out in the predawn darkness. But they weren't aimed at him. The sedan sped off across the parking lot, jumped the curb, and left. Still unsure what was going on, Austin aimed his gun toward the Saturn. The Saturn pulled up a little bit. The sound of its engine filled the silence.

Though the sun had only spit out an ounce of light, Austin recognized the guy sitting behind the wheel. Big. Bald. Brad Hulk.

Remembering getting beat with a toilet plunger, he kept his finger on the trigger. But grateful for the help, he didn't shoot.

"Get the girl out of here," Brad screamed. "They'll be back!" He squealed off.

Light spilled out of the back of the vet office from the back door. Leah Reece poked her head out. Sixty seconds earlier, she might have gotten shot.

Jumping out of the car, he stuck his gun in the back waistband of his jeans. Leah slammed the door. Austin took off, cutting his eyes to the road. No sirens rang out. Considering the street was nothing but businesses, and most weren't occupied before six a.m., they might not have been called.

He got to the door. "Leah, it's me, Austin. Open the door!"

The bolt turned. The door opened. Leah stood with her phone in her hands.

"What happened? I thought I heard a car wreck and then it sounded like cars backfiring, but then it sounded like...

gun shots." Fear rounded her eyes. "What's that all over you?"

He glanced down at his shirt, covered in air bag powder. "There was a wreck."

"You okay?" She touched his chest. "Should I call the police?"

He considered it but knew what they'd do. They'd take them to the station, and because he had a gun, they'd keep him and eventually let Leah go. It wouldn't matter if he told them the truth, they wouldn't offer her protection without proof that she was in danger. The Hulk in the car was right. He had to get her out of here.

"No. Where are your car keys?"

"Why?" She pocketed her phone.

"We need to get out of here."

She shook her head. "What?"

He remembered seeing her purse in her office the other day. She probably kept her keys there. Ushering her by the arm, he led the way.

"What are you doing?"

"There's a lot I have to explain, but right now I need for you to do as I say."

"No." She yanked free.

"Leah, we're getting your car keys and then we're getting the hell out of here."

"I have to work." She looked baffled.

He took her arm again and eased her down the hall.

"Stop this!" She jerked away at the office door.

He spotted her keys on the desk and forced her to look at him. "I can't stop, Leah. They're coming back."

"Who's coming back?"

"You were right. You heard gunfire. Your brother is try-ing to kill you."

She blinked. "What? You don't know Luis. He—"

"Not Luis. Rafael. Rafael DeLuna."

Her face paled. "How do you know... I never—"

He took her arm and got almost out of the office, when she started struggling. He spotted some masking tape on the file cabinet. He didn't want to do that, but...

She kicked him in the shin.

He released her. She reached for her phone, probably to call 9-1-1 on him. Without any other option, he snagged the phone from her, tossed her over his shoulders, and kicked the desk chair around. As gently as he could, he dropped her in the chair.

He bracketed his hands on each side of the chair's arms, leaned down, and looked her right in the face. She shot her knee up in his groin. He caught it. Good thing, because she had damn good aim.

"I don't have time to explain everything, but I'm going to give you the quick and dirty version. Then, you're gonna walk out of here with me. If you don't, I'm going to have to force you. Because if those men return, they'll kill us both."

She stared daggers at him, but she wasn't trying to bust his balls anymore. Call him an optimist, but he considered it a good sign.

"I'm a private detective. I came here to see if you knew anything about your half brother. DeLuna is running cocaine and guns. There's been some people on the inside sabotaging his deals. And he's got it in his head that Luis is doing it."

Her eyes tightened. "Why does he think that?"

The pressure eased from his chest. Asking questions meant she was listening. "I'm not sure. But let's go."

"Where's Luis?" she asked.

He hadn't wanted to tell her until later, but maybe it would force her to see how serious this was.

"He's in the hospital. DeLuna got to him and—"

She shot through the space between his arm and her chair. "What hospital? Where?" She held out her hands. "Give me my keys!"

"Let's go and we'll check on him as soon as we can."

"I'm not going anywhere with you! You've done nothing but lie to me. Now tell me where my brother is!"

He let go of a big gulp of frustration. "I told you what was going to happen."

He snatched the tape from the top of the file cabinet, looking away for two seconds. She didn't waste any time. She snatched the lamp off her desk and swung.

He blocked it with his forearm, and it hurt like hell. Yanking the lamp from her hands, he backed her against the wall. She screamed as he snagged her hands over her head. Using his teeth, he pulled the tape free and then finally managed to wrap it around her wrists. She started kicking. He squatted down and taped her ankles together. She slid down the wall and beat him in the head with her taped hands.

"You're going to hurt yourself," he growled.

Still screaming, she grabbed fistfuls of his hair and yanked so hard he was going to have bald spots.

"Stop it!" He stood. Dropping the tape, he carefully grabbed her around her waist, tossed her over his shoulders, and started out. She hit his back with her tied hands. He reached in his pocket for her keys and placed them in his hand, holding the back of her legs in place.

Pulling out his gun, he heard her gasp as if she'd seen it. He opened the back door. The rising sun had turned the night a dusky gray.

Just as he got to her car and clicked the locks open, headlights shot across the parking lot.

His gut clenched. She continued to scream.

"Fuck!" The sedan came racing at them.

Bullets hit the concrete at their feet. Opening the driver's door, he tossed her and then shoved her over as he got in. "Head down," he yelled.

He started the engine. The sedan rammed into the back of Leah's car. The impact knocked her on the floorboard. The back window shattered and the sound of bullets whizzed past. Turning, he shot at the sedan's windshield. Twice. Both shots hit. But if he'd gotten the person or persons in the car, he didn't know. He couldn't risk staying around to find out.

Yanking the car in drive, he turned the wheels on a dime, pushed the gas down as far as he could, and sped off.

With his focus flittering from the road to the rearview mirror, he finally glanced at Leah, still facedown on the floorboard. Had she even moved? "You okay?"

When she didn't answer, panic shot through him. Had she taken a bullet?

"Damn it, Leah. Answer me! If I have to pull over to check on you, they could catch up with us. Do you want that?"

She lifted up on her elbows and glanced at him. Her look punched him right in the gut. Tears rolled down her cheeks. She didn't trust him, but she was scared not to. She inhaled, and the sound of her shuddering breath filled the car and his chest gripped.

"I'm sorry, babe," he said.

She struggled to push up as if to get back in the seat.

"Not yet. Stay down there until I know they aren't following us. Please." He recalled how hard she'd fought him, and he inwardly flinched knowing how much she must hate him right now.

*   *   *

Sara's mom pulled up in front of Purrfect Pets. Sara's car needed a brake job and her mom had offered to play chauffeur. "Thanks, Mom."

"No problem," her mom said. "Brian and I are going to the park."

"Park, park, park," Brian chanted.

Sara crawled over the seat and kissed her son. "Be good for Grandma."

"I be good," he said in his big-boy voice.

Blowing him another kiss, Sara reached for the door handle.

"Is anyone here yet?" Her mom stared at the dark vet office.

"I'm sure Leah is. She parks in the back. She's in her office. On Fridays, Evelyn doesn't come in until one."

"Thanks again." A gust of wind tossed Sara's hair. Arriving at the door, she found it locked. Leah usually unlocked it for her. Grabbing her keys from her purse, she let herself in.

"I'm here." She dropped her purse on the counter.

A banging sound came from the back. "Leah?" As she cut the corner, she saw that the wind had knocked the back door against the building. "You left the door open." Sara went to close it.

She saw a wrecked silver car in the middle of the parking lot. Leah's car wasn't there. Yet a dark sedan was parked to the left.

Antsy, she shut the door. "Leah?" She poked her head in Leah's office. The place had been ransacked.

"Leah?" A bad feeling made her skin crawl. Had something happened?

She headed to the front, but she heard someone step out of exam room two. The footsteps too heavy to be Leah's.

CHAPTER TWENTY-EIGHT

"SARA?" THE DEEP voice sent panic spidering her veins, but recognition had her turning around.

"What are you...?" Visions of Leah's ransacked office filled her head. "Where's Leah?"

Roberto collapsed against the door frame. "With Austin."

"You know Austin?"

He nodded and squeezed the top of his thigh.

She saw the dark spot in the blue denim below his hand. Blood?

"I need a nurse, Sara," he said.

She recalled the wrecked car in the back. "What happened?"

"Don't overreact."

That made her overreact.

"I was shot." That's when she noticed what he had in his right hand. A gun.

Her breath caught. She'd known it. He was a criminal. She stepped back. "You need to go to the hospital," she said. "And then prison. And when you're there, say hello to Brian's daddy." She turned to run.

"Please don't go."

She got three steps, imagined him shooting her in the back, and swung around. He wasn't pointing the gun at her. "You rob banks, too, don't you? Am I a magnet for criminals?"

"I'm not a bad guy."

"Then I'll call an ambulance. They'll take you to the hospital."

"I can't, Sara." He moved closer.

"Because they'll take you to jail?"

"I didn't do anything. I'm the one who got shot."

She stared at the gun. He followed her gaze.

"Take it. Take the gun if it'll make you feel better." He grabbed her hand and put the gun in it. "If I was a bad guy would I do that?"

"It's not loaded," she accused, convinced he was tricking her.

"It is," he said. "It's ready to shoot. I didn't know who—"

"Really?" She raised the gun and put her finger on the trigger. The sound popped in her ears and her arm jerked.

Roberto dropped to the ground.

Leah crawled up in the seat as soon as he hung up from a call. He'd told her to wait. She was sick of waiting. Her heart pounded against her breastbone. She couldn't get enough oxygen into her lungs. Coffee churned in her stomach.

Who had he been talking to? She remembered him saying, *I have her,* and then, *I can't talk. They could be following me. I'll call you back. Answer this time.*

"Where's my brother?" she asked.

"In a hospital." His gaze shifted between the rearview mirror and the road.

"What hospital?" She envisioned Luis alone and hurt.

"I don't know." He frowned. "But I'll find out and have someone check on him."

"Take me to him now!"

His grip tightened on the steering wheel. "Not until I know it's safe."

"I don't care if it's safe. I want to see him."

He exhaled through his teeth.

She considered everything he'd told her. "You're lying. Luis isn't hurt. You just wanted me to stop fighting you." She wanted to believe Luis was okay.

"Did I lie about the men coming back?"

Her breath caught. She could still hear the bullets whizzing past her, the pings and clunks as they hit the cement. She'd never been shot at; never had her wrist and ankles taped, either.

"Then take this tape off me and let me call him."

He glanced at her. "I don't think he's answering the phone right now."

Tears blurred her vision. "How bad is he? Please take me to him."

His jaw tightened. "As soon as I know it's safe, I promise."

She shook her head. "You can't do this. This is kidnapping."

"I saved your life." He cut his blue eyes to her.

"You could be the bad guy and those guys back there were trying to rescue me."

"Do you really believe that?"

"Why wouldn't I? You've done nothing but lie. And for what? Money? Someone paying you to find Rafael?"

"No," he said.

"Liar!"

He didn't look at her. "When you calm down, I'll explain things."

"You could have asked me if I knew where Rafael was. You didn't have to humiliate me by . . . seducing me."

"I wasn't..." His jaw clenched. "If I'd asked about him, what would you have told me?"

"That I don't know where he is!" She said the truth.

"But you've spoken to him, haven't you? And you wouldn't have told me that."

Still on the floor, Roberto propped himself against the hall wall. He pressed a hand to his ear. A warm sticky substance met his hand. Blood. He looked at Sara. "How much ear do I have left?"

Shaking, she knelt. "It just nicked you. Oh, God, I didn't mean to shoot you." Tears filled her eyes.

He spotted reason in her eyes. "Help me, Sara. Please."

"You're a criminal," she muttered.

"I'm not. It's about Leah's brother. He's the criminal."

"Luis isn't—"

"Not Luis. Leah's half brother."

Sara frowned. "She only mentioned him once."

"That's because he's bad. And he's trying to hurt her and Luis."

Sara's eyes widened. "That's who broke into her apartment. And sent the chicken parts."

Chicken parts?

"Are you a cop?" she asked.

"No, I work for a private investigating company. Doing undercover work." The lie felt heavy. He didn't know what provoked him, but the real truth followed, "Leah's half brother killed my wife and kid. I've been trying to find him."

Her eyes widened. "You said they died in a car accident."

He nodded. "They were pushed in front of a train. My wife witnessed Leah's brother kill someone. Less than a week later, she was dead."

Sara shook her head. "Leah wouldn't have anything to do with that."

"I know. I was here to see if she knew where he was. When I didn't think she did, I left. But Austin came back to see if he could find out anything."

"Austin's a private investigator?"

He nodded.

"Does Leah know?"

"She probably does now. Her brother, or someone he sent, was here trying to hurt her. Austin saved her."

"You sure she's okay?"

"I'm sure. But I need your help, so I can help them. So I can find DeLuna."

"You're shot. You can't help—"

"Sara, I have to do this. I'm going to do this, with or without your help."

She bit her lip. "What do you want me to do?"

"Get the bullet out."

Her mouth dropped open. "I can't—"

"You told me you did it for a dog once."

"You're not a dog."

"It's the same thing."

"No, it isn't." She looked at his leg. "There're major arteries in there."

"It's not deep. Just get the bullet out, sew me up, and give me some antibiotics. And I'll leave."

She squeezed her hands together. "It's against the law."

"If you get caught, I'll say I forced you. I'll say you shot the tip of my ear off trying to stop me." His ear stung like hell, too.

She frowned. "I didn't mean to shoot you."

"I know. Help me? Please."

*   *   *

Austin saw Leah's brow twitch. "Be honest. You've spoken with him, haven't you?" This wasn't the right time, but he wasn't sure there would be a right time.

She hesitated a second too long. "No."

"You're lying." Disappointment pulled at his shoulder blades. She knew he was telling the truth about DeLuna's men coming after her. He'd hoped she'd be a tad more understanding.

"Why should I tell you anything when you're kidnapping me?"

"I'm not kidnapping you," he said.

"Then pull over, untape me, and get the hell out of my car!"

He stared at her. "Okay, I'm kidnapping you. But if that's what it takes to save your life then—"

"I don't want you to save my life."

"Don't be ridiculous," he said.

"You're going to jail for this. I swear you're going to jail."

That pissed him off. "I've already been there. Your half brother sent me there."

When that quieted her, he thought maybe she was ready to listen. "I was a cop. Me and two other cops were close to shutting his organization down when—"

"I have nothing to do with him, and this has nothing to do with you kidnapping me!"

"He framed me and two other guys for murder. We were convicted. Went to jail for sixteen months!"

"I don't believe you."

"Neither did anyone else until an undercover FDA agent heard him bragging about it and actually found the gun he used. But after all of that, some people still think we did it."

She stared at the window as if she was done talking. That was fine. He needed to figure out a plan. The only thing he knew was where he was going. His cabin outside of Austin. His mind raced with questions. Had DeLuna been in the car shooting at them? The realization hit. He hadn't gotten a good look at them, but they had seen him. And if they recognized him, they might go after Dallas or Tyler. Shit. He needed to warn them.

As Austin expected, Dallas was concerned and pissed. Concerned more about his wife and Tyler's wife than anything. But he was also concerned for Austin when he told him what he'd had to do. *She can have you arrested for this.*

Austin didn't mention that Leah had promised to do that. But what were his choices? Let DeLuna grab her?

As upset as Dallas was, he spewed laughter when Austin asked him to have someone grab his and Leah's cats and bring them to his cabin. And when he told Dallas he could find Leah's key in his kitchen drawer, she glared at him.

Dallas groaned when he'd asked him to also pick up his truck from the rental place and pay the guy outright whatever the owner felt his silver Cavalier was worth. Explaining why he'd had to rent a car so he could watch the vet office had Leah scowling even more.

The call ended. Several minutes later with nothing but the humming of the tires on the pavement, Leah spoke. "Even if Rafael did what you said, I had no part in it. I shouldn't be punished for what he did."

"I know. That's why I couldn't let him hurt you."

Tears filled her eyes. "Stop this nonsense and take me to Luis."

"As soon as I know it's safe, I'll take you. I give you my word. Dallas is going to find out where he is and make sure he's safe. Then we'll see about getting you there."

"I want to see him now! And as someone who lied to me, your word means shit."

He looked back to the road. Her words hurt. Not that he didn't deserve them. He'd been wrong to lie to her. Wrong to have ever kissed her. Or to let her kiss him.

But friggin' hell! He wasn't wrong to force her to come with him. And he wasn't wrong not to take her to the hospital until he knew it was safe.

He'd take her anger over her getting hurt or killed. He just hoped if he did time for this, he'd feel the same way.

CHAPTER TWENTY-NINE

ROBERTO'S PHONE RANG.

"We need to talk," Dallas snapped in lieu of a hello.

Why had he answered it? Because he was scared it was bad news about Leah or her brother.

"Can this wait?" The pain was almost unbearable, even with the doggy pain pills he'd chewed. The smell of antiseptic filled the small room. In the back, he could hear a cat meowing.

"Do you want me to stop?" Sara asked.

"No," he gritted out.

"No, what?" Dallas asked.

"I'm in the middle of something," Roberto said.

"You've been in the middle of something for a long time and neglected to tell us."

"I'm getting a bullet pulled out of my leg. I'll call you back."

"Shit. You got hit?"

"Yeah." Roberto hung up, slammed his head back on the table, and accidentally let out a four-letter word.

"I almost got it," Sara said. "I'm trying to be gentle."

"I know," he managed to say. "Just do it." He breathed in and tried not to pass out.

He couldn't. He needed the bullet out of his leg and then he had to get Sara out of here. But the black spots started popping off like fireworks in his vision.

Roberto heard a feminine moan. Was Anna upset?

Then, bam! He remembered.

Anna was dead. Gone. As was his son. How many times had he woken up and forgotten that? His subconscious simply didn't want to retain that information. But this time, the pain in his leg brought on another realization.

He'd been shot.

He'd talked Sara into helping him.

Now she was crying. And just like that, he remembered she could be in danger. Shit! Had Cruz come back?

He reached for his gun, but it wasn't there. His pants weren't there, either.

The pain in his ear had him remembering he'd given her the gun. She'd shot him, too.

He blinked the fuzziness from his brain and saw her standing there beside him.

"What's wrong?" He tried to sit up.

"Don't get up." She pushed him down. "You need to be still for a while." She frowned. "Please tell me I didn't do something stupid."

"What did you do?" Had she called the cops?

"I helped you. Tell me you aren't a criminal and just saw me as gullible. I have a son to worry about. He's my everything. I can't go to jail or get killed. I don't know what I was thinking." Tears filled her eyes.

"You're not gullible," he said. He'd thought of her in a number of different ways, but never that way. "I'm not a criminal. And I swear I won't let this come back on you." At least he hadn't been a criminal. Now he was beginning to wonder if it was a crime to get her involved. She didn't deserve this.

"I'm sorry." He rose up on his elbow and looked down at his leg. When he'd had to remove his pants earlier, he'd wished he'd worn his better boxers.

"You're done?" he asked.

She nodded. "You really didn't break some law? Rob a bank or something worse?"

"No. It's all about Leah's half brother. I promise you."

She didn't look convinced. "I've got some antibiotics and some more pain pills." She pointed to the pills on the counter. "They are safe for humans."

He started to get up.

"No. If you move too much you'll start bleeding."

He frowned. "How long have I been out?"

"Ten minutes."

"Where's my gun?"

"I hid it."

"Can you get it for me?"

She frowned. "You gonna shoot me now and prove to me just how stupid I am?"

He sighed. "No. But you need to leave in case the guys looking for Leah come back."

"I have to open the office. Clients will be here in an hour. And Evelyn will be here in . . ." She frowned. "Evelyn's gonna kill me for doing this." She bit down on her lip. "Leah, too."

"You don't have to tell them. But you can't stay here. Leah wouldn't want anyone to get hurt."

She seemed to consider that. "I need to talk to Leah. Call her. Now."

It seemed like a reasonable request. And just as soon as his head stopped swimming he'd do that.

*   *   *

Leah wasn't sure who she was angrier at, Austin Brookshire—if that was really his name—or herself. She knew better than to trust a man. Especially a good-looking one. Wait, she did know who she was angrier at. Him!

Luis was hurt. Luis was in the hospital, and this lying jerk wasn't letting her go. Yup, she was madder at him. She twisted her hands, trying to loosen the tape. A couple of times, she'd wanted to ask him to free her, but now she didn't want to ask him for anything. She'd eventually get herself free. She didn't need him.

She didn't need anyone. But her brother. She prayed he was okay while she continued wiggling her hands, loosening the tape with each twist.

Not that the tape was so tight it hurt. Had he purposely not gotten it too tight? Did he regularly tape up people and kidnap them? Yup, she was definitely angrier at him. The only thing that kept her from totally freaking out and believing he was a complete psychopath was realizing she could be dead right now if he hadn't been there.

Not that it made Austin right. Her gut started churning again with worry, and then anger for not being taken to see her brother.

Austin's phone rang again. "Did Dallas get you?" Austin asked. Pause. "Good. Did he get the...hospital information?"

She looked at him, unable to hide her concern about her brother.

He nodded at her, assuring her someone was checking on her brother. But she didn't want *someone* there. She wanted to be there.

Austin looked away and continued the conversation. "What's Brad Hulk's connection to DeLuna?"

Who the hell was Brad Hulk?

Austin continued, "Why did he break into—" Pause. "You trust him?"

Like earlier, it was killing her only being able to hear half the conversation.

"Shit. Are you okay?" Pause. He looked at Leah. "I don't think...so."

What didn't he think? It was about her. Frustrated, she twisted her hands harder.

"Let me call you back," he said.

She didn't look at him, but she felt him looking at her. Was he going to try to stop her from freeing herself? He pulled to the side of the freeway. If he touched her, she'd fight him!

"Let me help you?"

Shocked at his offer, she got angrier. She didn't want him to start being nice. She wanted to hate him.

"No." She was being stubborn, but it felt good. "I'll do it myself."

"Please."

"No." The tape loosened and she slipped her hand through. She threw the tape on the floor. Leaning over, she untaped her ankles. The question of what she'd do when completely free bubbled up inside her. She could get out of the car.

He exhaled. "We need to talk about something."

She faced him. "Unless it's to do with my brother, I'm not in a talking mood."

"I need you to be reasonable."

"Reasonable? You kidnapped me. You lied to me."

"I saved your life. And I'm sorry about lying," he said.

"You took advantage of me by...by making up some pathetic story about being a foster kid. You knew I'd fall for it."

"Everything wasn't a lie." He sighed. "Look, Sara wants to talk to you."

"Sara?" What did she have to do with this? "How does she...she knows who you are?"

"She does now. There's someone I know at your clinic with her. He doesn't think she should be there in case DeLuna's guys come back."

Leah's chest gripped as she remembered being shot at. She didn't want Sara hurt. Or Evelyn. "They should leave."

"She wants to hear it from you."

She tilted her chin up. "And you're afraid I'll tell her that you kidnapped me. Because you'd go to jail."

"Look, when you're out of danger, if you want to report me to the police, fine. But right now you need me to protect you." He held up his hand. "I know you don't want my help. And you're madder than a firecracker. I get that. I'll admit that I might deserve it. I didn't mean for this to happen. I didn't expect to be attracted...." He ran a hand over his face. "If you go to the police now, the most they'll do is send a patrol car to drive by your place a few times a night. It's not enough."

"But—"

He held up his hand again. "Think about your brother. I guarantee you that as soon as possible my friends will have someone at the hospital making sure DeLuna doesn't get to him. It was even someone working with us that took him to the hospital. If you go to the police, they'll make my friend leave. But they won't put a guard there. You and your brother will be unprotected."

She knew he was right, but hated it. Hated having to depend on him when he'd lied and used her. Hated knowing he was helping her. Then she realized something. She didn't have to feel beholden to him. He wasn't doing this for her.

He was doing it to catch Rafael. That had been his plan all along.

"Let me help you and your brother, please."

"Fine," she snapped. "But I want to see my brother."

His jaw tightened. "If possible, I'll take you later today or tomorrow. But not before I know it's safe."

Frustration gripped her chest. "Fine. But don't pretend that you're doing this for me. We know why you're doing it. To catch Rafael."

His jaw clenched. "Whatever."

His expression said he wanted to argue with her, but the sting of all his lies hurt like a deep paper cut right across the heart. Hurt. Until this moment all she'd felt was anger.

Tears stung her sinuses. She could deal with the anger; being angry felt good. Feeling hurt meant she cared. She didn't want to care. Caring meant he had the power to hurt her. Too many men had already done that.

She stared out the side window. "I'll talk to Sara."

Sara started cleaning up the work area. She felt Roberto watching her.

He'd said that Austin would call him back for her to speak with Leah. Couldn't he have just handed Leah the phone? Fear prickled her stomach. Not fear of Roberto. Fear that something wasn't right. Like the fact that she'd just pulled a bullet out of a guy's leg.

What kind of a mother was she that she took such a stupid risk? But even still she knew why she'd done it. She'd followed her heart. Like the time she'd pulled off the freeway to rescue an injured dog? Or the time she'd stopped and given a strange woman a ride when she ran out of gas. Sara could have gotten run over rescuing the dog; the woman could have been a serial killer. But she risked it because her heart said to. All she could do now was pray her heart had been right about this like in the past.

"Can I put my pants on now?" he asked.

She looked at him. It had been a while since she'd seen a man without his pants. She hadn't thought about that when she'd been digging the bullet out, but now ... she thought about it. He had nice legs, not too hairy. Though, she had shaved around his wound before she'd gone in for the bullet.

He rose up.

"Let me help you." She took his hand. "Are you dizzy?"

"Not anymore." His hand wrapped around hers. The touch seemed different now. Her heart raced, but not from fear. His closeness, his scent, it surrounded her.

She reached for his jeans folded on the counter. She shook them open and leaned down for him to put his legs in.

"Now ease off the table," she told him. "Don't put weight on your leg."

His warm palms came against her shoulders, and they weren't just holding on, they were touching her. He slipped off the edge of the examining table. She pulled his jeans up, reached for his zipper, then realized the back of her hand pressed against some private body parts.

She yanked her hand away and rose up. His hands remained on her shoulders. His eyes on hers. "I'm used to dressing Brian. But you're not Brian."

He smiled. "You're blushing."

That made her blush more. "I'm blond, we blush easy."

His grin widened. "It's pretty." He zipped his pants and eased back up on the table.

They stared at each other. Awkwardness slipped into the moment, but not so awkward that she wanted it to end. The ring of his phone brought it to an end. He picked it up from the table and looked at the number. "It's Austin."

Sara stood there, not even pretending she wasn't listening. She was in this too deep to pretend.

"It's Leah." Roberto handed her his phone. Their hands met. His thumb brushed over the top of her hand.

She brought the phone to her ear. "Leah?"

"Yeah," her boss answered. "Are you okay?"

"Fine." *Other than I just pulled a bullet out of someone's leg.* She wasn't sure she should tell Leah that. "It's you I'm worried about. Roberto said Luis is hurt. Are you okay?"

"Roberto? The guy who brought in Spooky?" Leah sounded confused.

Sara glanced at Roberto. "Yeah. He said he's been working with a private investigator. I think Austin is—"

"I know," Leah said. "Look, you shouldn't be at the office now. We should shut down for a week. Forward the client list to your home e-mail, or to Evelyn's, and cancel appointments." She paused. "We just have one patient in the overnight clinic, right?"

"Yeah, just Boots; he belongs to the Petersons."

"Can you call Eric Taylor and see if Heartbroke Veterinarian Clinic will take the cat in? E-mail him the file on the cat. Then let the Petersons know and that I won't be charging for my services. Tell Eric I said I had a personal emergency and I'll call him tomorrow. Tell him I'll agree to his business proposition and sign the papers when I get back."

"You sure about the business proposition?" Sara asked.

"Yeah. And put a sign in the door that says there was a family emergency and we'll open soon."

"You sound upset. You okay?" Sara asked.

"Just worried about Luis." It was more than worry, Sara thought. Leah sounded angry.

"Okay, I've got things here. You just take care of Luis."

"Thanks." The line went silent.

Sara handed the phone to Roberto. "The only other time I've heard Leah sound like that was when someone brought in a cat with cigarette burns on it. I think Austin's in deep shit."

Roberto shrugged. "Austin can handle it. Let's get you out of here."

"I have to do a few things first. Oh," she said. "My car's in the shop. My mom brought me."

He frowned. "I'll take you home, but hurry, and give me my gun. Please."

She eased it out of a drawer. Not chancing it would go off again. "Do you really think they'll come back?"

"I hope not."

Austin rolled his shoulders, completely uncomfortable. Looking at this from Leah's point of view right now, he was nothing but a guy trying to use her to get some information. Guilt filled his every pore and made him itch—guilt for not coming clean with Leah from the beginning. It didn't matter that if he'd been honest, she'd never have flashed one dimple at him.

She leaned against the car door as if not wanting to breathe the same air as him. Seeing a fast-food sign up ahead, his stomach grumbled.

"Hungry?" he asked.

"No."

"You have to eat."

She didn't answer. He swerved off the freeway and went to the drive-thru. He ordered himself a sausage biscuit and hash browns, then asked, "What's the lowest-calorie breakfast item you have on the menu with cheese?" He knew she liked cheese.

The female clerk spouted out a sandwich. He ordered it, then added two coffees, one with extra cream and sugar.

When the meal was delivered, he put their coffee in the cup holder, placed her sandwich in her lap. Then he drove off.

He half expected her to knock her food onto the floorboard. She didn't. But it took five minutes before she started eating.

"Your coffee's there," he said.

She nodded.

He should be good with the nod. It was too much to expect an actual *thank you*, or maybe, *I totally get why you did this.* Even with the guilt, he knew he'd done the right thing making her come with him.

His phone rang. Dallas.

"Yeah?" he said, and watched Leah add cream and sugar to her cup.

"Rick's at the hospital. The kid is going to be okay," Dallas said.

"That fast?"

"He was on his way up to Heartbroke and rerouted. He played the cop card and said he was friends with the sister who couldn't get there until later. The kid's conscious and worried about his sister. The local police have spoken with him. He pointed right to DeLuna."

"Good," Austin said. But then again, it could also mean DeLuna would run back into hiding. "Rick's staying there, right?"

"Yup."

"Any signs of trouble?" Austin asked.

"Not yet. But whatever you do, don't bring her there."

Austin frowned. Taking her to see Luis seemed to be the only thing that would make her happy. But not if she was in danger. "Have Rick video him and send it to me for her."

Leah swung around, surprise in her eyes.

"I don't know," Dallas said. "Rick said the kid looked bad."

Austin stared at Leah. "I'm sure he's better than what she's imagining."

Leah nodded.

"I'll see what he can do," Dallas said.

Leah blinked, and Austin could swear he saw reason in her eyes. Would she see he wasn't the bad guy?

"You still there?" Dallas said.

Realizing he'd gotten lost in her gaze, he asked, "Who's getting the cats?"

"Tyler and Nance are on their way. And I'm going to come to the cabin to talk to her," Dallas said.

"I got this," Austin growled.

"You could do time for this, Austin," Dallas said.

"I know."

Dallas made a deep, discontented sound. "Has she calmed down any?"

"Some," Austin said. But not nearly enough. He wanted to see her smile, to see her dimples winking at him again. He wanted her to lean on him like she'd leaned on him the day she'd gotten the bloody package. He wanted to be her hero, but he was pretty sure that ship had sailed.

Roberto watched Sara run around the office preparing to leave. His gut told him he needed to get her out of here. Every time he tried to help her, she refused.

"You just had a bullet pulled out of your leg."

He hadn't forgotten; it still throbbed, though not as much as it had. Then again, it could be the doggy pain pills Sara had given him.

"I'll sit here." He dropped into a chair.

"You need your leg up." She sounded like a worried someone who cared. He remembered his mom, and then Anna, fussing at him like that. He hadn't had anyone care in a long time. It felt nice. Then again, it could just be the pain pills.

He set his leg up on the counter. "Happy?"

"I'd be happier if you hadn't gotten up." She pressed her palm to his forehead. "Do you feel feverish?"

"No." He allowed himself a second to enjoy her touch, then... "We need to go."

"Almost done. I need to get Boots in a carrier." She popped up. "Stay here."

He followed her. Her hair shifted across her shoulder blades as she moved. He wanted to touch it. His gaze lowered to her ass. He wanted to touch that, too. Things in his jeans tightened. Oddly enough, he didn't feel guilty about those feelings.

Definitely the doggy pain pills.

She swung around. "You're a bad patient. You don't follow orders."

"You are a bad nurse. You shot me." He laughed.

She grinned, and damn if he didn't want to stop worrying about everything and tease her. See how many smiles he could coax out of her. Was that due to the doggy pills, too? *Not now,* his gut said. He needed to get her out of here. "Get the cat."

Minutes later, she had a cat carrier and her purse. He unlocked the back door and cautiously peered out.

He didn't see anyone, but his gut felt knotted. Pulling out Luke's car keys from his pocket, he unlocked the doors to the sedan. The taillights flashed in the hazy morning light.

"Let's go."

The door shut behind them. They'd only gotten a couple of feet when Roberto heard the car coming around the side of the building.

He swung to Sara. "Run. Get in the car now!"

CHAPTER THIRTY

THE CAR ROARING around the back wasn't another black sedan. The tension in Roberto's gut lessened, but not by much. Especially when the gun appeared out the driver's window. He pointed his Glock, then turned to see if Sara had gotten in the car. She had.

The car squealed to a stop.

The door to the Saturn opened. Brad climbed out. "Stop pointing that gun at me!"

Roberto didn't move, but everything around him seemed to. Brad, his car, the parking lot. Roberto fought to remain standing. "Have you forgotten you shot my ass?"

"That was a mistake." Brad looked toward the sedan. "Who's the chick?"

"She works with Leah Reece. And was kind enough to undo your handiwork. What are you doing here?"

"I lost Cruz and thought they'd come back here. I saw the sedan and thought it was them." Brad moved in.

Roberto lowered his gun. "Does Cruz know you're after him?"

"He does now," Brad said. "I helped that blond guy get Leah Reece away. The same guy at her apartment the other day."

"Good." Roberto thought about Brad's wife, Sandy, and what DeLuna might do to her and her girls. "Your wife?"

"She's taken off with the girls."

"What are you going to do now?" Roberto's head spun again. He swayed.

The big bozo stood there as if thinking. "That blond guy, you know him, don't you?"

Roberto nodded.

"He's one of those cops DeLuna set up, isn't he? DeLuna flashed his picture around once."

"Yeah." Roberto didn't see any reason to deny it.

"You're working with them? That's what you were doing the whole time?"

"I helped them, but I have my reasons for going after DeLuna," Roberto said.

"He hurt someone you cared about?" Brad asked.

Roberto didn't answer, but Brad must have read his expression. "Figured," Brad said. "It's the only thing that could make people like us do this."

Roberto shifted his weight off his left leg. Another dizzy spell hit.

Brad's gaze lowered. "How bad is it?"

"Bad enough." Roberto frowned.

"Sorry." The big guy's gaze shifted to the sedan. "Go take it easy."

"You're not the only one with an ax to grind," Roberto said.

"But I'm the only one who's not about to fall on his ass." Brad started to leave.

"Damn it, Brad. What are you planning on doing?"

"The only thing I can do. Finish what I started."

Roberto remembered how Sandy had looked, tears and love in her eyes. "If you walk away now, you might live through this and be there for your family."

"If I walk away now, I'll be running the rest of my life. Alone." He sighed. "Sandy's parents are in a nursing home. She wouldn't abandon them."

"If you keep this up, you'll wind up behind bars."

"I might. But I might've started this whole thing stupid... I don't plan to finish that way. I gotta plan. The only people who know I'm behind this are you and that blond ex-cop. The car was borrowed and the guns I'm using belong to my dear ol' brother-in-law. Actually that ex-cop probably has my gun. And I saved his and DeLuna's sister's ass, so I'm hoping he'll keep his mouth shut."

"You gonna try to make this all fall back on Cruz?" Roberto asked, and glanced back to see Sara peeking over the edge of the window. He waved to let her know it was okay.

"It's a long shot," Brad said. "But I'm kind of lucky sometimes."

Roberto hoped Brad was right. "Where do you think Cruz and DeLuna are now?"

"If they aren't here, they're probably worried about not being able to reach Luke and Don. I haven't seen any news out about anyone finding bodies at the warehouse, so they might go back to Austin to check on them."

Roberto tried to think. "Let me drop her off at her place and we'll go together."

"Nope. You look like shit. Lay low. I'll update you when I find Cruz or DeLuna. I'm not even sure they're still together. But when I know something, I'll call."

Roberto nodded. Brad held out his hand.

Roberto nearly missed it when he reached out. "Take care."

"You, too," Brad said. "I'm going to overlook the fact that you've been lying to me all this time."

"And I'll overlook the fact that you shot me."

"Deal." Brad smiled.

Roberto watched Brad get back in the Saturn before he limped back to the car. He almost fell getting in. Not from pain, but from the dizziness.

Sara popped up in the front seat, fury in her eyes. "Why did you tell me to run and make me believe the guy was going to kill us and then stand there talking with him while I'm sitting here thinking we're dead?"

"I didn't know if I could trust him. He's the one who shot me."

Sara's mouth dropped open. "He shot you and you just had a civil three-minute conversation with him? Are you nuts?"

Roberto grinned. "You shot me and I'm giving you a ride home."

She huffed. "That's different."

"Yeah, it is. You're a lot prettier than him." He dropped his head back on the headrest as his world spun again.

Sara stared. "I think I'd better drive."

He started to argue but realized she was right. "I think it's the pills."

"How many did you take?"

"Four before the surgery and four after. Like you said."

She frowned. "I told you to take four. Two before and two after."

"Oops."

Thirty minutes later, Austin parked in a Walmart parking lot. Leah hadn't spoken to him again since he'd hung up with Dallas. She'd leaned her head back, her eyes closed, but he didn't think she'd slept.

His phone dinged with a text. From Rick. The text read: *looks bad, but he's doing good.*

"Is it the video?" she asked.

"Yeah."

She held out her hand, her eyes moist again.

He handed her the phone.

She hit play. Tears slipped off her lashes as she watched. Shit! He'd messed up. Maybe she shouldn't have seen this. The sound kicked in.

"Hey, Sis. Don't go freaking out. I'm fine. Black and blue, but the doc says I'm fine. Listen, I'm told you're with a PI that works with the guy who's here. You do what he says. I know you don't like counting on people. But please don't go doing anything stupid. Rafael told me he was coming after you. And if something happened to you..." The kid's voice wavered. *"Just listen to him, okay? I'm fine. And I'll see you as soon as I'm out of here."*

She wiped her cheeks.

He wanted to touch her so badly it hurt—to offer comfort. But he didn't.

Without looking at him, she handed him his phone. He felt a thousand watts of emotion run through his hand straight to his chest when their hands touched.

"I need to see him." She stared out at the parking lot.

"I know it's hard," Austin said. And deep down, he wished that was completely true. Wished he knew firsthand the kind of family loyalty she had with her brother. Sure, he had his partners, and if one of them was hurt, he'd walk through fire to get to them, but there was something about real family ties that he felt he'd missed out on. As if not having family made him less human and somehow damaged. *Just like your ol' man.* Candy Adams's words played in his head.

Another silence filled the car. She looked out the window as if seeing it for the first time. "What are we doing here?"

He ran his hand over the steering wheel, relieved she sounded sensible now. "The cabin's just up the road. I figured we'd grab some supplies."

She looked in the backseat. "I didn't bring my purse, did I?" She shook her head as if remembering how she'd gotten in the car. "Of course, I didn't."

"You won't need it."

She looked up. "I'm paying you back every red cent."

He wanted to argue, but she had that look in her eyes again. Anger.

She opened the console between the seats and pulled out a pen and pad. She was actually going to keep a tally. But damn, she was hardheaded. Then a stray tear slipped from her lashes and rolled down her cheek, and he forgot about her being difficult and wished he could find a way to give her want she wanted—a visit with her brother.

Leah walked into Walmart; Austin pushed the cart beside her. He barely looked at her, and that was just dandy with her. On top of being hurt, Leah was back to being pissed—and for damn good reasons, too. Oh, sure, he'd gotten her the video and that had been nice, but if she'd understood half the conversation he'd had, Austin had kept one of her apartment keys. To do what? Snoop around her apartment?

Fine, she'd asked him once to break in, and he'd been nice to fix her locks, but did that give him a right to keep her key without telling her?

No.

And that made her wonder if he'd already been rummaging around her place when she wasn't there. Was he some panty pervert going through her underwear. Had he searched through her private things to find information on Rafael?

She wanted to kick Austin's ass.

But adding fuel to her fury was that she didn't know this man, and yet he'd wormed his way into her life and...made her care.

As furious as she was, the fact that she was more hurt than angry told her she still cared. Cared for Austin Brookshire, an admitted liar. Wait. Was that even his name? Heck, he could be married or involved with someone. All she'd been to him was possible information.

She recalled him saying: *I didn't lie about everything.*

"Define everything!" she wanted to scream. But asking was like poking around in an open wound. It didn't stop the questions from forming in her mind.

Was it a lie when you said you liked me?

Was it a lie when you said I was the most fun you'd had in...forever?

Was it a lie when you told me you didn't like broccoli and you'd had as terrible a childhood as I had?

Was the hard-on in your pants the night we rolled around on your wet kitchen floor a lie?

Yup, an open wound. Best not to know the answers. Best to just stay furious. She'd eventually stop caring.

He pushed the cart to the women's underwear department.

"You might want to pick up some basic essentials."

"Why don't you just pick them out?" she seethed. "Since you kept the key to my place, I figure you've been snooping in my panty drawer!"

Okay, she wasn't supposed to say that, but damn it felt good.

Looking slapped, he glanced around to see if anyone was listening. They weren't. Not that she'd checked before blurting that out. She'd just gotten lucky.

He came closer. "I didn't go through your drawers."

"Then why did you keep the key and not tell me?"

He inhaled. "Do we have to talk about this here?"

"Yeah," she said. "Because if I'm alone with you, and you tell me that you were trying on my panties, I might kill you. Here, you've got people to protect you."

A woman walking by snorted with laughter. Austin looked mortified.

"I've never tried on a pair of women's underwear... ever."

"Then why did you keep the key?"

He released a gulp of air. "In case I needed to get in. You'd already asked me to break in to your place once."

"Then why didn't you tell me that?" she seethed.

He ran a palm over his face. "Because you can be the most unreasonable person I've had the pleasure of meeting."

Her chest burned with anger. "And I thought you said you liked me. I guess that was a lie, too." Realizing what she was doing, poking around in the wound, she searched the buy-one-get-one-free stack for panties.

He moved behind her so close that his warm breath caressed her cheek. "I do like you. But you're still... pigheaded."

"Really?" She swung around. With him leaning down, her nose came even with his. "Are you referring to my pig-headedness *before* or *after* you hogtied me and threw me in my car?"

His jaw clenched so tight she was amazed his words came out. "I saved your life."

"So that excuses the behavior?"

He stared at her as if she'd grown two heads. "Yes, it completely excuses it! And if you'd been reasonable, I wouldn't have had to do it."

"And if you hadn't lied to me, and hadn't been worming your way into my life, pretending to have fun with me"—her voice rose—"and trying to get into my pants just so you could get me to give you information, then maybe I'd have been reasonable!"

"I wasn't trying to get into—"

"Really?" she spit out. "Where I come from, when a guy unhooks your bra and sticks his hand down your pants, it usually means—"

A woman with a young boy cleared her throat. "Come on, Joey." The mom hurried her boy past. "These people need some privacy." She frowned at Leah.

"She's mad like you were mad at Daddy last night," the boy said.

Austin shook his head. "Told you discussing this here wasn't a good idea."

She grabbed the basket and rolled to the bra aisle.

While she was picking one out, he came close. "I hadn't planned on being attracted to you. I wasn't trying to seduce you to get information, I was doing it because...I couldn't stop myself. But if you'll recall, I did stop it. I told you we needed to take it slow. I didn't want to sleep with you until I'd told you the truth."

Another knot of hurt rose in her throat. "You should have never lied." She grabbed a cheap white bra and some socks.

He frowned. "You wouldn't have told me anything if I'd told you the truth."

She went to the clothing racks and found a pair of jeans and a couple of cheap long-sleeve shirts. After grabbing a pair of sweats, she glanced up at him. "You fooled me into trusting you. Do you know how few people I trust? And now you're keeping me from seeing my brother."

"I'm sorry, but..." He ran a hand down the back of his head and squeezed his neck. "Have you realized that if I wasn't here, you and your brother might be dead? I'm not saying I'm right, but maybe you could cut me some slack and not hate me so damn much!"

His words bounced around her head, dropped to her chest like a lump of pain. Did she actually owe him gratitude for deceiving her?

He grabbed the cart and rolled over to the men's aisle. He picked out some boxers, socks, and a couple of T-shirts.

The words *I don't hate you, I hate what you did,* and *I don't know who you are* were on her lips. She couldn't get them out. It felt like admitting she cared, and while she'd admitted it to herself, admitting it to him was too much.

She followed him to the food section. He haphazardly tossed items in the basket, rushing down five or six aisles. "Is there anything you want?" Frustration rang in his voice.

"I'm not picky." She didn't want to talk anymore.

"What if I picked out Chinese food?" he asked.

"Then I'd go hungry. Without complaining."

He moaned and cut through the store to the registers. As they came upon the Halloween section, he stopped so fast, his shoes made skid marks.

"That's it!" He smiled like a kid at Christmas. She hadn't seen him smile since this went down, and it pulled at her heartstrings.

"What?" she asked, determined to ignore her heartstrings.

"Clowns." He waved to the display of costumes.

"What?"

His grin widened. "Pick out a clown outfit, Leah. We're going to see your brother."

CHAPTER THIRTY-ONE

LEAH SNATCHED THE receipt from the cashier's hand. Austin frowned, but she didn't care. She was paying him back. As they walked by the restrooms, she stopped. "We could change here and head to the hospital."

"Not yet. Tyler and Nance are bringing the cats. And I need to confirm with Rick that it's clear." They left the store.

"I thought the costumes made it okay." She envisioned Luis's face, swollen to the point that it hurt to look at him. Her chest clutched.

"They will. But better safe than sorry."

"But we're going today, right?"

"If not today, tomorrow."

She frowned.

He frowned back. "I'm doing everything I can." Damn if he didn't sound sincere and damn if she didn't believe him. But how could she believe him when he'd done nothing but lie to her?

"Who's Rick?" she asked as he loaded the bags in the trunk.

"He's with your brother." He shut the trunk.

She almost asked him to give her the keys, *her* keys, so

she could drive *her* car. But since she didn't know where they were going she didn't.

"I know that. But how did Rafael screw him over?"

"He didn't. Rick's a cop and works part-time with our agency." He unlocked the car and she got in. He crawled behind the wheel.

"And Roberto? You guys sent him to spy on me, too, didn't you?"

Austin nodded. "Yes, but Roberto believes that DeLuna killed his wife and child."

Leah heart clutched. Both shame and fury burned inside her for the things her half brother had done. "If I knew where he was, I'd tell you."

He glanced at her—his blue eyes open and honest. "I believe you."

She stared out the windshield, trying to decipher her roller-coaster emotions about the man sitting in the driver's seat: anger, then gratitude. All of it complicated by a sense of vulnerability. Vulnerable to her murdering half brother who almost killed Luis. Vulnerable to men in general—men like Austin, who waltzed into her life and tricked her into caring.

He pulled out of the parking lot. Five minutes passed when she suddenly couldn't stop from asking, "What's your real name?"

He glanced at her. "Austin Brook."

"Not Brookshire?" Sarcasm heightened her voice.

"No." Guilt sounded in his voice.

"You're not married, are you?"

His brow pinched. "No."

"Your mother never abandoned you at a day care, did she?"

"That wasn't a lie." Honesty deepened his tone.

"What else?" she asked.

"What else what?" He stared at the road.

"What else did you lie about? What else did you do besides keep my key?" Suddenly something dawned on her. "Was my apartment even broken into, or did you do it?"

He shifted in his seat as if antsy.

"It was you the whole time."

"No. I . . ." Guilt filled his eyes. "I was in your place when the guy broke in."

She tried to wrap her head around that. "You expect me to believe that you'd broken into my place, and then by some strange coincidence someone *else* broke in while you were there?"

He sighed. "That's what happened."

"Right." She scowled at him.

He pointed to his eye with the half-moon purple bruise. "Do you think I did this to myself?"

"You could have," she said.

"I'm not an idiot."

"As far as I'm concerned, that's still up for debate," she snapped. "What were you doing in my place? What did you expect to find? Rafael hiding under my bed?"

His hands on the steering wheel tightened. His knuckles turned white. He looked at her and opened his mouth to say something and then shut it.

"Do we have to talk about this now?"

"Yes," she insisted, knowing whatever he had to say, she wasn't going to like it. "What else did you do or lie about?"

An hour after she'd gotten home, Sara checked on Roberto. He was still asleep in her bed.

She studied him. Asleep, he looked less dangerous—though he had a serious case of five-o'clock shadow going. His chest, covered with a blue cotton T-shirt, moved up and down with his every breath. His bare leg extended from under the covers. He looked good in her bed. Okay, so maybe he still looked dangerous. Just in a different way.

After driving them to her apartment, she'd insisted he come in until the drugs wore off. He'd argued, but not much. The man was stoned on doggy drugs. After checking on the cat and putting him in her laundry room, she'd made Roberto remove his jeans so she could check the wound.

It had looked good, and he wasn't feverish. She still forced him to get into her bed. He'd argued about that, too, but she'd won again.

The first thing she did was check if the extra dose of medicine could be harmful. According to his weight, he hadn't taken enough to do any damage.

Assured he was okay, she called her mom and asked if she could keep Brian overnight. She might take a chance being around a handsome, totally hot guy who showed up with a bullet in his leg, but she wouldn't risk him being with her son. Frankly, she wasn't sure she'd let any guy near her son yet, bullet or no bullet.

The thought of the bullet, or more specifically, her removing it, sent her pulse racing. She'd broken the law. And she was going to have to tell Leah. Who would surely be upset. Would she understand that Sara's following-her-heart theory? And was bringing him home with her part of that theory?

Of course, when she'd requested her mom keep Brian, her mom had asked what was up. Sara lied and said she was going out with Leah. Leah…who was with Austin. Leah who'd sounded madder than a trapped raccoon. Sara wished Austin all the luck in the world at coming through this without being neutered. If there was one thing Leah excelled at, it was removing testicles.

Then Sara called Evelyn. She freaked when hearing about the whole mess. But, being professional, Evelyn agreed to help take care of business by calling the clients with appointments.

Of course, Sara hadn't told Evelyn about Roberto and her now being a criminal. Evelyn would have totally flipped. Sara knew because part of herself was flipping.

Roberto stirred, knocking the sheet off. Worried he might be feverish, she went in and sat on the edge of the bed. She touched his brow. He wasn't hot.

Her gaze dropped to his boxers and the oh-so-male frontal bulge. Okay, she had to amend that last thought. He was totally hot, just not feverish.

Leaning back against the headboard, she watched him sleep and fought the desire to reach down and brush his hair from his brow. He could have died, she realized. And if he hadn't come to her, infection could have set in and that could have killed him.

All of a sudden, helping him didn't seem so wrong. He'd already lost so much. His son. His wife. She sensed a goodness in him; he didn't deserve to die.

She just prayed her heart hadn't led her down a road she'd regret.

"I bugged your place." Austin knew sooner or later he'd have to tell her. He'd just been hoping for later. The car hit a jarring dip in the dirt road heading to the cabin.

"You did what?" She blew air out of teeth. "You put cameras in my apartment? You've been watching—"

"Not cameras." He parked at the cabin. "Just listening devices, so I could hear if you spoke with Rafael."

"So you've heard every conversation I've had?"

He felt every bit of the louse she considered him to be.

He could almost see her mind replaying her past conversations. Her eyes rounded; her mouth dropped open. Was she remembering the conversation about the battery-operated boyfriend? He knew he'd never forget it.

From the fury in her eyes, that was exactly what she was remembering. Bouncing against the seat, she crossed her arms over her chest, twisted away from him, and stared out the window. Silent. Deadly silent.

He waited for a good five minutes before he dared to speak. "We're here."

"I know we're here."

He kept his voice calm. "Do you want to get out?"

She unlocked her seat belt and bolted from the car. Stomping to the porch, everything about her, posture, pace, and expression, exuded anger. He deserved every bit of it.

Sara felt a tickle on her cheek. Her eyes shot open. Dark brown eyes stared at her with the same befuddlement she felt.

When had they wrapped around each other? Her arm under his neck. His leg on top of her thighs. His... impressive bulge, even more impressive now, pressed against her hip.

They untangled themselves at the same time. She scrambled to stand up. He scrambled to reach for the sheet. But not before she saw it. His boxers were the open slit kind, versus the button-up kind, and something, standing rather erect, had decided to come out for air.

"Sorry." She slapped a hand over her eyes.

She heard him continue to fight for the sheet.

"I checked on you and I must have dozed off," she explained.

"It's your bed." His voice sounded raspy from sleep. "It's safe now."

She split her two fingers and peered out.

He stared at her. And while he was olive skinned, she could swear his face was red. And that made her blush, too.

"I see that every day." The words spilled from her fogged brain. "My son's. And it's nothing." Laughter bubbled up inside her. "Not that you aren't..." She pressed a hand over her mouth. "I'm gonna shut up," she muttered from behind her fingers.

He smiled. Not just a smile, but one of those really sweet ones. Or maybe not so sweet as...sexy.

They stared at each other. Her knees wobbled; her skin tingled. She felt both energized and weak at the same time. Weak from wanting to press her lips to that smile. From wanting to run her fingers over his five-o'clock shadow and slip her hand down his hard abs and into those boxers.

The air suddenly tasted different. His scent, the one she'd been cozied up to while she slept, filled her nose. She wanted to breathe it in, to surround herself with it.

He stood up, wrapping the sheet around himself. "Do you mind if I use your bathroom?"

"No. It's right there."

She watched him step into her bathroom. Heart still racing, she didn't move. She'd never had a man in that bathroom before. The sound of him shuffling around filled her ears. Then she heard the shower. The visual of him standing naked beneath a hot spray of water filled her head. She envisioned water droplets rolling off his chin, landing on his wide chest. Rolling down past his hard abs, to his hard sex and then his...

"Stop!" She ran to the door. "You can't take a shower. Did you hear me?"

"Why not?" His voice echoed from the door.

"You can't get your leg wet."

The door swung open. He'd removed his shirt but held the sheet around his waist. His dark eyes, filled with heat and desire, met hers. A thousand butterflies stretched their wings in her stomach. She was nurse Sara, and he was her patient. She wouldn't let him do anything that cost him more than he'd already lost.

The sound of the shower and puffs of steam filled the small bathroom. Who knew that standing in a bathroom with someone could feel intimate, but it did. It felt good, as if she was suddenly a part of something, a part of someone's life. Was that why her heart led her here? She was so lonely for companionship, she'd taken risks?

"Why can't I get it wet?"

"It could get infected."

"So I'm not supposed to bathe?"

"A spit bath. Or, I can wrap it. With cellophane and tape. For a quick shower."

"I need a shower," he said.

"I'll get the cellophane."

They looked at each other again, and oddly she recalled the times she'd brought home an injured creature, a bird, or a baby squirrel, and her mom would say, "You know, Sara, eventually you have to set it free."

Her mom knew it always hurt her to let something go after she nursed it, and down deep Sara knew this was the same. She couldn't keep him.

But was it wrong to enjoy it just for a little while?

Austin let her into the cabin and then returned to the car for the purchases. When he brought in the bags, Leah was sitting sat at the small pine table staring at nothing. He set a few of the bags on the sofa. He put cold stuff away. She never glanced at him.

The one-room cabin, two if you counted the bathroom, wasn't what you'd call fancy, but rustic didn't describe it, either. The main room was divided into three areas: a full-size bed with a dresser and nightstand took over the back of the cabin, the stove and fridge with the dining table took up the center area, and then a small sofa, which made out into a bed, and a coffee table and television fronted the room. Other than the bathroom, it hadn't been built to offer privacy. He hadn't needed it. This wasn't a love nest, rather his own private getaway. Only his partners had visited it.

"I can't believe you bugged my apartment," she spit out.

He put the avocados and half dozen tomatoes in a basket centering the table.

He took a deep breath. "At the time, you'd hardly speak to me, and it felt like the only way to get information."

"You violated my privacy."

"I know. I regret it. But at the time, it didn't feel wrong. I'm sorry. If you want to hate me for it—hate me. But remember I'm doing everything I can to help you and your brother." He went to grab another bag.

"I don't hate you!"

He turned around. She stood up. "But I'm so angry I could..."

She grabbed a tomato from the basket and threw it. She got him in the thigh. The ripe fruit burst and tomato guts rolled down his leg.

He looked up at her. Another tomato came hurling at him. He took that one to the head. He wiped the juice from his ear. "This is childish, but if it makes you feel better, go ahead." He pointed a finger at her. "But you won't have tomatoes in your salad tonight."

She threw another one.

The juicy ripe fruit whizzed past him.

"What the hell?" a voice boomed behind him.

Dallas stood in the door. Plastered on his wide chest was a splattered tomato.

The look on Dallas's face almost had Austin laughing. But when he looked back at Leah, the hurt in her eyes, nothing seemed funny. She hurled another tomato at Austin.

He waved at Dallas to leave. As Austin followed, the last tomato hit the back of his head. Knowing there were still two avocados, he shut the door.

"Girl's got a good arm." Dallas wiped tomato off his shirt.

Different emotions ran amok in Austin's chest. He shook the bits of tomato from his hair. A noise erupted from Dallas. Laughter. He tried to disguise it. Just not enough.

"Don't!" Austin warned.

Dallas wiped a palm over his face. "I thought you said she'd calmed down?"

"She had until I told her I bugged her place."

"That'd have made me mad, too." Dallas looked back at the door. "Let me talk to her."

"No." Austin blocked the door. "I can handle this."

Dallas quirked a brow. "I saw how well you're handling it. Someone needs to intervene."

"I'm not letting you read her the riot act. She has a right to be mad."

"I'm not going to read her any riot act." Dallas frowned. "I told you from the beginning this wasn't a good idea. I'm going to try to convince her not to press charges against you. I don't want to have to visit your ass in prison."

"I'll deal with it," Austin said.

Dallas studied him. "You're awful protective of the little tomato thrower."

"I'm not . . . I know her better than you."

"And that's why she needs to hear this from me." He picked up his briefcase. "I'm just going to smooth things over." Dallas hesitated. "Did you sleep with her?"

Austin shook his head. "No." His gut knotted when he realized it didn't seem to matter. He didn't think she could hate him more.

Dallas sighed. "Thank God for small favors."

Austin watched Dallas step inside. "Watch out for the avocados."

CHAPTER THIRTY-TWO

SARA RETURNED TO the bathroom with tape and plastic wrap. She motioned for Roberto to sit on the toilet. He did but tucked the sheet between his legs. She saw his boxers on the counter and her breath hitched, knowing he wore nothing under the sheet. Kneeling in front of him, she put her hand behind his calf. The warm muscle melted into her palm.

He flinched and she looked up. "My hands cold?"

"No." His voice sounded deep.

She wrapped the plastic around his leg to cover the wound. To do a proper job, she had to inch her hands up his leg.

He caught her wrist. "I can do this."

"I just need to tape it." She saw the heat in his eyes; the same she felt low in her belly.

He nodded. She added the tape and then stood. She turned to leave, then swung around to offer him a towel, but ran right into him. He caught her by the forearms. Their eyes met and she felt the sheet puddle around her feet.

"Oh, hell." He pulled her against him. The kiss didn't start slow, but it wasn't too fast. It was perfect.

She ran her palms up his bare back, loving the feel of his skin. The next thing she knew she was against the bathroom wall and he was pressing against her in all the right places. His hand moved under her blouse and eased up to her breast. Her nipples tightened. She moaned.

His knee shifted between her legs.

Suddenly he pulled back. "If you want me to stop...?"

"No." She tugged him back, her mouth on his.

His hand slid between her legs. His touch through her jeans wasn't enough.

She heard him mutter a curse. He stopped kissing her and rested his forehead against hers. "I don't have..." He had to catch his breath. "Protection."

She smiled. "I do." She moved to the medicine cabinet and produced one foiled package. "My emergency stash." She set it on the counter.

He pulled her against him again. His sex, hard and ready, pressed against her. She shifted her hand down and wrapped her palm around him.

He let out a noise, half moan, half growl. Only then did she remember. She shifted her mouth from his. "Your leg... we probably shouldn't."

"I'm fine." He ran a finger over her lips. "If you want to stop, I understand, but not because of that."

"Then what are we waiting for?" She nipped at her bottom lip.

He smiled. "How about a quick shower?"

She pulled her uniform top over her head. Her hair spilled out and cascaded down her shoulders. He watched her, his eyes bright with want.

"You are so beautiful." He ran a finger from her chin down to her cleavage.

She reached back to unhook her bra.

"Let me." His arms came around her, and when he did, he kissed her neck.

She let her head fall back.

Her bra fell loose. He cupped her right breast, running his fingertip over her nipple.

She didn't remember removing her jeans. But they were both naked and kissing outside the shower. His hands roamed her body, touching and teasing. His sex pressed against her lower abdomen. His finger came between her legs, slipped inside her cleft.

He found her hot spot and ran his thumb over it twice. Her breath caught, and the sweetness of his touch nearly pushed her to orgasm.

He pulled her into her shower. Not that it took effort on his part. She'd have followed him anywhere. Hot water and warm steam filled the space. He reached for a bar of soap, then turned her around facing the shower. The spray of water hit her face. She closed her eyes. His soapy palms cupped her breasts. He teased her nipples until they tingled. Slowly, his right hand lowered between her legs. His fingers worked magic. Each time he touched the sensitive nub, she almost came, and each time he'd pull away.

Realizing he was teasing her, she turned around. "Two can play this game." Her gaze lowered to his sex. It stood completely erect, brushing against his belly button. With one fingertip, she circled his bulging tip and saw a pearl of liquid appear.

He moaned.

She caught his hot hard flesh in her palm, squeezed, and then slowly palmed him, up and down.

He caught her hand. "It's been a while," he growled.

"Me, too. Two years, eight months, and four weeks, and—"

"That long?" He laughed.

She reached for him again.

He pulled back. "I might explode."

"Then explode." She smiled.

He caught her hand and moved it to his chest. "Where I'm from, ladies always come first." He led her out of the shower, snatched the condom, and took her to bed.

The door opened. The dark-haired man who she'd pummeled with a tomato stuck his head in.

"Can I come in?" he asked.

She didn't know who he was, but she guessed he was one of Austin's friends. Friends who were behind this whole thing.

"It's not my cabin, so I can't say who can or can't come in." She sounded like an angry child. Hell, she felt like an angry child. She'd pretty much acted like one, too. What kind of reasonable adult threw tomatoes? Maybe one who'd been deceived and had her apartment bugged. Maybe one trying to hold on to her anger so she wouldn't have to focus on the other emotions raging inside her—like how much she'd grown to care about someone who'd only been deceiving her.

He stepped inside. "No more fruit ninja stuff?"

"I'm out of tomatoes." She hadn't meant it to be humorous, but he smiled.

"I'm Dallas." He pulled out a wooden chair.

"You know who I am," she said.

He sat down across from her. "Yeah, I know." He sat a briefcase on the table. "I have something I'd like you to see." He opened the case and pulled out an iPad. "And I'll warn you, it's not pretty."

Sara bounced back on the bed, ready to feel him touch her again. He stood there, just staring. For one second, she felt self-conscious, but then the way he looked at her had her back to just wanting, needing to be touched. He stretched out beside her.

His lips met hers, then those moist kisses moved to her neck. "What do you like? What do you want?" he asked. "You name it, and you got it."

She wrapped her hand around his sex. "I want this."

"You sure you don't need a little more of this?" He ran his hand between her legs, slipping inside her tight opening. "Or this." He took her nipple in his mouth. He suckled hard and it felt wonderful. She arched her back.

Unable to bear it anymore, she pulled him up. "I need you inside me."

He grinned. "I like a woman who knows what she wants."

He put the condom on. When he rolled on top of her, she felt the cellophane still wrapped around his thigh.

"Your leg's not hurting, is it?" She pressed her hands on his chest.

"No, but I'm gonna die if I don't get inside you." He adjusted his hips. His hardness pressed into her center. She raised her hips, and from the second she took him inside, it was heaven. He entered her slow. With each arch of his hips, he went deeper. Deeper until he filled every inch of her. She wrapped her legs around his waist. Wanting more. Wanting the dance and pace that would send her over the edge.

He leaned up on one elbow and brushed her hair from her eyes. "You okay?"

"Yeah." She shifted her hips up. "You ready?"

He moved faster. In and out. Deeper. The pressure built, the sweetness of wild passion, but with tenderness filling her every pore, then it burst into a rainbow of pleasure.

He'd accomplished what he'd wanted. For her to come first. He moved faster until every muscle in his body clenched.

The sounds of passion came from his throat.

When he came, he didn't fall on top of her—something that she hated that some men did—but he fell to her side and brought her with him. They stayed like that for several minutes, both trying to catch their breaths. Both holding on to each other.

The silence in her bedroom grew awkward. One of them needed to say something, but what?

That was good.

Thank you.

Let's try that again.

A dozen appropriate things whispered through her mind, but she wanted him to say it first. His arms held her. His heart raced beneath her hand.

As the magnificent tingling faded, and the silence grew longer, reality set in. She'd slept with a man she hardly knew. Yet for some unknown reason it didn't matter. She felt it. The connection. She buried her face in his shoulder and inhaled his scent—a little like fresh grass and earth. Closing her eyes, she swore she wouldn't regret this.

Roberto pulled away and leaped out of bed. He raked a hand through his hair and looked around the room. He finally glanced at her. What she saw in his eyes tore at her heart. She wouldn't regret this, but he did.

".I'm sorry," he said. "That was a mistake."

She didn't say anything. All the wonderful she felt melted away like a Popsicle dropped on a hot Texas sidewalk.

"Where are my clothes?" he asked.

Her throat knotted. She pointed at the dresser. Snatching the clothes, he stormed into the bathroom. He came out seconds later, dressed and with his keys in his hands.

Her heart clutched. She pushed up on her elbow. Why? she wanted to ask. Why was it a mistake? Then she remembered. He'd lost his wife.

It had to be that, didn't it? An uncomfortable feeling burrowed deep into Sara's chest and brought tears to her eyes. Was she wrong to be jealous of his dead wife?

"I'm sorry." He tossed the words at her and walked out.

"So am I."

When she heard her apartment door shut, she rolled over and cried.

"Is it another video from Luis?" Leah asked Dallas.

"No." He powered up the box. "Look, I won't pretend that what Austin did wasn't wrong."

"That's good," Leah said. "Because some of it was illegal."

"That's the reason we need to talk." He rubbed the back of his neck. "Austin calls it following his gut. Tyler and I call it stepping in shit." He grinned. "But the crazy thing is, most of the time he comes out smelling like a rose. Tyler concluded he got away with so much because Austin does the wrong thing, for the right reason."

He looked at his iPad screen. "You know he was a cop?"

She nodded.

"Did he tell you we were framed for murder?"

"Yeah. He also told me Rafael was behind it. I'll tell you what I told him. I don't know where Rafael is. I never have. And considering he's trying to kill me and my brother, it's clear we're not what you'd call close."

He nodded. "Have you ever thought what it would be like to be accused of something you didn't do? To have your peers believe the worst of you. To lose the woman you thought loved you because she"—he turned the iPad toward her—"believed you could do *this*."

The image looked like a scene from a horror flick. A lot of blood and two bodies. The woman almost decapitated.

Leah blinked. "You didn't have to show me that."

"Yes, I did. I wanted you to know how hard it was to believe that people we cared about thought we could do this. Sixteen months of our lives we spent in prison with this image flashing in our heads."

Her sinuses stung, but she refused to cry. "I told you, I don't know where Rafael is."

He frowned. "Do I want your brother caught and punished for what he did to us? Hell, yes! But I didn't come here about your half brother. I came for Austin." He cut her a pointed look. "You have the ability to send Austin back to prison."

He closed his iPad. "At first I figured Austin took the risks due to the anger over what happened to us. But"—he studied her—"after seeing…the tomato battle, I think it's more. I think he'd rather go back to prison than risk you getting killed." He exhaled. "You realize that he could have walked away and let you and your brother die. So, before you talk to the police, remember what he risked…for you."

Leah swallowed. She knew this, but hearing it made it more real. Made her half brother even more of a monster.

"I'm not going to the police. I never was. I know he saved my life, but I still have a right to be mad at him for…It's infuriating." Her voice shook.

He grinned. "I've felt the same way about Austin a time or two."

They sat there without talking, the silence awkward. His earlier words tiptoed through her head. *To lose the woman you thought loved you.*

So Peggy Darlene Delmar wasn't the only person who'd broken Austin's heart.

CHAPTER THIRTY-THREE

ROBERTO SAT IN his car in Sara's parking lot for an hour, his stomach sour. What the hell had he done?

He was an asshole. What kind of a man made love to a woman and then told her it was a mistake? An idiot. Maybe one still high on doggy pain pills.

No, he wouldn't give himself an easy out and use the drugs. It was the same dirty emotion he was feeling now. Guilt. He'd made love to her and enjoyed the hell out of it. And when it was over, and he'd held her soft body against his, he'd remembered holding Anna—remembered loving her.

He'd remembered how unfair it was that she was yanked out of this world. It had suddenly felt terribly wrong that he was so happy . . . and she was so dead.

His eyes grew moist. Anna was gone. He knew that. Logically he knew he wasn't cheating. Emotionally, though . . . Hell, he was screwed up. And he'd hurt someone else. Sara had gone over two years without letting a man close, without trusting anyone, because Brian's father had done her so wrong. And he'd had to come along and fucked her over again. She didn't deserve this.

He reached for his phone to call and apologize, then noticed he had messages. One was from Austin, the other from a number he didn't recognize for a second. Then he remembered; it was Luke's number. Luke was dead. He clicked on his voice mail.

"Hey, you don't know me. Or at least I don't think you do. But my friend, Cruz…"

Roberto's heart lurched. He'd never heard his voice, but he knew. Knew he was listening to the man who'd killed Anna and his son.

"…he filled me in on how you and Brad were buddies, and how you knew about the deal going south in New Orleans. I could be wrong, and you might be like Don and Luke, dead. But the whole time Cruz told me about you, I smelled a rat. Maybe one working with those ex-cops. If you aren't dead, well, I'm gonna find you, and then I'm gonna gut you like a pig. And I'm gonna enjoy it. Just like I'm gonna enjoy killing Brad and those three ex-cops I think you're both working with."

"Not if I don't gut you first." Roberto dialed Brad's number.

After Dallas stepped out of the cabin, Austin told Dallas about the clown suits.

"Damn it!" Dallas argued. "It's too risky."

"I got it planned out. I'll rent a car. Even if DeLuna is at the hospital, he won't know it's us."

"It's still risky!" Dallas snapped.

"It's her brother," Austin said. "If it was your brother, wouldn't you go see him?"

Dallas's expression hardened. "That's different."

"No, it isn't."

Dallas groaned. "I swear, if I had a tomato, *I'd* throw it at you."

Austin grinned.

Dallas frowned. "Shit! When are you going?" Dallas asked.

"As soon as the cats get here."

"Wait until tomorrow?"

"No. The longer he's there, the more likely DeLuna will find him."

Dallas frowned again, but instead of arguing, he started toward his car.

Austin glanced back at the cabin, then followed Dallas. "What did you two talk about?"

"About what a piece of shit you are." Dallas smiled. "I don't think I'm gonna have to visit you in prison."

"What did you say to calm her down?"

"It's not what I said. It's me. I'm a rational person, unlike some people."

"I'm rational."

"Right." Dallas opened his car door but stood outside. "Have you talked with Roberto?"

"I tried. He's not answering again."

Austin remembered that one of DeLuna's men might have recognized him. "Where are Nikki and Zoe?"

"We sent them on a shopping spree in New York."

Austin nodded. "That's good."

Dallas leaned against the car. "My gut says all this is about to come to a head. There was a time all I thought about was getting that bastard. Now, more important than catching him is making sure he doesn't hurt anyone else I care about. Vengeance isn't as sweet as I thought it would be."

"I don't know," Austin said. "I think it'll feel pretty damn good."

Dallas put one foot inside his car. "Watch out for your tomato thrower. She's the dangerous kind."

"There isn't anything dangerous about her."

Dallas quirked an eyebrow. "That's what I thought about Nikki. And look what happened." He crawled into his car and drove off.

"Bullshit," Austin said to himself, and went to face the tomato thrower. His tomato thrower? Damn if he didn't even like the sound of that.

She was resting on the bed, flipping through a magazine. All the tomato drippings were cleaned up.

She looked up.

"You didn't have to clean up. I'd have done it."

"I threw them," she said.

He wasn't going to argue with that. He moved in and stood at the table. "I'm sorry if Dallas came off like a jerk."

She stared at the magazine. "He didn't."

"Good." She looked good in bed. In his bed. His tomato thrower. In his bed.

She glanced up. "We're still going to see Luis, right?"

Had she heard them talking? It didn't matter. "I'm calling Rick to make sure it's safe. If so, we'll leave after Tyler gets here with the cats."

They stared at each other for a pulse of silence. Something felt different. Good different, but he was afraid to hope. He turned to grab a soda.

"I'm sorry, too," she said.

Standing at the fridge, he looked back. "For the tomatoes?"

"No. You deserved that." She half smiled, and damn if his heart didn't melt. "But you, and your two friends, didn't deserve what Rafael did. I'm sorry."

Hundreds of people had told him that, yet her words mattered when none of the others had.

Emotion tightened his chest. "Soda?" He held up a drink.

"No."

He shut the fridge and stared back at her. "I never blamed you. I didn't expect to like you, but I never blamed you."

Their gazes met and held. It felt like a new beginning. Could they find their way back to what they'd had before?

She's the dangerous kind. Dallas's warning rang in his head. He pushed it aside and reminded himself that they lived in different cities. Whatever this led to, it wouldn't be too serious.

The sound of a car echoed. He moved to the window. His truck and Tyler's car pulled in front of the cabin.

"It's Tyler and Nance. You ready for your cats?" *Friggin' hell, he knew he wasn't.*

The homecoming of cats wasn't as bad as he imagined. It was worse.

Tyler and Nance came in and Austin made quick introductions. Unlike with Dallas's introduction, there was no tomato tossing. But there was a second when Austin wished they hadn't shown up. Leah had actually smiled at him. Then bam, Tyler and Nance were there and Austin realized the probability of them exposing another of his lies. One he should have come clean on but simply forgot.

He hadn't had a cat that died. Those avocados were gonna hurt more than the tomatoes.

Tyler shook Leah's hand, as if assessing her. Was she friend or foe? Nance did the same. Leah was eager to bring the cats in. One by one, five cat carriers were brought in.

Like an idiot, Austin suddenly realized something; he'd be sleeping, or rather, not sleeping, in the same room with five friggin' cats. Unless he decided to turn the bathtub into his sleeping quarters. What had he done to deserve this hell on earth?

Yeah, he and Spooky had almost become friends. The cat peered out of the carrier at him. But that could have changed.

Sort of like his and Leah's relationship. It wasn't on solid ground.

Plus, the real problem was Leah's cats.

When the cats were free of their carriers, Austin noted Tyler and Nance watching him. Probably mentally laughing their asses off. How long, Austin wondered, before they exposed his fear of cats? Five minutes? Ten?

Austin went out to the truck to grab a bag of cat litter. Returning, he inspected the room for cat status. He set the litter by the pantry, spotting only three cats. Leah was on her hands and knees whispering sweetly toward the underside of the bed. No doubt, her two semi-feral kitties were in hiding.

Suddenly, Spooky moved around the sofa, heading right at him. The cat stopped at his feet, raised up on his hind legs, put his front paws on Austin's knee, and meowed. Austin touched the cat's head.

"I won!" Nance belted out. "He touched one! *You* owe me fifty bucks!"

"I don't believe it," Tyler said.

"What?" Leah stood.

Nance continued, "I told you if anything could get him over...what do you call it, ailurophobia, it would be a hot chick." Nance looked at Leah. "I say 'hot chick' with the upmost respect."

Leah didn't respond to the hot chick comment, she was obviously too busy trying to put two and two together. And Austin already knew where this would lead. Back to him being in the doghouse.

"Who's ailurophobic?" Her gaze shifted from Nance to Tyler, then him. And from the look in her eyes, it was a damn good thing they were out of tomatoes.

*   *   *

Leah, dressed in a baggy polka-dot clown costume, with a white face and a big painted-on red smile, had gone silent again. When Tyler and Nance left, he made them sandwiches, minus tomatoes. Leah ate in silence. Austin called Rick. He got the thumbs up, so the visit with Luis was on.

It was only a thirty-minute drive to Austin. He had suggested they get dressed in the clown outfits. She didn't argue. Probably because she wasn't talking to him.

On the drive, kids in other vehicles on the freeway pointed and waved. While not speaking to him, Leah waved like a happy clown. A mile from the car rental place, he informed her of how things would go down.

"We're only staying a few minutes at the hospital, okay?" She nodded.

He yanked off the red wig, which made his head itch like hell. "Are you ever going to talk to me again?"

She looked at him. "You never had a cat who died, did you?"

"No," he said. "I'm sorry. You put me on the spot by trying to get me to adopt one, and I had to come up with something."

"Why don't you tell me everything you lied about so I can get furious and get it over with?"

He exhaled. "The cat thing just about covers it." Then he remembered. "Except…the water gun. It was mine. I bought it the day I broke into your apartment."

She stared in total bafflement. "Why?"

"Because cats don't like water, and I don't like cats."

"You squirted my cats with a water gun?"

"No, I didn't have to. They didn't attack."

"But you were going to?"

"If they'd attacked, I would have." He frowned. "It was better than using a real gun."

She turned to the window. After a minute, she faced him. "Why are you afraid of cats?"

He gripped the steering wheel. "Because they're vicious."

"Please."

He pulled back his ear. "See the scar? A cat damn near took my ear off."

"I don't believe that," she said.

"Believe it. And I had sixteen stitches under my arm, too."

"Cat's don't just attack."

"This one did. I saw the cat carrying her kittens into a shed. I went to get a peek and she damn near killed me." He frowned. "Then because she disappeared, I had to have shots in the stomach for a month of Sundays."

"She was trying to protect her babies."

"I was four and not much more than a baby myself."

She sighed. "Why did you agree to keep Spooky if you're so scared?"

His chest tightened, but he told her the truth. "Because you said I'd be your hero. I wanted that."

She straightened her rainbow-colored wig and stared at him. But with her face painted, he couldn't read her expression.

She didn't speak again until they got into the rental car. "Give me the receipt."

He rolled his eyes. "It was my decision to rent the car."

"You're renting the car so you can take me to see my brother. It's my expense."

"Fine." Frowning, he handed it to her.

They were almost to the hospital when his phone rang.

"Where are you?" Urgency rang in Dallas's tone.

"Almost to the hospital. Why?"

"Turn your ass around and head right back to the cabin."

CHAPTER THIRTY-FOUR

"WHAT'S GOING ON?" Austin asked Dallas, seeing concern flicker in the eyes of the cute clown in the passenger seat.

"Roberto called," Dallas said. "DeLuna and his friends are in Austin. I'm ten minutes away. We're moving Luis Reece to a new hospital."

"Has anyone shown up at the hospital?" Austin asked.

"No, but—"

"Then let her see him for a few minutes?"

"I'm seeing Luis!" Leah seethed.

"Goddamn it." Dallas's voice boomed through the phone. "If they're here, then that means they are looking for the kid. In spite of what Rick told them, they have him listed under his real name. DeLuna probably knows where he is."

"You don't know that for sure." Austin stopped at a red light. "We're almost at the hospital. I'm going to ride around. If it's clear, I'm bringing her in. We're in costume; even if he's there, he won't know it's us."

"At least wait until I get there."

"That I can do." He paused. "What are you doing here, anyway?"

"I was worried."

Austin sighed. "You worry too much."

"You worry too little."

"Call me when you're at the hospital." He started to hang up, but added, "Be careful."

"All I want to say is I'm sorry. Please pick up." Roberto saw Brad step out of the sandwich shop, so he hung up.

"Who do you keep calling?" Brad crawled into the car. He dropped a sandwich in Roberto's lap. Roberto wasn't hungry.

He'd called Sara five times since he'd left her apartment. He'd met Brad at a service station and they were scouting out six locations where Brad knew DeLuna had stayed in the past. So far, they hadn't found him. Dallas had suggested they keep driving between the locations until hopefully they came across him.

Roberto pocketed his phone. Obviously, Sara wasn't in the mood to talk to him, or to forgive him. Not that he deserved it. He was an asshole.

"You calling that chick?" Brad asked.

"Yeah." Why lie?

"You like her, don't you?"

"Yeah, but I screwed up."

"What did ya do?"

"Nothing," he said, unwilling to share.

"I messed up with Sandy in the beginning. She forgave me."

"Yeah." Roberto doubted Brad had screwed up that bad.

After a pause, Brad asked, "What did your PI friends say?"

Roberto had realized that Dallas, Tyler, and Austin wanted DeLuna as badly as he did. Together they actually stood a chance of getting him.

"We're going to meet up and work out a plan as soon as they get Luis Reece moved."

"You sure about them?" Brad asked. "I beat up that blond cop pretty bad."

Roberto looked at Brad's face. "He got in a few licks, too."

"He might hold a grudge."

"You helped him save Leah Reece. He owes you."

"I hope so. You think they'll go along with my plan?"

"Yeah," Roberto said. Brad's plan might really work. Get the cocaine back to them and call the cops. But there was one flaw to Brad's plan. He thought he could find DeLuna and Cruz and simply sneak in the powder. That didn't sound so simple. They needed an inside man. And Roberto was it. DeLuna might think he was the rat, but if he showed up with a hole in his leg, and a good story, he could plant the evidence himself.

Was it risky? Yeah. There was a chance he wouldn't make it out of this alive. But he hadn't gone into this two years ago thinking he stood much of a chance. Of course, then he hadn't been so sure he'd wanted to live. Now, he couldn't say that.

He just wished he could talk to Sara. He wanted to tell her she hadn't been a mistake. She'd been one of those rare gifts, so wonderful he didn't deserve it.

Leah, scared she wouldn't get to see Luis, waited for Austin to pull over before she spoke up. "I'm seeing Luis. If you or anyone tries to stop me, I'll—"

"Slow down." Austin held up his hand. "I'm going to take you, but you need to know DeLuna could be there. And we're waiting until Dallas is there for backup."

Her throat tightened. Not from fear, but emotion. She wanted to see Luis. Needed to see he was okay.

"But"—he pointed a finger at her—"the moment we step out of this car, you are to do exactly what I say. If I tell you to do jumping jacks, you do friggin' jumping jacks. Got it?"

She nodded.

He exhaled. "Shit. If you get hurt, I won't be able to live with myself."

"I won't get hurt." Tears filled her eyes. "Thank you," she said.

"Thank me when this is over and you're not hurt."

Sara's phone dinged with another message. She ignored it and continued scrubbing the grout in her kitchen floor. It had been bothering her for a month since Brian had spilled grape juice on the floor. Who wanted purple grout?

Who wanted to be someone's mistake?

It didn't matter if the mistake was due to the unjust, untimely death of someone's ex-spouse. Sure, she sympathized with him. She knew how it hurt to have someone yanked from your life. But what was she? Chopped liver? Oh, no, he told her what she was. A mistake.

She dipped the toothbrush into the soapy bleach water and commenced to scrubbing. Scrubbing hard. Her sinuses stung. She blamed the bleach. She'd cried enough. It shouldn't hurt this much. It hadn't hurt this much when Brian's father walked out. But she knew why. There had been something about Roberto, something she couldn't explain. The connection. The feeling of fate. And yet she barely knew him.

But she did, a voice inside her said. She'd known him well enough that she'd risked her job to remove a bullet from his leg. She'd trusted him enough to bring him into her home. To get naked with him. To offer him the one emergency condom she'd bought a year after Brian was born just in case some knight in shining armor showed up to sweep her away.

He'd swept her away. He'd made her glow inside.

She'd thought he was her knight. She could still recall the talk she'd had with her dad less than a month before he died. She'd just broken up with a boyfriend and he'd told her, *Sweetie, he wasn't the one. You weren't shining from the inside out. You see, when you meet the right person, like your mom is my person, you'll glow. It's this feeling you get inside, as if you just discovered another part of yourself.*

Roberto had held her so tenderly and made love to her. Made that lonely knot she'd felt for months fade away like a rainbow faded from the sky after a rain shower. Just talking to him over the phone had infused her with...happiness.

Then he'd called her a mistake.

After she finished the kitchen grout, she might as well do the bathroom.

Leah tried to be patient. But Luis was in that hospital and they were driving around the building over and over again. Austin talked to Dallas twice. They hadn't spotted Rafael or Cruz. Enough already, she wanted to scream.

Finally, he parked. He glanced at her. "Wait until I open your door to get out."

"Why?" she asked.

Austin's clown face went stern. "What did I tell you about doing everything I said?"

"Sorry." She wasn't accustomed to taking orders.

He opened her door and pulled her to his side. His touch sent bolts of emotion coursing through her so strong that it physically hurt. It hurt more when she realized the reason for the closeness. He was shielding her. He was willing to take a bullet for her.

She held her breath until they entered the hospital. The knot of unease in her stomach lessened, but not so much for

Austin. His gaze flipped from side to side as if he thought Rafael might be inside.

They got in an elevator.

Stepping out on the third floor, another tall cop-looking guy stood at the door down the hall. He nodded. "Make it short. We're moving him to another hospital in ten minutes."

Ten minutes didn't seem like enough time, but she'd take what she could get. Austin motioned for her to go. So he trusted her enough not to think he had to come in and listen. Or was the room bugged? As soon as the thought hit, she sent it packing. He wasn't the enemy anymore. But what was he? Her heart seemed to know the answer, but she wasn't ready to listen.

She moved in. The door swished closed. The room's silence enveloped her. Luis was asleep. Emotional pain gripped her chest at the sight of his swollen face and bruises. Tears filled her eyes and her breath hitched as she imagined the pain he'd endured.

She inched closer, trying to find a spot on his body that wasn't black and blue to touch. Even his arms were purple. She rested her hand on the back of his.

His eyes opened, or tried to. He stared at her through swollen eyelids.

"Hey. It's me," she said, remembering her costume.

"Shit!" he muttered. "What are you doing here?"

"I had to come." Her throat thickened; tears spilled from her eyes. "I'm so sorry, Luis. Why did Rafael do this?"

"Because he's...a bastard. He thought I was somehow getting information to the police. A kid that he thought was behind this went to school with me. I hardly knew the kid. And then he had some deals go bad in Austin and then in San Antonio. And because I was in both places at the time he just assumed..."

"Shh." Leah could tell it hurt him to talk. She started to touch his lips but pulled her hand back when she saw the stitches on his bottom lip.

"I told that PI to keep you away. Rafael's one sick human. Enjoys seeing people hurt."

She pressed her hand over her mouth to keep from crying aloud. Breathing deep, she found a small measure of control. "Austin and his friends are moving you to another hospital so Rafael can't find you."

"I know. You leave," he muttered. "Go somewhere safe."

"I love you." More tears slipped from her lashes.

"Love you, too, but please leave. You're not invincible like you think."

Fury built in her chest for Rafael. She wanted to hit him, to hurt him like he'd hurt Luis. "Is anything broken?"

"Just a rib," he said. "I'm fine. Get out of here."

The door swished open and Austin stepped in. His gaze met hers as if saying her time was up. He glanced at Luis.

"I'm Austin Brook."

"You the clown who saved her?" Luis tried to smile, but it looked painful.

"Yeah," Austin replied.

"Thanks. Now get her the hell away from here before Rafael shows up. Don't let her push you around. Her bark is worse than her bite." He nudged Leah away. "Go."

Leaning down, she pressed a kiss to his forehead.

"Love you," she whispered.

Austin took her hand as they walked to the door. "You okay?"

Emotion swelled inside her. "Promise me you'll catch that bastard."

He smoothed his thumb over the top of her hand. "That's my plan."

Austin nodded at Rick as they stepped out. Leah looked at him. "Please keep him safe."

"Don't worry," he said.

Austin's phone rang. He checked the number. "Dallas." He took the call. "We're leaving," he said into the phone, then frowned. "Shit! Where?" He listened for a second and hung up.

"What?" Leah and Rick asked at the same time.

"Dallas spotted a dark sedan with tinted windows parked three cars over from our rental. They're here."

Rick pulled out a set of keys. "Take my truck. White Ford, parked outside the emergency room. Dallas and I'll hold the fort down here. Get her out of here."

"No," Leah insisted. "I'm staying with Luis."

"We're leaving," Austin growled.

"They don't know what room he's in," Rick told her. "We moved him. Go. We'll take care of your brother. If you're here, we'll have two of you to protect and that makes it harder."

Austin handed Rick the rental car keys. "It's a Chevy Cruze, silver, south entrance. My truck's at the rental place." He took Leah's arm. She followed. She didn't want to, but she did.

CHAPTER THIRTY-FIVE

IN THE ELEVATOR, Austin pulled the puffy, elastic-gathered sleeve over his hand. Leah saw the barrel of a gun poking out of the gathered fabric. A gun. Another thing he'd lied about, but she was too scared to care.

The elevator doors opened. He stepped out looking left and right, then motioned her out.

They walked down a long hall, following the signs to the emergency room. Anytime someone crossed their paths, his shoulders tensed. *Don't let him shoot anyone. Don't let him shoot anyone.* The mantra repeated in her head.

Her chest tensed, making it hard to breathe. They walked outside. Cold October air made her skin crawl. Austin's red wig stirred in the breeze. He pulled her against him again. Not to shield her from the cold, but from bullets.

She wondered if this meant he cared, or if this was just his protect-and-serve training coming out. Either way, she moved beside him.

"We're looking for a white Ford truck," he bit out.

She scanned the parking lot. "Is that it?" She pointed at the third row.

"Yes."

As they stepped off the sidewalk, she saw him. Cruz stood on the other side of the parking lot, but he stared right at her.

"There's Cruz!" she muttered, and the man came walking toward them.

"Keep walking. He doesn't know it's us."

Cruz called out, "Hey, clowns! I need to ask ya something."

"Damn!" Austin passed the keys to her. "Get in the truck and drive off."

"Where?"

"Away from here." He grabbed his phone out from under his clown outfit, hit a number, and muttered, "They spotted us. Outside the emergency room." He hung up.

"Go!" He motioned for them to do so.

"I'm not leaving you." Leah glanced back. Cruz was halfway across the lot. And damn if it didn't look like he held something in his hands. Something like a gun...or a knife.

"Go!" He shoved her forward. She took off.

"Stop!" Cruz yelled again.

Leah's pounding heart echoed in her ears as she ran. The metallic taste of fear coated her tongue. The memory of Cruz's forced kiss sent a sick feeling to her gut.

"What is it, buddy?" Leah heard Austin call out, no doubt drawing attention to himself.

She clicked the truck open, crawled in, but her hands shook so hard, she couldn't fit the key in the ignition. Then she made the mistake of looking up. Cruz and Austin were fighting. Why didn't he shoot him? she wondered.

A loud pop sounded, but it came from across the parking lot. She spotted a man running toward the fight. It wasn't Dallas or Rick. It had to be another of Rafael's men. She spotted a baseball bat on the floorboard. She stopped trying to fit the key in the ignition.

She snatched up the bat and leaped out of the truck, praying she made it there before the guy with a gun. Praying one of his bullets wouldn't get to her first.

When she got there, Cruz and Austin were rolling around on the ground. Cruz, on top, pushed a knife toward Austin's face, while Austin held the man's wrist back. It wasn't until she swung the bat at Cruz's head that she realized it was a plastic T-ball bat. It still caused a good whack upside his temple.

Startled, Cruz shot around. Austin bolted to his feet. He growled, then charged at Cruz. She spotted Austin's gun on the ground. Thinking it was a better weapon than a plastic bat, she started for it. Cruz caught her by the arm and slung her back. Austin went at Cruz.

Catching herself from falling face first on the pavement, she saw Cruz swipe his blade at Austin, missing him by inches. She took a flying leap onto the man's back. Wrapping her legs around his waist, one hand around his neck and the other around his eyes, she screamed. He stopped fighting Austin and started dancing and bucking to get her off his back. Austin, spitting out obscenities—that seemed aimed at her—charged Cruz again.

He hit Cruz in the upper gut with his fist. Cruz's knife dinged to the pavement, and then he went down, taking Leah with him. Slammed to the pavement, her lungs gave up their air in a gulp. Another bullet popped off. Leah saw the pavement splinter at Austin's feet. He scrambled for his gun, and Cruz bolted between two cars.

Austin snatched her up so fast, her feet dangled in the air. He forced her into a dead run toward the truck. Bullets pinged against the cars as they ran.

She must have left the door open, because Austin shoved her inside on the driver's side and then came in behind her, pushing her to the passenger side.

"Keys?" he snapped.

"Shit." She started looking around the truck seat.

She spotted them on the floorboard at the same time he did. He snatched them up. The engine roared to life as a spray of bullets hit the truck.

"Down!" He grabbed her head and buried it in his lap.

He kept his hand on her head, her nose pressed firmly in his crotch as he drove off. She couldn't explain it—hysteria, maybe panic—but she laughed. She tried to rise up.

"Not yet," he bit out.

He turned the truck on a dime. Tires squealed as he stomped his foot on the accelerator.

She waited another few seconds before sitting up.

This time, he let her. She looked back and didn't see anyone following them. She laughed again. "That was almost fun."

He looked at her with so much anger her exhilaration evaporated.

"What?" she asked.

"I friggin' told you to leave!" He yanked off his wig and tossed it into the seat.

"I saved you," she said.

"You could have been killed. You promised to do what I said."

"So I lied," she snapped back. "Seems to be the norm around here, Mr. I-have-gun-because-I-travel!"

Growling, he focused on the road, zipping in and out of traffic, getting them as far away from Cruz and his men as possible.

His phone rang. Snatching it from his jeans pocket he

answered it. "Tell me you got them." He sounded like an angry bear. "Damn!" he muttered.

"Is Luis okay?" she blurted out, certain it was either Dallas or Rick.

He glanced at her, nodded, then refocused on the road. "We're fine." He paused and his scowl deepened. "Give me hell later, not now." He hung up.

Shooting her another frown, he said, "Buckle up."

He drove without speaking. Never had she seen such an angry clown. When he stopped speeding, and she stopped shaking, she actually fell asleep.

Someone touched Leah's shoulder.

"Hey, sleepyhead, we're here."

Lifting her eyelids, she flinched at the sight of the blond clown standing outside the passenger door. Then it all came back. Seeing Luis, the fight with Cruz, Austin...Her heart raced, but his sweet expression sent her initial panic packing. He leaned in front of her. She thought he planned to kiss her. She had no intention of stopping him. He unsnapped her seat belt instead.

He smiled ever so softly. "You make an adorable clown."

Part of the conversation they'd had on the ride to the hospital replayed in her head.

If you're so afraid of cats, why did you agree to keep Spooky?

Because you said I'd be your hero. I wanted to be that.

"You okay?" he asked.

She nodded. Instinctively she knew she was done fighting. Done fighting with him.

Done fighting what she felt. Lies, no lies. She cared about Austin. The thought scared her, but less than before.

"You want me to carry you inside?" he asked.

"No."

He stepped back. She caught him by the arm.

"You are," she said.

He tilted his head to the side, looking like a confused clown. "I'm what?"

"My hero. Thank you for taking me to see Luis."

His painted smiled turned upside down. "I almost got you killed."

"No. You saved me. Then I saved you," she reminded him.

"That still pisses me off," he said, but he was smiling, especially when she caught the ruffled collar of his clown costume and tugged him closer.

"Thank you." She pressed her lips against his.

She was kissing him. Austin could hardly believe it. It started out soft, sweet, but went to hot and hungry in seconds. And it was she who took it there. He'd been too afraid to react. Her tongue slipped inside his mouth. She pulled him closer and deepened the kiss. At some point, he stopped thinking about being kissed and started kissing back. He almost climbed into the truck, but instead he caught her under her arms and pulled her out.

So light, yet he'd never felt anything so right. She wrapped her legs around his waist and her arms around his neck. He placed his hands on her ass, loving how the round flesh fit into his palms. The V of her legs came right at his pelvis. Each step he took, she brushed against him, causing him to grow harder behind his zipper.

All he could think about was how it would feel to hold her like this without clothes. To take her, slip inside her body, while standing up. To have his hands on her bare ass and shift her back and forth, in and out.

He made the three steps up his porch, kissing her the

whole time. He pulled away one second to unlock the door but didn't let her down. Walking into his cabin, he was kissing her again. When three felines came running up, he barely hesitated before he went back to kissing her. Would it be presumptuous to head straight to the bed?

Not wanting to chance ruining this, he asked, "Bed, sofa, or...kitchen table?"

Her brow pinched. "Kitchen table?"

He laughed. "To talk." He prayed she wouldn't go for that option.

"About what?"

He grinned. "About how badly I want to take you to bed."

She bit her bottom lip as if considering. "How about I shower first?" Her tone came out bashful.

"Together?" He held his breath.

Hesitation filled her eyes. Okay, he needed to slow down. "You go first." He lowered her to her feet. Sliding her down him, feeling every inch of her. Another thing he wanted to do when they were naked.

"I'll hurry." She smiled, now sounding bashfully sexy.

"You do that." He kissed her again. "If you get lonely, just holler. I'll wash your back."

She grinned. He noted a touch of insecurity in her eyes, but then the sexy look she sent him over her shoulder before shutting the door made his breath catch.

The running shower echoed behind the door. He had to reach into his jeans and adjust his dick. Suddenly, one of Leah's gray cats shot out from under the bed and hacked up a hair ball on his shoe.

CHAPTER THIRTY-SIX

LEAH STEPPED UNDER the spray and let the water hit her face to remove the clown paint. She hoped the warm water and steam would calm her nerves. Not that she wanted to back out. It was just that... it had been a long time, and old insecurities bubbled to the surface. Did she remember how to do it? Was it like riding a bicycle?

Hell, she obviously had never been much of a biker chick—had been so bad at it that her ex had gone and biked with an older, less attractive neighbor. Not to mention, he'd turned to phone sex. She closed her eyes, accepting she had good reasons to be concerned. Then she remembered feeling the hardness between Austin's legs as she'd slid down his body. He wanted her. She wanted him.

She could do this. Turning off the shower, she realized she hadn't brought in a change of clothes. She started to re-dress in what she had on, then stopped. Snagging a towel from the rack, she wrapped it around herself. Feeling a surge of confidence, she shifted the slit to be a little sexier. She finger-combed her hair and did a leg check for bristle. No bristle.

Picking up her clothes, she gave herself a quick pep talk.
Ready or not, here I come.

*   *   *

Hair ball removed from shoe, Austin sat at the kitchen table. He hadn't moved his eyes off the bathroom door since the water shut off. Leah walked out wearing nothing but a towel and a sexy smile. Some really nice body parts played peek-a-boo in the slit of her towel.

Did he really need a shower?

He wanted to undo that knot under her right shoulder and watch that piece of nubby cotton cascade down to her feet. He wanted her completely naked. He wanted to touch, to taste. He wanted her so much it hurt.

He wanted to make her want him equally as much.

She held her folded clothes in her hand, then set them on the end of the bed. The bed where he'd like to take her right now.

"My turn." He forced himself to do the right thing.

The right thing ended up being the shortest shower he'd ever taken. Seconds later, naked and dripping wet, he searched his bathroom cabinet for condoms. He'd brought a pack a couple months back when he'd considered inviting someone up for the weekend, but had decided he'd rather keep the cabin his own. Oddly, he didn't mind sharing it with Leah.

What did feel wrong was that he only had four condoms, which meant they were going to have to make a run to the store. Soon.

Checking the mirror to make sure he'd scrubbed off his clown face, he ran a hand through his wet hair. She'd set the dress code and he'd follow it. He tied the towel around his waist. Glancing down, he noticed a problem. He'd already pitched a tent under the nubby cotton. An impressive tent, too. Taking a deep breath, vowing to make this good for her, he hid two condoms in his palm and walked out.

She sat on the edge of the bed, frowning. "Do we have... protection?"

He turned his hand over.

She sighed. A touch of hesitation and sweet innocence showed in her smile. It only made him want her more.

She's the dangerous kind.

He ignored Dallas's warning and went to her. Dropping the condoms on the bedside table, he reached for her hands and pulled her up. He wrapped his arms around her and pulled her in for a kiss. He had to lean down, but not so much it was uncomfortable. When the kiss turned hot, he pulled back and brushed a damp strand of dark hair from her cheek. Her skin felt like silk.

He reached for the knot holding up her towel. "Think we can lose this?"

She cut her eyes up at him. "I'll show you mine if you'll show me yours."

Grinning, he released her knot and watched the towel sweep down her naked body. He tried not to stare, but couldn't help it. "You're so damn beautiful." His gaze moved over the sweet dips and curves of her body. He'd seen her without her shirt, but completely unclothed was amazing. Her breasts were round, tipped with soft-rose nipples. Her abs were flat, her waist so tiny that... He reached down and fit his hands around it. Her hips flared out. She had a perfect hourglass shape. So feminine. So... perfect. Between her legs was a dark triangle of hair. Not shaved the way some women did to attract attention. No, Leah was... real.

Her legs were like the rest of her, shapely. He glided his hands up her rib cage to her breasts. He traced her nipples with a fingertip. Her breath hitched.

"You like that?"

She nodded. "I thought we had a deal." Her voice came

out a little raspy. She pulled his towel loose. It slipped from his hips to the floor.

Her gaze lowered one second, then came back up, almost as if embarrassed. There was something charming in her bashfulness.

"Happy now?" He grinned.

"Yes." She blushed.

He took her hand and pressed it against his chest and slid it down. The whole time he watched her expression. If he saw any hesitation, he'd stop.

She showed none.

When her hand found his dick, she cupped her palm around him and rubbed her thumb over his swollen tip.

"You like that?" She tossed his question back to him.

"Oh, yeah."

He moved to the bed and pulled her with him. He rested on his side and let himself feast on her. Her hair, still wet, looked almost black. He brushed it off her shoulder, wanting to see all of her. "I feel like a kid in a candy store. I don't know where to start."

She smiled and then he did know. He touched her dimple. Then he leaned down and kissed the same spot. His mouth didn't stay there long, though. He moved to her lips, to her neck, to her breasts. Bringing her tight nipple in his mouth, he suckled her with barely any pressure, not knowing if she was into gentle, or not so gentle.

He slipped his hand down to the soft patch of hair of her sex. Slowly, he slipped his finger between her cleft. When he found her wet with want, his dick got harder.

Moaning, she rocked her hips against his hand. But she kept her thighs closed.

Wanting some part of him inside her, he slipped a finger into the tight opening between her thighs. Moving his lips from her breasts, he breathed kisses down her rib cage. Stopping at her navel, he flicked his tongue inside.

When she arched her hips off the mattress, and her thighs parted just a bit, he took advantage and moved down, positioning himself between her knees. Keeping one finger inside her, he parted the soft wet flesh and moved his tongue over the little nub that he knew would offer her the most pleasure.

Her taste, her scent, made his own hips rock. Her soft moan reached his ears. She tightened her thighs around his head.

"Slow and easy," he whispered against her sex. "Make it last."

Seconds later, he knew she hadn't taken his advice. Her tight opening clenched on to his finger, and all he could think about was that squeeze around another body part.

When her orgasm stopped, he moved up. He reached for the condom; she reached between his legs. She tightened her fist around him, moving her palm up and down his length. The next thing he knew, she'd sat up and snatched the condom from his hand.

"Let me." She pushed him back on the bed. Sitting straddled over his knees, she opened the condom with her teeth. He feasted on her, her eyes bright, her hair dancing on her shoulders. As she shifted, her breast juggled and her nipples stood tight and erect. Her thighs were open, exposing the pink wet flesh he'd just tasted. He didn't think it was possible, but he got harder.

He waited for her to slip the condom on, but instead, she scooted down his legs, leaned over, and took him in her mouth. She moved her tongue around his engorged tip. It took everything he had not to explode. He reached down, grabbed her by her shoulders, and pulled her up. His dick almost slipped inside her as he got her where he wanted her.

He snatched the condom from her hands, reached between them, and slid it in place. Then because he couldn't forget how good it had felt standing with her legs around him, he stood up and took her with him. Holding her bare ass in his hands, he guided her in place. Her sex surrounded him like a glove. He almost orgasmed right then.

"You're tight," he muttered.

"You're just big."

He laughed. "Just what a man wants to hear." Holding her sweet ass in his palms, he shifted her closer, moving in and out. As good as it felt, he suddenly needed to be horizontal. Not pulling out, he lowered her to the bed, keeping most of his weight on his elbows.

She arched her hips up and took him deeper. Her lids fluttered closed. He whispered, "Look at me."

She opened those brown eyes, wild with passion. She moved, setting a slow, easy pace. But then her legs came around his waist, and the position allowed him to go even deeper. Their pace quickened. She moaned again. When he felt her sex spasm around him, he let go. The orgasm shook him to the core. He rolled over and pulled her on top of him. He wrapped his arms around her. She dropped her head on his shoulder.

Her short in-and-out breaths against his chest felt both hot and moist. Holding her close, her heart thudded against his chest. He couldn't remember any moment ever feeling this right. No woman had ever felt like this against him.

He moved his hand up and down her back. "That was..." He paused to find the right word. "Real."

She raised her head and looked at him, a smile in her eyes. "Real? That's all I get?"

He laughed and ran a finger over her cheek. "Let me try again. That was friggin' amazing! You're amazing."

He kissed her. "We're going to have to make a run to get some more condoms. I only have three more."

She made a cute face. "I think that's enough."

He rolled on top of her. "Then clearly you didn't enjoy that as much as I did."

An hour later, they were still in bed, still naked, and down two condoms. He slipped his hand under the sheet, drew circles around her navel, and kissed the side of her neck.

Leah couldn't decide if Austin was just a champion at sex, or if she'd just forgotten how good it was. She decided it was him. Especially when she saw the tent in the sheet.

He noticed where her eyes went. "It's not my fault. You turn me on."

She leaned in to kiss him. "If we keep this up we really will have to run to the store."

He laughed. But stopped when Socks, her tuxedo cat, jumped up on the bed.

"He's not going to hurt you," Leah assured him.

"Right." He raised his arm and pointed to a jagged scar. "How do you think I got this? And you've seen my ear."

She kissed his scar. When she pulled back, he was sneaking a peek down the gaping sheet.

She pressed the sheet to her chest. "Seriously, they won't attack you." Spooky jumped up and slowly tiptoed over to Austin. "He really likes you."

He studied the cat with caution, but didn't push him away. "We sort of bonded. But your cats don't like me."

She frowned. "Probably because you squirted them with a water gun."

"I didn't squirt them. I only threatened to." He eyed Socks, then watched Spooky curl up next to him. His expression softened. "He purrs when I pet him."

She didn't have the heart to tell him that most cats did. "Because he likes you."

"Yeah." He carefully touched Spooky, then glanced at Socks. "That guy hisses at me."

"He doesn't know you."

"It's rude." Austin stopped petting Spooky, and his eyes went back to the sheet that had glided down her chest. He stopped petting the cat and slipped his hand under the cover and fit his palm into the curve of her waist. "You sore?"

"Not too sore," she said, loving his touch.

That's when it hit her. She was a kitten's whisker away from falling in love with this man.

And that was a dangerous place to be.

But as his hand slid past her waist and slipped between her thighs, she decided she could use a little danger in her life.

Feeling brave, she rolled on top of him, straddled his thighs, and sat up. The sheets tangled under her knees. She ran her hands over his chest as he gazed up. He was so perfect he almost looked Photoshopped.

Skitter, sitting in the window, suddenly hissed. Leah glanced that way and saw the cat leap through the air toward the bed. Then she saw not one but two faces peering in the window.

Screaming, she tried to snatch the sheet, but in her desperate rush to cover herself, and Austin's desperate attempt to get up, she fell sideways off the bed and plopped her naked butt onto the wooden floor, facing the window.

CHAPTER THIRTY-SEVEN

"IF YOU'D HAVE answered your damn phone, you'd have known we were coming," Dallas ranted back. "But no, you don't, and that led us to think someone followed you back here and something bad had happened."

"You could have knocked instead of behaving like Peeping Toms." After recognizing the faces in the window, Austin had assured Leah it was okay. But naked, embarrassed, and sitting bare-assed on the floor, she'd bolted into the bathroom. He'd snagged his sweats from the bag on the sofa and went to give his two partners hell.

Before he got to the door, he'd heard their laughter and considered killing them.

"We thought someone might be in there holding you at gunpoint. Knocking didn't seem smart," Tyler said. "Besides, we didn't expect to find you—"

"Just shut up before you piss me off more." Austin considered another reason they were here, one that would tear Leah's heart out. And that would tear his heart out. "Is her brother okay?"

"Yeah. We moved him to a hospital outside of Austin."

"So y'all really came because I didn't answer the phone?"

That's fucking nuts. He was a grown man and was trying to do grown-man things.

"No, we were coming anyway. Roberto and that friend of his are on their way, too. They have a plan to catch DeLuna. I wanted all of us to go over it together."

"Is Luis okay?" At the sound of Leah's tight voice, they all turned to see her standing in front of the kitchen table. She'd donned his clothes. In one hand, she held his jeans, which were about eight sizes too big, bunched up on her waist. On her other side, his shirt hung clear to her knees.

Austin's breath hitched in his lungs. He'd never seen a more adorable sight. She looked like a little girl playing dress-up. But he knew below all that cotton was a woman whom he'd just had incredible sex with...twice. And it would have been three if they hadn't been interrupted.

For reasons he didn't understand he liked the thought of her in his clothes. Liked how her hair danced around her shoulders as she shifted her gaze from him to his two partners. Then Austin noted the concern in her eyes.

"Luis is fine." He fought the need to bundle her up in his arms. But not one to show affection in public, he didn't move. Still he couldn't look away.

She shuffled to the side of the bed, his jeans bunched up at her feet. She retrieved a stack of her folded clothes, then waddled back into the bathroom.

He stared at the closed door, unsure why his chest suddenly felt like an open vault.

Tyler cleared his throat.

Austin turned. The two of them stared at him. "What?"

"Nothing," Tyler said, but his expression said it was something. "She's cute." He grinned. "Well, she's more than cute."

"Don't go there."

"Hey, both of you walked in on Zoe naked." Tyler laughed. "The only one of our girls we haven't gotten to see naked is Nikki."

Austin and Tyler looked at Dallas. "Over my dead body," he growled.

They all laughed, but then Austin realized they were putting Leah in the same category as their wives. It wasn't like that. Was it? "But Leah and I aren't . . . you know."

"Looked like you were . . . 'you know' to me." Dallas cracked a grin.

"I mean, it's not . . . serious." But damn if it didn't feel serious.

"Looked serious." Tyler glanced at Dallas. "Didn't it to you?"

Dallas grinned. "She threw tomatoes at him and he didn't get mad."

"Shit!" Tyler said. "It's definitely serious."

"Stop this!" Austin snapped, uncomfortable in his own skin.

Uncomfortable with his own thoughts.

Uncomfortable with the feeling in his chest.

"We didn't start this. You did," Dallas said. "And for the record, I warned you she was the dangerous kind."

It was twenty minutes before Leah came out of the bathroom—wearing her own clothes. She still looked adorable, but it didn't hit him so hard now that she wasn't wearing his. He pushed his silly concerns about his feelings aside and reminded himself that each of them had their own lives and lived almost two hundred miles apart.

Dallas had called Roberto, who was supposed to be pulling up anytime. Wanting to warn her about what was going down, Austin met her in the kitchen.

"A couple other guys are coming here." He hesitated. "I just wanted to warn you that…we're going to be discussing your half brother."

She nodded. "I want him caught. He's a monster."

"I know." Austin studied her. He wanted to touch her so badly, he had to poke his hands in his pockets.

She glanced toward the opened door where Dallas and Tyler stood on the porch.

"Are you okay?" he asked.

She leaned in. "They saw me naked."

Unable to resist, he pulled one hand out and passed a finger over her cheek. "You want me to kill 'em?"

She giggled.

He slid his finger to her dimple. And he wanted to keep sliding his touch. He exhaled. "I can't wait for them to leave."

And just like that, he realized how hard it was going to be—only seeing her on the weekends. What he'd seen as his safety net was beginning to feel like a trap. But it was better that way. Wasn't it?

He pulled his hand back and tucked it in his jeans. Snared. Trapped. He cared. He cared too damn much. Yet his eagerness to run wasn't nearly as strong as it should be. How the hell had this happened?

When Austin stepped out on the porch, he heard a car pulling up. Roberto and Brad Hulk, the big guy who swung a mean toilet plunger, got out of the car. Brad nodded a silent apology at Austin.

Austin nodded back, letting the guy know there were no hard feelings, but he couldn't deny that it felt damn good when he saw the man's swollen nose and bruised eyes. Sure, his own eye still carried a mark, but not as bad.

They brought chairs out on the porch and Roberto told

them of the plan. He'd call Cruz, claim he missed DeLuna's call because he'd been shot, say he still had the cocaine from the New Orleans deal gone bad, and offer to drop it off. Once he got the cocaine there, they'd have the cops raid the place, finally placing DeLuna with the drugs.

"It's too dangerous," Dallas said.

"He's right." Normally, Austin didn't shy away from a little risk. But after hearing the message DeLuna left on Roberto's phone, it seemed apparent that DeLuna would shoot first and ask questions later.

"Tell me another way," Roberto said. "And make it fast. The longer I take to contact them, the more suspicious they'll be."

Leah stepped out onto the porch. "What's going to prevent Rafael from killing you?" she asked Roberto.

Austin had known she'd been listening. At first he worried it would be too much for her to hear, but then he realized she had a right to know.

Roberto met her gaze. "If he thinks I'm working for him, he won't."

"But when the police show, he'll know you set him up."

"I'm going to try to be out of there by then."

"Yeah, *try.* But I listened to your plan, and you never mentioned how you were going to do that."

"It's risky, I know, but I haven't come this far to walk away."

"But have you come this far to die? Because that's what's going to happen. And my half brother has hurt too many people already."

It was almost seven, dark, and quiet, except for the voices on the front porch. Leah had offered to make sandwiches for everyone. They'd declined. So she sat at the table staring at her hands. The cabin door opened. She expected it to be Austin; he'd come in earlier and just held her. It had felt so good, his arms around her, resting her head on his shoulder.

She looked back. Roberto shut the door and eased inside. "Can I sit down?"

Leah nodded, and suddenly she couldn't help thinking of Sara. She'd been mesmerized by this man, and yet now he was probably going to go off and get himself killed. And it was Leah's half brother who was probably going to do the killing. She wondered how she could even be related to that monster.

"Sorry for upsetting you," he said.

She looked at him. "Don't do it."

He dropped his hands on the table. "When you went to see your brother, didn't you know it would be dangerous?"

She took a deep breath. "Luis is still alive. But your wife—"

"I know, and as crazy as this sounds, until I get justice for them, it feels like my wife and son are alive, too."

Deep down, Leah knew if Rafael had killed Luis, she'd feel the same way. "I just want the ugliness to end."

"I do, too." He ran his hand over the edge of the table as if considering his next words. "About Sara and what she did. I'm hoping you're not upset with her. I know she was worried about it."

Leah leaned in a bit, confused. "What happened with Sara?"

He closed his eyes a second. "I just thought...she said she was going to tell you."

"Tell me what?"

He appeared to debate speaking up.

"Sara's my friend, I'm sure that whatever she did was... fine."

He nodded. "She's the one who took the bullet out of my leg."

"Okay." Leah gulped, trying not to think of the consequences if . . . if police got word of that.

"I put her in a bad spot. Don't blame her."

"I don't." And Leah wouldn't. But then she couldn't help adding, "She really likes you."

He frowned. "She *did*. I pretty much ruined it."

Her protective nature for her friend surfaced. "What did you do?"

His expression filled with remorse. "I was an idiot. I tried to apologize, but . . ." He raked a hand through his hair. "Just tell her I'm sorry."

As soon as Roberto walked out, Leah went on a witch hunt for Austin's cell phone.

Sara's car was done early, so she'd had the shop bring it to her. She dropped off the cat at the other vet clinic and was picking up Brian, when her phone rang. Again. She let it ring.

Her mom looked at her suspiciously. "You aren't going to answer that?"

"Nah," she said.

Her mom, already suspicious since Sara had asked her to keep Brian, and was now there to pick him up, propped her hand on her hip. A hand on her mom's hip usually led to being referred to by both her first and middle name.

"Sara Jane, sit your butt down and tell me what's up."

A frog-size knot tightened her throat. "I'm not ready to talk, okay?" She grabbed her phone to cut it off and saw it wasn't Roberto.

Shit! It's confession time. She looked at her mom. "I gotta take this."

Sara walked into the bathroom. "Hello?"

Leah didn't bother with formalities. "Are you okay?"

"Fine. Why?"

"I just spoke with Roberto and—"

"I'm sorry. He was bleeding, and then I shot him, and—".

"*You* shot him?" Leah asked.

"Not in the leg. He was already shot there. He gave me his gun and it went off. It…it only grazed his ear, but I felt bad. If you want to fire me, I'd understand."

Leah exhaled. "No. I don't care about that. Well, I do, but it's okay. He said something about needing to apologize to you. What happened?"

Sara hesitated. "I did something stupid."

"You mean besides shooting him?" Leah sounded perplexed.

"Yeah," Sara answered. *I had wild, wonderful sex with a man I hardly knew even when he'd practically told me he still loved someone else.*

"Well, according to him, he thinks he's the idiot."

"He was!" Sara said, still bitter. "But I'm not without fault."

"Do you want to talk about it?" Leah asked.

"No. I want to forget it." She pushed her own problems aside. "How's Luis?"

"He's black and blue, but he's going to be okay." Leah paused. "I'm sorry, Sara. You shouldn't have gotten caught up in this. Even you meeting Roberto is on me. I've got this lunatic half brother and he's…evil."

"Why are you apologizing? It's not your fault." Sara hesitated.

"Is Evelyn okay?" Leah asked.

"She's worried about you. You know how she is, she thinks she's the mother hen. She's been bugging me to give her Austin's number, do you mind?"

"No, give it to her," Leah said.

"How's Austin?" When Leah didn't answer right away, Sara asked. "He won you over, didn't he? I knew he was a good guy." She sighed. "Why is it I can pick 'em for other people, but when I pick one for myself it turns out to be a clusterfuck?"

"Was it that bad?" Leah asked.

"It feels like it right now."

"Okay." Leah exhaled. "Shit. I probably shouldn't say this, but I don't think Roberto is all bad, either."

"You're right," Sara muttered. "You shouldn't say that."

"I know, and I wouldn't, but he's about to... You're right. Forget I said anything."

Sara paused. "Damn! You can't start to say something, then not finish. What is it?"

"You better have a damn good reason for disappearing!" Cruz snapped.

"I do." Roberto looked at the four guys standing on the other side of the porch. He'd first tried to reach DeLuna by calling Don's phone, but it had gone straight to voice mail. Probably already buried with Don's body in some landfill.

"Then why the hell didn't you take DeLuna's call?"

"'Cause I was getting a bullet dug out of my leg."

"What the fuck happened?" Cruz asked. Roberto heard someone in the background. DeLuna?

"Don and I had just got to the warehouse and Luke showed up. I was opening the door to the warehouse when a white Saturn pulled up and bullets went spewing everywhere."

"Did you see who was shooting at you?"

"No. It was dark, then I must have passed out. When I woke up, Don and Luke were dead."

"Then why are you still alive?"

"Hell, I don't know. Luck? Whoever did it probably thought I was dead. Do you know who it was?" He put some anger in his tone.

"Forget that. Who got the kid to the hospital?"

"How the hell would I know?" Roberto asked. "The last thing I remember was Don getting the kid out of the trunk. When I woke up I was bleeding like a stuffed hog and grabbed the keys out of Don's dead hands and got the hell out of there. I found an emergency vet clinic and held the damn bitch at gunpoint and made her dig the bullet out. I've been holed up in some damn hotel, eating doggy pain pills." Lies. He was getting too good at telling them.

"Who's got the product?"

"I do. And I don't like driving around with the shit."

He heard the voice in the background again; this time he was certain it was DeLuna.

"Hang on," Cruz said.

The line went silent. He knew Cruz was filling in DeLuna. And he couldn't help wondering if they weren't onto him and weren't already planning where to hide his body. God, he hoped it wasn't in some landfill beside Don and Luke.

"Hey," Cruz said. "I'll call you tomorrow and tell you where to meet us. Make sure you answer this time."

CHAPTER THIRTY-EIGHT

LEAH HAD JUST hung up from checking on Luis. Rick said he was asleep. She'd almost set the phone down, when Austin's phone rang. She glanced at the number and it was Evelyn. Her friend had dozens of questions, and Leah tried to answer them matter-of-factly. But when she asked Leah if Austin was behaving and Leah said, "Very well," Evelyn somehow knew more than Leah wanted her to know.

"So he's that good, is he? I should have known; he has big feet."

Leah laughed, but she didn't deny the implications. Heck, she didn't want to deny them. She'd slept with Austin and it had been wonderful. It had been amazing. But...

"You deserve to be happy," Evelyn said.

"Yeah." Leah traced her finger along the table's edge.

"Is that hesitation I hear?"

"I just... it happened fast and I'm not even sure we want the same thing."

"What do you want?" Evelyn asked.

"A real relationship." *Everything my parents didn't have.* Dallas stuck his head in the cabin to say good-bye; Leah said good-bye to Evelyn and walked outside to offer her farewell to the others. The night was dark, making the stars shine brighter, and the breeze came with night noises—insects and birds. The cool air whipped her hair around her face. Austin came and stood beside her. As everyone drove away, he dropped his arm around her and pulled her close. She leaned into his side, his scent mingling with the woodsy night air.

"You could have sat in on everything. We weren't trying—"

"I think it would have made everyone uncomfortable." It would have made her uncomfortable. She held no loyalty to Rafael. She wanted him caught, wanted him to pay for his sins. But down deep existed a thread of shame. Rafael shared her blood. He should have mattered, just as Luis mattered, but he didn't.

All this time, she'd thought Rafael had been the lucky one to have had their father—to have had his love. Now she couldn't help surmising if Rafael's upbringing hadn't somehow contributed to the terrible person he'd become. Who would have ever guessed it turned out that she and Luis had been the lucky ones.

Leaning into Austin's warmth, she asked, "Did you talk Roberto out of seeing Rafael?"

Austin glanced down at her. "No, but we're going to be close in case—"

"We?" she asked.

"Dallas, Tyler, and I. They're supposed to call Roberto tomorrow and tell him where to meet. Early tomorrow, I'm taking you to a hotel in Austin and have another of our PIs with you just in case."

Leah's heart clutched. "What? You're going to see Rafael, too?"

He squeezed her arm. "We're going to be close. In case—"

She shook her head. "Someone could die. Just call the police."

He ran a hand down her cheek. "Leah, we were the police. We've been trained to deal with this, plus we're calling the police as soon as we know for sure he's there and it'll be a good arrest."

"Or you kill him, right?" she asked. "Isn't that what you're really after?"

He hesitated, a mix of emotions on his face. A mix of emotions in her chest. "We want justice. Not blood."

She looked at him, doubting his words.

He exhaled. "Okay, at one time we all wanted blood. But it's not like that now. I want him caught because some people still think we did this."

She walked to the edge of the porch. How could she blame him for that? She couldn't. She wanted justice for what he'd done to Luis, too. "I hate that he's my brother. I hate knowing that we share the same DNA." Tears filled her eyes.

Austin came behind her, wrapped his arms around her middle, and pulled her against him. "I think about that, too. I don't even know who my father was, but he can't have been much of a man to have walked away from my mother and me. But I tell myself that our destinies are our own. We make our choices, not DNA." They stood on that porch for the longest time. Just holding on to each other. It felt so right.

"It's so quiet here." She listened to the night.

"I know. I love it." He held her even closer. "There are a few cabins around, but I own twenty acres. There's a slight hill about an acre back. I dream of putting a house there."

"It would be nice." They didn't talk for several more minutes.

"I'm starved. Let's fix dinner." He rubbed his palms up and down her arms.

She nodded and tried to forget what tomorrow might bring.

They made grilled cheese sandwiches. She noticed he'd bought margarine to cook with, and she knew he'd remembered her saying she preferred it. After dinner, he talked her into taking a shower, together.

He undressed her—slow and easy. Her modesty peaked, but as soon as she started removing his clothes, she didn't mind her own state of undress.

They took turns washing each other—more touching and teasing than cleaning. Between the warm steam, hot kisses, and soapy hands, she was past ready when he guided her out of the shower. Before she walked out of the bathroom, she made him drop the window blinds.

"So no exhibitionist fantasies, huh?" he teased.

"Tons of them," she teased back, "but I've lived that fantasy today."

He laughed. When the blinds were lowered, they dropped into bed wearing nothing but smiles. Their lovemaking was less urgent this time, and somehow more meaningful than earlier.

He held her as they caught their breath. She rested her head on his chest and he ran a finger over her cheek, then lifted up and stared at her ear.

She cut her eyes up at him. "If they're dirty, you're going to have to talk to the guy who bathed me."

"Just checking to see if any cat has ever tried to remove one of *your* ears." Laughing, he tugged on her earlobe.

She chuckled.

"Do you have pierced ears?" he asked.

"Yes."

"Do you wear jewelry?"

She felt her heart clutch a little, remembering the jewelry her dad always brought her mom. "Remember, I don't like gifts."

"Why?"

"Just because." That's all she gave him.

They lay there talking about crazy things. Movies they liked. Which Saturday cartoon they watched as kids. Favorite things to do on a Sunday afternoon. His was to come to his cabin. Hers was to read an entire book in one sitting.

He fell asleep. Leah fell back into worrying. Her heart raced with the thought that tomorrow he would confront Rafael. His hand shifted and rested on her hip, and his touch sent bolts of emotion to her chest. Would she lose him before they ever really had a chance?

The pain of that thought made her chest hurt, and she wanted to wake him. She had questions. She wanted to know everything about him. His favorite candy bar. His favorite meal. Where had he gone to school? How many years had he worked on the police force?

What was this thing happening between them? Did they have a stab at a future? Had he ever been married?

Tears filled her eyes. She brushed them away before they fell on his bare chest. But fear, fear of where all this was leading, whittled its way into her heart.

She didn't know him well enough to care this much. And yet, here she was, up to her eyeballs in caring.

"Can we really trust them?" Brad asked Roberto when Tyler and Dallas left the table to grab a beer. They'd been sitting at the hotel bar, going over the plans.

"They're good guys," Roberto said.

"I know, but when the cops get there, am I gonna end up in jail? Do they know that I—"

"No. They don't know. I told them just what I told Cruz. That I didn't see who shot at me and the others. And if that whole thing comes up, that's what I'll tell the cops, too."

Brad sighed. "And if you don't make it out, what's going to happen?"

Roberto's gut clenched. Why did everyone think he wouldn't make it out? "Austin will take care of you."

Brad nodded and kept quiet when the two guys returned.

Roberto's phone rang. His heart jolted. Cruz was supposed to call tomorrow. Was he ready to do this now? He checked the number. His heart did another tumble.

"Is it them?" Dallas asked.

"No." He stared at the number. "I gotta take this." He stood and started out.

Then, afraid she'd hang up, he answered. "Hi, Sara. I've tried to call you a dozen times."

He walked into the hotel lobby and headed to a quiet corner. "Sara, this is you, isn't it?"

"Yeah." Her voice sounded hesitant. "What are you doing, Roberto?"

"I was having a beer."

"No. I mean...I talked to Leah. She said you were going to get yourself killed."

Another person who already had him dead. "That's not my plan."

"But whatever you're doing is dangerous. Don't do it."

A couple moved across the room, catching his eye with their loving embrace. "Look, the reason I called you was because...because I was an ass. I'm sorry, I didn't mean—"

"You still love your wife, I get that."

"No." He scowled at the wall. "I mean...a part of me will always love her, but she's gone, and I know that. But what you and I shared—"

"I shouldn't have crawled in bed with you. It was my fault. You don't have to apologize."

"Damn, Sara, I'm not apologizing for making love to you, I'm apologizing for what I said. It wasn't a mistake. It's the first thing in my damn life that's felt right since I lost my family. I want that, Sara. At least I want a chance at it. A chance at us. At us being an *us*."

"Dying won't bring her back," Sara said, as if she wasn't listening to what he said.

"I'm not planning on dying. We could start all over. I could take you to dinner. A real date."

"I didn't pull that bullet out of your leg and risk losing my job for you to go and get yourself killed."

Roberto closed his eyes. "You want me to live?"

"Of course I do."

"Then give me something to live for, Sara. Tell me, no, promise me, that you'll see me again when this is over."

Austin woke up feeling anchored and warm. He opened his eyes. A smile bubbled up inside him at the sight of the petite brunette pillowed on his chest. Damn, she was pretty. And sexy. And...real.

A thread of fear wrapped around the ball of happiness filling his chest. Could it last? It never did. People walked away—dropped you off at day care, left you to sit outside on a porch, when they weren't coming. People told the foster program they couldn't keep you anymore; people who promised you forever handed you back your ring and said good-bye.

He pushed the thought away. He was just going to enjoy

this now. He'd pay the price later. He always did, didn't he? And he survived it.

She stirred. Her gentle weight against him felt so damn right. So right, he wondered if he could survive losing her. But it was too late to stop it. He cared. Cared too much. All he could do was make it last as long as he could. And the fact that she lived in another city might even help it last. It would always feel fresh. Maybe she wouldn't be so eager to walk away like the others had in his life.

Glancing at the clock, he realized it wasn't even five. He'd set the alarm for five thirty so they could meet Dallas and the others at their hotel by seven. He leaned down and kissed her. She bolted up, eyes wide, as if shocked to wake up with someone.

"Morning," he said.

"Sorry," she muttered. "I'm not used to…" As if realizing she wasn't wearing anything, she snatched the sheet off him and clutched it to her chest. Her eyes traveled down his naked chest to his sex, standing at its normal morning salute. She pulled the corner of the sheet from around her legs and tossed it over him, the tent in the sheet still evident.

Her face reddened and he grinned.

"You are unscrupulous," she said, a slight tease in her tone.

"You are gorgeous." He pulled her in for a kiss that led just where he wanted it to go.

The sun hadn't risen yet, and while they were on their way to Austin in Rick's truck, Leah was on her way to worrying again. In twenty minutes or less, he was going to leave her in some hotel with another man. Fear for Austin's safety, and fear for her heart, started building with the sound of the wheels rolling down the freeway.

As the first golden rays of sun spilled light from the pink sky, her unasked questions from last night popped off like fireworks in her head.

Unsure how to start, she blurted the first question out. "Have you ever been married?"

He sent her an odd glance, as if she should have known the answer. But how could she, he'd been pretending to be someone else?

"No," he said.

"Engaged?"

His lips tightened, as if he didn't like that question. "Once."

"What was she like?"

He focused on the road, silent for several seconds. "Blond, about five-nine. Green eyes."

She frowned. "That's not what I meant. What was her personality?"

He took one hand off the wheel and rested it on her thigh. "I don't know how to describe someone's personality."

She put her hand on top of his. "Try."

He moved his hand back, and his fingers tightened around the wheel. "Why are you asking this?"

"You asked me about my ex."

"Not to describe his personality." He chuckled.

She waited a few seconds. "It's just, you know a lot about me and I don't know a lot about you."

He shifted his shoulders as if he didn't feel comfortable. "You know more about me than most people."

She considered his words. "You mean about your childhood?"

"Yeah." He frowned.

"Why did you tell me about that?" She hoped he'd say it was because he'd felt connected to her—something that

would assure her she wasn't alone in her feelings—feelings
that were a kitten's whisker away from falling in love.

He shrugged. "I don't know, it just came up."

She nodded, disappointed in his answer. "So what was
she like?"

"I told you she abandoned me."

"Your fiancée?"

He flinched. "I thought you meant my mom." Another
silence filled the cab. "Cara was a mistake, just like your ex."

"Did you love her?" She filed away the name. Cara.

He looked at Leah, his eyes tight with what appeared to
be frustration. "If you're worried she's still a part of my life,
then don't. She's not."

"I'm not worried about that," she said. "I just..."

"Just what?" He sounded puzzled.

Suddenly insecure about her...insecurities, she said,
"I..." How could she explain it? She decided to be honest,
mostly honest. "I'm nervous."

"About what?" He paused. "Today?"

"Yeah. And tomorrow." She waved a hand between them.
"About this. Us. About what it is."

"This?" He waved his hand between them. "This is
friggin' great. It's awesome." He offered her a sexy smile.
"Didn't you enjoy this morning?"

She pointed out the obvious. "We live almost two hundred miles apart." *And that's if you don't get killed today by
my half brother.*

Then an epiphany hit. The thought of losing him physically was making her question if she actually had him
emotionally. Everything had happened so fast. It was as if
she'd woken up and found herself almost in love. And she
wasn't sure if she'd gotten here by herself, or if he'd made
the trek with her. If he wasn't really into "this," she needed

to know—needed to start putting on her emotional brakes. Brakes she'd kept locked until he walked into her life.

"That's part of what makes it great." He sounded as if he'd given it some thought.

"What?"

"The fact that you live in Heartbroke and I'm in Miller. We won't get in each other's way. Then on weekends, we can hook up. I'll keep my apartment next to yours. Some weekends we can meet at the cabin."

"You think I'd get in your way?"

"No." He frowned. "I didn't say that."

"Yes, you did." She quietly folded her hands in her lap, her chest tightening. A bright spray of sun spilled into the cab. Then she realized what else he'd said, that he'd keep his apartment. He didn't even want to stay at her place.

Good golly. She was at an emotional place where she was ready to offer him forever, yet he wasn't even going to offer her his weekends. She mentally reached for the emergency brake.

"Well, I didn't mean it like that. I meant that... we both have our jobs and lives, and this way we won't have to deal with that kind of stuff with each other."

"But that 'stuff' is life."

"It's the drudgery of life. I won't need to worry if I have to work late. When we're together, we just have fun. No daily crap to worry about."

"So just sex, huh?" The question bubbled up from somewhere inside her.

His brows tightened. "Don't do this."

"Don't do what?"

"Don't make what I said into something bad."

Was that what she was doing? True, he hadn't said anything about sex, but... "I'm just feeling vulnerable."

"You don't have to," he said. "Like I said, this is the best-case scenario."

Why was it best? Didn't he know that statistically, long-distance relationships didn't last? Why was everything beginning to feel wrong? Even her asking questions felt wrong, as if she was some clingy girl he'd slept with and who was now seeking promises.

He reached over and passed a hand over her cheek. "Hey...absence makes the heart grow fonder."

If the brakes weren't all the way pulled, they were now. That clarified his emotional status. Austin wanted the fun, but not the commitment. Just like her ex, who swore he still loved her but didn't want to be monogamous. Just like her dad, who wanted her mom but didn't want to live with her or be a part of his own kids' lives.

She tried to swallow the emotion, but it hung on her tonsils. She felt eight again, being abandoned by her father at the cemetery.

The temptation hit to tell Austin the distance quote was bullshit. But logic intervened. Now wasn't the time. He was about to step into a dangerous situation.

While they wouldn't have a future, she didn't want his future to be cut short because of her or her half brother. Good-bye would come soon enough.

She stared out the window. Fury burned her chest, but not at him. Not now. When he'd lied, she'd had a right to be furious, but he'd come clean. And he'd never confessed feelings for her at any time. Austin's only admission was his attraction.

He hadn't made promises. She hadn't asked for promises. He'd saved her life. Probably saved her brother's life. But they hardly knew each other. So what if they'd had sex? Great sex. It wasn't his fault she'd let her heart get involved—that she wasn't into recreational sex like ninety percent of the adult world.

It wasn't his fault that her absent father had messed with her head and had her waiting for some knight in shining armor to sweep in and promise her a fairy-tale ending—one that included forever.

It wasn't his fault that she couldn't accept anything less.

CHAPTER THIRTY-NINE

AUSTIN KNOCKED ON the hotel door. As soon as Rick opened it, he saw the look of concern on Leah's face.

"Who's with my brother?" she asked.

"Another PI's with him," Austin answered.

After knowing she was comfortable, he needed to head out. The others were waiting on him in the lobby. But Leah had gone quiet on him again on the ride. What was wrong? Was she just scared? Worried about him? Worried about Rafael? Was she still worried about him not wanting to talk about Cara? But damn, this whole thing was so mixed up.

He motioned for Rick to step outside. Alone, he moved over to her and tilted her chin up. "You going to be okay?"

"I'll be fine." But the look in her eyes said differently. "Make sure you stay safe."

He leaned down to kiss her and felt her hesitation. Finally, she leaned into him. The kiss ended too soon. He brushed his finger over her lips, still wet from his kiss.

"I need to go."

"Go." She offered a smile, but it didn't reach her eyes.

* * *

Roberto made his way to the free coffee in the hotel lobby. He'd barely slept. His thoughts were torn between Sara and her hesitant "yes" that she'd go out with him, to the fact that he was finally going to come face-to-face with the guy who'd killed Anna and Bobby.

His past and possible future played tug-of-war with his heart. Amazingly, he didn't feel the guilt anymore. It was time. He even got the feeling Anna would have wanted him to move forward. And in spite of how many times he assured himself that today would go okay, he couldn't deny the unsteady feeling of fear.

He looked around for Brad. He'd knocked on his door as he walked out of his room, and the guy hadn't answered. Dallas, Tyler, and Austin were already there. He grabbed some coffee.

"Where's Brad?" Austin asked as Roberto stepped up.

"I knocked on his door. He didn't answer. Probably overslept." Roberto pulled out his phone and hit the man's number.

Brad picked up on the fourth ring. "I found them."

"What? Where are you?"

"I couldn't sleep, and I remembered another place they could be. One of Sandy's cousins owns a cabin up north of town. And damn if it ain't right there by Austin's place. They're here."

"Shit!" Roberto snapped. "We're supposed to do this together." He instantly recalled Brad's hesitancy last night, but after Sara's call he'd forgotten about it.

If Brad messed this up, or worse, got himself killed, it was on Roberto. All three of the men surrounding him frowned.

"I got this," Brad said. "There's a shed in the back of the

property; I'm gonna stash the drugs and the gun there. I'll let you know when to call the cops. You don't have to get mixed up in this."

"Damn it! Where exactly are you?"

Thirty minutes after Roberto pulled the address from Brad, Austin parked at his cabin. He led the way through the thick line of trees and underbrush. Oddly enough, the cabin where DeLuna and Cruz were holed up was less than a mile from Austin's. He was glad he'd taken Leah to the hotel instead of having Rick come to the cabin. He didn't want DeLuna anywhere near her.

As briars hung on to his jeans, thoughts of Leah clung to his heart. Was it the thought of DeLuna's demise that had caused her to lapse into silent mode? "You sure you're going the right way?" Roberto's concern for Brad heightened his tone.

"It's right up here." Austin had spent the last year walking his property lines, debating building a house. No, not a house, a home. He hadn't started, because building a home for just him felt wrong.

The clearing lay ahead. Knowing that DeLuna could have been here off and on over the last year left a bitter taste in his mouth. He couldn't help wondering if he'd ever passed the asswipe on the road. His need for revenge peaked.

Then he thought of Leah and his resolve wavered. Not revenge. Justice.

Roberto tried to call Brad again. "It's still cut off," he muttered.

"If he gets hurt, it's not your fault," Austin said. "You didn't ask him to do this."

"I should have checked on him last night. He was antsy." Roberto pulled at the ballistic vest Dallas has insisted everyone wear. Austin found the damn heavy piece of shit just as annoying, but he'd seen that look on Dallas's face when he'd passed them around. If Austin had refused to wear one, they'd still be at his cabin arguing.

They walked the next few minutes in silence. The sound of their steps crunching the underbrush seemed loud. The clearing appeared about fifty feet away. In the far distance, a car engine rumbled by.

Pressing his finger to his lips, Austin looked back at the guys. Moving silently, they inched forward.

Austin peered out from behind a tree. Three men got out of a dark Chevy Malibu and went inside the cabin.

Dallas inched forward. "It's time to call in the cops."

"No," Roberto said. "Not until I'm sure Brad's not in the shed or they haven't got him inside."

"And how are we going to know if he won't answer his damn phone?" Dallas asked.

"Like this." Roberto took off through the line of trees toward the shed, the limp in his left leg only slightly noticeable.

"Fuck," said Dallas.

"Yeah, fuck," Austin muttered, and took off after him.

Austin made the shed about five seconds after Roberto, his weapon drawn.

They made eye contact. There were no windows in the shed. Roberto motioned that he planned to go around and enter the building.

The sound of voices interrupted the tense moment. Roberto and Austin plastered themselves to the back of the shed.

"How long are we gonna hang out here?" a nasal-sounding voice said from the other side of the shed.

"Until the Boss says we can go," another answered. A slight accent hung to this man's words.

Cigarette smoke snaked around the cabin. "You called Rivera yet?" the first guy asked.

"Boss wants him to sweat a while. Hell, let him stay alive a little longer."

"You think he's lying?" Nasal-voice asked.

"What I think doesn't count. The Boss thinks he's dirty."

"Damn, I don't wanna bury another one. I got blisters from Luke's and Don's graves."

Roberto's eyes widened. Austin sympathized. Nothing like hearing someone bitch about burying your ass before you're dead.

The thud of footsteps drew closer.

Austin tightened his grip on his gun, ready for hell to break loose. He saw Dallas and Tyler shift back a few feet out of sight. He didn't have a clue how many guys were in the cabin. Could they take them—without one of them getting hit?

He imagined Dallas had already alerted the officials. For once, Austin appreciated Dallas's less-risk policy.

Time crawled by as the two men continued to shoot the shit. *How long could they be here without being caught?*

"Fuck! Did you see that?" Nasal-voice asked.

"What?"

Austin's breath caught.

"I could swear I saw someone move between the trees."

Austin's gaze shot to where Dallas and Tyler had been. He didn't see them.

"Where?"

"Straight back."

Austin glanced toward the woods again. Sure as hell, he saw someone—a big someone. Toilet-plunger guy was going to get them killed.

Austin motioned to the woods, and Roberto frowned.

"Not to the left," the nasal-sounding guy spit out. "Straight back."

Austin's finger tightened on the trigger. Brad slipped behind some trees.

"I don't see anything," the other man said. "But go check it out."

Footsteps moved at the side of the shed. Austin and Roberto aimed their guns where the man was about to appear. Roberto cut Austin a quick glance that said exactly what Austin thought. They were fucked.

CHAPTER FORTY

TENSION FILLED AUSTIN'S chest as the man continued forward. Then a bullet popped off from the woods. Brad?

"Motherfucker! I'm hit." The man, sounding only a foot away from the back of the building, slammed against the shed.

Bullets shooting into the woods came from behind the shed.

"Throw down your weapons, you're surrounded!" Dallas's voice boomed from the trees.

So not smart, Austin thought. Gunfire blasted off in the direction of Dallas's call. Austin hated being right.

A barrage of voices now echoed behind them, along with the sound of glass breaking. More gunfire exploded. His gaze shot to the woods, praying Dallas and Tyler had taken cover.

"Is it the cops?" someone asked.

"Don't know," another person shot back.

Austin nodded at Roberto and held up three fingers. He hoped the man understood. On the count of three, he was going to go around his side of the cabin and shoot like hell.

One. Images flashed in his head. Leah's dimple winking

at him. The sight of her asleep on his chest. The scent of her hair, waffle ice cream cones. He needed more time with her.

Two. He imagined the house he'd wanted to build. Would Leah be interested in helping him?

Three. Don't kill her brother.

There were five guys, and five guns shifted at Austin. Roberto suddenly appeared. Austin fired at the same time Roberto did. One guy took a bullet in the leg—another dropped to the ground. A car engine roared in the front. Probably DeLuna trying to escape. If the guy was good at anything, it was running.

As bullets whizzed past, he heard the sirens. Backup had arrived.

"Police!" voices yelled. Had they stopped DeLuna? More gunfire exploded. Shit, had they killed DeLuna? He thought of Leah.

A cold pain hit Austin's arm, but it was the one that hit him in the chest that knocked him on his ass. He drew in air, but none came.

Leah sat in the chair and watched the television. He'd been gone for four hours. She couldn't relay what was on TV if someone paid her a million bucks. The flickering flat screen was simply a place to stare. A focal spot while her heart continued breaking.

Rick sat on the other chair in the room, in front of the door, staring with the same intensity. She had a feeling he wasn't watching TV, either.

His phone had rung thirty minutes ago. All he'd told her was it was over. When she asked specifically about Austin, he'd said, "Alive." When she'd inquired about Roberto, he'd said the same. When she'd inquired if anyone was hurt, he said Austin should arrive soon.

She accepted this meant that Rafael hadn't come out of this alive. A thread of shame whispered through her heart. Shouldn't she care? Tears filled her eyes, but she wiped them away. Shame should be enough. It had to be, for she couldn't even determine whether her tears were for Rafael or for her own personal heartbreak.

She'd already called a friend of Luis and asked if he would take her to Austin's cabin to get her car. Prolonging good-bye would make it harder.

The hotel door opened and Austin walked in. His gaze zeroed in on her, his brows pinched with concern. His light blue chambray shirt held bloodstains. She stood up, her heart aching, and her tears doubled. "You okay?"

She expected him to send Rick out, but he walked over and reached for her. His arms encircled her. She let him pull her into his embrace, knowing it would be one of their last.

Sweat dampened his shirt. She breathed in his scent, so warm, so comforting. Was this what her mom had felt for her dad? Was this feeling why she accepted that having a little of him was better than losing him entirely? She wasn't her mother. She wanted more.

Then, remembering the bloodstain on Austin's shirt, she pulled back.

"You were shot?"

"Just nicked in the arm." He tilted her face up so he could look right at her. "I'm sorry."

She knew he meant Rafael. Nodding, her chest tightened.

"He drew on the officers. I wasn't anywhere near him to stop it." He used his thumb to brush away a tear. "Even if I was close, I'm not sure I could've stopped it."

"It's not your fault." She inhaled and noticed a hole in the chest of his shirt. She pulled it open and saw a bright purple bruise. "What happened?"

"I was wearing a vest, but I took one to the chest."

Her breath hitched. "You could have died. Anyone else hurt?"

"Roberto was nicked in the leg. But he's fine. Several of DeLuna's men didn't make it. Cruz is dead."

A numbness spread to her chest. "So much death for nothing."

He pressed a kiss to her forehead. "I'm supposed to take you to the police station. But if you're not up to it, I'll tell them I'll bring you in later."

"No." Another tear slipped down her cheek. "I'm okay." And she would be, eventually. As soon as she got back into the rhythm of her own life. As soon as Austin returned to Miller and she was back to living with her emotional brakes on.

It wasn't like this was real love. A kitten's whisker away.

A Detective Sullivan took her back to a room to talk. Austin squeezed her hand before she walked away. "I'll be here when you get out."

The detective asked her questions, some of the same ones more than once. She told him the truth, omitting the part about Austin kidnapping her.

"If you'd reported it when your place was broken into, this could have been avoided."

She looked him right in the eyes. "Please. You'd have made a file and it would have never gone anywhere."

He muttered something under his breath. "But at least there would've been a report."

"I'll remember that the next time my place is broken into." It was hard not to be sarcastic—he looked a little bit like the guy who took the report on Snowball's death.

Before the detective finished, she interrupted him and asked to use a phone. She called Luis's old roommate and asked if he could pick her up now. Face it, she sucked at long good-byes.

Austin felt useless waiting in the lobby. He knew how hard some cops could be on witnesses. Hell, he'd been hard on a few in his day. Dallas and Tyler walked in.

"They still have her?" Tyler asked.

Austin nodded. "I'm giving the guy five more minutes and then I'm going in after her."

Dallas shot Tyler an odd look.

"What?" Austin asked.

"Nothing." Dallas shrugged.

"Don't give me that shit. If you two know something that concerns Leah—"

"No." Tyler said. "He just meant you're awfully protective of her."

"She didn't deserve this shit." Austin ran a hand through his hair. "DeLuna was her half brother. This has to be hell on her."

"Probably." Tyler glanced at Dallas.

"Then stop acting like I'm overreacting," he bit out.

"We don't think you're overreacting," Tyler said.

Dallas jumped in. "You're acting like a guy who cares about a woman. It's new for you."

"Am I that big of an asshole?" Austin asked.

"Not an asshole," Dallas said. "You just don't let a lot of people close. Especially women."

Austin cupped his hands behind his neck, squeezed his elbows in, and dropped in a chair to wait. "Did anyone mention Brad Hulk to you?" he asked his partners.

"No," Dallas answered. "As far as they know he was never there."

"Good." The seconds were torturous. He needed to

see Leah. Wanted to make sure things were okay...okay between them. "Have you seen Roberto?"

"They were still questioning him," Dallas said. "But I don't think it's going to be a problem."

After a few minutes, Austin spoke up again. "This isn't the way I saw us after we caught him." He let out a deep moan. "Shit! I can't even be happy about this. I didn't know what to say to her."

"'Revenge has its own special taste.' I think it was Job who said that." Tyler sighed. "But DeLuna needed to be stopped. Look what he did to Luis Reece. We can't feel bad."

"Yes, we can," Austin admitted. "I feel bad for Leah."

Dallas nodded. "I understand you feeling that way. But we didn't do this to him. He did it to himself. Leah can't blame you."

"I don't think she does," Austin said. "I just...everything feels so crazy."

"It is crazy," Dallas said. "I'm not happy Leah's brother died, but I'm happy this is over. I would have been happy to have seen him behind bars. He didn't have to die; that was his choice."

"I know." Austin felt confused, about everything. And damn it, he didn't blame them for being happy. If he wasn't so concerned about Leah, he'd feel differently. Not thrilled at DeLuna's death, but at least relieved that the person who had caused them so much pain, and continued to hurt others, had been stopped.

The door swung open and Leah walked out. She met Austin's gaze. He went to her and, needing to touch her, ran his palms down her forearms. "Hey. You okay?" He didn't care who saw him. He pulled her in for a hug. And he held on. She allowed it for only a second before pulling back.

"What do you need?" he asked, loosening his hold. "Food? Wine? You want to go back to the cabin? You want to go see Luis? Whatever you need, we'll do it."

She looked at Dallas and Tyler, then moved to the glass doors. "I...called a friend of Luis. He's going to take me to my car, and I'll go see Luis by myself."

Austin didn't think he'd heard her right. He replayed her words in his head. "Why would you do that? I can take you. I figured you'd want to see him. I just thought you might be hungry or..." God, why was he rambling like this? Because he didn't know how to act. Not about her half brother being killed and not about...his feelings.

She bit down on her lip, a sure sign she felt agitated, or nervous. Amazing how he could read her after such a short time, but this...this "by myself" crap blindsided him.

Inhaling, she started talking again. "I thought you'd have plans with your partners."

"I don't. So I can take you. It's fine."

He reached to touch her again. She pulled back. Who knew a couple of inches could hurt more than the bullet to the chest? "What's going on, Leah?"

She glanced down, then up. "Everything happened so..." She paused. "This..." She waved a hand between them. "I'm not sure it's..."

"Whoa," he said. "I thought it's been great."

She shook her head. He saw her gaze shoot to the glass doors again. "I can't..."

A car pulled up. He was losing her; his heart dropped. "Is this because of DeLuna?"

She didn't answer. "Thank you for...everything. I owe you. I'll send a check. But I can't do this." She waved a hand between them again.

He watched her leave. Watched her walk away. He

couldn't breathe. Dallas and Tyler came to stand beside him.

"Something wrong?" Dallas asked.

"No," Austin said. "Everything is as it always is." They fucking walk away. Why had he expected anything different?

Leah got back to her car at the cabin. She packed up four cats. Remembering Austin's newfound relationship with Spooky, she didn't take his cat, but she left a note saying if he decided he didn't want him to please drop the cat off at her office. Then, with her cats in tow, she drove to Luis's new hospital. It was almost seven when she got there. The cats weren't happy. But she didn't plan to stay long. And a good thing, too. She barely kept herself together through the visit. While his swelling had gone down, he was almost completely purple. What she wanted to do was weep. Fall to the floor and cry.

But crying hadn't seemed smart with Luis's girlfriend there. As soon as Luis had been told it was safe, he'd called her. She was there holding Luis's hand, worrying over him like...like she loved him. It only made Leah want to sob harder.

So she kissed her brother, hugged his girlfriend, and told them she'd see them the next day. Then she drove back to Heartbroke. Damn if the name wasn't appropriate.

When she passed her vet clinic, she dropped in and grabbed her phone and purse. She had several missed messages. She held her breath as she went through the recent calls, thinking she'd hear Austin's voice. She didn't.

Of course not.

Absence made the heart grow fonder.

Austin went to the cabin, hoping maybe she'd still be there. Thinking she'd say she hadn't meant it. He'd have forgiven her, just like he'd have forgiven his mom when she'd come back into his life the first time. Just like he'd have forgiven Cara if she'd come running back saying she'd made a mistake.

But Leah wasn't at the cabin.

She'd left the damn cat and a note, though. Not about them, or about how she'd been wrong, but about the cat.

On the way back to Miller, cat in tow, he went by the liquor store. He hadn't wanted to stay at the cabin. It reminded him of Leah now.

He wanted the numbness of a heavy evening with some Jack Daniel's. He stayed away from the wine. It would have reminded him of Leah, too. He tried to be happy about DeLuna getting his just dues, but that reminded him of Leah, too. So he pushed that out of his mind.

He settled into his townhome, and after about four drinks, he decided he needed a distraction. He picked up his phone to call Holly Macon, the flight attendant.

Hadn't she said something about having a few days off this week? Maybe she'd fuck Leah out of his mind.

He never hit her number. He tossed the phone on the other side of the sofa and let out words that a sailor would have kicked his ass for saying. Spooky didn't seem to appreciate it, either. Austin had a couple more drinks. Doubles.

He was passed out on the sofa when he heard his doorbell. Over and over again. Leah? His forced himself to get up, stumbled to the door, and stood there a second trying to remember how to open it.

He knew it had something to do with the knob. When he got that puzzle solved, and the door open, he latched on to the frame and tried to focus. The room started spinning, and no matter how hard he tried to make the blurry figure look like Leah Reece, it didn't work. But didn't he recognize this woman?

And then it hit. Not clear vision. Not recognition. Nausea. He bent at the waist and hurled. Several times. Wiping his mouth with the back of his hands, he saw the pair of old-lady pumps swimming in barf.

For some stupid reason it seemed funny. He looked up and tried not to laugh. And that's when recognition hit. Son of a bitch!

CHAPTER FORTY-ONE

WITH MORE JACK Daniel's in his veins than he'd ever had, his emotions went wonky. He continued to laugh. He couldn't help it. "Hi, Mom," he said. But the moment he said the word "mom," the humor escaped him.

"Let me help you." She stepped inside, kicked off her shoes, caught him under his arms, and guided him to the sofa. He should've been madder than hell, her showing up here, and part of him was. Yet the half a dozen times he'd actually drunk this much he'd been told he was a happy drunk.

But once his butt hit his leather sofa, he looked up, and happiness faded. "You can go. The door's that way."

She picked up his almost empty bottle of whiskey and turned toward the kitchen.

"What're you doing?"

"Putting it away," she said. "And making coffee."

He scowled. "Don't pretend to care."

"I'm not going to pretend anything," she said. "But I know from personal experience when someone's had enough."

She walked toward the kitchen. He should insist again

that she leave, but another wave of nausea hit. He collapsed back and shut his eyes. The smell of coffee stirred him out of his stupor. He opened his eyes. A cup waited on the coffee table. The woman had pulled a kitchen chair beside him and sat there staring.

"I want you to leave," he muttered.

She handed him a damp washcloth.

He wiped it across his face. "The door's that way."

She leaned forward. "Let me say a few things first. Chances are you won't remember them anyway."

"I'll remember. I don't forget things...like leaving my kid at day care for over two decades."

She frowned. "I deserve that."

"Yup," Austin said. "But why do you think you deserve a chance to clear your conscience?"

She held her chin high. "I don't deserve anything, but I thought *you* might deserve to know some things."

He pushed a palm over his face. "I've had a shitty day, so leave."

"What happened?"

He propped his elbows on his knees and then dropped his pounding head into his hands. After a second, he looked up. "I had another woman walk out on me. This makes the third. No, fourth. You got me twice."

She frowned. "Did she leave because of your drinking?"

His sour stomach clenched. She had no right to judge him. "You think I'm like you? I'm not a drunk or a druggie."

She just stared.

"Okay, tonight I'm drunk. But I've only done this...Oh, hell, why am I talking to you?" Because he was drunk.

She sighed. "Why did this woman walk out on you? She meet someone else?"

Austin felt compelled to defend Leah. "She's not like

that. I did something she can't forgive me for." *I got her brother killed.* At least that was part of it. He didn't know what the other part was. She obviously hadn't cared enough. "Isn't the whole forgiving thing ironic? Because I can't forgive you for…" He needed to shut up. Why the hell had he opened the door?

Oh, yeah, he'd thought it might be Leah.

Candy walked toward the door, but instead of leaving, she grabbed her purse and came back.

She pulled out an envelope and dropped it on the coffee table, and a couple of pictures slid halfway out. "Do you know the saying, 'If you love something, let it go'? Well, that's what I did. Now I realize that the saying's nothing but bullshit." She paused. "Then again, I'm not sure if I wouldn't have messed you up worse if I had come back. I'd get clean, swear to stay clean, and then something would happen and I was back at it."

She didn't cry, she said it matter-of-factly, as if a practiced speech. "But there wasn't a day that I didn't think about you. I know I wasn't in your life, but you were always in mine. I had a lawyer friend call CPS and check on you every few months, and I'd find you. I took pictures." She dropped back into the chair. "When you graduated high school…I watched you walk across that stage. I was so proud because I never did finish school. And when you graduated from the police academy, I was there, too. I know I didn't deserve to be there. But, like I said, I thought you might deserve to know that I was."

He didn't pick up the pictures, just stared at the steam floating off the coffee. What the hell did she expect him to say?

"I've been sober and clean for ten years. It's taken me this long to get the guts up to come see you." She stood. "I hope you remember some of this. And if you ever need anything, my number is on the back of that envelope."

She walked to the door, but turned. "Do you love her? The girl?"

He didn't answer.

"If so, go tell her how sorry you are. She might not forgive you, but if you don't at least try to make things right, there may come a time that you can't forgive yourself." With those parting words, she left.

The click of the door closing echoed in his chest. "Leah said the same thing about you," he muttered. Right then, Spooky came out from under the sofa and bumped his head to Austin's knee.

Tell her how sorry you are. An overwhelming need to talk to Leah swelled inside him. He reached for his phone. No, a call wouldn't do. He had to look her in the eyes, so she'd know he meant it.

Sort of like his mom had done. Right in the eyes. He pushed that thought away.

He needed to make sure Leah knew how sorry he was that her brother died. Hell, maybe she was just grieving and he should have tried harder to explain...explain what?

The question hung in his mind.

Do you love her?

He loved Leah. He'd known it, deep inside he'd known it for a while, but he just hadn't admitted it to himself. And he hadn't told her. Standing up, he tried to remember where he'd put his keys, but when he stumbled, he accepted he couldn't drive.

Turning, he found his phone again. This time he dialed.

Roberto raised his hand to knock, then checked his phone for the time. After nine. Was she already in bed? He should wait. Call her in the morning and set up a date.

Hell, he didn't want to wait. He knocked.

He heard footsteps. Saw the peephole go dark. Heard her opening the door.

She didn't say anything, just stared, eyes wide. "You're alive," she finally spit out.

He nodded and waited to see if she was going to invite him in. Waited to see if she meant what she'd said about giving him another chance.

"Brian's asleep," she said.

That didn't sound good. "So it's not a good time?"

She hesitated. "I thought you wanted to go out on a date next weekend?"

He wanted to touch her so bad his teeth ached. Wanted her to help remind him he was still alive, yet that didn't seem to be what she wanted.

She looked back inside. "I...He's young and impressionable and I don't want...I have to be careful not to...I don't won't people walking in and out of his life."

She didn't trust him with her son. Damn that stung. He nodded. "Later." He walked away, his chest aching.

"You look drunk," Dallas told him as he and Tyler walked inside. When Austin called, they were still at the office coming to terms about DeLuna. Or maybe celebrating. But Austin couldn't celebrate. It felt wrong.

"If I wasn't drunk, I'd have driven myself."

Tyler gave him a hard look. "You sure about this?"

"Positive. Let's go. It's gonna be midnight before we get there." Not that it mattered. Their wives wouldn't be back until the next day.

Dallas cocked a brow. "This can't wait until morning?"

"Damn, I thought of all people, you two would understand. Besides, you two owe me."

"We owe you?" Dallas asked.

"Yeah, your wife got me in the eyes with pepper spray and yours..." He looked at Tyler. "Zoe brought that damn ugly cat into my life and made me look like a scared little boy."

"What do our wives have to do with this?" Dallas asked.

"I love Leah like you two love them."

Tyler laughed. "Never thought I'd see the day you turned into a wuss for a girl."

Dallas elbowed Tyler. "You and I are wusses."

Austin frowned. "If loving her makes me a wuss, then call me a wuss. I'll get it tattooed on my ass, too."

Dallas and Tyler chatted all the way to Heartbroke. Austin sat in the back, his eyes closed, but awake. What the hell was he going to say to Leah? How was he going to convince her that they belonged together?

Every time he'd start working on his speech, he'd hear something Candy Adams had said. Why did she somehow seem connected with the whole Leah issue? Then he understood. She was the reason he'd worked so hard not to let Leah close. His mind turned to the photographs Candy had left. He hadn't looked at them. He wouldn't.

Or would he?

Shit! He was confused about Candy, but he wasn't confused about Leah anymore. He knew what he needed to tell her: I love you.

Roberto made it all the way down the steps before he realized how stupid he was for feeling this way. The fact that she cared about her son was one of the reasons he'd fallen for her.

He turned around and started back up the stairs. He had to tell her he respected her. He had to tell her he'd wait until this weekend. Hell, he'd wait as long as it took.

His phone rang as he stopped at her door. He looked at the number and flipped open the phone.

"Please come back," she said before he could answer.

"I'm already back. I have to see you, just for a few minutes."

She swung open the door, tears in her eyes. "I'm just scared—"

"It's okay," he said, and smiled. "I respect you for putting him first. I lost my son, so I know how precious they are. And I'd never do anything to hurt you or him. And I still want the chance to prove that to you."

She stepped out. He reached for her. She came up on her tiptoes and kissed him. He wrapped his arms around her, needing her touch. When it ended, she took his hand and started in.

He stopped. "I don't have to come inside."

"It's—"

"No, let's do this the way you wanted it. Slow. I respect that."

She blinked. "Is it over?"

He knew what she was asking. Was DeLuna dead? He nodded.

"I'm glad," she said.

"I'm glad it's behind me, but oddly enough that's not what's fixed me," he said. "You did that."

He leaned in one more time and kissed her. "I'll see you next weekend."

Almost midnight that evening, Leah lay in bed. Her head hurt from crying. Her heart hurt from missing Austin. She wasn't a kitten's whisker away from falling in love with him. It had already brushed up against her heart.

Why hadn't she told him the truth? Told him she didn't

want to be his weekend bootie call? Why had she walked away without trying harder?

Several answers whispered back at her. Pride. Being in love was one thing; admitting to it when the other person wasn't feeling it was another stupid thing altogether.

But wasn't denying it even more stupid? Then there was the fear. Fear that saying it aloud would make it hurt worse. But it couldn't hurt worse than now, could it?

Sitting up, she reached for her phone. What was she going to say to him?

If he cared about her, wouldn't he have called? She hesitated, her finger hovering over his number.

Austin sent Dallas and Tyler packing. He stood in front of her door, his hand poised to knock, but fear held him back. What if she slammed the door in his face? What if she didn't even answer? What if she told him she never wanted to see him again?

But what if she didn't?

He had to do this.

His phone rang. He didn't want to talk to anyone. He went to cut it off and saw the number. His heart lurched.

"Hello?"

"Were you asleep?" Leah sounded nervous.

"No. Wide awake."

Silence filled the line.

"Leah—"

"Austin—" They blurted out at the same time.

"You go first," he said.

She hesitated. "We need to talk."

"Wouldn't you rather do that in person?" he asked.

"I don't think it can wait." She sounded disappointed.

"How long does it take to get to your door?"

"You're at my door?" she asked. Was that a smile in her voice?

"Yup."

He heard her scrambling out of bed. The bolts clicked and the door swung open.

She ran at him. He picked her up. She wrapped her legs around his waist. They kissed. Kissed like they hadn't seen each other in weeks. Kissed like she hadn't told him she didn't want him.

As quickly as it began, she stopped kissing him. "I won't be your weekend bootie call."

"What?" Hands on her bottom, he held her close.

"I won't be your mistress."

"My mistress?"

"Yeah, I loved my mom, but I refuse to make the same mistakes she did."

His heart wrapped around what she said. "That's what you thought I wanted?"

She put her hand over his mouth. "Just listen. I'll be your girlfriend, but I won't be excluded from the drudgery parts of life. I want it all. The getting mad because you're late from work, the day-to-day headaches. The arguing over who gets the remote and whether or not we use butter or margarine. I want to cook grilled cheeses with you."

"Leah—"

She pressed her fingers tighter over his mouth. "I'm still talking."

He bit her.

She frowned; he laughed.

"It's my turn to talk. I love you."

Her eyes widened. "You do?"

"It scares the hell out of me, but I do. And you know that saying that if you love something, you let it go? Well, that's a bunch of bullshit. I'm not letting you go. So how about building a house with me—on my property? How about being a part of the drudgery of my life?"

Her grin crinkled her eyes and her dimple winked at him. "I'd love to build a house with you. I love drudgery. And... I love you, too."

He went back in for another kiss and stopped. "One thing, I'm ambivalent about sharing you with your boyfriend."

"My what? I don't have—"

"Your purple, battery-operated friend."

She thumped him in the chest with her palm, and then they both laughed. And Austin had a feeling that with Leah in his life he was going to be doing a lot of that. Real, Austin thought. He'd found the real thing.

EPILOGUE

Five months later

"HOLD HIM A second!"

Leah turned around as LeAnn, Dallas's sister-in-law, dropped five-month-old Denver into Austin's arms.

"Wait," Austin called out, but too late. LeAnn had already rushed inside the cabin to grab some more barbeque sauce for her husband, Tony, who was busy manning the grill. "Shit," Austin muttered, and, walking as if he might drop the baby, he came inching toward her.

"Take this," Austin said, sounding as if he was in pain. "I don't know how to hold it."

"He," Leah said. "He's not an it. And you're doing good."

"What if I break it."

"He," she repeated. "And you're not going to break him. Besides, you said you wanted one someday, so you could probably use the practice."

"I'll practice on mine. If I break it, no one can get mad at me."

Leah rolled her eyes. "I'd be mad at you. And hey . . .

look, he's smiling at you. He likes you." She brushed a hand over the boy's rosy cheeks.

Austin glanced at the baby. The baby chuckled. Austin's pained expression softened. "He does like me, doesn't he?" It was the same look he got when he discovered her cats didn't actually hate him.

Leah leaned into him. "Yeah, you're just so irresistible."

"True," Austin said, and grinned.

Leah watched as the man she loved pulled the baby a little closer to his chest. He studied the infant and then he inched closer to her. "He's kind of funny looking, isn't he?"

Leah elbowed him in the ribs. "No, he's beautiful."

"I'll bet ours will be better looking," he whispered. They had officially gotten engaged a month ago, and Leah had brought up the idea of having kids. While Austin had admitted to being nervous, he hadn't shied away from the idea. As a matter of fact, he'd even brought up the subject several times.

The smell of grilling hamburgers flavored the air. Spring had sprung, and the sound of birds added to the chorus of laughter from the partygoers. Leah loved being surrounded by the people who had become her second family. All the friends and family of the Only in Texas gang. Another car drove up, Roberto and Sara.

"Thanks," LeAnn said, and grabbed her baby from Austin's arms.

"Anytime," Austin said. "He likes me."

"Yeah," Roberto said, walking up. "He's not old enough to have acquired taste yet."

"Bullshit." Austin grinned and then motioned to the cardboard tube in Roberto's hand. "Is that what I think it is?"

Roberto had agreed to design their house.

"Yeah, this is just a rough draft."

"Pee pee. Pee pee." Brian, Sara's son, chanted, and started tugging on Roberto's jeans.

"Pee pee?" Roberto belted out. "Yes!" He swung the kid up in his arms.

"Can I see the plans?" Austin asked as Roberto started off.

"No, I want to show it to you," Roberto said. He darted off toward the cabin but turned back and spoke over his shoulder. "We're potty training him and this is the first time he's asked to go." He looked back at Brian. "That's a big boy."

Leah smiled at the devotion Roberto was showing in Brian's life. Austin wrapped his arm around Leah. "Where's Luis?"

"Helping Tony at the grill. Trying to prove his manliness."

Austin grinned. "Yeah, well, when you can really cook, you don't have to prove anything on the grill anymore."

"You're that confident in your maleness, are you?" Leah teased.

"I didn't hear you complain this morning?" He wiggled his brows.

"Where did Roberto and Brian go?" Sara walked with Nikki at her side. Nikki, whose baby bulge was really beginning to show, and early. There was already talk that it might be twins. The doctor was going to do a sonogram next week.

"Brian told him he had to go pee," Austin said.

"Really?" Sara squealed, and took off to the cabin to join her two men.

Austin shook his head. "The pissing thing must be a big deal."

They laughed. Ellen walked over. "Did you want me to make some more iced tea?" she asked.

"Yeah, let me help you. I think it's time we got out the

potato salad, too." Leah gave Austin a quick kiss and then she, Nikki, and Ellen walked inside.

"Where's the kids?" Leah asked as they walked into the cabin.

Ellen rolled her eyes. "In the back, watching Tony and Tyler trying to obliterate each other at badminton. Tony said he brought the game for the kids. I swear, men are nothing but big boys." She grinned.

"Yeah, but I still love 'em," Nikki said.

"Love what?" Zoe asked, walking in.

"Men," Nikki said.

"Well, being that you're knocked up, I'd say that's pretty evident," Zoe said.

"So call me a slut," Nikki said.

They all laughed.

LeAnn walked in. "What's so funny?"

"Just Nikki admitting to being a slut," Leah said in a low voice as the bathroom door opened and Sara and Roberto followed Brian out, praising him for being such a big boy.

Roberto, noting the number of women in the room, took Brian's hand. "Come on, big guy," Roberto said, "this is a chick fest. Let's go hang out with the men and tell everyone you peed in the potty."

Grinning, Sara watched her two men walk out.

"He was a good catch," Leah said.

"Yup," Sara answered. "A keeper."

"Hey." Zoe lowered her voice. "Did Austin agree to see his mother?"

Leah looked to make sure no one was at the door. "Yeah. We're having dinner with her next week. I don't know what will happen, but the fact that he agreed to see her is a good sign."

They stepped outside, carrying bowls of potato salad and chips in their hands.

Two more cars pulled up, Brad Hulk and his family and Evelyn and her bunch. As everyone ate, played badminton, and passed the day enjoying the spring weather, Leah realized how large her circle of friends and family had gotten.

"What are you thinking about?" Austin asked, stepping up.

"About how lucky I am that less than six months ago you blew a horn and made me drop all my groceries, bugged my place, and ended up kidnapping me."

He smiled. "And you took one look at me and decided you wanted my body."

"You just keep on believing that," she said, and slipped her hand in his.

"Oh, I will," he said. "And I'll remind you of it at our fiftieth anniversary."

"Is that a promise?" she asked.

"You're damn straight it is."

Austin's Thick-Crust Pizza Recipe

Pizza Dough

1 cup lukewarm water (105–110 degrees F)
1 envelope yeast (fast-rising if possible)
2 tablespoons sugar (3 or 4 tablespoons if sweeter dough is preferred)
1 tablespoon olive oil
¾ teaspoon salt
2 to 2½ cups flour

1. Stir warm water, yeast, and ½ teaspoon of the sugar together, cover with plastic wrap, and let stand 5 to 6 minutes until yeast is dissolved.
2. Add the oil, remaining sugar, and salt to above mixture.
3. Slowly add flour until stiff.
4. Knead dough 5 minutes, then cover with cloth.
5. Let rise in a warm place 1 to 1½ hours until it doubles in size.
6. Poke down and use or refrigerate (dough can be frozen).

Pizza

½ cup pizza sauce (more or less, depending on taste)

Pizza toppings: fresh veggies and meat should be lightly sautéed before garnishing pizza

Nonstick spray or 1 teaspoon olive oil

1½ to 2 cups shredded pizza cheese blend or mozzarella cheese

1. Preheat the oven to 475–500 degrees F.
2. Put pizza dough in a slightly greased 9 x 11 glass or metal casserole pan or a round deep-dish pan of equivalent size.
3. Spread pizza sauce on dough.
4. Spread ½ cup cheese on pizza crust (bottom cheese will help keep toppings from falling off).
5. Garnish pizza with desired toppings.
6. Add remaining cheese on top.
7. Cook for 9 to 12 minutes on lower rack of oven. Remove pizza when bottom crust is brown and dough is fully cooked.

Enjoy!

Nikki Hunt is accused of killing her no-good, cheating ex-husband.
But hunky PI Dallas O'Connor thinks she's innocent—and hopes a little "undercover" work will help him prove it…

Please turn this page for an excerpt from

ONLY IN TEXAS.

CHAPTER ONE

"It's the right thing. It's the right thing."

At five o'clock on the dot, Nikki Hunt drove past the valet parking entrance to Venny's Restaurant and turned into the one-car alley lined with garbage Dumpsters. She eased her car over potholes big enough to lose a tire in, and parked her Honda Accord. "It's the right thing," she repeated then rested her forehead against the steering wheel. After one or two seconds, she squared her shoulders and mentally pulled up her big-girl panties. Letting go of a deep breath, she stared at the Dumpster adjacent to her car and hoped this wasn't a foreshadowing of the evening.

Though no one would guess it—other than that one bill collector, her bank, and the McDonald's attendant who'd waited for her to dig out enough change to pay for her sausage biscuit this morning—Nikki couldn't afford valet parking.

Her local gallery barely made enough money to cover the rent. Who knew that a little downturn in the economy would prevent the general population from appreciating art?

Okay, fine, she knew. She was financially strapped, not stupid. And yeah, she'd also known that opening the gallery had been risky. But at the time, she'd had Jack to fall back on if things got tough. Good ol' Jack, charming, financially stable, and dependable—dependable, that is, as long as one didn't depend on him to keep his pecker in his pants.

She pulled a tube of lipstick from her purse, turned the rearview mirror her way, and added a hint of pink to her lips.

Please, Nikki, meet me at Venny's. I made some mistakes, but we can fix it.

Jack's words skipped through her head.

Was Jack really going to ask her for a do-over? Was she really contemplating saying yes? And was saying yes the right thing? The questions bounced around her brain, hitting hard against her conscience.

Rubbing her lips together to smooth the pink sheen on her mouth, she looked at the back of the restaurant—probably the most expensive restaurant in Miller, Texas. The one where Jack, the man she considered the love of her life, had proposed to her four years ago. This wasn't the first time she'd heard from Jack since the divorce. The flowers he'd sent had gone to her grandmother's retirement center. Someone should enjoy them. The messages where he begged her to take him back went unanswered. She hadn't even been tempted. Until today.

Today he'd called the gallery right after Nikki had received a call from the retirement home, reminding her that her grandmother's cable bill was due. Right after she realized she was going to be short paying Ellen, her one and only part-time employee. There'd been desperation in Jack's voice and it had mimicked the desperation Nikki felt in her own life.

She focused on the rearview mirror again and gave herself a good, hard look. She fluffed her hair, hoping her thick, blond curls would appear stylish and not impoverished.

Nana's cable trumped her regular clip job. Her grandmother had spent thirteen years taking care of Nikki, so the least she could do was allow the woman to watch the cooking network.

And Ellen—how could she not pay the woman who'd become her best friend? The woman who singlehandedly dragged Nikki out of the done-wrong slumps kicking and screaming.

Nikki stepped out of her car. The heat radiating from the pavement assaulted her. She could almost feel her hair frizz. Humidity thickened the air, making it hard to breathe. Or maybe that was just the anxiety of seeing Jack, of making a decision to reenter the holy union—a union that turned out not to be so holy for him.

Passing the Dumpster, she wrinkled her nose and walked faster. The ring of her cell brought her to a stop. She grabbed the phone from her purse, and checked the number.

"Hello, Nana?"

"You're my one call," Nana said.

"Shoot." Nikki hurried her steps to escape the garbage smell. Common sense told her Nana was playing the timed crossword game with her Ol' Timers Club. A game that allowed the participant a single one-minute call to someone who might be able to help. But the first time Nana had used her one-call line, she'd been in jail. Sure, Nana had only been arrested once, but bailing your grandmother out of the slammer was not something one tended to forget.

"Name of the club you join when you get it on at high altitudes, twelve letters," Nana said.

"What kind of crossword puzzle is this?" Nikki asked.

"Smokin' hot."

Figures. The Ol' Timers Club members, on average, had a better sex life than Nikki did. "Mile High Club. Not that I belong." She cut the corner to the restaurant, welcoming the warm scents of Venny's menu items.

"You should," Nana said.

"Gotta go," Nikki said before Nana started ranting about Nikki's less-than-exciting social life.

"You're coming to the dress rehearsal tonight?" Nana asked.

What dress rehearsal? Then Nikki remembered. Her grandmother and several of the Ol' Timers had gotten parts in a small neighborhood theater show.

"I can't, but I'll come to the show." If she could afford the ticket.

"Where are you?"

"About to walk into a restaurant."

"A date?" Nana sounded hopeful.

"No." *Just possibly coming to get proposed to for the second time by the man I used to love.*

Used to? Nikki stopped so fast she almost tripped. Didn't she still love Jack? Weren't there still feelings underneath the pain of his infidelity? Because if she didn't really have feeling for him then...

"Who are you meeting?" Nana asked.

It's the right thing. "No one," she lied, flinching.

In the background, Nikki could hear Nana's friend Benny call out, "Five seconds."

"Gotta go," Nikki repeated.

"Nikki Althea Hunt, do not tell me you're meeting that lowlife scum of an ex—"

"Love ya." Nikki hung up, dropped her cell back into her purse, and tried to ignore the doubt concerning what she was about to do. Instead, she wondered what the hell her mother had been smoking when she named her Althea. Then again, figuring out what her mother was smoking when she'd dropped six-year-old Nikki at Nana's with the request that Nana raise her was a much better puzzle. And not one Nikki liked to think about, either.

Walking into the restaurant, pretending she belonged in the rich, famous, and lawyer circle, Nikki was embraced by the scents of beef burgundy. Her stomach gave one last groan, then died and went to heaven without looking back. The biscuit she'd scraped change together for this morning was a forgotten memory.

"Meeting someone?" the hostess asked as Nikki peeked into the dining room.

"Jack Leon." Nikki spotted him sitting at the table—the same table where he'd proposed to her—talking on his cell phone.

"This way." The hostess started walking but Nikki caught her arm and yanked her back. The woman's eyes rounded.

"Just a second, please." Nikki continued to stare at Jack and waited. Where was it? Where was the heart flutter when her gaze landed on him? A light flutter would do. That's all she was asking for.

No flutters, damn it. The only emotion bumping around her chest was residual fury at finding him in her gallery office, on the sofa, banging her hired help.

Not a good memory to be hanging in her mental closet tonight. Not if Jack was going to propose. Because if she said yes, then she might be the one banging her ex.

"Crappers," she muttered, and her heart did a cartwheel, hitting the sides of her ribs. Nikki had no problem with sex. Not that she'd had any pleasure in a *long* time. A really long time. Like...since Jack.

The truth rained down on her. She wasn't here because she loved Jack. If she went back to him it wouldn't even be for pleasure. It would be for money. Sure, the money was to pay Nana's cable, to pay Ellen, and to keep her gallery afloat, but still...the hard fact was she'd be having sex for money.

"Oh shit!" Could she stoop that low?

My name is Nikki Hunt, not Nikki Name Your Price.

"I don't think I can do this," she muttered and tightened her hold on the hostess's arm.

"You don't think you can do what?" asked the hostess.

"Oh hell. It's not the right thing."

"What's not the right thing?"

Nikki stared at her feet. "How important are the cooking shows anyway?"

"Which one?" asked the hostess, still mistaking Nikki's muttering for conversation. "I like Rachael Ray."

Releasing the hostess's arm, Nikki turned to go, but stopped short when a waiter carting a tray of yeast-scented bread and real butter moved past. He left a wake of warm tantalizing aroma.

Crapola. She wouldn't have sex with Jack. She wouldn't remarry him, but could she sit through a dinner for some mouthwatering food? Yup, she could stoop that low.

Call it payment for defiling the much-loved antique sofa in her office. No way could she have kept it after seeing him and her employee going at it doggy-style on the piece of furniture.

Mind made up, Nikki swung around and, without waiting for the hostess, shot across the dining room and plopped down at Jack's table.

Still on the phone, Jack looked up. His eyes widened with what appeared to be relief, and he nodded. Dropping her purse at her feet and not waiting for a bread plate, she snagged a hot roll and smeared a generous amount of sweet butter on it. Her mouth watered as the butter oozed over the bread.

"No," Jack snapped into the phone and held up an apologetic finger to her.

She nodded, smiled, and took a bite of the roll. Her stomach growled as if it were saying bread alone wouldn't silence or satisfy it. She noticed a bowl of gumbo sitting in front of Jack. She'd kill for gumbo. Too bad Jack had a thing about sharing food.

"Fuck, no!" Jack seethed. "I can't do this."

The F word brought Nikki's gaze up from his gumbo. Jack, a refined lawyer trying to make partner and always concerned about public decorum, seldom cursed. Amazingly, from his viewpoint, screwing your wife's part-time help wasn't considered bad manners.

"Listen to me," Jack muttered.

Nikki recalled Jack taking offense at her occasional slip of "shit," "damn," and "hell"—a habit she'd obtained from hanging out with Nana and the Ol' Timers. Jack had almost broken her of it, too. Then, staring at his Armani suit and his hundred-dollar haircut, Nikki had an epiphany.

Jack had spent the entire two years of their marriage, not to mention the year they'd dated, trying to turn her into someone else—someone who would look good on the arm of a partner of the Brian and Sterns Law Firm. *Don't say this. Say that. Wear this. Do you have to spend so much time with your grandmother?*

Glancing down at her black pants and knit top, she knew he wouldn't approve of her wardrobe. How odd that she hadn't even considered dressing up for the event. Or maybe not odd. It should have been a clue that their reconciling was a joke. Seriously, she hadn't even put on sexy underwear. Her gaze shot back to his gumbo.

Screw Jack's apparel approval and his no-share policy. She reached for the bowl and, suddenly feeling lowbrow and proud of it, dunked her roll in the roux and brought the soupy mess to her lips.

Heaven.

Spotting a floating shrimp in the cup, and not lowbrow enough to use her fingers, she went for Jack's spoon.

He slapped his hand on top of hers and frowned—a disapproving, judgmental frown that pulled at his brown eyes.

Big mistake on his part.

Slipping her hand from under his, she fished out the shrimp with two fingers and ate it. Even made a show of licking her fingers. Jack's mouth fell open at her lack of manners. Not that she cared. Considering the way things were going, the gumbo and rolls were all she'd be having for dinner. She might as well enjoy them.

A tuxedo-wearing waiter ran up and placed a spoon in front of her. Nikki smiled at his pinched, disapproving look, which matched her husband's frown.

"Thank you," she said, proving she wasn't totally lacking in the manners department.

"Something to drink?" the waiter asked, his expression still critical of her lack of etiquette.

"A Budweiser, please." She didn't like beer, but it fit her mood. And just like that, she knew why. All this time—even after she'd caught Jack bare-ass naked with her employee, even after she realized how badly he'd screwed her with that prenuptial agreement—she'd never given Jack a bit of comeuppance. And why? Because she'd been more hurt than angry. Now, realizing she'd stopped loving him, the hurt had evaporated and she was just angry. And it wasn't altogether a bad feeling, either.

Jack stood up. Frowning, he pressed his phone to his shoulder. "Order for us," he said. "I'll be right back." He snatched up his gumbo and handed it to the waiter. "And she'll take a glass of Cabernet." He took off.

Nikki tightened her hands on the edge of the table and considered walking out, but another waiter walked by with a plate of chicken marsala. She inhaled and eyed the waiter clutching Jack's gumbo as if afraid she might fight him for it. And she might have, but suddenly she got an odd after-taste from the gumbo. "Bring us one beef burgundy and one chicken marsala. *And my beer.*"

After one disapproving eye roll, the waiter walked away.

She'd already sipped from the frosty mug and devoured another roll when Jack returned. He sat across from her and frowned. She snatched another bite of bread, pretty certain her free meal had just come to an end.

His frown faded. "You have no idea how glad I am that you came."

Nikki nearly choked on her bread. What? No condescending remark about her lack of manners? Jack was playing nice. Jack never played nice unless he *really* wanted something.

Did he want her back that badly? It wouldn't change anything, but whose ego couldn't use stroking?

He picked up his linen napkin and dabbed at his forehead where she'd just noticed he was sweating. Sweating was right up there with playing nice. Jack didn't sweat.

Her pinching gut said something was up and it had to do with more than just her. She leaned in. "What's going on, Jack?"

Dallas O'Connor walked into the building that housed both his business and apartment. Stopping just inside the doorway, he waited. Five seconds. Ten. When Bud didn't greet him, Dallas looked over at the coffin against the nearby wall. Someone had opened the dang thing again.

He growled low in his throat, "Get out of there."

One soulful second later, Bud—short for "Budweiser"—raised his head from inside the coffin and rested his hanging jowls on the edge of the polished wooden box. The pain of being chastised flashed in his huge bug eyes. Bud, an English bulldog, hated being chastised.

"Out," Dallas said, lowering his voice. "It's not a doggy bed."

The prior owners of the building, which had been a funeral home, had left the damn casket when they moved out six months ago. Dallas had called and left numerous messages asking them to remove the dang thing, but no response. The last time he'd told them they had one more week, and he was going to sell it on eBay. He was tired of having to explain the casket to his clients.

The dog leaped out of the coffin and barreled over to Dallas. After one swipe over the dog's side, Dallas glanced at his watch and shot back to the office. He found Tyler, one of his Only in Texas Private Investigations partners, listening to the police scanner as he watched the television. Tyler's expression had worry stamped all over it, too.

"He hasn't called yet?" Dallas removed his gun from his holster and placed it in his desk—a habit he hadn't broken from the seven years he'd worked for the Glencoe Police Department. Seven years he wished he could get back. The only good thing that had come from those years was the friendship of his PI partners, Tyler and Austin.

Tyler glanced away from the television. "Not a word. Any luck at the park?"

"There were two female joggers, but neither of them fit the description Nance gave."

Frowning, Tyler leaned back in his chair. "I'm afraid we're not going to get anything to save this kid. He's going to go down for robbery."

"It's not over." No way would Dallas let that innocent boy do time. But right now, both he and Tyler should be worried about one of their own. Dallas motioned to the police scanner. "Have the cops been called out yet?"

Tyler nodded and concern pinched his brows, making the two-inch scar over his right eye stretch tighter. "Thirty minutes ago."

"Shit," Dallas said. "Why the hell hasn't he called?"

"You know Austin," Tyler said. "He's a lone wolf."

"That's not how we operate," Dallas said, but in his gut he knew they were all lone wolves. Life had taught them that was the only way to live. Getting set up by a lowlife drug dealer named DeLuna and then having almost everyone you believed in turn their backs on you—not to mention spending sixteen months in the slammer—well, it did that to you. It made you feel as if the only one you could trust was yourself.

Dallas glanced at the silent television. "Any media coverage?"

"Not yet," Tyler said. "But the cops called for another unit to help hold them back, so they're there."

"Have you tried to reach him?" Dallas dialed Austin's number.

"He's not answering." Tyler grabbed the remote and ramped up the volume. "We got something."

Dallas glanced at the redheaded reporter on the screen, but listened to his cell until the call went to Austin's voice mail and he hung up. The camera closed in on the reporter as she announced a breaking news segment.

"God, she's hot," Tyler said.

Dallas studied the redhead as she held a microphone close to her lips. "You need to get laid."

"Okay," Tyler said. "You want to give my number to that hot brunette I saw leaving here last week? Or tell your ex to pay me a visit. She could leave her underwear at my place, too."

"Funny," Dallas said, and regretted telling the guys about his screwup with his ex. Then again, he hadn't told them. His dog had. Bud had come traipsing into the office the next morning with a pair of red panties hanging from his jowls. Thankfully, Suzan—aka, the hot brunette—was careful to take her underwear with her when she left his bed. And she didn't expect—or want—more than he was willing to give. The perfect relationship—pure sex. Twice a month, when her ex got her kids for the weekend, she showed up at his place. Most nights, she didn't even stay over. Sex and the bed to himself—what more could a guy ask?

The news reporter started talking. "We're here at the home of Blake Mallard, CEO of Acorn Oil Company. An anonymous caller said Mallard's dirty shenanigans, both with the company and his personal life, were about to be made public." The reporter paused.

"He had to have gotten out." Tyler traced his finger over the scar at his temple. He'd earned it during their stint in prison. While Tyler never talked about the fight, Dallas knew the guy who'd given Tyler the mark hadn't walked away unscathed. Rumor in the pen had it the guy hadn't walked away at all, but had to be carried out on a stretcher. Jail time was never a walk in the park, but Dallas suspected Tyler had had a harder time behind bars than both he and Austin.

The reporter started talking again, and a smile threatened to spill from her lips. "According to sources, Mallard was found handcuffed to his bed with a call girl. The missing files Mallard swore were stolen from his office were found in the room. We're told the cops were called to the residence by Mallard's wife, who was worried someone had broken in."

After a few beats of silence, the reporter continued.

"We're told the girl found with Mallard is claiming a guy dressed in a clown costume handcuffed them to the bed and pulled the files from Mallard's private safe."

"Did y'all try to call me?" Austin's voice came from the doorway.

Dallas glanced up. "You..." Words failed him.

"I love it," Tyler said and laughed.

"You mean this?" Austin motioned at his bright red-and-blue polka-dotted clown suit and multicolored wig. Whipping off the wig, he tossed it up and caught it.

Dallas shook his head. "You love theatrics, don't you?"

"Theatrics? Are you kidding? This was brilliance. It's a gated community. I had to get past security. A birthday party was happening next door to the Mallards. They wouldn't let in a guy wearing a ski mask, but a clown? Not a problem." Austin looked at the TV. "Did I make the news?"

"Oh, yeah," Tyler said.

Austin tossed his wig on his desk. "It's not every day we get to solve a cheating-spouse case and a real crime at the same time. It felt good. And now we can put this case to bed and I can focus on proving Nance is innocent."

Dallas raked his hand through his hair. "I'll bet a hundred bucks my brother will be calling me within five minutes, wanting to know if we're behind this."

Austin dropped his clown-suited ass into a chair. "Tell him Miller PD owes me a beer for solving their case."

The reporter appeared on the screen again. Austin looked at the television. "She's hot."

"That's what I said." Tyler grinned.

Austin looked back at Dallas. "Did you get anything at the park?"

"Nothing," Dallas said.

"I'm going to try a few different parks around here,"

Austin said. "Maybe the chick swaps off and jogs at different places."

"Maybe," Dallas said.

"Did you hear from Roberto?" Austin asked Tyler.

"Yeah," Tyler answered. "None of his leads point to DeLuna."

"Then tell him to get some new leads," Austin said, his frustration clearly showing at having so much time pass since they'd had anything on DeLuna.

Dallas's cell phone rang. He checked the number. "See," he told Austin. "It's my brother."

"I thought pissing off the guys in blue was our goal." Austin crossed his arms.

"You're wrong." Dallas stared at the phone. "Pissing off the lowlife drug runner DeLuna is our goal. Pissing off the guys in blue..." He looked up with a grin. "Well, that's just an added benefit. My brother being the exception, of course."

As his partners chuckled, Dallas answered the call. "What's up, Tony?"

"Damn, Dallas, tell me that wasn't you," Tony demanded.

"What wasn't me?" Dallas shot Austin an I-told-you-so frown.

"Why do I think you're lying?" Tony came back.

"Because you're a suspicious son of a bitch."

Tony sighed. "Can you meet me for a burger at Buck's Place in half an hour?"

"Why?"

"To eat," Tony said.

Dallas wasn't buying it. Not that he and his brother didn't do dinner. They had weekly dinners with their dad. But something told Dallas that Tony wanted more than a burger and fries. To confirm it, Dallas asked, "You paying?"

"Sure," Tony said.

Yup, Tony wanted something. His brother never agreed to pay.

Nikki watched Jack rearrange his silverware in an attempt to avoid her question. "What's going on, Jack?" she asked again.

He shook his head. "Just trouble at work."

"What kind of trouble?"

He shifted his arm, knocking the linen napkin off the table. Scooting back in his chair, he reached to collect the cloth. Falling into old habits, she signaled for the waiter to bring a clean napkin.

"It's okay," Jack said, sitting up.

That's when she knew something had to be seriously wrong. Jack, a germ freak, would never use a dropped napkin.

"Look, the reason I asked you here is...I need a wife on my arm."

"A wife?" Had she heard him right? He didn't need *her*. He needed a wife. Anyone would do. As long as they were trainable and, damn it, she'd proven she was. Only not anymore.

"I realize I slipped up."

"Really, you think screwing my part-time help was a slipup?"

He frowned but before he could answer, his phone buzzed again. He looked at the caller ID. "I have to take this." He put a hand on his stomach and swayed when he stood up. Even though she was furious, she almost suggested he sit down, but then he grabbed her beer and set it down on a table that a busboy was cleaning.

Damn him! She popped up, tossed her napkin on the table, and went to rescue her beer. Eying the busboy, she grinned. "I think I lost this." Then she plopped back down in her seat. She wasn't Jack's to train anymore and when he returned she would, for the first time, tell him exactly what she thought of him. After she enjoyed her dinner, of course.

Five minutes later, dinner arrived but Jack still hadn't. Considering manners were optional tonight, she started without him. She even enjoyed some of Jack's beef burgundy. She'd been so involved in savoring the food, she hadn't realized so much time had passed.

"Is he coming back?" the waiter asked.

"Of course he is." Panic clenched her stomach and she nearly choked on the steak. "He has to."

She waited another twenty minutes, even had the busboy check the bathroom, before she accepted the inevitable. Jack wasn't coming back. The waiter returned with the check and eyed her suspiciously as if to say any woman who would stick her finger in her date's soup was thoroughly capable of the eat-and-run offense.

Glancing at the check, she muttered, "I'm going to kill him!"

"Kill who?" the waiter asked.

"Who do you think?" She peeked at the bill and moaned. A hundred and eighty without tip, then there was the fee the bank would charge her for overdrawing her checking account.

Her stomach roiled again, this time in a bad way. Snatching up her purse, she found her debit card. Thankfully, she had overdraft insurance. With anger making her shake, she handed the card to the waiter. Her stomach cramped. She considered complaining that something she'd eaten had upset her stomach, but she knew how that would look.

"Yup, he's as good as dead!"

*   *   *

"I'm killing him," Nikki muttered fifteen minutes later as she pulled out her already overdrawn debit card again.

The grocery store cashier scanned the Pepto-Bismol, Tums, Rolaids, and antidiarrheal meds before looking at Nikki. "Kill who?"

Why did people think just because she was talking, she was speaking to them? Was she the only one who talked to herself? Nevertheless, with the cashier's curious stare, Nikki felt obligated to answer. "My ex." She placed a palm on her stomach as it roiled.

Holding her purchases in a plastic bag, Nikki couldn't escape quickly enough. She darted out the door. The ball of orange sun hung low in the predusk sky. Her eyes stung. She almost got to the car when the smell of grilled burgers from the hamburger joint next door washed over her and the full wave of nausea hit. A woman with two kids dancing around her came right at Nikki. Not wanting to upchuck on an innocent child, she swung around in the opposite direction, opened her bag, and heaved as quietly as she could inside it.

Realizing she'd just puked on her medicine, she lost her backbone, and tears filled her eyes. *Only the weak cry.* The words filled her head, but damn it, right now she was weak.

She rushed to her car, wanting only to get home. Tying a knot in the bag, she grabbed her keys, hit the clicker to unlock the doors, and then popped open the trunk.

Tears rolled down her cheeks. Her stomach cramped so hard her breath caught.

She got to her bumper, was just about to drop the contaminated bag into the trunk when she saw...She blinked the tears from her eyes as if that alone would make the image go away.

It didn't.

There, stuffed in the back of her car, was a body.

She recognized the Armani suit first. Then she saw his face. His eyes were wide open, but something was missing.

Life.

Jack was dead.

Jack was dead in the trunk of her car.

Her vision started to swirl.

She tried to scream. Nausea hit harder. Unable to stop herself, she lost the rest of her two-hundred-dollar meal all over her dead ex-husband's three-thousand-dollar suit.

THE DISH

Where Authors Give You the Inside Scoop

♥ ♥ ♥ ♥ ♥ ♥ ♥ ♥ ♥ ♥ ♥ ♥ ♥ ♥ ♥ ♥

From the desk of Jaime Rush

Dear Reader,

Enemies to lovers is a concept I've always loved. Yes, it's a challenge, and maybe that's what I like most. It's a given that the couple is going to have instant chemistry—it is a romance, after all! But they're going to fight it harder because they have history and a good reason. Each person believes they're in the right.

That's how Kade Kavanaugh feels. Being a member of the Guard, my supernatural world's police force, he has had plenty of run-ins with Violet Castanega's family. They live in the Fringe, a wild and uncivilized community of Dragon shifters who think they are on the fringe of the law as well. And mostly they are, except when their illegal activities threaten to catch the attention of the Muds, the Mundane human police. Because Rule Number One is simple: Never reveal the existence of the Hidden community that has existed amid the glitter and glamour of Miami for over three hundred years. Mundanes would panic if they knew that Crescents—humans who hold the essence of Dragons, sorcerers (like Kade), and fallen angels—lived among them.

Violet is fiercely loyal to her Dragon clan, even if it does sometimes flout the law. But when one of her brothers is murdered by a Dragon bent on firing up the clan wars, she has no choice but to go to the Guard for help. There she encounters Kade, whom she attacked the last time he tried to arrest her brother.

My job as a writer is to throw these two unsuspecting people together in ways that will test their loyalties and their integrity. And definitely test their resolve to resist getting involved with not only a member of another class of Crescent, but a sworn enemy to boot. Juicy conflict, hot passion, and supernatural action—a combination that truly tested my hero and heroine. But their biggest lesson is never to judge someone by their name, their heritage, or their actions. I think that's a good lesson for all of us.

We all have magic in our imaginations. Mine has always contained murder, mayhem, and romance. Feel free to wander through the madness of my mind any time. A good place to start is my website www.jaimerush.com, or that of my romantic suspense alter-ego, www.tinawainscott.com.

Jaime Rush

From the desk of Kristen Ashley

Dear Reader,

While writing MOTORCYCLE MAN I was in a very dark time of my life. An *extended* dark time, which is very rare. Indeed, it's only ever happened that once.

In fact, I wrote nearly an entirely different book for my hero, Tack. He had a different heroine. And it had a different plot. Completely. But it didn't work for me and it has never seen the light of day. I abandoned it totally (something I've never done), gave it time, and started anew.

I had thought it was rubbish. Of course, on going back and reading it later, I realize it wasn't. I actually think it's great. It just wasn't Tack. And the heroine was not right for him. But never fear, I like it enough; when I have time (whenever that is in this decade), I intend to rework it and release it, because that hero and heroine's story really should be told.

Nevertheless, when I finally found the dream woman who would belong to Kane "Tack" Allen in MOTOR-CYCLE MAN, I was still questioning my work because things in life weren't going so great.

You see, sometimes I battle my characters. Sometimes they urge me to take risks I feel I'm not ready to take. Sometimes they encourage me to glide along an edge that's a little scary even as it is thrilling. And when life is also scary, your confidence gets shaken in a way it's tough to bounce back from.

But Kane "Tack" Allen is an edgy, risky guy, so he was pretty adamant (as he can be) that he wanted me to just let go and ride it with him. Not only that, but lift up my hands and enjoy the hell out of that ride.

But as I was writing it, I still fought him. Particularly the scene in Tyra's office early on in the book, where they have a misunderstanding and Tack decides to make his feelings perfectly clear and in order to do that, he gets Tyra's attention in a way that's utterly unacceptable.

I fretted about this scene, but Tack refused to let me soften it. I even sent it to my girl, a girl who knows me and my writing inside and out. If I remember correctly, her response was that it was indeed shocking, but I should go with it.

Ride it out.

In releasing MOTORCYCLE MAN, I was very afraid that my life had negatively affected my writing and the risks Tack urged me to take would not be well received.

As you can imagine, I was absolutely *elated* when I found I'd done the right thing. When Tack and Tyra swiftly became one of my most popular couples. That Tack had rightly encouraged me to trust in myself, my instincts, my writing, and give myself to my characters to let them be precisely what they were, let them shine, not water them down, and last, give my readers the honesty. They could take it. Because it was genuine. It came from the soul.

It was real.

And because of all this, MOTORCYCLE MAN will always hold a firm place in my heart. Because that novel and Kane "Tack" Allen gave me the freedom I was searching for. The freedom to ride this wave. Ride it wild. Ride it free.

Lift up my hands and ride it being nothing but me.

Kristen Ashley

♥ ♥ ♥ ♥ ♥ ♥ ♥ ♥ ♥ ♥ ♥ ♥ ♥ ♥ ♥

From the desk of Christie Craig

Dear Reader,

Here are two things about love I took from my own life and used in TEXAS HOLD 'EM:

1. Love can make us stupid.

Sexy PI Austin Brook is a smooth-talking good ol' boy Texan. Where women are concerned, he wings it. Why not? He's got charm to spare. But one glance at Leah Reece and he's a stumbling, bumbling idiot. First he accidentally blows his horn as she's passing in front of his truck, causing her to toss up her arms and drop her groceries. Wanting to help, he snatches up a plastic bag containing a broken bottle of wine and manages to douse Leah with Cabernet from the waist up. And since he likes wine and wet T-shirt contests, it only makes her more appealing and him more nervous.

For myself? On a first date with a good ol' Texan, we were both jittery. I'd dressed up in a short skirt. The guy, thinking he should be a gentleman, pulled my chair out in the crowded restaurant. I had my bottom almost in the seat when he moved it out. *Way out.* *He* might've looked like a gentleman, but there was nothing ladylike about how I went down. All the way to the floor, legs sprawled out, skirt up to my yin-yang. Laughter filled the room. Snickering in spite of his apologetic look, he added, "Nice legs."

Later when he dropped me off at my apartment, I struggled to get the door of his sports car open. Forever the gentlemen—hey, that's Texans for you—he rushed to open my door, and then shut it. Standing close, he heard my moan, and completely misunderstood. He dipped in for a kiss.

I stopped him. "Can you open the car door?"

"Why?" he asked.

I moaned again. "Because my hand's still in the door."

With a bruised butt, and three busted fingernails, I eventually did let him score a kiss. It's amazing I married that man.

2. Love is scary.

Divorced, and a single mother, I wasn't looking for love when I met Mr. Craig. Life had taught me that love can hurt. And I'm not talking about a sore backside or fingernails. I'm talking about the heart.

Neither Austin nor Leah is open to love. Isn't that what makes it so perfect and yet still so dad-blasted frightening? We don't find love; love finds us. And like me, Leah's and Austin's pasts have left them leery.

At age six, Leah realized her daddy had another family, one he obviously loved better because they had his name and he called that home. Oh, when older, she still gave love a shot, got married, expected the happily-ever-after, and instead got a divorce and a credit card bill for all his phone sex. It's not that Leah doesn't believe in love; she just doesn't trust herself to know the real thing.

Austin, abandoned by his mother at age three, passed from one foster home to another, and learned caring about people gave them power to hurt you. His last and final (he swears) heartache happened when his fiancé dumped him after he got convicted of a murder he didn't commit.

As scary as love is, Leah and Austin give it another shot. Not to give away any spoilers, but I think it'll work out fine for them. I know it has for me. I'll soon be celebrating my thirtieth wedding anniversary. So here's to laughter, good books, and getting knocked on your butt by love.

Happy reading!

Christie Craig

♥ ♥ ♥ ♥ ♥ ♥ ♥ ♥ ♥ ♥ ♥ ♥ ♥ ♥ ♥

From the desk of Laura Drake

Dear Reader,

There's just something about the soft side of a hard man that I've never been able to resist—how about you?

Max Jameson looks like a modern-day Marlboro Man. He's a western cattleman, meaning he's stubborn, hard-working, and an eternal optimist. But given his current problems, there's not enough duct tape in all of Colorado to fix them.

To introduce you to the heroine of NOTHING

SWEETER, Aubrey Madison (aka Bree Tanner), I thought I'd share with you her list of life lessons:

1. Nothing is sweeter than freedom.
2. It is impossible to outrun your own conscience.
3. "When you're going through hell, keep going."
   —Winston Churchill
4. There are more kinds of family than blood kin.
5. A stuck-up socialite can make a pretty good friend when the chips are on the table.
6. Real men (and bulls) wear pink.
7. "To forgive is to set a prisoner free, and discover that the prisoner is you." —Louis B. Smede

I hope you'll enjoy NOTHING SWEETER. Keep your eyes open for a cameo of JB and Charla from *The Sweet Spot*, and watch for them all to turn up in *Sweet on You*, the last book in the series!

From the desk of Rebecca Zanetti

Dear Reader,

I met my husband camping when we were about eight years old, and he taught me how to play Red Rover so he could hold my hand. He was a sweet, chubby, brown-eyed boy. We lost touch, and years later, I walked into a bar (yeah, a bar), and there he was. Except this time, he was six-foot-five, muscled, with dark hair, a tattoo, a leather jacket, and held a motorcycle helmet under one hand. To put it simply, I was intrigued. He's still the sweet guy but has a bit of an edge. Now we're married and have two kids, two dogs, and a crazy cat.

People change…and often we don't know them as well as we think we do. In fact, I've always been fascinated by the idea that we never truly know what's in the minds or even the pasts of the people around us. What if your best friend worked for the CIA years ago? Or the mild-mannered janitor at your child's elementary school is a retired Marine sniper who didn't like retirement and has found a good way to fill his life with joy? What if your baby sister was a criminal informant in college?

What if the calm and always-in-control man you married is one of the deadliest men alive?

And what if you're now being threatened by an outside source? What happens to that calm control now? That was the main premise for FORGOTTEN SINS. Josie Dean, a woman with a lonely past, married Shane Dean in a whirlwind of passion and energy. Then he disappeared two years ago. The story starts with him back in her life, with danger surrounding him, and with the edge he'd always partially hidden finally exposed.

Of course, Shane has amnesia, and in his discovery of finding himself, he reveals himself to the one woman he ever truly loved. He'd always held back, always treated her with kid gloves.

Now, not knowing his deadly training, there's no holding back. The primal, arousing man she'd believed existed has to take the forefront as he protects them from the danger stalking him from his past. Yeah, he'd always been fun and sexy…with hints of dominance in the bedroom. Now the hints disappear to unveil the true Shane Dean—the man Josie hoped she'd married.

I hope you truly enjoy Shane and Josie's story.

Best,

Rebecca Zanetti

RebeccaZanetti.com
Twitter, @RebeccaZanetti
Facebook.com/RebeccaZanetti.Author.FanPage

From the desk of Kate Meader

Dear Reader,

FEEL THE HEAT is the first in my smokin' Hot in the Kitchen series, about an Italian restaurant–owning family and the sexy, sizzling chefs who love them. And don't we all want a hotter-than-Hades, caring, alpha chef like Jack Kilroy in our lives? A man who cooks, defends his lady, and knows how to treat her right both in the kitchen *and* in the bedroom is worth his weight in focaccia (and the British accent doesn't hurt). But sometimes we've got to work with what the gods have given us. So if you have a husband/boyfriend/sex slave who believes guy cooking = grilling, but outside of the summer months, you won't catch him dead in an apron, read on.

"But he just makes a mess" or "I'm a better cook," I

hear you whine. Who cares? The benefits to encouraging your man to cook are multifold.

1. Guys who cook know how to multitask. If he can watch a couple of bubbling pots, chop those herbs, and pour you a glass of wine, all while *you* put your feet up, it'll eventually translate to other areas. Childcare, taking out the trash, maybe even doing the dishes as he whips up that *coq au vin*.

   Guys who cook know how to get creative. You might ask your man: "Is this made with sour cream, babe?"

   Cue worry crease on guy's brow that looks so adorable. "No, I didn't have any so I used Greek yogurt instead. Does it taste okay?"

   Hold praise for a beat "That's so creative, babe, and less fattening."

   (Positive reinforcement is key during the early training phase.)

2. Guys who cook have a direct correlation to a woman's TBR list. He's brought you that glass of Pinot and he's back in the kitchen where he belongs. Now you can get down to the important stuff—making a dent in your stories about fictional boyfriends who probably cook better than your guy. (In the case of Jack Kilroy, Shane Doyle, and Tad DeLuca, the sexy heroes of the Hot in the Kitchen series, this conclusion is a given.)

3. Guys who cook will evolve into guys who shop for groceries. Nuff said.

4. Guys who cook make better lovers. Chefs have very skillful hands, often callused and scarred from years

of kitchen abuse. Those fast-moving, rough hands are going to take your sexytimes to the next level! As long as your guy is burning himself while he learns, it can only be beneficial to you further down the road.

So get your guy in an apron and let the good times roll. Remember, chefs do it better...

Happy cooking, eating, and reading!

Kate Meader

www.katemeader.com